# WHAT WOULD LAVONDA ROBINETTE DO?

Kirsten Maron

Printed in Australia

First Printing: Feb 2021

Shawline Publishing Group Pty Ltd
www.shawlinepublishing.com.au

Paperback ISBN- 9 781922444424

Ebook ISBN- 9 781922444431

*For all my girls*

*Above all, be the heroine of your life, not the victim.*

NORA EPHRON


*Bang! Bang! Maxwell's silver hammer*
*Came down upon his head.*
*Bang! Bang! Maxwell's silver hammer*
*Made sure that he was dead.*

THE BEATLES: MAXWELL'S SILVER HAMMER

# PROLOGUE

The first two murders weren't deliberate. Not really. Neglecting to help until it was too late, well you couldn't call that murder, could you?

The second one, well yes, *technically* that was murder, but it was accidental... almost. She'd been a bit drunk and upset, and she hadn't realised what she was doing at the time. She was just fantasising about killing him; she hadn't meant to *actually* kill him. It was just bad luck. Or good luck, depending on how you looked at it.

Not this time. There was nothing accidental about this time.

# ONE

Three things happened on the morning of LaVonda Robinette's 49th birthday that set her on the path to murder. Although two of those things didn't seem particularly important at the time. So, if you had asked LaVonda what happened on her 49th birthday, she would have said, 'Oh, that was the day my husband told me he was leaving me.'

To be fair, he hadn't meant to pick her actual birthday to leave her; he'd intended to wait until after Easter. But apparently his new girlfriend Jemima (yes, the birthday surprises kept coming!) had thrown a bit of a spanner in the works when she booked the two of them a romantic getaway for the weekend, so he'd been forced to move up his departure date, so to speak.

'I'm literally gutted to be doing this to you.' Dave put his coffee mug down on the granite kitchen counter and ran his hands through his thinning hair.

*Figuratively, not literally,* thought LaVonda, as her toast popped up. *If you were literally gutted, Dave, I'd be calling for an ambulance right now. On the other hand, maybe not.*

'Are you okay? I mean, I know this must be devastating for you. It's just that, well, this feels like my last chance for real happiness. A proper life, a passionate life. Jemima makes me feel alive. You understand, don't you?'

No, she didn't. This couldn't be happening. Dave wasn't a particularly sensitive man, and their relationship was hardly the love affair of the century, but he couldn't actually be walking out on her on her *birthday*, could he?

Apparently, he could. LaVonda watched in growing disbelief as her husband shuffled out of the kitchen, reappearing a minute later carrying a suitcase. She shivered. The early morning sunlight had washed brightness into their large kitchen but hadn't yet warmed it up. LaVonda picked up her mug of tea and cradled it to heat her hands. Dave cleared his throat.

'I'll be back next week to collect the rest of my things. I'm sorry, LaVonda. I didn't mean to hurt you. I just need to be true to myself and live my... my authentic life.'

Oh, for heaven's sake, had the man gone mad? Authentic life? If this was a joke, it was in particularly bad taste. Not that Dave generally made jokes, because he didn't have much of a sense of humour, did he? The number of times she'd pulled him aside at barbeques or parties, explaining the punchline until his confused expression finally cleared...

And if he was serious? Well, if he thought that was the end of the matter, he could jolly well think again.

'Dave...' Her mobile started ringing. They both glanced at it, vibrating on the marble island bench.

'Is it Em?'

'Yes, I'll just...' Her finger hovered over the answer button.

'I have to go.' Dave took advantage of her uncharacteristic dithering to hurry to the back door, open it, and carry his suitcase out of the house. Just like that. LaVonda glared after him as she picked up the phone.

'Happy birthday, Mum!'

'Thank you, darling.' She made her voice sound light and easy. She'd had to perfect that particular trick over the years.

'I hope your day is filled with magical blessings. Did Dad surprise you with something nice?'

*If only you knew, Em.*

'I'm sure it will be filled with... magical blessings. How are you? How's... Jasper?' She didn't care how Jasper was unless her daughter's boyfriend had also packed his bags this morning and left. Now *that* would have been a nice birthday surprise.

Emmett chuckled. 'He's wonderful, Mum. Thank you for pretending to care. Have you got anything exciting planned for today?'

'Nothing special. Your aunts are taking me to lunch next Saturday, assuming we can find a place that serves wine by the boatload to keep Maxine happy. Are you still coming home for Easter?' LaVonda glanced at her toast still perched in the toaster. It would be unacceptably cold now.

'Yes, definitely. We were planning on leaving here Thursday evening, but Jasper is giving an advanced STER class, so we'll head off early on Friday instead.'

LaVonda rolled her eyes so hard, she half expected them to tumble out of her head. STER was a made-up program Jasper ran for other like-minded hippies in the coastal town where he and Emmett lived. As far as LaVonda could tell, STER's sole purpose was to enable Jasper to potter around aimlessly and avoid getting an actual paying job. He'd tried to explain the concept to her once, so she knew STER stood for Serenity Through Emotional Release, but what it actually involved was still a mystery. A mystery she wasn't the slightest bit interested in unravelling.

'Don't do all the driving yourself, will you? It's a long trip. Make sure you share and watch out for all the idiots on the roads.'

It seemed to LaVonda that other drivers were getting increasingly more aggressive, and impatient, and far less courteous. She often arrived at work with a frown etched firmly into her forehead.

'We'll be fine. I'm looking forward to seeing you and Dad. We have something to tell you.'

*We have something to tell you, too.* LaVonda sipped her now cooling tea. Normally a statement like this from Emmett would have set off several thunderous alarm bells, but this morning's episode was overwhelmingly distracting. She stared at the back door. Had that really happened?

'Is Dad there? I thought I'd just say hi.'

LaVonda pursed her lips. 'No, he just left.' There was an unintended, almost imperceptible, emphasis on the last word. Emmett didn't seem to pick up on it.

'Okay, well, have a serene and blissful birthday, Mum, and we'll see you in a couple of weeks.'

A couple of weeks. Presumably by Easter, when Emmett and Jasper arrived, Dave would be back from his little fling with Jocelyn... Jasmine... whatever her name was. Or maybe he wouldn't. Maybe he was planning to move in with this new woman. Did he want a divorce? Was LaVonda supposed to break the news of their separation to their daughter all by herself?

Oh, this was nonsense. Dave couldn't possibly be leaving. It was absurd. He was a middle-aged man, a responsible husband and father, and he wouldn't walk out on the life they'd built together over so many years. It was unthinkable. Ludicrous.

That was the word. Ludicrous. Dave was being *ludicrous*. He couldn't simply up and leave her.

After all, he was the one who had relentlessly pursued LaVonda all those years ago. She'd agreed to this marriage because she'd had a small child and a broken heart, and she'd desperately needed safety and security. And she'd kept up her end of the bargain, hadn't she? She'd been a good wife; hard-working, reliable, and yes, maybe a little bossy, but she'd made a lovely home for the three of them. And this was her reward? Being left for another woman? LaVonda didn't think so. No, not at all.

She reached over and pulled the toast out, tossing it straight in the bin. Yes, it was a terrible waste, but she couldn't bear reheated toast. Particularly not this morning. Years of ensuring Dave and Em had good hot breakfasts, while she'd taken the leftovers had been enough. She earned the right to have crunchy, hot toast. Especially on her birthday.

LaVonda gathered herself. She would go into work as usual, and then tonight she and Dave would talk, properly, and work everything out. Yes, that was the best thing to do under the circumstances. Act normal. Go into work. Besides, it was her birthday, so people would expect her to turn up. Her colleagues would have bought her a cake for morning tea, and decorated her desk with balloons, streamers and annoying bits of tinsel glitter, just like they did for every single person, every single year. Birthdays were big at the Department of Environmental Services: Land, Waste, and Clean-up Division.

LaVonda placed two more pieces of bread in the toaster and filled up the kettle. Then she pulled open the back door, which her husband had walked through only a few minutes ago, and looked out. Her car was in the driveway, but his was gone.

Across the road, Doreen Worthington, her neighbour and fellow book club member, waved enthusiastically. LaVonda raised her hand and reluctantly waved back. Damn. If Doreen had seen Dave leave carrying a suitcase, she was bound to bring it up at their gathering next Tuesday. She'd better go over and do some damage control.

As she hurried across the road, LaVonda forced the corners of her mouth into a big smile. Three... two... one...

'Doreen, hello! What a lovely morning.'

'A bit cold for my liking, but they say it will get warmer later today.' Doreen pulled her cardigan firmly around her waist and shivered theatrically.

'Do they? Well, that's good.' LaVonda's smile grew tighter. Doreen nodded towards the driveway.

'I was just coming out to get the morning paper when I saw your Dave leaving with a suitcase. Off on holiday, is he? Hahaha.'

Doreen never actually laughed. She said things like hahaha, with a big smile on her face. It was extremely annoying.

'A business trip, actually. He'll be back in a few days.' LaVonda forced a note of nonchalance into her voice.

'I didn't know accountants took business trips, hahaha. Will we see you on Tuesday at book club?' A smirk appeared on Doreen's face.

'Wouldn't miss it for the world.'

That was a bare-faced lie. LaVonda would have preferred to go to a STER session than attend the neighbourhood book club. Almost. What had started out as a few neighbourhood women having a discussion about their favourite novels, had turned into a wine-and-gossip fest. The only reason she kept turning up was because she knew she'd be talked about if she didn't.

LaVonda left Doreen, walked back across the road, and pushed open her back door. The kitchen felt strangely deserted. The kettle had boiled and switched itself off, so she flicked the switch to boil it again, then rinsed her mug and opened the tea tin. Empty. She was completely out of teabags. She glanced over at the toaster where her second lot of toast had popped up and gone cold.

This was becoming a very irritating birthday.

'Happy birthday!' The chorus went up the minute LaVonda stepped out of the lift onto the third floor. Six women and one man stood grinning at her and, oh yes, there was her desk, sticking out like a dog's balls, as Dave would have said. It was draped in environmentally hazardous tinsel and colourful balloons and looked ridiculously out of place among the drab grey cubicles that made up the rest of the office.

Her forced smile felt more like a grimace as Sylvia, chief birthday organiser and unofficial branch mother hen, blew a paper party whistle in her face and gave her a birthday hug.

LaVonda kept her grin in place as she fielded 'good-natured' jokes about her age. *Actually, Colin, I'm three years younger than you, so who are you calling an old duck?*

Then there were the endless well wishes from staff of other business units who had wandered over in an attempt to delay the start of their working day with a little festive distraction.

Left alone at last, LaVonda switched on her computer, frowning as she pushed a silly purple balloon aside. Maybe coming into work was a mistake. She felt far too distracted and irritated to be of any use to anyone today.

'This is our senior policy strategy manager, and birthday girl, LaVonda Robinette. LaVonda, this is Royce.'

And how dare Dave confess to an affair on her birthday? Her *birthday*! A tight feeling in her chest made it hard to breathe. If she had a heart attack this morning and dropped dead, it would be all his fault. Perhaps she should write that down somewhere, so if the time came everyone would know who to blame.

'LaVonda?'

She looked up. Colin, and a man she didn't recognise, stood next to her desk. The man's arm was extended towards her. Belatedly, she realised he had been standing there holding out his hand for an awkwardly long time. She reached up, just as he gave up and withdrew.

'Nice to meet you,' he said stiffly, and turned away. LaVonda froze for a moment before she turned back to her computer. Her homepage had 'Happy Birthday LaVonda Robinette' in pink cursive writing, scrolling across the departmental background of garbage trucks, landfill, and flooding waterways. LaVonda sighed.

She could hear Colin introducing the newcomer to the rest of her team, and she thought briefly about going over to reintroduce herself, but it all seemed like far too much trouble right now.

LaVonda was justifiably proud of herself. It was mid-morning, and by fine-tuning the departmental policy on home water wastage, she had successfully put off thinking about her situation for the past hour and a half. Self-discipline. That was the key.

Then she smelled it. Wafting over her cubicle wall, floating through the ridiculous balloons, burrowing into her nostrils and scratching the back of her throat. The nastiest, most offensive smell in the world. Tinned tuna.

It was, wasn't it? Someone had the absolute gall to be eating smelly tinned tuna *at their desk.* LaVonda hated tuna. Pungent, fishy cat food; it tasted bad and smelled worse, and the stink lingered on people's breath long after it had been consumed.

LaVonda stood up. She pushed aside a green balloon and looked over the partition at the newcomer sitting on the other side. He was eating tuna *straight out of the can!* Not even putting it on a plate, let alone going into the kitchen where food was *supposed* to be consumed. She watched in disbelief as he scraped the last bit into his mouth and tossed the empty can into his wastepaper basket. The basket meant for paper waste, thank you very much. Not stinky cans covered in tuna juice that would make the whole workplace smell like Whiskas.

The scream building up in LaVonda was fighting to get out. But she was renowned for her professionalism here. It took years to develop a reputation like that, and one shriek to lose it, however justified that shriek might be. She kept a lid on it, just, and fought the urge to gag, and told herself he was new here and might even appreciate being made aware of the 'no eating at your desk' policy. In the nicest possible way. She took a deep breath.

'Excuse me. Oh, yes, hi.'

He looked up at her over the partition, and she couldn't help noticing he had rather lovely brown eyes that crinkled attractively at the corners.

'Royce, is it? Royce, it is departmental policy that we don't eat at our desks. Would you mind eating that... that food in the kitchen please?'

She smiled widely to take any possible perceived sting out of her words. He smiled back. He had a gorgeous grin. Wide and welcoming; it made his eyes crinkle even more, and it caused a little flutter in LaVonda's chest. What a lovely looking man. Even if he did eat tuna.

'Would you mind... minding your own bloody business?' he replied as he replaced his smile with a narrow-eyed glare. He opened his desk drawer and took out another can of tuna. He ripped back the lid, and the smell assaulted her nostrils again, making her reel back in shock.

LaVonda sat down quickly. The gentle flutter in her chest had morphed into a harsh thump. Thud, thud, thud. Good grief, how awful. What a rude man. How dare he speak to her like that?

Her face started to prickle, and the images on her computer blurred. A rogue tear escaped over the bottom of her eyelid before she had time to blink it back. She stood up again, grabbed her handbag and hurried over to the toilets where she locked herself in a stall, and dabbed at her eyes with environmentally friendly (and therefore grey and horribly scratchy) toilet paper.

*Don't cry, don't cry. Don't dare cry.* LaVonda dug her nails into her palms as she tried to pull herself together. This was a rubbish birthday. Everyone was supposed to be nice to her today, and instead they were making her angry and upset, and now she was crying all over the shop.

The nail digging wasn't working. She couldn't pull herself together. Oh, enough already. She pulled her phone from her bag.

'Syl, I have a terrible headache. It came on suddenly and I have to go home immediately. Yes, it is a shame. Yes, I know the cake won't keep until Monday. Yes, I know Colin has been looking forward to it. Well, that's very nice but I don't need... oh, okay. Lovely. Oh, you're not done; there's a second verse. Of course there is. Okay. Well, thank you for singing 'Happy Birthday' down the phone to me Sylvia, but I do have to go now. See you on Monday.'

To hell with Dave. To hell with horrible new Royce. It was her birthday, for heaven's sake. How dare people treat her like this? She hurried from the toilets into the lift, stabbing blindly at the buttons until she was transported to the basement car park. The lift doors opened, revealing the gloom of the underground.

LaVonda's hands shook as she turned the key in the ignition. This simply wasn't fair. She deserved to be surrounded by love and attention today. Her husband should be at home waiting to spoil her, and her sisters should be taking her out for a champagne lunch *today*, not next weekend, and her colleagues should be gathering together to sing 'Happy birthday to you', at her.

She shouldn't be driving to her empty house in furious tears, because of her silly husband leaving her, and a *tuna-breathing pig* being nasty to her. LaVonda stopped at a traffic light, reached for a tissue and blew her nose loudly. She wouldn't let her birthday continue like this. If no one else was going to make a fuss of her, then she would jolly well make a fuss of herself.

The light turned green. LaVonda pressed her foot down and drove straight to the local supermarket. She swung the car expertly into the nearest spot.

Because it was late morning on a weekday, the place was teeming with sluggish old people, and mothers dragging around tiny, whiny children. Why did everyone have to move so unbearably slowly? LaVonda ducked around two elderly women who were having a leisurely chat in the biscuit aisle and managing to block several shelves. Honestly, didn't they realise they were in everyone's way?

'Happy birthday,' one of the women was saying to the other. 'It's hard to believe you're turning ninety. You don't look a day over seventy-five. What are you doing to celebrate? Family coming over?'

'No, there's only me now. They've all gone. That's the trouble with making it to ninety; you outlive everyone. But I can't complain. I have my health, well, mostly. And I have a little cake to celebrate.'

LaVonda looked into the ninety-year-old's trolley. A plain, cheap sponge cake sat in the bottom next to a packet of dried macaroni.

'At least you have your health,' the first woman nodded. 'My diverticulitis has flared up and I could simply explode with diarrhoea at any moment...'

LaVonda darted into the next aisle before she had to hear any more details, let alone witness a possible explosion.

*How sad,* she thought, as she steered her wobbly trolley towards the refrigerator section. *To be ninety and all alone. That will probably be me one day. Emmett will marry that awful Jasper, and Dave will be happily remarried to whatever her name is.* (Yes, she knows full well her name is Jemima, and no, she is not going to call her Jemima, because that makes this real, and this cannot be real.) *They'll all be gone, and it will just be me, alone at ninety, buying plain sponge cakes in the supermarket for my birthday and having no one to celebrate with me. No one who cares.*

Sadness bloomed in her chest, and LaVonda felt tears welling again. She shook her head. Honestly, these savage mood swings were becoming ridiculous. Yes, Dave walking out on her was more than a bit unnerving, but the man would eventually come to his senses and come home. She was sure of that. And yes, the altercation with her new colleague was unpleasant, but it wasn't the first time she'd had a disagreement with someone at work. Truth be told, they were all a little stupid and irritating at times.

Why was she having a mini breakdown over a poor lonely ninety-year-old and projecting the same future on herself? It made no sense. She was a woman of *action*, not morose contemplation. So, how to fix this?

*I'll buy that woman a cake,* LaVonda thought. *A lovely birthday cake from a complete stranger, to celebrate her ninetieth birthday and show her people still care.*

LaVonda was extremely pleased with herself. It was a thoughtful idea; whimsically delightful, and it put good karma out into the world. Plus, it reaffirmed her true character; kind and gracious and controlled. Not wound up, furious, and hysterically weepy.

She stared down at the cakes displayed so prettily on the fridge shelves. *Let's see. The Black Forest chocolate for the old woman, and the red velvet sprinkled with tiny gold hearts for me. Perfect.*

LaVonda pushed her trolley, with the two birthday cakes, up to the checkouts, noting with satisfaction a new one opening up just in front of her. Excellent. She rolled the trolley towards the end of the conveyer belt.

A young woman in purple activewear came up from her left and bumped her trolley into the end of LaVonda's. LaVonda stopped in surprise and waited for an apology. The woman didn't even look at her. She manoeuvred her trolley around LaVonda, parked it at the end of the checkout and started unloading her groceries. LaVonda's eyes widened in astonishment.

'Excuse me? You just hit my trolley, and I was lining up here.'

The activewear woman ignored her. Just completely ignored her. How dare she? How incredibly rude. LaVonda felt anger bubbling up. She took a slow, deep breath in to soothe it away.

'Excuse me? I said I was here first. You can't just bump me out of the way.'

The other woman stopped unloading her groceries and swept her gaze briefly over LaVonda. She gave a nasty half-smile, more of a smirk really, and then turned back to her task. LaVonda was livid.

Heat rushed to her cheeks, and she opened her mouth to object again, when she realised the warmth in her face was intensifying and spreading down her neck into her chest. Her heart pounded in a horrible, terrifying way, as sweat broke out across her forehead. What on earth was happening to her? Was she *actually* having a heart attack? Or maybe a stroke?

LaVonda let out a moan and pulled at her shirt. Her skin was burning. She was on fire and she had to get her clothes off. Now. The rude woman glanced at her again, then stopped unpacking her trolley and stared as LaVonda pulled her shirt out of her skirt and flapped it in a desperate attempt to cool her skin. She was hot, so unbearably hot. All she could focus on was ridding herself of the fire consuming her body. Through her red haze, LaVonda noticed a bag of frozen peas in the other woman's trolley. She reached over, snatched them up and pressed them to her face.

Oh, sweet relief! The peas helped take the heat from her poor flushed face, so she shoved them gratefully against the back of her neck, then pushed them down the front of her shirt. The cooling sensation was wonderful. She was calming down now; the heat was subsiding, leaving her head and her shirt soaked in sweat. She felt weak with relief. She was still hot, but it was manageable now. Almost tolerable. She closed her eyes in gratitude, then opened them again.

Several shoppers had stopped and were staring at her. Good grief. How mortifying. She was all sweaty and dishevelled, and probably a bit smelly now too. LaVonda clenched her teeth. Should she just run out? Get back to her car and drive well away from here?

No. No, she was not going to run. She was going to have her birthday cake, and she was going to see to it that the elderly woman had her birthday cake too.

LaVonda gathered up the shredded remains of her dignity. Ignoring everyone, she dropped the now thawed peas back into the other woman's trolley, then picked up her precious cakes and marched up to the checkout man.

'This *person* pushed in front of me. I'd like to pay for these now, please. Separate bags and receipts.'

He gawped at her, eyes widening, then silently reached out to take the cakes. LaVonda smoothed her damp hair back from her face. She deliberately avoided looking at the woman behind her. No one said another word.

After paying for the cakes, LaVonda squared her shoulders, picked up her bags and hurried back into the shop to find the ninety-year-old woman in the biscuit aisle. They were *both* going to have a nice birthday; she'd see to that.

Later, when she thought back to her 49th birthday, LaVonda would shake her head in annoyance. Dave leaving her for another woman, meeting rude Royce, experiencing her first hot flush; any one of those events, let alone all three, would be enough to make her think: *That was a particularly awful thing to happen on my birthday.*

But it was far worse than that. What LaVonda didn't know then, what she couldn't *possibly* have known, was that those three things would set off a chain of life-changing events. Events that would, over the next few months, lead LaVonda Robinette to commit murder.

# TWO

'Good riddance I say.' Maxine took a sip of wine, then clanged her glass down on the metal café table, as if daring the other two to disagree. The table wobbled on the uneven cobblestones.

'Max!'

'She's right, Von. Emmett is almost thirty; she doesn't need her parents to stay together for her sake, and you've said yourself that you and Dave pretty much lead separate lives.'

'Independent lives, Ann, not separate lives.' Good grief. LaVonda hadn't expected vast amounts of sympathy from her sisters, but this seemed a bit harsh. At the very least, there should be a show of comforting support, plus the reassurance that, of *course*, Dave would eventually come to his senses and return home. After all, it had only been a week. A week wasn't nearly long enough for a middle-aged man to get over his mid-life crisis and return to the comfort and security of the family home. She just had to be patient and give him a bit more time.

Actually, she wouldn't mind if he took quite a lot more time, because it was surprisingly nice to have the house to herself. She didn't have to prepare meals, or pack his lunches, and she chose what she wanted to watch on television in the evenings. And she certainly did not miss having to pick up his dirty clothes from the bedroom floor. Twenty-five years of having a convenient laundry basket in their otherwise tasteful bedroom, and he *still* dropped his clothes where he took them off. How hard was it to go over, lift the lid, and drop his undies in the basket? Apparently too hard for Dave Robinette.

'You can't fool us with semantics, Von. We know you too well.' Ann put down her own wineglass, picked up a menu, and started fanning herself with it. 'Balls and bastards! This change of life stuff is a nightmare. I'm a bloody walking furnace.'

LaVonda felt hot just looking at her, even though the breeze swirling around them was cool. She would have preferred to sit inside the café, where it was dark and a bit gloomy, but at least sheltered. Leaving the lunch booking to their younger sister had been a mistake; naturally Maxine had booked an outdoor table so she could smoke. As it turned out, the café banned smoking within several metres of the entrance, so there was no reason why they couldn't have sat inside after all.

LaVonda leaned forward and lowered her voice.

'I had my first hot flush the other day in the supermarket. Fifty people stopped and watched my body roast itself in front of them. It was terrible; I thought I was going to die. Isn't it a bit too early for us to be going into... menopause?'

Ugh. Such an awful, clinical, but somehow primal, word. Could she actually be going into menopause? Wasn't she too young? She felt too young. Menopause seemed like a doddery old lady thing to happen, and LaVonda might be middle-aged (another revolting word) but she was not an old lady.

LaVonda had done her research online and, yes, it had almost definitely been a hot flush. Of course, she'd had to double-check, because there was always a possibility it might be a brain tumour. LaVonda had had several symptoms of brain tumours in her lifetime, but no actual brain tumour to date, so it seemed more likely that this was, in fact, a symptom of *menopause.*

Maxine snorted. 'You're on the cusp of fifty, so no, it isn't early, not at all. In fact, if anything, you're late. I started my perimenopause last year at forty-five.'

'*Perimenopause?*'

'Pre-menopause. Von, it's not smart to be so dense about your health.'

'I am not dense.' LaVonda was stung. Maxine was a nurse, for heaven's sake. It was her *job* to know all about the human body, and what it did and didn't do. LaVonda would just love to see her sister try to write a ministerial sewage proposal. Ha! She wouldn't know where to start.

'Well, I can't wait to be post-menopausal. This has been going on for far too many years now.' Ann flapped her menu even more vigorously.

'Could everyone please stop saying menopause?' LaVonda cast about for a subject change, but the only topic she could think of was her failing marriage, and she definitely did not want to bring that up again. Her sisters didn't understand. It wasn't about Dave, per se, it was about what he represented. Familiarity. Security. Control.

Ann put down her menu and scooped some ice out of the ice bucket. She held it against the back of her neck.

'The odd hot flush isn't that bad. The worst part of getting older is becoming invisible. The other day I was in the middle of addressing a group of law graduates, and one of the other partners, a man obviously, interrupted me and all the graduates immediately turned to hear what he had to say. I had to wave my stump at them to get their attention back.'

LaVonda was giddily appalled. 'Ann, you didn't!' She reached over to thump Maxine, who had started choking on her wine.

'No, of course not, but I was tempted. I've never used my deformity to my advantage before but, honestly, if it helps me shed the cloak of invisibility, I'd definitely consider it. Oh, bloody balls, Maxie, it isn't that funny!'

Ann rarely talked about her disability; the forearm that had been amputated just below her elbow as a result of a childhood accident. She'd stopped using her prosthesis several years ago, claiming it was too uncomfortable to wear, and if people didn't like looking at her stump, they could just get over themselves.

It seemed to LaVonda that this was a mistake. Ann struggled with tasks that her prosthetic arm had seemed to make so much easier. Not for the first time, LaVonda wondered what it had been like for Ann growing up with a disability. When they were children, they had just accepted it as one of her differences, the way kids do. Ann was smart, but only had one arm, LaVonda was pretty and Dad's favourite, and Maxine was the baby who cried a lot.

'Are you ladies ready to order, or should I give you a few more minutes?' A young waitress sporting a nose ring had come outside and was smiling at them.

'A few more minutes,' Maxine told her, as Ann nodded. LaVonda frowned.

'Max, we need to eat. We've been here for an hour. If I don't get some food soon, I'll make you responsible for dragging my emaciated body back to my house. We can't all exist on wine, cigarettes, and sarcasm.'

The waitress laughed. 'I can bring you some garlic bread while you're making up your minds.'

'No, we'll order now. Look at the menu, Max. Ann, what are you going to have?' LaVonda knew she was being annoyingly bossy, but sometimes she *had* to take charge, or nothing would get done.

The waitress took their orders and repeated them back.

'And more wine, please.' Ann lifted the empty wine bottle from the ice bucket. 'Another bottle.'

'Why would you do that to your nose?' Maxine barely waited until the waitress was back inside. 'And those tattoos. Covering her whole arm. Why disfigure your skin like that?'

Ann grinned. 'It's the fashion, Maxie. It's edgy. We're all old now so we don't get it.'

'But it is so ugly. Plus, they fade and become blurry with age. She won't look edgy when she's fifty. She'll look ridiculous.'

LaVonda said nothing. She had a tiny, secret tattoo just above her hipbone. She and her first boyfriend, the love of her life; Mark, had gotten them when they were both nineteen. Neither one of them was good with pain, so they'd chosen the smallest tattoos they could, each other's birth signs, and thought themselves very rebellious. They'd been so turned on by their own outrageousness, they'd spent the rest of the day having sex while trying not to knock each other's bandages off. LaVonda liked to think that was the night Emmett was conceived. Although they were having so much sex in those days, it could have been one of a number of times.

LaVonda could almost feel her left hip tingling where the (now admittedly blurry) Chinese symbol for Scorpio was located. Mark's tattoo had been the symbol for Aries on his right hip. Her tiny tattoo made her feel connected to him, even all these years later. She'd let Dave assume the symbol was her own birth sign, and Dave wasn't a particularly curious man. She doubted he'd ever bothered to check.

'Have you heard from Dull Dave at all since he left?' Maxine prodded LaVonda to get her attention.

LaVonda started to defend her husband, saying 'Don't call him Dull Dave', then realised she didn't care. *Call him what you will.*

'Not since early last week. He came back to pack up some more stuff while I was at work. He's moved in with the girlfriend.' LaVonda refused to say the woman's name, not because it upset her, but because Jemima herself was irrelevant.

'Have you found her on Facebook yet?'

LaVonda shook her head. 'No, of course not. I have no interest in her whatsoever.'

'Oh, come on, you must want to at least know what she looks like.' Maxine pulled her phone out of her handbag and opened the app. 'What's her name? Do you know her surname?'

'No. Max put it away. You know our rule; no phones when we're together. We're supposed to be focusing on each other, not social media.'

LaVonda loved her daughter more than anything in the world, but it drove her mad the way Emmett would endlessly scroll through her phone when they were together. Lately, she'd noticed both her sisters doing the same thing. It was so rude. That's why she'd had to instigate the rule.

Ann was clearly on Maxine's side, as usual. 'This is about you, Von. This is about your replacement. Aren't you even the slightest bit curious about her?'

LaVonda thought about it. She wasn't at all curious, she decided. She couldn't care less about this other woman. She was just annoyed that Dave was threatening to undo everything they'd spent two-and-a-half decades building together. They'd recently paid off their mortgage, and they'd done it without any help from Dave's dreadful, but extremely wealthy, father. They had a nice secure life where they both knew what to expect from each other. Of course, there wasn't much passion, but surely passion wasn't to be expected when you were in your late forties and early fifties.

Dave and LaVonda had plans. Solid, well-thought-out plans. They were both going to work full time for another ten years, let their investments build up, then sell the house and retire somewhere along the coast. She would spend her days reading, baking, and gardening, and Dave would do... well, whatever it was he wanted to do, and she would probably (hopefully) have grandchildren by then, who could come and stay for school holidays. LaVonda was already looking forward to spoiling them.

In the meantime, they had a pleasant, perfectly predictable, existence. They had a few mutual friends, plus she had Ann and Maxine, annoying as they might be from time to time. They had Emmett, they both had good jobs where they were liked and respected, and they both enjoyed excellent health, even if they'd succumbed a little to the dreaded middle-aged spread.

Naturally, there were inevitable flies in the ointment; her mother for one, Dave's appalling father for another and, of course, Emmett's completely unsuitable partner, Jasper Brown. But she couldn't do much about any of that.

LaVonda made sure her voice was measured and slow as she replied because, frankly, this was the only way to shut down either of her sisters for good.

'I'm not the least bit interested in her. And you are not to try and find her. Don't you remember what happened when you tried to stalk Ines's ex-girlfriend, and you ended up accidentally liking one of her old photos?'

Maxine blushed to the roots of her cropped, blonde hair, as well she might. It took a lot to embarrass Maxine, she could be outrageously brazen, but she'd been mortified when she'd been caught looking up her young girlfriend's ex-partner. Ines had eventually forgiven her, and Maxine should have learnt her lesson. Clearly, she hadn't.

'I'm going for a cigarette.' Maxine rose quickly from the table and walked over to a nearby park bench. Ann watched her leave.

'She's still embarrassed about that. Don't worry, we were only teasing; we're not going to look up Dave's girlfriend. Now, what are you up to this afternoon? I've got to take the twins to soccer since Sam is in Singapore, otherwise I'd happily come and burn Dave effigies with you.'

LaVonda laughed. There was no point in insisting that she and Dave would work things out. Her sisters simply didn't want to hear it.

'I'm visiting Mum. Don't look at me like that, Ann Avenell. We made a promise to Dad.'

Ann snorted. 'You made a promise to Dad, I didn't, and you know full well he didn't expect us to put up with weekly abuse from that witch for the rest of our lives. I don't know why you bother; I certainly don't, and Maxie hasn't seen her in years.'

LaVonda had given up trying to explain herself. She resented her mother every bit as much as her sisters, but she had to support Maude, because it was the only thing she could still do for the man she'd loved so much.

George had died early on the morning following Emmett's second birthday. Mark stayed at the house to keep the birthday party going, while LaVonda hurried to the hospital to join her sisters and their mother.

She had sat by their father's bedside long into the night. At some point, both her sisters had fallen asleep in the waiting room, and LaVonda was left alone with her father, holding his bony, grey-speckled hand, listening to the death rattle in his chest. She would not sleep. She needed to focus all her attention on keeping Dad alive through sheer force of will.

George's lungs heaved in his frail body as he slowly suffocated to death. The nurses kept coming in and topping up his pain medication, and Maude had drunkenly staggered about, abusing the staff until she finally passed out in the visitor's lounge. Through all of this, LaVonda held her father's hand gently in hers and concentrated ferociously.

Just before 3am, George, drifting in and out of consciousness, had lifted his hand weakly to his oxygen mask.

'What is it, Dad?' LaVonda helped him pull the mask aside.

'Vondalin.' It was his pet name for her, and he'd seldom called her LaVonda, even though she'd been named for his favourite aunt.

'What, Dad? What do you need?'

'Maude.'

'Do you want Mum? I'll go and get her.'

She didn't want to leave and find her mother, who was passed out in the hospital somewhere. She didn't want to leave his side. But she would have done anything for the dying man who had protected the three girls from the worst of their mother's abuse.

'No. Mum...' he waved weakly towards a woman who wasn't there, '...needs help. Sick... needs support. Please, darling...'

He closed his eyes again, and LaVonda fitted the mask back over his face. Tears rolled unchecked down her cheeks and dripped off her jaw onto the hospital sheets.

'I will, Dad. I will look after her. You don't need to worry; I'll be there for her. Don't worry, Dad. Just rest.'

George died an hour later without waking up again.

Looking out for her mother was the one thing LaVonda could still do for her dad, and she would continue to do it until the woman died.

That day couldn't come soon enough.

It was so unfair that their gentle, loving father had been struck down at fifty, while their alcoholic, abusive mother continued to live on. Now and then, LaVonda allowed herself to think about her life without Maude in it. No more middle-of-the-night abusive calls, no more criticism, no more picking up empty vodka bottles. It wasn't the charitable thing to wish your mother would drop dead, but she did. In her heart of hearts, she did.

Maxine returned to the table just as their meals and wine arrived. She attacked her salad with rapture. LaVonda took a more measured approach, delicately spooning on a little dressing and carefully folding it through the leaves. Maxine reached across with her fork and stabbed one of LaVonda's croutons, lifting it to her mouth.

'So, given that we're not allowed to talk about the most interesting thing that has happened to any one of us since I came out of the closet, and given that LaVonda pulls the 'squick' face when we mention menopause, what do we want to talk about? Politics? Sex? Work? By the way, I don't want to talk about my work. We had two deaths yesterday, and I'm still feeling traumatised.'

LaVonda frowned as she thought about her own work. That was another topic she wasn't ready to think about. Because the new guy, Royce, was proving to be quite horrible. He hadn't spoken to her directly since the Tuna Incident, but his attitude remained cocky, and he seemed to be undermining her in small, discreet ways.

She couldn't quite put her finger on it, but there was definitely something going on. At their team meeting on Thursday, she'd been presenting the outline for the waterworks project when Royce started sniggering. She'd hesitated, looked up to see him regarding her blandly, and then lost her place when she glanced back at her notes. When she got to the statistics page, he'd openly snorted.

'Your data is out of date. Look. It only goes up to the year before last. Are we doing a project based on old data? Seems a bit strange to me.' He'd looked around at the rest of the group.

LaVonda had been mortified. Surely, she hadn't used the wrong data. She'd fumbled with her reading glasses and looked at the page again. He was right. The data was from two years ago.

'I didn't realise, I mean I thought...'

'Don't worry, LaVonda.' Her manager's smooth voice had cut across the room. 'Just redo it with the correct data, and then you can present to the group next week. Good pick up, Royce.'

'Thanks, Deborah.'

LaVonda went hot and cold at the memory. It was a simple mistake that anyone could have made, but she was used to catching other people's mistakes, not making her own. And for Royce to be the one to call it out! Although, come to think of it, he hadn't noticed the mistake earlier when he'd reviewed her presentation before the meeting. Had he? Maybe he had, but he'd chosen not to say anything until it was too late. Oh, good grief, was she starting to get paranoid? This wasn't like her at all.

She looked up. Maxine was lifting the fresh bottle to refill her wine, and Ann was pulling rocket leaves out of her sandwich. LaVonda bit her lip.

'Ann, I need to ask you something. A legal question.'

'Frankly, I don't think you can afford my rates, but because you're my favourite sister, and because this is your birthday celebration, I'm prepared to make a rare exception. Fire away.' Ann took a huge bite of her sandwich. Dressing dribbled down her chin, and LaVonda resisted the urge to lean over and wipe it away for her.

'There's a guy at work and he's... well... I don't know.'

Ann's eyes flared with interest. She held up her hand, chewed vigorously, swallowed, and then patted her chin delicately with her serviette before speaking.

'Cute?'

'No, actually yes, a bit, but that's not what this is about. I think he is undermining me.' She didn't just think it, she knew it.

'What do you mean, you think he is? What is he doing?'

'Well, it's a bit hard to pinpoint; he's friendly with everyone else in the team but not me. He always checks if anyone else wants a coffee when he goes to buy his, but he never asks me.'

'You don't drink coffee,' Maxine pointed out, not unreasonably.

'That's beside the point. It is more that he deliberately doesn't ask me. Then, the other day, he pointed out a mistake I'd made in front of everyone. I think we got off to a bad start on his first day when I asked him not to eat tuna at his desk.'

'Why did you do that?'

LaVonda rolled her eyes. 'Because it is stinky and horrible, and we have a 'no eating at your desk' policy.'

Ann laughed.

'Well, it does sound like maybe you annoyed him. Look, Von, no one likes being told off, especially on their first day. Maybe you should have a chat with him and get it out in the open. You're probably not imagining some hostility from him; women tend to have a pretty shrewd instinct for this stuff, but it won't get better until you address the core issue.'

LaVonda thought about it as she took another sip of wine and forked her salad. Ann was probably right; she should tackle this issue with Royce directly. She could apologise for upsetting him, even though he'd been the one to upset her, and then things would probably be better.

She pushed her plate aside and picked up a piece of bread, chewing it slowly. She even felt a little bit sorry for Royce now. It would have been awful to have someone tell him off on his first day. Well, that was the way forward. That was the action she would take. She'd approach him first thing tomorrow, apologise, and get this sorted out.

# THREE

'Royce, may I have a word?'

LaVonda felt uncharacteristically nervous as she approached her colleague's desk. Silly. He was hardly going to yell at her, was he?

'Just a minute.'

He continued to type an email as LaVonda stood there awkwardly. She glanced around. Angela and Sylvia were at their desks and Deborah was in her office, but no one else was in yet. Good heavens, he was taking his sweet time though, wasn't he?

'I can come back if you're busy?'

'No, I'm nearly done.' He continued to type, and she continued to stand, waiting and feeling faintly foolish. Finally, he pressed send and swivelled his chair around to face her. He put his hands behind his head, a deliberate power move, and regarded her coldly.

'What can I do for you?'

All LaVonda's carefully rehearsed words went out of her head. She'd practised her lines on the way to work until she was word-perfect, but now she went blank.

'Oh, I um... well, I wanted to apologise, you see. For telling you not to eat tuna at your desk that day. I should have realised you didn't understand the policy.'

Oh dear, that didn't sound right, did it? She sounded like she was patronising him. Sure enough, his eyes narrowed. The smile dropped from LaVonda's face.

'No, I didn't mean it like that. I just wanted to say I am sorry for saying anything to you. About the tuna. You weren't to know the policy, of course, and I should have realised that. I was just trying to be helpful. Well, actually, I hate the smell of tuna, but you didn't know that, and if you want to eat tuna then, of course, that is your prerogative.'

Royce turned back to his desk.

'Thank you for the apology, LaVonda, and for graciously allowing me to eat tuna. Now, I need to get back to work, and might I suggest you do the same. So that you don't make any more stupid mistakes?'

Well, that was rude. LaVonda was taken aback. She'd been trying to apologise, but it felt as though she had made things worse.

Things were definitely worse. Over the next few days, Royce was openly hostile to her when no one else was around, and coldly polite when they were. It seemed to LaVonda that he was making a special effort to ingratiate himself with the rest of the team while blocking her at every turn.

To make matters worse, she had another hot flush. It came on just as she stepped into the lift on her way to deliver the completed project to the Managing Director. Only, this one was even more terrible than the first one. Trapped in the tiny elevator alongside Deborah, Colin, and Royce, LaVonda wanted to tear her skin off, as heat radiated through her torso and up into her head. It was unbearable; she could feel the sweat breaking out all over her body as she desperately fanned her flaming face with her project folder.

'Are you alright?' Deborah asked, stepping towards her, as the two men stepped hastily back.

'Just a hot flush,' LaVonda managed through gritted teeth. Sweat rolled down her back and her face, dripping off her chin. Oh god, if she could just get these clothes off. She wanted to scream, but instead she bravely endured the fires of hell for the next few seconds until the lift stopped on the 14th floor.

As soon as the doors opened, she burst through and ran into the nearest ladies' room. Once safely inside, she tore off her jacket and blouse and splashed cold water on her burning face and chest. She looked up, panting, and realised to her mortification that Deborah had followed her into the toilets.

'Are you sure you're alright? You look terrible.'

She did look terrible. Her face was red and wet, her hair was damp and starting to frizz. Her jacket and blouse lay in a soggy pile on the floor. LaVonda wanted to be anywhere but standing half-naked, flushed and sweating in the 14th floor toilets, as her manager looked at her with concern.

'I'm fine,' she said bravely. 'I just need a minute to sort myself out. Please start without me and I'll join you in a few minutes.'

Deborah nodded and left the room. Once the flush had passed, LaVonda splashed some more water on her face and set about fixing herself up. She didn't need to look in the mirror again to know she looked awful. She probably should have let Royce and Colin present the project but, after all, she'd done the lion's share of work to make sure it was a success.

By the time she walked into the boardroom, Royce had already started presenting and was taking the credit for the delivery of the project. She took the seat next to him and waited for the opportunity to point out her own contribution. But Royce didn't give her a chance. He spoke smoothly and rapidly about the milestones and achievements, and then finally acknowledged Colin and LaVonda's help.

'Of course, we couldn't have delivered on time without the dedication of the project staff. Colin has done an amazing job, working long hours and driving things along. And LaVonda, as well.'

Did he say LaVonda 'as well'? She'd been the project manager, for heaven's sake. Royce and Colin had each produced some work for the project, but she'd been the one to pull it all together and drive the timelines. How dare he?

'Actually, as the project manager–' she started to say, but Royce interrupted her.

'Sorry, I should say LaVonda has done *brilliantly* on the project. She should *definitely* be given most of the credit for her contribution to the outcomes. It wouldn't have been nearly as successful without her.'

'That's good of you to say Royce, but I'm sure it was a group effort.' The Managing Director beamed at all of them, though his smile faltered slightly at the sight of the bedraggled LaVonda. 'You should all be proud of your teamwork.'

LaVonda's anger soared, and her chest tightened, but she managed a bright little smile as the group walked out of the boardroom.


'Yes, it does sound like he's targeting you.' Ann wrapped her pashmina around her shoulders as she and LaVonda walked out of the chemist. The wind whipped at their hair and clothes as they continued their Sunday morning shopping. LaVonda used one hand to pull her woollen hat down firmly over her ears. The temperature seemed to have plummeted several degrees overnight, and it was freezing. Maybe it would help if she had another hot flush.

Ann stopped to look at a window display, and LaVonda took the opportunity to shift the bag containing her new cushions to her other arm. Her home was decorated in the neutral tones Dave preferred; he would hate the deep red and orange colours she'd chosen. Too bad. Perhaps he should have thought of that before he walked out. LaVonda mentally stuck her tongue out at her husband.

'What did Deborah say to you?'

LaVonda refocused her attention. 'She said I should be proud of my team's efforts. She knows I did most of the project work myself, so why didn't she tell the Director that I was the project lead and did almost all the work?'

'Think about it, Von. She was hardly going to contradict her boss in front of her staff. If he liked the idea of it being a team effort, then she wouldn't have done you or herself any favours by pointing out that it wasn't.'

'I guess so, but it still seems horribly unfair.'

'Since when is life fair? Is it fair that I lost my arm? Is it fair that you lost Mark? Is it fair that Maxie... well, anyway, back to this guy. It sounds like he is definitely harassing you in a subtle way. Gaslighting you.'

'What am I supposed to do about it?'

Ann turned away from the window display, heading back down the street, and LaVonda had to trot to keep up with her. For a small, round woman, Ann set a cracking pace. As kids they'd been so similar, three plain, little brown birds; but Ann had stayed short, as LaVonda grew taller, and Maxine taller still. Now no one would mistake them for sisters. A curvy redhead, an average-sized brunette, and a tall, skinny blonde; they'd never looked less alike.

'As I see it, you have three choices. You can put up with it; I don't recommend that option, by the way. You can leave and find another job. Don't look at me like that, Von, it is just an option. Or you can fight it.'

'Fight it. Definitely.'

'Okay, but I have to warn you it isn't that easy, and it could be a long and painful process for you both. If you're determined to go down that path, you should start taking notes of when, and what happens, and the details. On their own, each of these incidents don't sound like much, but they all add up to bullying and harassment.

Once you have some evidence, you can go to your HR department and lodge a formal complaint against the man. They'll have him investigated and, depending on the outcome, he could be reprimanded or even lose his job.'

Wouldn't that be wonderful? Royce gone, and everything back to how it was before. That seemed like the best solution.

'Alright, I'll do that. Thanks for the advice. Now what else do you need to get? I think I've got everything on my list.'

'Nope, I'm done too. Let's grab a couple of hot chocolates to warm us up a bit, and I'll text Sam to come and pick me up. I'm dragging him away from an afternoon in front of the football to see the new Renoir display at the art gallery. Want to come along?'

'I can't, Emmett and Jasper arrive on Friday for the Easter weekend and I want to get everything ready for them. I still haven't told her about her father's temporary insanity.'

'It doesn't sound temporary to me. He's been gone, what, two weeks now?'

Yes, just over two weeks, and it both surprised and annoyed her that he hadn't been in touch. She certainly wasn't going to be the one to reach out. She was starting to settle into her own routine, and it was surprisingly enjoyable. Dave would return soon because, after all, they'd made a commitment to each other and they were too old, *she* was too old, to start a new life at this age. In the meantime, she would make the most of the peace and quiet.

'You need to get your finances separated and sorted out,' Ann declared, as they joined the small queue at the café counter. It was warm inside, even if the place was a bit too bohemian for LaVonda's liking. She glanced around at the mismatched chairs and tables. A faint smell of patchouli wafted through the air. Emmett would be right at home here.

'That seems a bit premature. He's bound to want to come home soon.' Privately, LaVonda was starting to lose confidence that Dave would return. But she wouldn't admit that to Ann.

'What if he does? You don't have to take him back. In fact, in light of all this, I don't think you should.'

LaVonda glanced around and lowered her voice, even though no one in the queue seemed to be paying them any attention. 'Ann, he's my husband.'

Ann snorted. 'So what? Do you love him?'

'Of course, I do. One skinny hot chocolate and a pot of tea, please. Ann. I do.'

'You don't sound at all convincing. And a muffin, please. The date and walnut. Do you want one?'

LaVonda shook her head.

'Okay, just the one. My shout, you go and grab us a table near the window.'

LaVonda left Ann to pay and walked across to one of the few vacant tables. She settled her shopping on one of the chairs and herself on another. *Dave and I do love each other,* she thought. Maybe not in the way that some people do, not *actively*, like the two young men at the next table, but they had a mature companionable love born from years of marriage. Dave did do quite a lot of things that annoyed her, and she possibly did some things that annoyed him, but surely that was typical of most mature marriages. Moving through life, side by side, feeling slightly irritated by each other most of the time, but with the occasional sweep of mild affection.

One of the men next to her stood up from his seat, banging his chair against LaVonda's. She smiled up at him and waited for an apology that never came. It seemed as though he simply couldn't see her. She glanced at his companion, who was still sipping his coffee. He ignored her as well. Was she invisible?

'Are people getting ruder, or am I just more intolerant?'

Ann sat down and handed LaVonda a plate. 'Here, I got them to cut my muffin in half so we could share. Half the calories, half the guilt. Now what did you say?'

'I've become invisible, Ann. People keep bumping into me as though they can't see me.'

'It's our age. We're not relevant to society anymore so we're overlooked.'

'That can't be true. You're a partner in a law firm and I'm a *senior* policy manager. We are both important, busy, and *relevant* women. We can't be sidelined like this. Marginalised.'

'Sure, at work we're still valued. But in the eyes of the rest of the world, we're sliding into middle-aged obscurity.' Ann popped a piece of muffin into her mouth.

'It makes me furious. Actually, it really does. Any minor irritation flares straight into rage these days.'

'It's the change. I get wild at the slightest thing too. I swear the other day; I was so in the mood to slap someone. Very. Hard. Sam and the boys were giving me a wide berth, and that just made me angrier. If someone had just come over and taken one for the team...'

LaVonda laughed, but she still felt concerned. 'Surely it can't be normal to be angry all the time?'

'I find taking off my bra helps. As soon as I take off my bra, I am instantly less annoyed.'

'I don't think that's an option I can use at work. They already regard me warily after witnessing my hot flushes.'

She wasn't exaggerating. It was like she'd suddenly become an alien or something. Even Sylvia, who was about as subtle as a steamroller in overdrive, had taken to approaching her carefully, like someone trying to defuse a particularly tricky bomb.

'You should see someone, because you don't have to put up with that. I'll give you the number of my doctor. She's great. Once you get on the hormone pills, things will turn around. Or so I'm told. Nothing seems to be working for me yet, but I'm not giving up. Now I wasn't going to ask, because god knows I do not care, but how is our mother doing?'

'Terrible. She's getting worse. One of the community nurses told me last Saturday she needs to be moved into a nursing home, so when I visited yesterday, I thought I'd talk to her about that. You can imagine how that conversation went down.'

'Not well, I take it?'

No. It hadn't gone well at all. The whole visit had been a disaster. As usual.

The familiar panicky feeling drenched LaVonda the minute she'd arrived at her childhood home. This happened every Saturday but knowing what to expect didn't make it any easier. Her stomach churned, and diarrhoea threatened. She'd clenched her buttocks as sweat patches formed under her armpits.

*Come on,* she'd told herself. *You're all grown up, and she's just a harmless old woman. She can't hurt you now. No need to act like a frightened child. You're not going to poo your pants.*

She gave herself this same pep talk every time, and every time it made little difference. She'd forced herself to walk briskly towards the front door, even though no part of her felt the slightest bit brisk.

The fleur-de-lis wallpaper in the hallway was long faded, but LaVonda felt the familiar pang of loss when she'd stepped into the house. Dad had hung that wallpaper, letting her help by stirring the thick paste with a stick and handing him the brushes. She'd struggled with the glue, but by using both hands and all her force, she managed to mix it all in. Ann couldn't help because of her missing hand, and Maxine had been too small. LaVonda had been Dad's helpful little assistant.

*Dad. I wish you were still here.*

Ignoring the voices in her head telling her to leave, LaVonda had taken off her jacket and scarf, and draped them across the hall table, then steeled herself by taking several deep breaths. She would go through with this as though she was an actor playing a part. A devoted daughter visiting her poor house-bound alcoholic mother.

'Mum? It's me, LaVonda.'

No response. She'd heard the sound of the television coming from the living room and known exactly what she would see when she entered the room. Maude, dressed in one of her old dresses, tracksuit pants, and her favourite knitted jumper, slumped in her favourite chair, gaze fixed on the television screen.

'Hi, Mum. I brought you some nice biscuits. I'll make us a cup of tea if you like?'

Maude was staring straight ahead. As LaVonda came closer, she saw a dried line of saliva running from the corner of her mother's mouth to her chin. LaVonda shuddered in revulsion. Maude was only sixty-nine, but she seemed twenty years older. She coughed, then turned rheumy eyes towards her daughter, as LaVonda sat down on a stool near her chair.

'What do you want?'

'I've come to have a little chat, Mum. How are you? Do you need anything?'

'I need you to bugger off and leave me alone. Trying to take my house, little devil. I know your games.' This outburst brought on a coughing fit and she spat into the sleeve of her jumper. LaVonda stared in disgust at the glob of mucus on the dirty pink wool.

'Mum, no one is trying to take your home. We're just looking at some possible options. Would you like some tea?'

'I don't want your tea. I want you to go away. Where's Margaret?'

'Margaret left two years ago.' *Because despite being overpaid as a live-in carer, she couldn't stand living with you, Mum.* 'You've got the community nurses now. One of them will be back this evening before you have to go to bed.'

'I want Margaret.'

*Well, you should have thought of that before you drove her away.*

'Margaret is gone, Mum. But I'm here now. Do you want me to do anything for you?'

'Who the hell are you? And where is Margaret?'

Oh dear. Yes, she could see what the nurse meant. Her mother was definitely getting more confused.

'How about a cuppa? Would you like that?'

'Bugger off, you fat cow. Get me my glasses.'

'Mum, please don't talk to me like that.' She wasn't frightened of Maude, not now that she was an adult, but she still trembled in response to her mother's abuse.

'Fat cow, fat cow,' Maude crowed.

'Stop it. That's enough.' Why was she getting upset? Her mother was just a silly, confused old woman. She couldn't really hurt her. Not now. Come on LaVonda, get a grip.

Maude's eyes flashed pure hatred.

'Fat cow, coming here and trying to steal my house. Get out before I smack your fat face. Go on, get out!'

She had. LaVonda had stood up, flustered, and walked straight out of the house.

'No, it didn't go well.' She gave Ann a wry smile, but her hand trembled slightly as she picked up her tea and took a sip. To her great annoyance, she realised she had accidentally left her jacket and favourite scarf behind.

For the millionth time, she asked herself why it couldn't have been her mother who died instead of her beloved father? Why wouldn't Maude die now? Alcoholics were supposed to die young, weren't they? LaVonda's life would be so much easier if only her mother wasn't around. *Just hurry up and die a peaceful, quick death in your sleep, Mum. Is that too much to ask for?*

Apparently, it was. It seemed her mother would outlive all of them at this rate.

Oh, good grief. She was becoming morose again. If it wasn't rage she was feeling, it was self-pity. Her emotions were bouncing all over the place. She smiled weakly at her sister, who was waving at someone in the doorway. She turned to see Sam, Ann's towering husband, duck under the doorway and head towards them. Ann turned back to LaVonda.

'Are you sure you don't want to come to the gallery? We'd enjoy the company and uh... Sam's friend Gavin said he might join us later for a drink.'

LaVonda's eyes narrowed. *Oh no you don't, Ann. You're not setting me up with one of Sam's friends.* Quickly, she drained the rest of her tea and stood up.

'Hi, Sam. Sorry to rush off, but I have a million things to do. Enjoy your Renoirs.'

'You're not coming?' That high, slightly squeaky voice coming from such a giant man still had the ability to shock her slightly whenever he spoke. She covered her reaction with a broad grin.

'No, and don't think I don't know what your conniving wife is up to.' She turned to her sister, who was wearing an expression of innocence.

'Thanks for the drink and the chat. I'll talk to you later.'

She was *not* going to let herself get talked into blind dating. Or any sort of dating. No. If Dave didn't come back, if he was gone for good, she would spend the rest of her life alone. She'd been married twice, and that was enough for one person in their lifetime. She might not have control over the past, but LaVonda did have some control over her future.

Her mind wandered back to her mother. There must be some way she could convince her to move into a nursing home where she'd be looked after. Then at least LaVonda would have other people around for support when she visited. She frowned as she remembered the jacket and scarf she'd left behind at Maude's house. She would have to collect them next Saturday. Although knowing her mother, she'd have probably thrown them out by then. Damn. LaVonda adored that paisley orange scarf with the black fringe. It was a present from Emmett last Christmas, and it was the only thing her daughter had given her in the past five years that didn't smell and look like it had come from a flea market. She should probably just go and get it.

*But I don't want to go back. Oh, be quiet,* she thought crossly. *You're a woman of action. Stop procrastinating.*

She turned the car at the next intersection and headed for the house. If she was lucky, one of the community nurses might be there, and she could just duck in and out without Maude even knowing she'd been in the house.

No such luck. There were no other cars parked in the driveway. LaVonda hesitated for a moment. Perhaps she could come back another time? Oh, good grief, this was stupid. She lifted her bag and got out of the car, shutting the door firmly behind her.

Maude's front door was locked, but she used her key. She could hear the television blaring in the living room. Good. Perhaps if she were quiet enough, she could grab her things and leave again without her mother hearing her. She pushed the door open and stepped into the hallway. Her jacket and scarf were no longer on the hall table. Damn.

She crept a little further. Perhaps the afternoon nurse had found them and put them somewhere for safekeeping? She'd just pop her head around the living room doorway and take a quick look.

Her mother was asleep in her recliner, the images on the television dancing colours over her flaccid face. Despite being the middle of the day, heavy curtains were drawn, casting a depressing gloom over the living room. LaVonda scanned for her belongings and her gaze swept back onto her mother. Maude's face was turned slightly towards the doorway, her eyes were closed and her mouth hung open. She was still. Too still.

LaVonda's voice was a whisper. 'Mum?'

Maude didn't move. LaVonda crept closer. The television was showing some kind of game show, and electronic beeps and chimes almost drowned out the compere's voice. LaVonda reached forward and switched it off.

'Mum?'

Still no movement. A bolt of adrenaline shot through her, and every impulse begged her to turn and run, but she had to check. Of course, she did. She had to make sure her mother was alive. LaVonda reached out and gently touched the cold hand resting on the arm of the recliner.

Maude's arm shot up and nearly hit her face. LaVonda jumped back as her mother sprang up in her seat and screamed as though she was being murdered.

'What the hell! Get out! Get out of my house right now!'

'Mum, it's me.' Her breath caught in her throat. Maude's face was turning red, and her eyes were wild and unfocused.

'Out! Get out now!' She spluttered and clutched at her chest. Oh god, was she alright?

LaVonda watched in horror as her mother gasped and then flung herself forward in her chair. Then she lurched back, her hands tearing at the neck of her jumper. Her face was now purple.

'Mum!' She moved towards her mother; her hands outstretched to help.

'My pills! Get me my heart...' Maude croaked. LaVonda spun around and ran to the bathroom. She flung open the cabinet, revealing several bottles of pills on the shelves. Oh god, which ones?

She snatched up a bottle. Vasotec. There was no information on the label. She grabbed another one. Temazepam. What was that for?

Clutching them, she ran back to the living room. Her mother was still gasping for air, flinging herself back and forth.

'Which one, Mum? What pills do you need?' She held out the two bottles, and her mother grabbed them both, yanking off the lids, and tipping the contents straight into her mouth.

'Mum! Stop!'

'Get out!' The words were hissed. LaVonda froze.

*Fine. Go to hell, Mum. Do not pass go, do not collect $200. Go directly to hell, you miserable old woman.*

She ran from the room.

LaVonda sat in the car, staring at the clock on her dashboard. How long would it take? Ten minutes? Fifteen? Oh, holy hell. She'd left her mother to die.

The sprint up to the house took less than thirty seconds, but she was breathless when she shoved open the door and ran into the living room. Maude was lying on the carpet now, but no longer struggling for breath or grasping at her neck. She lay face down in the semi-darkness of the room, a pool of acrid urine spreading underneath her body.

LaVonda fumbled with her phone. 'Ambulance, please. My mother. She's taken some pills. Tempa-something, I don't know. No, I don't think she is breathing. Okay, yes, I can check.'

She dropped to her knees near her mother's body. She wasn't moving, but LaVonda thought she could see her mother's eyelids fluttering slightly. She put the phone back against her ear.

'She's still breathing. The address?' Her mind had gone blank. What was the address? She was in a thick fog of panic, and her brain seemed to be working so slowly. Only one thought stood out with any clarity. *Hurry up.*

Once the ambulance had been dispatched, LaVonda dropped the phone in her lap, took a deep breath, and closed her eyes, letting her breath out in one slow, steady stream. She kept quiet, kneeling next to her mother, that one thought continually rolling through her mind. *Hurry up, hurry up. Please hurry up.*

She could feel cold air blowing into the lounge room from the open front door, and she shivered violently, but she didn't move from her spot on the carpet near Maude's body. Her ears strained for the noise of the siren. *Hurry up.*

*Please hurry up and die before the ambulance arrives.*

# FOUR

$A$t least Dave had the decency not to bring his new girlfriend to the funeral. Although in truth, they could have done with the boosting of numbers. LaVonda looked around for the third time at the pitiful crowd assembled to farewell Maude Martin.

Emmett and Jasper had made it; the funeral coincided nicely with their planned Easter holiday. Maxine and Ann sat in the second row; Ines and Sam awkward, but stoic, on either side of them. Ann's twelve-year-old twins were still outside playing on her iPhone, having steadfastly refused to actually come into the chapel. A small scattering of elderly people sat right at the back. LaVonda thought they were church parishioners most likely, since her mother didn't have any actual friends. They were all respectfully quiet, eyes downcast, each holding one of the few Order of Service copies LaVonda had printed.

And there was Dave. Sitting halfway back on his own, dressed in his morning suit (She hadn't even realised he'd taken that with him. Why *had* he taken it?) and looking appropriately sombre. He should be next to her, supporting one of the chief mourners. Not halfway down the aisle, as if he were intending to make a run for it at the first opportunity.

She wanted to make a run for it herself. The chapel was unbearably stuffy, and she couldn't wait for the service to be over. It was still surreal. Her mother was gone, and she, LaVonda, was the cause of her death. Or at the very least, the reason Maude hadn't been saved in time. She *should* feel guilty, but instead, a tiny bright flame of joy flickered deep inside. Her mother was dead, and she was free.

She looked down at the Order of Service in her hands. She'd picked the one photo she could bear to look at as the cover. Maude, on her wedding day, standing next to twenty-year-old George. He was beaming with pride at the pretty teenager next to him. Maude looked lovely and serene in her white lace gown; her face gave no hint of the emotionally abusive drunk she would become after Ann's accident. Even then, George took his wedding vows seriously and always forgave Maude her screaming fits, her depression, and her wild accusations. He'd explained to LaVonda and her sisters that it was the alcohol swearing and cursing at them, not their mother.

*You should have left her, Dad. You should have packed us all up and left the first time she threatened to kill herself. She used emotional blackmail to tie you to her through the final years of your life. She denied you any chance of happiness, and yet you remained loyal to her until the day you died. Kept your vows, despite the pain she put you through.*

Tears filled LaVonda's eyes.

'Mum?' The bangles on Emmett's wrist jangled as she placed her hand on her mother's arm. LaVonda looked up and her face fell. Emmett's outfit was in no way suitable for a funeral. Faded blue and long-sleeved, her dress had a high collar and the full skirt brushed the ground as she walked. The hem was already filthy. Around Emmett's neck was a leather cord threaded with orange wooden beads and her hair was scraped into a loose topknot. LaVonda stifled a sigh. Her daughter used to dress so nicely and conservatively, before she met Jasper and transformed herself overnight into this strange, messy-looking hippie.

Emmett smiled her beautiful smile at her mother. 'Don't be sad, Mum. She's in a better place now, and wouldn't she get a kick out of being farewelled on Easter Friday?'

That was exactly why the wretched woman was being cremated; so there would be absolutely no chance of a resurrection in three days' time. But LaVonda kept quiet. Better for Emmett to think her mother's tears were for the woman in the coffin in front of them. She'd spent thirty years protecting her daughter from Maude and the truth about their relationship. She could keep up the façade a little longer.

The service was mercifully short (she'd deliberately picked the condensed version), and then Maude's body was taken away to be turned into ashes. It was over. They all walked sombrely outside into the pale sunshine, Ann making a beeline for her sons, who were fighting over her iPhone.

LaVonda looked over at Ines and Maxine, who were both lighting up cigarettes near the car park. What on earth was her sister wearing? Some kind of bright yellow jumpsuit covered with zippers, and flat, black sneakers. If Emmett's outfit was unsuitable, Maxine's was screamingly inappropriate, but LaVonda knew better than to say anything. It would have been a deliberate choice on Maxine's part; a middle finger to the woman who'd given birth to her but had failed to be a real mother.

Sam walked up to LaVonda.

'How are you holding up?' His tone was a little lower than usual to match the solemnity of the occasion. It suited him much better.

*Pretty good actually, Sam. Yes, she was our mother, but she was a horrible, miserable woman, and I think I killed her, and I'm not sorry. Thanks for asking.*

She smiled in response and squeezed his arm, before turning to see where Dave was. He was standing near a little bench seat talking to Emmett and Jasper, who was smoking one of his filthy herbal cigarettes. LaVonda glowered as she took in Jasper's scruffy little beard, his dark hair knotted at the back of his head, his loose linen shirt, and his pants that appeared to have a *drawstring* holding them up. At least he was wearing shoes for a change, so she didn't have to be repulsed by his long hairy toes.

'Will you excuse me, Sam?'

'Do you want me to come for moral support?' He grinned down at her.

'Thank you, but no, I'll be fine.'

LaVonda marched over to the little group.

'Put that out, will you?' She waved her hand in front of her frowning face. Jasper grinned, revealing stained grey teeth, then nodded agreeably and stubbed the end of his cigarette out on the grass. Emmett took his arm supportively, and LaVonda felt cross.

'Dave. Thank you for coming.' LaVonda turned her attention to her husband. Well, her *ex-husband*, she supposed. Who would have thought that when he walked out three weeks ago, the next time she'd see him would be at her mother's funeral? He looked shockingly familiar, yet strange at the same time. He also looked embarrassed as he cleared his throat.

'I'm sorry for your loss.'

*Oh, cut it out, Dave.* LaVonda resisted the urge to roll her eyes. He knew better than anyone what a dreadful person Maude had been. His own father was just as bad, if not worse.

It was one of the few things they'd had in common; part of the reason they'd been drawn together. Both survivors of abusive parents. Though Maude had never been physically violent towards her children, unlike Brian Robinette, who'd walked the narrow line between harsh discipline and outright domestic violence, handing out punishments to his only son for the slightest transgression. If anyone would understand why LaVonda had done what she'd done, it was Dave. She was half tempted to tell him.

'Will you be coming back to the house for the wake?'

'No, I'd better get back.' He looked nervously at Emmett.

'It's alright, Dad. Mum told us about your new... ah living arrangements.'

Well, she hadn't had much choice, had she? Emmett and Jasper had arrived late last night, and Dave's absence was overwhelmingly conspicuous. She hadn't known what else to say. She could hardly claim he was off on a business trip, could she?

Emmett had taken the news surprisingly well, not seeming at all shocked or upset. It was probably all the hippie Zen stuff she was now into that made her so calm and tranquil. Although, she'd always been peaceful and unruffled, even as a tiny child. She took after Mark in that way. LaVonda had barely had one peaceful and unruffled day in her entire life. There was always far too much to worry about.

'How was your holiday with...?' Now she was deliberately trying to make Dave feel uncomfortable, and it made her feel happy to see him drop his gaze to the grass and awkwardly wring his hands.

'Oh, um, Jemima. We ended up cancelling because she, um, she had a thing at work. We're going away tomorrow instead.'

Oh, great. So, he had cancelled his holiday because Jemima had a *thing*, but he couldn't postpone it to dump LaVonda on a day other than her birthday? What a dickhead he was. If he had a sudden heart attack, she wouldn't even *pretend* to call for an ambulance.

'Well, don't let us hold you up. Thanks for coming.' LaVonda waved her hand dismissively towards the car park, but her daughter reached out and gently touched her arm. She looked up. Emmett's eyes were brown and wide set, framed by long lashes. Mark's eyes.

'Actually, Mum, while we've got you both, we need to tell you something.'

LaVonda watched her daughter smile at Jasper, who grinned back. Ugh, those teeth. The thought of that mouth kissing Emmett's lips made her shudder. Emmett reached out and took Jasper's hand, then turned back to her parents.

'This obviously isn't the way we'd planned to tell you, at Gran's funeral and all, but we have some exciting news. Jaz and I, we're having a baby.'

LaVonda reacted instinctively and badly.

'Oh god no!' She clapped her hands to her cheeks in horror.

A look of shock spread over Emmett's face at her mother's reaction. It appeared she could be flappable after all.

'Congratulations, darling. What wonderful news.' Dave smiled widely.

Hypocrite. LaVonda knew full well Dave was as appalled as she was. Their beautiful daughter having a baby with this smelly, chain-smoking, unemployed hippie? It was unthinkable.

'Thanks, Dad.' Emmett glared at her mother.

'Sorry, darling. You just took me by surprise. It's... wonderful news. When are you due?'

Could Em have made a mistake? Oh, how could she even think that? This was her *grandchild*. She wanted grandchildren. She just didn't want Jasper Brown's genetic material to be part of her grandchildren.

*Don't shudder. Whatever you do, don't shudder.*

She should have guessed when Emmett first hinted over the phone. This was Dave's fault too. If she hadn't been so distracted by him leaving, she'd have had time to prepare her reaction to the news.

Emmett was still frowning.

'July, or thereabouts. I've been talking to our naturopath, and we estimate our little peanut is about twenty weeks along.' Her face softened as she spread both hands across her belly. There was a definite round bump that LaVonda hadn't even noticed before. Jasper reached out and placed his hand over Emmett's. It took a tremendous effort, but LaVonda managed not to slap it away.

'You haven't seen a doctor yet?' She was *trying* not to sound judgemental, but honestly, a *naturopath*?

'We're exploring natural alternatives, Mum. Try not to worry.' Emmett smiled as Ann came over and joined their little group. She looked almost as distracted and irritated as LaVonda felt.

'Von, are you okay if we skip the wake? The boys are driving me mad and I'm not up to wrangling them into behaving all afternoon.'

What about all the sandwiches and pastries she'd spent the morning making? She'd made far too much food for the one, two, oh god, *five* of them who would be coming back to the house. She glanced at Emmett, who looked immediately guilty.

'Aren't you coming back either?'

Emmett squirmed under her mother's frown. 'If it's okay, Dad, I thought we might come over and meet Jemima before you go away for the weekend. We won't be back down until after the baby is born so...' she glanced at Jasper, '...it might be a good idea to meet her now.'

LaVonda kept her expression neutral so she wouldn't give away the thoughts pounding through her head. *You little traitor, Em. You're my daughter, not his. Your loyalty is to me, not him. How dare you go and condone this... this relationship with another woman by meeting her?*

Her voice was calm and cool. 'Fine. Will you be home for dinner?'

'Yes, we should be back by six.' Emmett dropped her gaze. Ann looked from mother to daughter.

'Congratulations, Em. You too, Jasper. What wonderful, exciting news.'

She reached out to LaVonda, touching her lightly on the arm. Her smile was warm and comforting.

'I'll send Sam and the monsters home. Let's grab Maxie and Ines, and we'll go and open some wine.'

LaVonda squeezed Ann's hand gratefully. Her big sister understood. She turned her back on her duplicitous daughter, spineless ex-husband, and that awful Jasper, and walked away.

'More wine?' Ann didn't wait for an answer, filling LaVonda's glass to the brim again. LaVonda had already had two glasses and had sunk into a pleasant, blurry buzz. She rested one elbow on her island bench and picked up a sandwich from the plate in front of her, pulling it apart before dropping it back onto the plate. She didn't need to eat. She didn't need anything but this delicious wine and her family. Her lovely, lovely sisters.

'This pastry, amazing!' Ines was tearing into the food. She waved a sausage roll at Maxine as she bit into a handmade samosa. Crumbs landed on the clean kitchen floor, but LaVonda didn't care, because she needed to concentrate on staying seated on her stool. Were they always this small, or had her bottom suddenly gotten bigger?

'Please, keep eating. It will all go to waste otherwise.' Her words were coming out a tiny bit slurred, but probably no one had noticed.

'Are you getting blind drunk because of our mother, your daughter, or Dull Dave?' As usual, Maxine missed nothing. Ann put her glass down, leaned over, and slung her arm around LaVonda.

'Probably all three, aren't you, Von? Nothing wrong with the occasional pity party, as long as it doesn't become a lifelong habit. Speaking of lifelong habits, shall we toast Maude?'

Maxine lifted her glass. 'Ding-dong, the witch is dead. Thank God, or whatever celestial being decided to finally remove her from the earth.'

LaVonda thought this seemed a little harsh, but frankly, she was in no position to object, given the role she'd played in Maude's death.

'Thank you both for coming today. I know you didn't want to.'

Maxine snorted. 'Oh, no, my darling sister; you've got it all wrong. I've been looking forward to going to that woman's funeral for the best part of forty years. I had my outfit planned from the first time I saw Kill Bill, and I only wish I'd had the chance to dance on her grave. Can I have her ashes? We could have a little party before I flush them down the toilet.'

Ines frowned. 'Maxine, you are being disrespectful.'

Maxine spun around to look at her. '*Excusez moi*, Ines, but mind your own damn business. Our mother was a terrible person, and I will not pretend otherwise.'

Ines pouted and bit hard into another sausage roll. Gosh, she was making a mess, wasn't she? Not that LaVonda cared. She was just *noticing* the crumbs. She wasn't actually bothered by them. The kitchen didn't need to look perfect all the time. Imperfect was fine.

There was a knock at the back door. Ann walked over and opened it as LaVonda swung her stool around. Her neighbour Doreen, stood in the doorway, holding a dish covered with a tea towel.

'I hope I'm not interrupting. Only I just heard your mother died, LaVonda, and I'm so sorry for your loss. I would have come to the funeral, to pay my *respects*, but no one told me.'

She strutted into the kitchen and set the dish down on the kitchen counter. 'I had to find out about the *tragedy* from Florence Jessup, next door, and I'm afraid I didn't have time to make my special sausage casserole, but I did whip up a Tuna Mornay for you and Dave. Here, enjoy. Where is Dave by the way? I haven't seen his car in weeks. Still on his business trip, I suppose? Hahaha.'

Maxine laughed. 'Dave's not on a business trip. He's shacked up with his new girlfriend.'

LaVonda groaned and dropped her head into her hands. From the corner of her eye, she could see Doreen looking Maxine up and down, clearly taking in the yellow jumpsuit, the spiked, blonde hair, the inappropriate bright red lipstick. A slight sneer appeared on Doreen's face.

'Really? Well, not that it is any of my business...' she trailed off expectantly. Ann's eyes flashed, and she set down her glass.

'You're right. It isn't any of your business.'

'I'm sorry? Excuse me, but I'm a close friend and neighbour of LaVonda, and I am simply concerned—'

'No, you're not. You're being nosy.' Ann walked over to the back door and pulled it open. 'This is a private wake for our mother. Perhaps you should go?'

Doreen looked at LaVonda. Her overbearing confidence faded, and she seemed suddenly uncertain.

'Look, I *am* sorry for your loss. If I can do anything... well, will we see you at book club next Tuesday? We've missed you these past few weeks.'

LaVonda kept her head in her hands and didn't reply. Doreen walked towards the back door, turning as she reached it. 'Listen. Just look after yourself, LaVonda, and don't worry about returning the dish. I've got dozens of them.'

Ann shut the door behind her. 'Well, that's lucky.' She lifted the Tuna Mornay, still covered in the tea towel, and dropped the whole thing into the kitchen bin.

Maxine burst out laughing. Ines chuckled. LaVonda reached out for the wine bottle and topped off her drink. Ann high-fived Maxine as she returned to her stool at the kitchen counter.

'Seriously, who brings tuna bake to a wake? Horrible, stinky, stodgy thing.'

Maxine snorted. 'What? The dish or the neighbour?' She glanced at her girlfriend, who smiled and reached out for another sausage roll. Ann pushed the plate closer.

'Both. Now, enough about her, let's talk about Gavin.'

'Who?' asked Maxine, at the same time as LaVonda said, 'Let's not.'

'These little beef rolls, simply superb. You're a good baker, LaVonda.'

'Thanks, Ines.' LaVonda took a sip of her wine and wondered vaguely how long it would take the neighbourhood grapevine to spread the news about Dave leaving. To her surprise, she found she didn't care. Let them gossip. She was done with the book club. She was done with worrying about the women in her street. She shifted slightly. She definitely needed to get some bigger stools though, preferably bright red ones. She'd go to Ikea tomorrow.

'Who is Gavin?' Maxine reached over and took a sausage roll, biting into it. 'She's right, these are great.'

Ann smiled. 'Sam's mate from rowing. Divorced, no kids, no baggage, owns two homes. He works in finance. He's a lovely man and would be perfect for LaVonda. Pass the plate over, will you, before your girlfriend eats everything.'

'I'm not dating Gavin.' LaVonda slid off her stool and walked over to the kitchen sink, unbuttoning her shirt as she did. She was having another hot flush, although, thankfully, this was one of the milder ones. She still had the occasional being-roasted-alive sensation, but mostly her flushes were just an unpleasant and uncomfortable heat that usually went away after a few minutes.

'Welcome to the wet t-shirt competition part of the wake,' Ann announced, as LaVonda scooped a handful of cold water onto her chest. Ines looked confused.

'She's joking. Von is having a hot flush.' Maxine stuffed another sausage roll into her mouth, laughing at Ines's expression as she did.

'Oh. How... terribly horrible for you.'

Yes, it was terribly horrible, thank you Ines. Oh, to be twenty-three again and years away from this heavy, hot misery. Although, at twenty-three, LaVonda had been a newly forged widow with a tiny child and still a year away from meeting Dave. Twenty-three hadn't been a particularly good year for her.

She didn't remember much of that time. After Mark's accident, she'd toppled headlong into an endless abyss of overwhelming guilt and grief. Time ground to a halt, and absolutely nothing mattered. She didn't matter. Her child didn't matter. Staying alive didn't seem to matter.

Her sisters had flown into action, taking control, caring for Emmett, and allowing LaVonda to do nothing but sink down, breathe, and try to bear it. It was all she could manage. Breathing in and out, over and over, day after day, month after month. Eventually, time started moving, and the episodes of pain and panic, which brought her figuratively and literally to her knees, became less frequent, and LaVonda, who hadn't expected to survive this heart-crushing event, found she had.

At the time, she had thought she would never get over his death. Decades later, she knew she wouldn't. Every day, for the rest of her life, she would continue to miss Mark and wish he was still here. Mark, and her dad. It was true; you didn't get over grief, but time did make the pain more manageable.

Sunlight streamed in through the French doors, warming LaVonda as she stretched out on the couch, one of her bright, new cushions stuffed behind her back. Her sisters and Ines had left an hour earlier, and although she had stopped drinking, she was still pleasantly tipsy. The house was quiet; a serene quietness, not a lonely one, and LaVonda felt deliciously relaxed. A few sprigs of daphne, cut from her garden and placed in a water glass, perfumed the living room air.

LaVonda inhaled deeply, smiled, and stretched her arms above her head. Life was gifting her one of those rare, precious moments of undiluted pleasure in the moment, and she had a sense of impending joy, as if she was anticipating a particularly lovely gift.

Did she regret not saving her mother? Even a little bit? No. She didn't. She felt extraordinarily light and happy, as though someone had reached inside her, lifted out the heavy stone of tension she always carried, and replaced it with a frothy bubble of excitement. She wouldn't be visiting her mother this weekend, or any other weekend. She didn't ever have to endure another one of Maude's abusive phone calls or run interference when the home care staff complained about their treatment at her mother's hands. LaVonda was finally free.

Mentally, she ran through her to-do list to ensure there were no outstanding issues or things she had to think about. Emmett and Jasper wouldn't be back until later, but dinner was already made and just had to be thrown in the oven. She certainly didn't have to worry about what *Dave* was doing anymore. The housework was up to date, and the kitchen back to its usual tidy state, with no crumbs on the floor. It was so delightful to realise there was nothing pressing on her list that she went back through it, just for the sheer pleasure of realising anew that she had nothing she needed to do.

She had a mug of hot tea, her new murder mystery, and her gleeful little secret giving her the much-needed feeling of control she'd been missing for so long. The rest of the afternoon stretched out lazily in front of her. She didn't have anything she had to do, no pressing needs, just time. Perfect time. She could even have a little snooze if she wanted.

She reached out to pick up her mug and noticed a small fly walking across her coffee table, near the daphne. She flicked her hand languidly at it. The fly moved off, flew around a bit, then landed on her knee. She jerked her leg, and the fly disappeared. LaVonda returned to her book.

She read a few lines, then realised she was thinking about Royce and what he might do next to sabotage her. No! She would not allow thoughts of him to interrupt her lovely afternoon. She stretched again and wriggled her toes. The fly landed back on the coffee table and began walking towards her tea. She flapped her hand at it, and it flew off, returning a few seconds later. Oh, for heaven's sake.

She watched it for a bit. *Just go, would you? Just buzz off to another room.* The fly stubbornly refused to cooperate. It was deliberately provoking her now, rubbing its forelegs together and dancing towards her. LaVonda regarded the insect with increasing annoyance. At first, it had been a tiny, slight bother, now it was a growing irritant. She tried to wave it away again. It responded by landing ticklishly on her bare foot. Well, that was a bridge too far.

LaVonda flung her book down and got to her feet. She stomped into the laundry and, after what seemed like a stupidly long time, finally located the fly swat. She marched back into the lounge room, brandishing the swat. The fly had disappeared. She looked for it for a few minutes, but there was no sign of it. She sat back down on the couch, looking around warily. She gripped the handle of her weapon and waited.

The fly was back. Little bastard. She watched as he crawled along the back of the couch, before she lifted her swat, aimed carefully, and brought it down quickly. The fly shot away and flew to the other side of the room. Damn!

She got up and stalked it, bringing down her swat again and again as she chased it around the room. It finally landed back on the coffee table and *thwack!* The fly lay squashed and flat on the surface.

LaVonda felt gloriously triumphant. *Serves you right.* The sound of the fly being splattered was just so satisfying! *Serves you right,* she thought again.

She felt inordinately pleased with herself for dispatching the fly. It had annoyed her over and over, and she had successfully removed it from her life. Of course, she had killed an otherwise harmless creature, but did that make her a bad person?

Okay, it probably didn't make her a *good* person, but heavens, it was only a fly. Although perhaps she wasn't quite the generous, honourable person she'd always presumed herself to be. If she could kill an animal (were insects considered animals?) with such pleasure.

Oh, come on. Why was she having an existential crisis over a fly? She tried to get back her feeling of pleasure. Ah, there it was. She was *happy* she'd killed the fly. It was annoying her. She'd had all the power in this situation, and she'd chosen to exercise her power. The fly was dead, and LaVonda was not sorry.

# FIVE

Jasper had used up the last of the milk. Because of course he had.

There had been just enough left for a *civilised* person's serve of milk on cornflakes and one cup of tea. LaVonda leaned her hip against the kitchen sink and pursed her lips. Drinking her tea black was doing nothing to improve her mood towards the father of her impending grandchild.

'So, what are you two up to today?' Her voice was tight with annoyance, but neither Jasper, who reeked of cloves and tobacco, nor Emmett seemed to notice. Emmett was dressed in yet another ridiculous outfit. She had on a loose, grey knit draped over a long-sleeved t-shirt, and a red velvet skirt with a frilled hem. The pervasive bangles and beads adorned every limb, and her hair was again knotted into a careless bun. LaVonda itched to brush it out. Emmett looked up from buttering her toast and beamed.

'We're going to meet my friend Alice for lunch and see if she'll be the baby's goddess-mother. This afternoon we're visiting Jasper's Uncle Kelvin, who is a wood-whisperer. We're going to ask him if he might consider making a baby's cradle out of recycled railway sleepers.'

LaVonda blanched. 'That sounds...' *completely horrible,* '... lovely. Don't forget we're going out for dinner with Max and Ines tonight. I hope you like Mexican, Jasper?'

Jasper stopped slurping his breakfast and looked up at her. Hopefully the baby would inherit Emmett's lovely eyes and not his little piggy ones.

'Yeah, sure. Great. I'm vegan, mostly, but as long as they have sustainably grown legumes and rice, it should be okay.' He returned his attention to his cornflakes.

*A vegan who drinks all the milk, and who devoured two-thirds of last night's beef lasagne,* thought LaVonda. *No problem, Jasper. I'll make sure you get a whole pig's worth of bacon to have with your bean enchiladas tonight.*

Emmett smiled across at her partner. 'Jaz doesn't like to make a fuss, do you, babe? It's okay, I'll call the restaurant this afternoon and make sure they can accommodate your dietary needs.'

Jasper continued to slurp his cereal without replying. He was a man of few words, and most of what did come out of his mouth was brain-numbingly tedious. LaVonda clenched her fists.

Emmett picked up her empty plate and took it over to the dishwasher, patting LaVonda's shoulder as she passed.

'Mum, we'll meet you at the restaurant. Uncle Kelvin suffers chronophobia. Don't roll your eyes, it's a real thing, so he doesn't like to be rushed. We might be there for a while.'

'That's fine.'

In fact, it was better than fine. LaVonda would drive to the hospital and leave her car in the overnight parking so she could have some time before dinner to complain to Maxine about Jasper. And Emmett, who was dressing and acting even weirder under Jasper's influence. And Dave, who was off on his stupid romantic holiday, having monopolised their daughter's attention all yesterday, even though it was *LaVonda's mother's funeral,* and Emmett should have rightly been paying attention to her.

She didn't deserve attention though, did she? She didn't deserve anything after deliberately letting her mother die. Yes, she'd gone back inside the house, and, yes, she'd eventually called the emergency line back and given them the correct address, explaining her panic had made them give her own address, but she'd let Maude die alright. She *should* be wracked with guilt and remorse; instead, she carried this nasty, happy little secret deep inside. She'd love to share it with Emmett, Maxine and Ann, even with Dave. *Hey, guess what? I'm not the boring, morally righteous, perfectionist you all think I am. I deliberately let my own mother die.*

And wouldn't Jasper sit up straight if he knew she was an (almost) murderer? Look at him, hunched over his breakfast, the ends of his long, straggly hair brushing the bowl. He was quite revolting. Emmett deserved so much better. She should be married to someone like her dad, her real dad, someone kind and sensitive, loving and smart. LaVonda felt the familiar pull of grief. *Mark. Oh, Mark, if you were still alive, there is no way our daughter would be dating Jasper.* Her nose prickled. *Don't cry. Not now.*

'So, how was yesterday afternoon?' She kept her tone deliberately light.

She had waited all last night for either of them to bring up the subject of their visit to Dave and Jemima. Not that she cared, but it would be nice to get a feel for when, or indeed *if*, her husband might be returning home.

But neither Emmett nor Jasper had said a word. Their conversation had centred almost entirely on Emmett's pregnancy, and LaVonda had put a lot of enthusiasm and effort in to make up for her earlier faux pas at the announcement. Never had a grandmother-to-be expressed more interest in a pregnancy than LaVonda had last night.

Emmett immediately looked shifty, as Jasper gave a rude snort of laughter. LaVonda felt a buzz of impatience. What was wrong with them?

'Of course, if it is *private*, you don't need to tell me anything.'

'No, no, Mum. It's not that. Jemima is... well she's quite...'

*Spit it out, Emmett.* LaVonda took a sip of her black tea to curb her irritation. Ugh. *Jemima is what?*

'She's very young. Maybe a few years younger than me. Slim. She's quite plain though.'

The last part of her comment had almost definitely been added to soothe the sting of the earlier part. But Emmett had underestimated her mother. So, Dave's new girlfriend was young and slim, Well, good for Dave. LaVonda actually preferred to be left for someone better than her; imagine if he'd left her for someone middle-aged and frumpy. That would have stung. Plus, young women were universally self-absorbed and boring so, once the novelty wore off, Dave would undoubtedly come crawling back. Back to familiarity. Back to his normal, secure life where he was well looked after by his middle-aged, but definitely not frumpy, wife.

'Is she excited about the baby?'

Emmett's eyes shone. 'Oh, yes! She's thrilled for us. She kept laughing and saying she was much too young to be a granny, but she welcomes the chance to love and spoil little Peanut.'

'How nice. I'm quite looking forward to spoiling... little Peanut too. I've kept all your baby dresses for her.'

Emmett laughed. 'Oh, Mum. I know you have your heart set on a girl, but it might be a little boy, you know. A mini Jaz running around.'

Good grief.

'Grandpa is excited too. We called him while we were at Dad's place to give him the good news. He's promised to come up and visit when Peanut is born.'

LaVonda felt her upper lip curl with distaste. If she had her way, Brian would have nothing to do with his great-grandchild. He was almost entirely estranged from Dave, and LaVonda hadn't seen him for more than twenty-five years. But for some reason, the old man had a soft spot for Emmett; his only grandchild, even if she wasn't actually related to him. LaVonda had never stood in the way of their relationship as long as Emmett was safe, but that didn't mean she had to like it.

Oh, and by the way, it wasn't 'Dad's place', thank you very much. It was *Jemima's*. 'Dad's place' was here. At home.

Emmett beamed over at Jasper, who sniffed and then drew his hand across his nose. LaVonda felt a belt of nausea and quickly turned towards the sink. She rinsed her mug under the tap before turning back to face them.

'Well, enjoy your day. I'm heading off to the shops. Do either of you need anything?'

Emmett shook her head, as Jasper picked up the empty milk carton and stared somewhat stupidly at it.

'Yeah. I think we're out of milk.'

'Wouldn't it be *nice* if you could just dispatch the people who annoyed you? Just swat them down like flies?'

'I think our definitions of the word 'nice' vary wildly.' Maxine blew a stream of smoke towards LaVonda, who coughed dramatically and waved her hands.

They were standing outside the hospital entrance waiting for their Uber to take them to the restaurant. Maxine had just finished her shift and had changed out of her uniform into a navy-blue pants suit. She looked... severe. LaVonda, in her yellow cardigan and pink skirt, felt frivolous and overtly feminine next to her. The skirt had been flattering when she'd put it on earlier, but now she felt like she was trying much too hard to look young.

'I'm being serious, Max.' Her tone was low; she was conscious of trying to sound serious to make up for looking slightly ridiculous. 'Imagine if you had the power to simply eliminate anyone or anything that annoyed you.'

'Some people do have that power, Von, and it generally doesn't end well for their countrymen. Thankfully, we live in a civilised society.'

*Do we?* LaVonda wondered. *Is it civilised, or are we all just animals existing under a thin veneer of social obligation?* After all, look what happens when you put people together in terrible situations such as the Holocaust, or being stranded out at sea. The ones prepared to put themselves first and sacrifice others, they're the ones who survive. There is no room for generosity and kindness when your life is at stake.

LaVonda shivered and pulled her cardigan more firmly around her shoulders.

'So, who are you thinking about killing?' Maxine grinned, pushed her spiky fringe out of her eyes, and took another deep drag on her cigarette.

LaVonda laughed. 'I can think of three or four people I could cheerfully dispatch, right off the bat. Jasper. Dave's horrible father. Possibly Dave, right now. The new guy at work. How about you?'

'Hmm. Well, maybe Ines? We're not getting on that well at the moment. She's so fucking *French*, pardon my French.'

'I'm being *serious*. You can't want to kill your girlfriend.' LaVonda rolled her eyes dramatically.

'No, not really. She's a pain in the bum, but most people are, aren't they? Present company included. But seriously? The only person I ever wished dead was our mother, and praise the powers that be, she's gone now.'

'What about Walter...' LaVonda watched Maxine's eyes narrow, but she ploughed on regardless. 'Max, he hurt you!' She knew 'hurt' didn't begin to describe what Walter had done to her sister, but she couldn't bring herself to use the word 'rape'.

They'd never spoken about it. Not since the night Maxine crawled into Ann's bed, crying, as LaVonda hurried across the bedroom and hopped in beside them. Not once since then, in more than thirty years.

Apple shampoo. LaVonda could still smell Maxine's freshly washed hair spread damply across the pillow. She'd buried her nose in the silky-soft strands, trying to breathe support and comfort into her little sister. Ann had spoken quietly, prompting Maxine, who sobbed out enough details for them to realise what had happened. LaVonda was seized with fury, mingled with distress, as the three sisters huddled together. She'd wanted to strangle Walter Durbin, and then storm into their mother's room and strangle her too, for allowing that awful man into their lives.

Maxine had sworn them to secrecy.

'It would kill Dad if he knew. You mustn't say anything. Promise me you won't.'

LaVonda knew Ann had been as torn as she was. Neither of them could bear to let Walter get away with what he'd done, but George had been recently hospitalised and had to use all his strength to fight the lung disease wracking his body. It was too much; Dad's terminal illness, on top of Maude's unrelenting abuse, and now the horror that Maxine had endured. It seemed easier to bury the knowledge and keep quiet. Rally around each other and protect themselves, the way they had since they were children. Fortunately, Walter disappeared from their lives as quickly as he'd entered.

There was no point in saying anything to Maude. Even on the few occasions when their mother was sober, she treated them like annoying, unwanted pets.

Particularly Ann. After the accident that took Ann's arm, Maude couldn't bear to look at her daughter.

How different things might have been if they'd had a proper mother, one who cared, and looked after them. But a mother like that wouldn't have started bringing strange men home as soon as her husband was hospitalised.

So the sisters concentrated on supporting each other, and looking after their father, with Maude set in the background, irrelevant and uninvolved apart from the outbursts of verbal abuse. No one spoke about that night, but LaVonda noticed Ann acting more protective of Maxine; hurrying her out of the living room when Maude started ranting at them. Going in late to her university classes so she could give Maxine a lift to school. Making sure Maxine had a packed lunch every day. LaVonda understood. She'd noticed herself fretting over her little sister too. She'd had to be careful, though. Prickly Max noticed and firmly rejected, any hint of fussing.

Not talking about the rape had been their way of protecting Maxine.

As adults, it was there, but like Mark's death and Ann's disability; buried in their shared past, seldom acknowledged, and never discussed in detail. They were as close as three sisters could be, having bonded over their childhood traumas. So why hadn't they ever talked about the biggest things to happen to each of them? Why hadn't they ever spoken about what happened to Maxine?

'Max?' The Uber was two minutes away, and this wasn't a good time for a conversation about the past, but LaVonda couldn't stop herself now she'd opened Pandora's Box.

'No. Leave it, Von.' Maxine's voice was a low growl.

'But he completely ruined your life.' LaVonda realised, with a small shock, as she said the words, that she thought this was true. Maxine's drinking, her dependency on cigarettes, her inability to hold down a relationship, were all a result of the terrible thing that had happened to her when she was barely a teenager.

'What the hell? My life isn't ruined, you demented cow. How dare you?' Maxine's face had turned blotchy and red. LaVonda had seen her angry before, but not this furious. She immediately tried to backtrack.

'Max. I'm sorry, I-'

'You know what? I'm sick and tired of listening to you complain and whine about your life, while the whole time you're looking down on me. Thinking yourself so superior. You're not, Von, you're every bit as fucked up and annoying as the rest of us. How dare you judge me?'

LaVonda was appalled. She wasn't *judging* Maxine. She wasn't. Yes, she was *concerned* about her sister, naturally, but she didn't judge her choices any more than she judged Ann's or Emmett's. Although, she wasn't exactly *delighted* with her daughter's choices.

'No, I just...'

'Go to hell. What happened to me was unpleasant, but it didn't ruin my life. I'm perfectly fine, better than fine, I'm great. You can just piss off.' Maxine dropped her cigarette and stomped it into the pavement. 'Here's your Uber. Enjoy your dinner.'

LaVonda watched Maxine stride back into the hospital. What had she done? She'd managed to upset and offend her younger sister. Why had she blurted that out? It was completely out of character because she was usually so measured. What was *wrong* with her?

Although, let's be honest; Maxine had *totally* overreacted, and now LaVonda had to get into the Uber, go to dinner, and explain to everyone why her sister wouldn't be joining them. She frowned. It was *typical* of Maxine to get wound up over the slightest thing.

See, it was happening again. Her own emotions, lurching from self-pity to annoyance, then swinging into anger. Surely it wasn't normal to feel irritated all the time. Irritation that boiled over so easily into fury.

Ann was right; she needed to see someone and get some help managing her moods. Although even *that* made her feel annoyed, because it was *yet* another task on a never-ending list of things to do. She shouldn't *have* to see someone, because this shouldn't be happening. Didn't she have enough in her life to worry about without this emotional rollercoaster going on at the same time? LaVonda climbed into the Uber and leaned back against the seat. She felt utterly exhausted.

'Max is refusing to answer my calls, Ann. It's been three days.'

LaVonda spoke quietly into the phone, even though she was alone in the office. The rest of the team had gone out to lunch, organised, as usual, by Royce. LaVonda hadn't been invited. She could have gone anyway, it wasn't like anyone would have stopped her, but she decided to stay in silent protest. Also, Deborah was wound up about something that had happened on the Easter weekend, so she might need LaVonda's support.

'Yes, she's pretty upset, but she's a bit sensitive at the moment. She and Ines aren't getting on well. Give her a few more days to calm down, and I'm sure she'll come around. Hang on, I'm just going to put you on speaker so I can drink my coffee. I've only had one this morning, so I'm still being quite insufferable, and my poor staff are all hiding under their desks. There. Now what about Gavin?'

'Ann. Drop it, please. I don't want to date Gavin. I am still married, you know. And Dave is going to come back at some point.'

The words rang hollow now. LaVonda wasn't at all convinced Dave was coming home any time soon. And how did she feel about that? Truth be told, she wasn't particularly perturbed.

After Emmett and Jasper left last night, she'd expected to feel lonely, maybe even a bit bereft, but she didn't. She felt quite content. Well, apart from the stuff with Maxine, of course, and the mess at work with Royce. And the hot flushes. And the slight guilt she felt for not feeling guilty about Maude's death. But *apart* from all that, she felt absolutely fine. She didn't need Dave, or anyone else for that matter. She was perfectly happy being irritated by the people in her life, all by herself.

'There is no harm in going on just one date.' Ann spoke quickly, as though she could convince LaVonda before she'd have time to think. 'It would be good for you to get out of the house, and who knows? Maybe Dave will hear about it and be jealous enough to come rushing back.'

'You don't think that.'

'No, I don't, but I'd love you to go out with Gavin anyway. Just one date. Von, he's perfect for you. I'll book somewhere nice for next Saturday night, my treat, okay?'

'If I agree to this, will it get you off my back?' LaVonda rolled her eyes and enjoyed the sensation so much she did it again.

'Yes! I promise if this doesn't work out I will never, ever try to set you up again.'

'You've got your fingers crossed behind your back, haven't you?' She knew her sister.

'Absolutely.'

'Listen, I'd better go. Deborah is on the warpath. Someone screwed up the security system by coming in on the weekend and not turning off the alarm. She'll want the culprit hung, drawn, and quartered, and I'm just in the right mood to help.'

Ann laughed. 'Listen, don't worry about Maxie, you know she burns bright and fast. I guarantee she'll be fine in a few days. I'll invite her shopping with us next Sunday. She'll have cooled off by then.'

'I hope you're right.'

'I'm always right. I'm right about Gavin, too.'

'Goodbye, Ann.'

LaVonda wandered back to her desk, thinking hard. She didn't want to go on a date with Gavin, so what had possessed her to agree to it? Could she change her mind? No, because then Ann would just start up again. Easier just to go along and then report back to her bossy older sister that her date had been a disaster. Because there was no doubt in LaVonda's mind; it would not go well.

'LaVonda, could you pop in here for a moment, please?'

LaVonda pasted a smile on her face as she walked into Deborah's office and shut the door behind her. To her surprise, the Director of Security was seated at the small conference table, along with one of the HR staff. Adam something? Andrew? LaVonda tried to act cool, even though she suddenly felt inexplicably guilty. Heat warmed her cheeks.

'Please, take a seat.' The Director gestured towards the empty seat next to him. LaVonda sat, praying the heat in her cheeks wouldn't become a full-blown hot flush. Oh, how ridiculous. Her body was reacting as though she were suddenly ashamed, which was completely absurd. She hadn't come in on the weekend. So why did she feel like she was the culprit? She continued to smile nervously as Deborah, the Director, and the HR man looked at her silently. Finally, the Director spoke.

'As you're probably aware, LaVonda, someone came into the office on Sunday and set off the alarm system. That in itself isn't an issue, however, instead of following protocol and contacting the security company to advise, the person in question simply exited the office, leaving the front door open, and the building completely unsecured. The police had to be called to search the entire premises for possible intruders, and the security company is issuing an invoice for the time they've wasted investigating the matter. Naturally, my department is taking a fairly dim view of this incident.'

LaVonda nodded. Her face was flaming now, a completely ridiculous reaction to the situation. She wasn't the culprit and, really, if they wanted to know who it was, why hadn't they simply checked the swipe card data records? All employees had a pass card they used for entering the building and certain parts of the office, so it should be easy to identify who had been here on the weekend.

'We've checked the data records...' Well, there you go then. '... and we know who the person was.'

Then why was he wasting her time? Why had she been brought in, when they already knew who the culprit was? He should just go and seek out that person...

Oh. No. It couldn't be, could it? A rogue bead of sweat tickled its way down LaVonda's spine, and she pressed against the back of her chair to stop it. The Director leaned forward; his fleshy face closer, his voice threatening.

'We need to get to the bottom of this.'

Royce. He must have stolen her pass card and used it to frame her. What could she possibly say to prove her innocence? LaVonda cast her mind back to the weekend. She felt frantic. Did she have an alibi? She'd spent the morning of Easter Sunday with Emmett and Jasper, but then they'd gone to visit friends. In the afternoon, she'd done a little baking, some cleaning, and then taken her book out to the garden to read in the sun. It had been unexpectedly gorgeous weather.

But there was no one to vouch for her movements. If she hadn't had the blow up with Maxine, she might have joined her at her self-defence class, and then she'd have had several alibis for the afternoon. Right now, she had none.

'What time... did this happen?'

If it was in the morning, she could prove it hadn't been her. If it was the afternoon, she was done for. But how had Royce managed to take her card and then return it to her handbag without her noticing, in time for her to swipe herself in this morning? It didn't make sense. Unless... he'd followed her home and broken into her house? LaVonda felt a lurch of fear. She brought her hands up to her face and pressed her fingertips against her temples.

The Director scowled. 'Shortly after 2pm. LaVonda, as Angela's direct supervisor, we wanted to speak to you before we talk to her. Angela is relatively new, so we need to know if you've given her the organisational security briefing.'

Angela? What did she have to do with this? Had Royce used her to get LaVonda's pass? LaVonda looked at the Director in bewilderment. His frown deepened, and he glanced over at Deborah, who nodded back at him and then looked directly at LaVonda.

'LaVonda, Angela's pass was recorded coming into the office on Sunday, and she failed to enter the security code. It appears she left a few minutes later, and we assume she probably panicked when the alarm went off. Has she had a security briefing, or not? Because if she hasn't, then I'm afraid some of the responsibility for this event lies with you.'

LaVonda tried to wrap her head around this, but she felt fuzzy and wrong-footed. Royce *hadn't* framed her? Had he framed Angela? But what would be the point? He *liked* Angela. He was always hanging around her. It was only LaVonda he disliked. She could hear the rest of the staff returning from their lunch, and she turned her head towards the closed door.

'LaVonda.' Deborah spoke sharply. 'Did you give Angela a security briefing when she started?'

Yes, of course she had. She gave all new staff a security briefing; it was part of her job, and a part she took very seriously. LaVonda raised her chin to nod, then stopped. Had she given Angela a briefing? She couldn't remember.

'I... think so. I'm sorry, I can't actually recall when, but I'm sure–'

The Director snorted rudely and interrupted her.

'You'd better stay while we bring Angela in and question her. Perhaps her memory is better than yours.'

Question her? Who did this bastard think he was? No one had committed a crime, yet he was behaving like an obnoxious prick. He was the Director of Security at Environmental Services, not sodding ASIO.

Deborah left her office, returning a minute later with Angela trailing behind her. The poor girl was visibly trembling, and LaVonda's heart went out to her. She was so young. A recently single mother to a little boy; she reminded LaVonda of herself at that age. She moved her seat nearer to Angela's in a show of solidarity.

The Director seemed to puff himself up before he spoke. A burst of fury shot through LaVonda. He was deliberately trying to intimidate poor Angela. Bastard. LaVonda itched to smack his face.

'Angela, we have evidence you entered this building on Sunday, and you subsequently set off the alarm system. Were you aware that if you come in after office hours, you need to enter the security code?'

LaVonda held her breath. Part of her wanted Angela to admit that yes, she'd had the briefing and knew the procedure and had just forgotten, and part of her wanted Angela to tell them no, she hadn't known. LaVonda was happy to take some of the blame for the incident if it meant the poor girl was let off lightly.

Angela looked terrified. 'It's my son's birthday.' Her voice was a whisper. 'I wanted to use the printer to make his party invitations.'

The HR man spoke up. 'That's against company policy, you know. Using office equipment for personal use.'

The Director glared at him. Obviously, he didn't want anyone derailing his Very Important Investigation for a lesser crime. The HR man looked down at the table. The Director turned his attention back to Angela.

'When you started with this organisation, you would have received induction training, correct?'

LaVonda hated him more with every passing moment. She slid her hands under the edges of her thighs so they wouldn't suddenly reach out of their own accord and slap him.

Angela nodded.

'Did you, or did you not, receive a security briefing from your supervisor, LaVonda Robinette, as part of your induction?'

Angela looked at LaVonda, her eyes widening. The poor thing looked completely panicked. The Director leaned back in his chair. For a moment, no one spoke. Then LaVonda's voice filled the room, surprising even herself.

'No. She didn't. I'd intended to give her the security briefing, but frankly there were *far* more important induction items to cover off on, so I simply forgot.'

It was utterly delightful to watch the Director's corpulent smackable face turn puce, and his nostrils flare in anger. A tiny thrill of defiance pulsed in LaVonda's veins, and she let it show by grinning widely at him.

Unfortunately, her body chose that moment to betray her again. The now familiar heat shot across her face, seeping into her neck, and spreading out across her body. LaVonda pushed her chair back and undid the top buttons on her shirt. When the bad ones hit, they left no room for social niceties; she had to do anything and everything to combat the heat.

The HR man's water glass was snatched up and pressed against her cheeks. Deborah's notepad became an impromptu handheld fan. The only good thing about this overt display of female biology was the stunned look on the Director's face. She would have laughed if she hadn't been so distracted trying to cool herself down.

Deborah took charge. 'Angela, you may go. I will schedule some time this afternoon to go through your security briefing in full. Andrew, I'll report back to HR on any disciplinary action taken with LaVonda, so you can leave now, too.'

She waited until Angela and the HR man had left the room, then turned to LaVonda. 'Why don't you go and cool down and then come back when you're ready.'

LaVonda nodded gratefully. As she closed the door behind her, she heard Deborah say to the Director, 'It's a hot flush, Shane; there is no need to act like the woman suddenly grew horns.'

Safely in the toilets, LaVonda stripped off her shirt and patted her skin with damp paper towels. Damn, this change of life stuff. It was so... undignified. She looked at herself in the mirror. Her face was still flushed, and her eyes glittered. Actually, aside from the slightly frizzy hairline, she looked surprisingly attractive. She turned her head and sucked in her cheeks. Not bad for almost fifty.

*Oh, way to get distracted, LaVonda. You've just embarrassed yourself. You've let a subordinate get into trouble, you're about to face disciplinary action, you've made yourself a brand-new enemy, and you've let yourself leap to paranoid conclusions about one of your colleagues. But please, carry on admiring how sexy you look standing in the office toilets in your bra. That's far more important.*

The door to the toilets swung open, and Angela crept in, her eyes widening as she met LaVonda's gaze in the mirror.

'Are you alright?'

'Yes, fine. Just a hot flush. Something for you to look forward to when you're older.' LaVonda picked up her shirt and covered herself.

'I wanted to check on you and say thank you for sticking up for me.' Angela twisted her fingers nervously, and she avoided looking directly at LaVonda.

'Don't worry about it. As your supervisor, I should have made sure you knew about the security stuff. Anyway, it is done now.'

Angela nodded and backed out of the room, shutting the door behind her.

LaVonda exhaled. She didn't feel the least bit sexy anymore; she felt foolish. She'd been so forgetful lately, and on top of that, she was becoming completely paranoid. Why did she immediately jump to the conclusion that Royce had somehow been involved and had set her up? Yes, he was rude and awful, but she was letting herself get carried away. He wasn't likely to break the law to get her into trouble, was he? And yet, that is what she'd immediately thought. How stupid.

She slipped her arms into her shirt and buttoned it up, before running her hands through her hair. Might as well go and face the music. She didn't regret sticking up for Angela, even if she was almost 100 percent sure she had gone through *all* the induction training briefs, including the oh-so-important security one.

LaVonda left the toilets and headed back to the office, passing the lifts on her way. One of the lift doors was closing, and as she hurried by, she caught a glimpse of the people inside. Royce, grinning, holding his suit jacket hooked over his shoulder in the annoying look-how-cool-I-am way he had. There was a wide grin on his horrible smug face. His other arm was around a woman, who had one hand pressed against his chest, as she laughed up at him.

Angela.

# SIX

'Shut your mouth, bitch, or you'll taste my knuckles.'

LaVonda's head jerked upright, and she almost dropped the chip she'd been about to put in her mouth. What on earth?

Across the table, her date stiffened, shock reddening the tips of his ears, before he returned his full attention to cutting his steak. LaVonda was momentarily stunned. Then the now familiar rage bubbled up in her chest, shooting out in all directions through her entire body. This was completely unacceptable behaviour.

The evening had started out pleasantly, although admittedly there were no great sparks between her and Gavin.

He was nothing to look at. But then most men over fifty weren't, were they? In LaVonda's humble opinion, based on nothing more than a general observation of her age group, most women tried to keep themselves attractive and presentable, whereas most men slid gracelessly into old age, allowing baldness and fatness to spread across their bodies in a way no self-respecting woman ever would. After all, how many anti-wrinkle creams were there for men?

And if she was completely honest, she was slightly offended Ann had thought Gavin was perfect for her. LaVonda didn't have tickets on herself, of course she didn't, but she'd pictured her perfect match as someone quite a bit better-looking than Gavin. Someone like Ann's husband, Sam. Tall, broad, nice-looking, but probably without the squeaky voice. Oh dear, that was completely shallow of her, wasn't it? But Gavin just seemed so ordinary. So uninspiring. So bland.

But look, he was agreeable; he was solicitous, plus he smiled a lot and made good eye contact with her when she spoke. He certainly didn't monopolise the conversation, and apart from a momentary lapse in composure when he mispronounced the name of the wine, he'd ordered for them, he seemed unruffled by the sheer awkwardness of their blind date. She liked him, LaVonda decided, although not in that way. He was a pleasant middle-aged person. A nice man. But she already had a pleasant middle-aged man, (even if he was suffering temporary insanity and living with a woman half his age) so she really didn't need another one.

The man at the table behind them clearly wasn't a nice man at all. LaVonda felt sickened by his tone. Why on earth would anyone speak to their partner, or anyone, like that? Let alone in a trendy bar like this, where the lights were dimmed, and the noises of diners and drinkers were muffled by soft carpeting and wood panelling. Dave would never speak to her like this, and Gavin wouldn't either. What was wrong with some men?

LaVonda deliberately and carefully pressed her napkin to her mouth, then folded it and placed it beside her plate, as she prepared herself to unleash the full force of her anger. Had she considered the probable outcome; she might have thought twice about the wisdom of this decision. But her focus was purely on standing up for the poor woman behind her. She needed, no *deserved*, to know that she didn't have to put up with this man's abuse.

LaVonda knew all about putting up with abuse. Maude had made her life a misery as a child and impacted on her sense of worth for all of her adult life. But LaVonda had finally fought back, even if it had been in a passive way, and now she was righteously empowered. She owed it to this woman, this stranger, to stand up and defend her. To show her the way out.

Slowly, LaVonda stood up. The entire bar seemed to draw quiet as she moved into the spotlight of her moment. She drew herself up to her full height and glared down at the obnoxious man. A fleeting thought shot through her mind; he looked slightly familiar. Did she know him from somewhere? Was he someone famous? She shook her head slightly to rid herself of the thought. It didn't matter. What mattered was standing up for a fellow victim. LaVonda knitted her eyebrows more firmly together, her gaze fixed unwaveringly on the man seated in front of her.

'Who do you think you are, speaking to her like that? Show some respect!'

For that one wild, brief moment, looking down on him, she felt utterly powerful and invincible. She could squash him like a fly. She, LaVonda, was brave, and strong, and sticking up for the sisterhood.

The woman gaped up at LaVonda, her eyes widening in obvious panic. LaVonda smiled reassuringly, because there was nothing to be concerned about. The poor woman could relax; her partner was about to be shamed into contrition and apology. At least, that was what LaVonda later imagined she'd been expecting when she challenged an abusive man in public.

The man's head snapped back and LaVonda felt a sudden, overwhelming impulse to smile at him. To soften the impact of her words and smooth over the potential awkwardness she had created. She could feel the corners of her mouth tugging upwards.

In the next second, the man was on his feet, sending his chair flying behind him. As he towered over her, menacing and huge, ice-cold horror replaced LaVonda's righteous smugness. She glanced to her right, hoping to curb her panic with the reassuring sight of other people backing her up. No one was there.

Her breath caught in her throat. Time stood still for a second, an eternity, then sudden, shocking pain flashed through her, as the man seized her shoulder and shook her so violently her teeth actually rattled in her head. A metallic taste filled her mouth. She'd bitten into her own tongue.

'Who the fuck? I'll kill you, bitch. I will fucking tear you in half.'

'Frankie.' The other woman's soft word was a plea for mercy; a tiny, possible lifeline. LaVonda tried to turn towards it, but she was pinned against the giant.

His response bit through the quiet room with savage intent.

'Shut up. Go home. Wait for me, because I'm going to deal with this bitch, then I'll deal with you.'

Part of LaVonda's brain registered the woman gathering her things and scurrying out of the bar, but she could only focus on the terrible, terrifying situation she had deliberately put herself in. The man was gripping her shoulder, painfully crushing and bruising her skin, but even in the raw terror of the moment, she was still waiting for, still *expecting*, some form of rescue.

Someone please. Anyone. Where was everyone?

'Want me to kill you, bitch? Do you? I could kill you.' His breath was hot and sour in her face, and she had never felt so frightened in her life. No one was pushing in between them to help. She was completely on her own in front of a man who was about to hurt her badly.

'I'm sorry,' she begged, desperate to undo the last few minutes and her actions that had brought them to this point. Tears sprang to her eyes, and she badly wanted to cry, but she was too terrified. She was dangerously close to wetting her pants. All she could do was babble; 'I'm so, so sorry. I'm sorry. Please. I'm so sorry.'

The man regarded her for a minute, then pulled her face close to his.

'I could kill you,' he repeated, and then thrust her away from him so violently she almost fell. He turned and strode out of the bar, and through the buzzing in her head, LaVonda could hear him yelling out viciously after his partner.

'Are you okay?' A young waitress put her arm around LaVonda. She tried to nod her head, but she wasn't okay. She was trembling, her tongue ragged and bleeding, and she wanted to go straight home and never leave the safety of her house again. What had she done? She'd tried to help, and all she'd done was to probably make things worse for that poor woman. Not to mention putting herself at risk of injury, or worse. Nausea swelled in her throat. She wanted to vomit up all the panic and dread churning inside.

Gavin was in front of her, his face creased in concern and something else... repulsion?

'Why did you do that? LaVonda, he could have killed you.'

*Where were you? Why didn't you step in to help?*

She knew she wasn't being fair. Gavin would have been no match for that brute, and it had been her own fault the situation had escalated. Still. He could have tried to help. Dave would have tried. Mark would have torn that monster apart. Tears spilled over and ran down her cheeks.

She missed Mark. She still missed him so badly. At the time, his death had been so shocking, so overwhelming; she hadn't expected to survive it. But she had, and decades later, she was standing in a bar after a terrible altercation, still wishing Mark was here. Wishing he was alive. Wishing with all her might she had never sent her young husband out that night.

LaVonda tortured herself regularly by imagining Mark's death. It hadn't been quick or painless. He'd been driving through Pine Forest and swerved suddenly to avoid something, a kangaroo most likely, and driven straight into a tree. His chest crushed, his arms broken; he'd been unable to move, barely able to breathe, and he couldn't call out for help.

All evening he lay there dying, while LaVonda waited at home, at first irritated because Emmett's favourite pink stuffed bunny was in the car, and the little girl refused to go into her cot without it. But when Emmett finally did drop off to sleep, and Mark still hadn't returned, LaVonda became increasingly panicked. Finally, she'd called the police; by the time they found him, it was too late. If he'd been discovered earlier, if she'd acted sooner, he might have survived. LaVonda could never forgive herself for waiting so long to call for help. She couldn't forgive herself for the reason he was out so late at all.

She'd sent him for chocolate. She hadn't had cravings; she'd just felt like something sweet, and there was nothing in the cupboard. She was using her pregnancy as an excuse to make Mark run around after her. Of course, she had actually been exhausted. Emmett was a lively toddler, and her second pregnancy was much harder than her first. But even so, she didn't need chocolate. She'd just felt tired and sore, and she missed her darling dad, and she wanted to cheer herself up a bit. So she'd told her husband she had a sudden craving for chocolate.

'Are you sure it's a craving?' Mark looked tired too. Emmett was unsettled and had woken up several times the night before, so they were all operating on very little sleep. At least she'd been able to have a rest when Emmett went down for her midday nap, whereas Mark had had to go to work and try to concentrate all day.

How easy it would have been to laugh, and shrug, and admit that, no, she didn't need chocolate; she just felt like some. How many times had she pictured that exact moment? Rewritten history to remember a scene where she cared more about him than herself and her greedy desire? Mark might have gone anyway, just to please her, because he always went out of his way to make her happy. But perhaps he wouldn't have gone. He might have simply grinned back at her and said he'd bring home a whole truckload of chocolate tomorrow. Then he would have had a tomorrow.

'I'll call you.' Gavin had faded into the background, along with the past. He was simply noise now. LaVonda wanted nothing more than to curl into a ball, and cry, and sleep, and simply forget about everything. What was that song? *Make the world go away.*

'Please don't.'

Three days later, when Dave rang, LaVonda was still feeling weepy and a little sorry for herself. She'd cancelled her Sunday morning shopping trip and told her sister the date had been fine, just fine, but there were no sparks between her and Gavin, and Ann was not to try setting her up ever again. Then she'd taken a few days off work, tucked into bed, and fed herself hot toast and endless cups of tea. She did not feel up to facing either Royce or Angela in her current state of mind. She hadn't worked out what to do about that situation and her suspicions. There probably wasn't anything she could do, apart from note it in her evidence journal and hope Royce would eventually lose interest in harassing her.

But the altercation with the man in the bar, as well as her continued distress over her situation at work, meant LaVonda wasn't feeling particularly resilient when her phone rang early on Tuesday morning. She put down her magazine, rolled over in bed, grabbed for the mobile, and glanced at the screen. Dave.

'Hello?'

'Hi LaVonda. It's me, Dave.' His voice was warm, familiar, and comforting, like a hot drink on a cold night, and she felt like bursting into tears. She took a deep, slow breath to try to control her emotions. *Come home, Dave. All is forgiven. Just stop all this nonsense and come home now.*

Dave cleared his throat.

'LaVonda. I have something I need to... ah... discuss with you. A preposition, as it were.'

'Do you mean proposition?'

'Yes... proposition. Of sorts. Actually, it is more of a request, although it doesn't need to... hmm. Are you still there?'

'Yes, Dave. I'm still here.'

'Oh. Good. As I was saying, I have an idea, a thought really. I was wondering...'

LaVonda felt the comforting warmth slide away and the usual irritation rise. *Just spit it out, will you? Stop making a pudding out of everything.*

'...if you might be free tomorrow evening. I could come over for dinner. I think this is something we should discuss face to face.'

So, either he wanted to ask her forgiveness and come home, or he wanted to make their separation more permanent and get a divorce. LaVonda sighed. Either way, she wanted a resolution to this stupid situation. She nodded, then spoke.

'Yes, alright. I have the day off so come over whenever, any time you want.' Good heavens. She had almost asked him what he would like her to make for dinner. Perhaps she shouldn't be quite so accommodating until she knew what he wanted. 'Actually, Dave, I have plans until early evening. Come at 6pm. I assume you won't be bringing your friend?'

'No. Just me. I'll see you at 6pm tomorrow. Thanks, LaVonda.'

He hung up, and LaVonda stayed lost in thought for a few minutes. So what was it? Did he want to come home to her, or was he committed to that girl? Would he ask her for a divorce? Would she give him one? Idly, LaVonda wondered what would happen if she refused. Just put her foot down and said no. *Sorry, Dave, but I don't think I feel like getting divorced.*

Could you force someone to give you a divorce?

She'd make one of his favourite meals anyway. Whatever the flip of the coin, divorce or forgiveness, it wouldn't hurt to remind him about one of the things he loved about her. Her cooking.

She'd roast a chicken. Dave loved her chicken. LaVonda started planning the menu in her mind. Duck-fat potatoes and minted peas. Homemade rolls, and maybe lemon cheesecake for dessert, even though it was her favourite, not his. Dave loved chocolate more than any other sweet, but she couldn't tolerate having it in the house. She'd recently removed his 'secret' stash and now her home was finally, blessedly free of chocolate. And smelly socks on the bathroom floor. And the infuriating sound of him clearing his throat; something he did seven or eight times every day.

LaVonda frowned. It was nice not having Dave in the house. Did she truly want him back if he wanted to return?

Yes, she did. They were still husband and wife. She'd been treating his absence like a mini holiday for them both. She got the house to herself for a few weeks, and the freedom that came from not having to consider another person in every decision she made, and Dave was, well, he was off getting his more basic needs met.

The break from each other had probably done them good, although Dave being the one who instigated the break (and therefore the obvious villain in the piece) would have to make it up to her (the obvious injured party). She was quite looking forward to seeing how far she could push his guilt. Especially when she reminded him, as she would, he had chosen to leave her on her birthday.

She wasn't going to make it easy for him if he did want to come back. She might be feeling a bit vulnerable right now, but LaVonda Robinette was no pushover.

'She listens to me and she actually focuses on me when I speak. She's so considerate of my feelings. She doesn't cringe when I cough, LaVonda, and she doesn't correct my language all the time.'

'Well, she probably doesn't know enough words yet. She's how old? Twelve?'

Dave threw her a look.

'Sorry. Carry on. Do keep telling me how amazing this new girl, sorry, woman is.' LaVonda reached into the fridge and pulled out a bottle of wine. If ever a situation called for alcohol, this was it.

He'd been prattling on for ten minutes now, demonstrating yet more appalling lack of judgement in assuming his wife would want to hear all about the various merits of his new girlfriend. She hadn't interrupted him though, not much anyway. She would simply let him get to his eventual point. She wasn't sure what his point was, although she was currently leaning towards the 'LaVonda-I-want-a-divorce' side of the coin. There could still be a 'Jemima-is-amazing-but-I-want-to-come-home', though, so she wasn't rushing him.

At any rate, LaVonda was glad she'd changed out of her jeans and flattering red top, and into yoga pants and a loose t-shirt. The last thing she wanted to do right now was look like she cared too much. She reached over and opened the oven door. The smell of roasted meat and vegetables filled the kitchen. Dave sniffed deeply, before clearing his throat. Ugh. The sound was like nails down a chalkboard, setting her teeth on edge for approximately the millionth time.

'Smells wonderful. I've missed your cooking.'

*Your cooking, LaVonda. Not you.*

'Go and sit down in the dining room and take the wine. Dinner is almost ready.'

He trotted off obediently as LaVonda reached into the oven and pulled out the baking dish. The chicken was nicely browned, and the potatoes were golden and crunchy looking. She put the rolls in the oven to warm, then quickly drained the peas and stirred through a knob of butter and some freshly picked mint leaves.

Dave was pouring wine into her glass when she carried their plates into the dining room. She looked around, pleased with the effort she had made in the room. The overhead light was switched off; the room lit by a pair of glowing lamps on the sideboard. The wine glasses caught the soft light and sparkled. She'd set the table using a plain white tablecloth and a little vase of dried flowers for decoration. It was enough. Comfortable, homely and elegant, and not the slightest bit romantic or contrived.

Dave looked appreciatively at the meal she set in front of him. Without waiting for her to sit, he picked up his fork and broke open a potato. Steam wafted out.

'Amazing.'

Of course it was. Because she could cook. It seemed unlikely young Jemima, despite her myriad of incredible qualities, would be able to produce a meal like this.

LaVonda took her seat on Dave's left-hand side. Close enough to seem friendly, but not too close. She wasn't hungry at all, she wanted to know what his plans were, and her patience was just starting to run thin.

'So, are you going to tell me what this is all about?' Her tone was friendly. Whatever he had to say to her, she would react calmly and coolly. She took a sip of wine and smiled encouraging at him.

Dave smeared butter onto his potato, sprinkled salt liberally, then cleared his throat. LaVonda ground her teeth behind her smile and took a bite of her chicken. It was delicious.

'LaVonda, I know this is a bit out of the blue, but I... I want to move back into the house. With Jemima.'

LaVonda was dumbfounded. How was that supposed to work? All three of them, cohabitating under the same roof? Of all the stupid ideas her husband had had in the past few decades, and he'd had a few, this was possibly the stupidest.

'I'll pay you market rates, of course. I thought we could get someone in to do a valuation, then once we know what it is worth, I'd pay you half.'

Oh. He wanted her out. That was what this was about. He wanted her to leave her home so he and his amazing, considerate, illiterate girlfriend could move in. The chicken stuck in her throat. She grabbed for her wine to wash it down.

'No. I'm not leaving my home. You're not kicking me out, Dave. Absolutely not.'

Dave looked pained. 'Look, I know it isn't ideal, but Jemima wants to live here. There aren't many houses in this area for sale, and she wants to be in the zone for schooling for when...' he cleared his throat, 'for when we start a family.'

Of all the... LaVonda couldn't believe her ears. She'd never contemplated Dave wanting to have a family with Jemima. She'd thought it was a fling, a stupid, impulsive, but brief affair. And even if it wasn't, even if he did decide to stay with that woman, to have an actual family? To have a child with someone else when they'd been unable to have any of their own together? It was *inconceivable*. Pun intended. She let out a short bark of laughter.

'Are you alright?' Dave cleared his throat again, and LaVonda nearly hurled the dried flower arrangement at his head.

'Get out.'

'LaVonda, please.'

'I said, get out. You are not taking my house, my home. In fact, you are no longer welcome. Get out.'

'Let's just be reasonable about this.' He looked at her imploringly.

A blanket of cold determination settled on LaVonda. She pushed back her chair, stood up, and in one swift movement, picked up both their plates and flung them hard at the wall behind him. They hit the target with a satisfying smash, food smearing across the paint, then oozing between the pieces of broken crockery on the carpet.

Dave froze, looking stunned and holding his fork, a piece of potato still wedged in the prongs. He didn't seem to know what to do with it. LaVonda reached over, took the fork out of his hand, and flung it after the shattered plates.

'I'm happy to call the police if you'd like help leaving.'

'No, I'll go. I'm going. But LaVonda, we have to do this. You know we do.' He blinked at the mess behind him. 'Do you need a hand...?'

In general, LaVonda didn't approve of profanities. But if there was ever a time...

'Dave, just get the hell out!'

# SEVEN

The man from the bar was back. LaVonda could taste his beery breath and feel his strong fingers digging into the soft flesh of her shoulder. But this time, her mother was there as well, egging him on.

'Do it. Stab her. She doesn't deserve to live.'

Skinny, young Jemima picked up one of LaVonda's new cushions and threw it at her. LaVonda ducked, and her mother laughed nastily.

'I'll buy you a nice muffin to make up for it. That will fix it, won't it, LaVonda?' Jemima picked up another cushion.

'Stop!' LaVonda cried out. 'Stop wrecking my house.'

Her dad shook his head. 'I'm very disappointed in you, LaVonda.'

Her mother nodded in smug agreement. 'I told you we should have called her Sissy.'

LaVonda jerked awake. Her heart was racing wildly, and her bed was hot and soaking wet. It was still dark, but a faint light shone through where the curtains didn't quite meet. Early morning.

She lay quite still, waiting for her heartbeat to slow, and the heat to leave her body while she reviewed her dream. It was one of those horribly realistic dreams that felt like it had all actually happened. LaVonda rolled onto her side. The sheets were damp and chilly. She needed to get up.

After a warm shower, LaVonda stripped the sheets off her bed. She thought about remaking it with fresh bedding, then decided against it. Although it was still dark, she didn't think she could go back to sleep, and anyway, she had sweated down to the mattress. It was probably better to leave it to dry out.

Instead, she went into the kitchen to make herself some tea. She yawned as she waited for the kettle to boil, and her gaze settled on the smashed mess on the floor of the dining room. Sodding Dave. After he'd left last night, she'd pulled off her wedding ring and dropped it ceremoniously into the toilet. Then she'd finished the bottle of wine, all the time singing loudly to Aretha Franklin and dancing wildly around the lounge room. She was not going to be forced out of her beautiful home. No way. She felt powerful and resolute. Let him try to get rid of her. Let them all try. She'd outlast everyone. LaVonda kicked her legs high, spun in circles, and punched at invisible enemies, singing until her voice was hoarse. At some point, she'd suddenly felt very tired and dragged herself off to bed.

Now, in the early morning dawn, her eyes felt raw and scratchy from lack of sleep, and her head ached. She was supposed to go back to work this morning, even though it was the last thing she felt like doing. But LaVonda was a professional, so despite wanting to stay cocooned at home, she would go into work today and hold her head high. She would ignore Royce and act professionally towards Angela, and she would finish her briefs on recycling measures in rural communities.

LaVonda groaned aloud. It was going to be a very long day.


Deborah assembled the division staff in the general office area.

'Thank you, everyone, for your attention. I have an important announcement. As some of you already know, my husband has been offered a posting in Washington, and after much consideration, I have decided to accompany him for the next six months to settle our family in the States. I may or may not return, but in the meantime, I have appointed an Acting General Manager to run this department.'

A few heads turned towards LaVonda. She smiled nervously.

It wasn't her. Deborah would have discussed it with her beforehand if she were planning to appoint LaVonda. But if not her, then who? No one else held the same seniority. No one else knew the department as well as she did.

Deborah beamed at the group.

'There was only one obvious candidate. A person whom, since joining the organisation, has proven himself to be dedicated, capable, efficient, and above all, utterly committed to our strategic vision.'

Oh no.

'I am thrilled to announce Royce Butler has agreed to act in my position for the foreseeable future, and I know I can rely on each and every one of you to give him your full support in his new role. Congratulations, Royce.'

Deborah nodded towards Royce, who stepped forward, grinning and adjusting his tie in a self-conscious gesture that was anything but.

'Thank you, Deborah. As we've discussed at length, I can assure you, and the rest of the team, I am 110 percent committed to fulfilling the duties of this role, and I'd personally like to thank you for giving me the opportunity to demonstrate my commitment to you and the organisation.'

Smarmy, smug bastard. LaVonda felt sick. How could Deborah have asked Royce instead of her? She was part of the organisational succession planning, and she was the obvious candidate to look after things in Deborah's absence. Ultimately, it was Deborah's decision, of course. But she should have chosen LaVonda; it was unthinkable to choose someone so new and who had no idea how anything operated around here.

The staff crowded around Royce, congratulating him. LaVonda didn't want to draw attention to herself, so she forced herself to join in. She had to be gracious, for now, and deal with this later, calmly and professionally.

'Congratulations, Royce.' She reached out her hand. He ignored her, turning to Colin and slapping him on the back.

'Team dinner tonight. My shout. Sylvia, can you book us a table at El Rancho? Thanks.'

Sylvia simpered.

'Oh, my goodness, isn't he wonderful? He will make a fantastic General Manager.'

'Temporary manager,' LaVonda couldn't help adding.

'Oh, yes temporary, but I mean to say, my money is on Deborah staying in Washington, and Royce taking over permanently. I think he is just the breath of fresh air we need. I mean, you would have been great in the role too, LaVonda, of course. It's just that sometimes the best man for the job is... well... a man.'

'Thank you for seeing me, Deborah. I wanted to talk to you about your decision to have Royce acting in your role while you are away.'

Sitting across the desk from her manager, LaVonda could feel her heart thudding under her neatly buttoned jacket. She hated this sort of confrontation, but she had to stick up for herself. This was a bad decision on Deborah's part, and she needed to let her manager know her feelings on the matter.

Deborah raised one eyebrow. Her mouth was set in a thin line.

'I can understand your disappointment, LaVonda. However, Royce was the obvious choice. He comes with years of experience in managing staff, and since he has been here, overall productivity has increased substantially. The entire culture of the team has improved, and as far as I can tell, this is due in no small part to his efforts in bringing everyone together.'

LaVonda thought this was complete rubbish. But she could hardly say so, could she?

'That might be the case,' she said carefully, 'but I have been with the department for almost twenty years. I'm your second-in-charge. I know this place inside out.'

Deborah sighed.

'If I'm completely honest with you, that is part of the problem. We need fresh ideas, a new perspective. Royce brings that. Also, well look, LaVonda, you haven't been on your game the past few months. The business with Angela... your concentration, and your memory, aren't what they used to be. I feel Royce is a better fit to lead the team right now.'

LaVonda felt as though she had been slapped. Her mind whirled, but she couldn't think of anything to say.

Deborah sighed again and picked up a pen, spinning it between her fingers.

'Also, I know your upcoming divorce is tough on you, so you're probably not up for additional responsibilities right now.'

What? How did Deborah know about Dave leaving? Sodding Sylvia. That woman could not keep her mouth shut about anything. LaVonda gritted her teeth.

'I am not getting a divorce, Deborah. I don't know where you heard that gossip, but I can assure you it isn't the case. And even if it was, I wouldn't let anything affect my professionalism. I may have made a few mistakes lately, but my record over the past two decades speaks for itself. I'm not asking you to reconsider your decision, but you could have done me the courtesy of informing me first, so I didn't have to find out at the same time as everyone else.'

Deborah looked embarrassed. Good. So she should.

'You're right, LaVonda, and I am sorry. I should have spoken to you first. And look, I didn't mean to upset you. You must know how highly I value your contribution.'

It would probably be a career-limiting move for LaVonda to roll her eyes at her manager, so she refrained. Although who knew how much longer she would have a career, once Royce was in the General Manager's seat. If he'd made her life hell before, imagine the damage he could inflict on her as her boss.

LaVonda left Deborah's office and walked straight to her desk. She opened her handbag and took out her notebook. Then she took the lift directly to the seventh floor to Human Resources.

The HR woman turned the last page of LaVonda's notebook and closed it carefully. She placed her index fingers on opposite corners of the book and swivelled it around. LaVonda wondered if she had practised this move. It looked practised.

'So, the thing is, LaVonda... well, now that Mr Butler has been promoted, and into a position you wanted, I think, I mean your actions could be construed as a little... hmmm. Petty?'

LaVonda stared at her in dismay.

'No, no, not at all. This has nothing to do with his promotion.'

'I'm not saying it does.' The HR woman's voice was cool, non-emotive, but she was blinking quite a lot. 'I'm just saying it could look like you are trying to seek vengeance...'

Vengeance? What are we, in an old Western movie? Who talks about vengeance?

'...and that makes your case weak. You might want to have a good think about whether or not you want to pursue this claim. Because Mr Butler would be well within his rights to bring a case of wrongful harassment against you.'

LaVonda could hardly believe what she was hearing.

'But he wouldn't. He'd have no proof.'

'I'm not saying he does.'

LaVonda narrowed her eyes, not bothering to hide her contempt, as the woman continued. 'I'm saying he might. And for that reason, you should think long and hard before you formalise this complaint.'

'But I...' LaVonda looked down at her notebook, at the meticulous entries documenting all the hurt, embarrassment, and humiliation she had endured in the past month. Her evidence. Worthless. She could feel a mass of despair forming at the back of her nose, causing tears to prick her eyes.

'I'm not trying to talk you out of your complaint, LaVonda. I'm just pointing out Mr Butler is in a stronger position than you are right now, and you should take that into consideration when deciding whether or not to pursue this decision.'

LaVonda picked up her notebook. She couldn't think straight. She needed time to process her thoughts and work out what she needed to do next, and she couldn't think while sitting in front of this snotty cow with her HR attitude and HR smugness. Something else bothered LaVonda about this whole interaction, but she couldn't work out what it was.

'I'll... I'll have to speak to my union rep and decide on my next course of action. I will be in touch in due course.'

The HR woman nodded formally, although LaVonda knew she wasn't the least bit fooled by the show of bravado or the subtle threat. She could probably see right through LaVonda and knew not only did LaVonda not have a union rep, but that she wouldn't be following through with her complaint.

*So that's it then*, she thought as she walked back down the corridor, holding her notebook in front of her like a useless shield. *Game over. C'est la vie. It is what it is.*

'I hate that expression!' Oh heavens, had she spoken out loud? Was she turning into one of those homeless people who ranted to themselves in public, causing everyone else to deftly avoid them?

*I do hate it. It isn't what it is. Also, I'm not homeless.*

Well, not yet.

It wasn't until LaVonda got back to her desk that she realised what else had been bothering her about her meeting. Throughout the conversation, the HR woman had referred to Royce as Mr Butler, whereas LaVonda had been constantly, and somewhat condescendingly, called by her first name.

It was cool in the taxi, and LaVonda shivered. She reached for her coat and then realised it was back at the restaurant. What a nuisance. She leaned as far forward as the seatbelt would allow and waved her hand at the driver.

'I'm so sorry, but I've forgotten my coat.' Good grief, she sounded a bit sozzled. She'd had a few drinks, naturally, but surely, she wasn't that drunk. She tried again. 'Excuse me, but would you mind if we went back please? I've left my coat behind.'

The taxi driver scowled at her in the rear-view mirror. Did he understand her? Perhaps he didn't speak English; after all, he was quite dark-skinned. Oh dear. Was she being racist? It seemed like she might be, but if the poor man didn't understand... She tried again, speaking louder and slower, as if that might help.

'My coat. I left my coat, you know, coat? At the rest-au-rant. Please, we go back now?'

'Yes, I heard you the first time. I'm looking for somewhere to turn around.'

'Oh. Sorry.'

She was slightly shamefaced at both her inadvertent racism, and her obvious excessive drinking, but then promptly forgot both, as she thought about her coat. It was strange that she had forgotten it; the weather was chilly, and she'd had several minutes standing outside the restaurant waiting with the others for their taxis and Ubers. Yet until now, she hadn't noticed the chill at all.

They'd been busy laughing about... something? What had they been laughing about? It was only ten minutes ago, but LaVonda couldn't for the life of her remember. She couldn't remember calling the taxi either. Someone must have called for her. Clearly, she was far more drunk than she'd realised.

She had been drinking a lot, it was true. But who could blame her? She'd had to sit there all night and celebrate Royce's promotion, while the smug prat sat at the head of the table being... well, smug. Accepting all the congratulatory remarks as though they were his due. LaVonda had caught herself looking at him on several occasions, wishing he would choke on his steak, or fall off his chair and break his stupid neck. But no. Royce remained resolutely and annoyingly intact throughout the whole evening.

She sat back in the taxi, balancing her handbag on her knee. It took them another ten minutes to return to the restaurant car park. The driver pulled up outside the front door. He turned to face her.

'Eighteen dollars.'

'I'm just getting my coat. I'm coming right back.'

'Eighteen dollars.'

'But I'm coming back. I'll just be... oh alright then.' She fumbled in her purse and took out a twenty dollar note. The driver snatched it out of her hand. Gosh, that was a bit rude, wasn't it?

'Now you will wait, won't you? I'm coming straight back. Can you just wait here? I will be back right. Okay? Right back. Don't go anywhere.'

The walk into the restaurant was wobbly.

Inside, the place was almost empty. Their table was still littered with dirty glasses and plates, and her coat was draped over the back of her chair. Everyone had left. Oh, not quite everyone. LaVonda noticed Royce standing at the counter, obviously fixing up the bill. He was the last person she wanted to see right now. She snatched up her coat and fought the urge to duck down so he wouldn't see her. He wasn't paying any attention anyway; he was questioning some of the items on the bill. Of course, he was. Prat.

She dashed back outside and hurried over to her taxi... which was gone. LaVonda blinked in disbelief. She'd been inside for less than two minutes! How could he just leave? She looked around desperately, but the car park was almost empty. She'd just have to call another taxi. What was the taxi number? Come to think of it, what was the address of this place? She peered up at the sign. El Ranchos. Well, that wasn't very helpful.

The wind picked up, and she shrugged into her coat. Royce was going to come out any minute, and she absolutely did not want to see him. Her car was parked at the edge of the car park near two other cars. She hurried over, dug her keys out of her bag, opened the door and hopped into the driver's seat.

Ducked down in her car, she tried to look up the taxi number, but her glasses were all smeary. She tried to polish them on the edge of her skirt. There. Oh, that was worse. The battery warning light flashed, and her phone suddenly shut down. Great. Now what?

She could go back into the restaurant and ask them to call her a taxi, but she hadn't seen Royce come out yet. She shivered, then turned on the car to switch on the heater. That was better, but now she needed to pee. Damn. Surely Royce would come out in a minute, then she could go back inside. She waited. And waited.

Oh, sod it. She would just drive herself home. If she drove slowly and sensibly, she would be fine.

She took off the handbrake, applied her foot gently to the accelerator, and started pulling carefully out of the parking space. She was probably driving a bit too slowly. She pressed her foot down a bit harder, and the car sped up just as the restaurant door opened, and Royce stepped out into the car park. His head was down, his collar turned up, and his hands were cupped against the wind, protecting his match as he lit a cigarette.

*I could run right over him,* LaVonda thought, suddenly gleeful. *I could just press my foot down, and swerve a bit, and I could knock him right off his stupid feet.* Her little car seemed to speed up of its own accord and then pull itself hard to the left. LaVonda closed her eyes, and for one thrilling moment, she could almost see Royce looking up, shock darkening his face. She could hear the sickening thud of his body slamming against the bonnet, rolling up into the air, and smacking down hard against the solid ground behind her.

*I could have done it,* she thought elatedly. *I could have struck the bastard down once and for all. Take that, Royce!*

She opened her eyes. The car park was clear in front of her. Royce was gone. Carefully and slowly, she drove herself home.

# EIGHT

Pale light filtered in through the bedroom window, washing across LaVonda's sleeping face. Correction. Passed out face. After fighting head spins for an hour last night, she'd finally fallen into heavy, hot unconsciousness, trapped in strange, disturbing dreams. The man from the bar was there, along with Royce. The two of them swirling in her head, anger smeared across their faces, fists raised towards her. She was trying to hide something in the ground, but they were pulling her away. Exposing the mess she'd made. Hurting her.

She'd tried to get undressed when she got home but had given up when it all got too hard. The early morning light revealed her lying on top of the covers, her skirt twisted, and her bra still fastened, but with one arm wrestled free.

LaVonda blinked, then tried to burrow away from the light. Too late. The brief seconds of consciousness had brought awareness of a pounding headache and a dry, scratchy throat, and the longer she tried to ignore it, the worse the pain became. She needed water. Water and painkillers. *Come on,* she tried to coax herself. *Just get up and sort that out, then you can flop back into bed.*

It took several more minutes before she could persuade herself to move, and even then, they were the slow, laborious, tortured movements of the heavily hungover. Three painkillers and two glasses of sipped water brought on a bout of nausea. LaVonda fought against it by standing very still and doing some shallow mouth breathing. Once the nausea was under control, she staggered back to bed.

When LaVonda woke the second time, the sun was completely up and beaming through her window in a way that was far cheerier than the situation called for. LaVonda lay still and took stock. Her head still thumped, but the pain was dull and manageable now. Her stomach felt tender; had she actually vomited? She couldn't remember. She was slightly sore, as though she'd taken a sudden blow to the chest.

Her bra was still half on and causing her breasts to feel tight and uncomfortable. Her throat was dry again, but she'd had the forethought to bring a glass of water back to bed, although not enough forethought to close her bedroom curtains.

By far, the worst thing was this strange feeling of low-level dread mixed with nervous anticipation. It was the same feeling she got whenever she had to catch a plane. Slightly sick excitement. LaVonda frowned. She was being silly. There was no reason to feel like this.

She sipped her water carefully and looked around for her phone. Dead. She'd forgotten to charge it, so the alarm hadn't gone off. She plugged it into the charger next to the bed. What day was it anyway? Friday, it must be Friday as they'd gone out for dinner at 'All-you-can-eat-Thursdays' at El Ranchos. So, Friday. A workday.

*I do not want to go in to work. I'll just lie here and go back to sleep for six months, and when I finally wake up, Royce will no longer be my manager, and everything will be back to normal.*

LaVonda groaned. She'd already had several days off this week; she couldn't possibly take another one. Besides, if she called in sick with a hangover, she'd never hear the end of it. No, she would go in, force herself through the day, and then crawl back into bed as soon as she got home. She could sleep all weekend if she wanted.

A cool shower followed by two more painkillers and a few cautious sips of water helped. By the time LaVonda left the house, fumbling around in her bag for her sunglasses to lessen the intense glare of the sun, she was feeling halfway human again.

She stopped at the sight of her car parked crookedly in the driveway. Good grief, she'd driven back home last night. Driven drunk. How utterly awful. LaVonda was rightfully horrified at her own behaviour, and she could feel her hot cheeks telegraphing her shame. She looked around quickly, as though expecting someone to be pointing an accusatory finger at her.

Doreen was standing near her letter box, her hand raised in greeting. LaVonda lifted her own hand and gave a casual wave, one that said, *Sorry, running late, no time to chat, I must go.* She did not want to talk to Doreen. She needed to focus on her own dreadful behaviour and reassure herself this had been a one-off act of temporary insanity, and one she would never repeat.

Thank goodness no one had been hurt.

LaVonda got into her car and backed into the street, well aware she was driving particularly cautiously this morning, as though to make up to the universe for her extremely poor judgement last night. Kept both hands on the wheel. Indicated properly for a full three seconds before turning out of her street. The slight feeling of dread remained, although it was probably due to her anxiety about Royce's new role as her manager.

As she merged onto the highway, LaVonda thought back over the past few weeks. She had been drunk several times since Dave left, and she knew that was the slippery slope to losing complete control. She had absolutely no intention of losing control, or ending up like Maude. Before Ann's accident, Maude didn't drink, although LaVonda couldn't remember that time at all. Her earliest memories were of her mother sitting in the living room, steadily gulping her afternoons away.

Ann's accident had been the catalyst for the alcoholism. LaVonda had been three years old, Maxine a newborn, and Ann was just six. LaVonda had no recollection of what had happened; she'd been so traumatised that her mind had rejected the memory. But she did remember afterwards, when Ann finally came home from the hospital, how Maude had turned her back on all of them.

LaVonda had followed her big sister everywhere when they were small. On that day, they were riding their Christmas tricycles along the footpath outside their house. Ann had turned, perhaps accidentally, perhaps deliberately, into the neighbour's driveway instead of their own. The little girls had been completely oblivious to the chained dog sleeping near the back of the driveway, until it woke and attacked. Ann had been dragged from her bike; the damage done before the frantic owner could stop the attack. She was lucky to have survived, but her hand and forearm couldn't be saved.

The accident, and the loss of her arm, had been traumatic enough, but Ann could never forgive her mother's rejection, and LaVonda didn't blame her. She, herself, couldn't remember any differently, but Ann had memories of a mother who had been sober and loving, instead of drunk and abusive.

LaVonda shuddered. She might not have witnessed the transformation, but she had seen first-hand the effects of alcohol addiction on a family, and it wasn't a road she planned to go down. The drinking had to stop. Last night's behaviour was unforgivable, and she would not allow herself to get in a situation like that again.

She had little memory of last night. She remembered feeling delighted at something that had happened, but she couldn't think for the life of her what it was. Something she'd said... or done. Now what was it? LaVonda changed lanes to let a truck past. What on earth had happened? Had she told the team a funny story or a joke? It seemed unlikely; she could never remember the punchline to jokes. She pulled back in behind the truck. Good grief, why couldn't she remember anything?

A glance in her rear-view mirror showed a car coming up fast behind her. LaVonda flicked on her indicator to pull back into the slower lane and get out of the way, but a van blocked her. She kept the indicator on, slowing slightly to wait for her opportunity to move over, but another glance in the mirror showed the car behind was gaining on her fast.

*Slow down,* she thought crossly. *You're going to get someone killed.* Another glance. Gosh, he was coming up fast, wasn't he? Didn't he see her? Or at least the mammoth truck in front of her? She glanced desperately at the van blocking her in from the side. The driver seemed unaware of her peril. Should she honk or wave or something?

*Bang!* She barely had time to react as the car behind her ploughed into her and shunted her forward. Instinctively, LaVonda jammed her foot on the brake and gripped the steering wheel tighter, as the front of her car was forced into the back of the truck. LaVonda's head was flung forward. She thought, *Oh, no...* as her little car crumpled like a tin can.

The next hour passed in a blur of noise, and flashing lights, and overly concerned faces peering down at her; far too close for comfort. Someone's warm, minty breath, a torchlight flicking in and out of her eyes, being asked questions that flew away as soon as she answered. Darkness, and the disturbing appearance of a huge man, wearing a turban, grinning widely, and laughing at her. He was missing several teeth, and his red raw gums made LaVonda feel sick.

Then she was in a quiet room, blinking, while a woman wearing a dark blue dress covered by a white coat, looked down at her.

'LaVonda, my name is Dr. Aklish. Do you know where you are?'

She was lying down in a bed... in a hospital room. Hospital? LaVonda took a deep breath in; the antiseptic smell she inhaled caused another wave of nausea. Emmett's birth, her father's death, viewing Mark's crushed body; the sterile, chemical, hospital odour was associated with gut-punching, life-changing events. She clenched both fists, causing her right hand to jerk in pain.

'You had a car accident. Do you remember that?' A second woman, a nurse, was standing on the other side of her bed.

A car accident? No... wait, yes. Someone had crashed into her car and pushed it into the back of a truck. She could have been killed!

'I... I... am I hurt?'

Dr. Aklish smiled.

'No, you're very lucky. You have a sprained wrist and a nasty bump on your head. You've been slipping in and out of consciousness, so we will have to keep you in for a day or two under observation. But otherwise, you seem to have come through remarkably unscathed.'

LaVonda nodded and immediately wished she hadn't, as sharp pains rocketed through her skull.

'You'll have a sore head for a while, I'm afraid. We can't give you anything while you are under observation, so for the next few hours, try to keep still and not move. I'll check on you again in the morning.'

The doctor left the room and LaVonda turned her attention to the nurse, who was unwrapping a blood pressure cuff.

'Lift your arm, would you? That's right, that's lovely. Now a little pressure, that's it. Excellent. Just going to check your temperature.'

LaVonda endured the processes stoically, waiting impatiently until the nurse had finished her checks and left the room.

Her wrist hurt, and her head ached, but she needed to get her thoughts straight. She should call Emmett and let her know what had happened. And Ann, of course. And Maxine, who couldn't possibly stay annoyed now she'd been in a near-fatal accident. She wouldn't bother calling Dave. Her eyes narrowed at the thought of her ex-husband. He was not going to force her out of her own house. She made a mental note to talk to Ann about Dave's ridiculous request.

Her handbag was sitting on the chair near her bed. Wincing against the pain, LaVonda reached for it, hoping her mobile phone had survived the crash.

She was in luck.

'Ann, it's me. You're not going to believe this, but I've had a car accident. Some idiot drove straight up the back of me. I'm fine. Mostly. My wrist is sprained, and I was briefly knocked out, so I have to stay in hospital overnight. Otherwise, I'm okay.'

'Bloody balls, Von. Are you sure you're okay? Where are you? I'll come and see you as soon as I can. Do you need anything?'

'No, I'm fine, but could you call into work for me? My phone battery is low, and I'm not up to explaining everything to Sylvia. I have a shocking headache. I'll give you the number.'

After she had called Emmett and sent a text message to Maxine, LaVonda sank back against her pillows. Her head ached badly, and she tentatively touched the lump on her temple. It was raised and sore, but the skin didn't seem to be broken.

She closed her eyes and tried to go back to sleep. It felt like the pain would never subside enough for her to relax, but at some stage she must have dozed off, as she was awakened by the nurse coming back in to check her vital signs. LaVonda watched sleepily as the woman ripped the cuff from her arm.

'You have a visitor waiting outside, but I'm afraid she can only stay a short time. We have to get you back down to imaging to take another scan of your head and see if the swelling has gone down.'

A visitor? Ann? Or maybe Maxine? She looked towards the door. To her surprise, Sylvia bustled in and made a beeline for her bedside.

'Don't worry, I won't stay long.'

Sylvia seemed flustered, and as she plonked herself into the plastic visitor's chair, LaVonda noticed her eyes were all red and puffy. Had she been crying? LaVonda was touched, both by the unexpected visit, and by Sylvia's obvious distress. The poor woman must have been so worried about her. Actually, it would have been a dreadful shock for all the staff to hear of her terrible accident.

'It's alright, Syl. I'm fine. A few bumps and bruises, and I won't be doing any typing for a while thanks to this.' She held up her bandaged wrist. 'Other than that, I'm good as gold. The concussion stuff is just a precaution. I'll probably be let out tomorrow morning.'

'Oh, I'm so glad you're alright. To think, two accidents in less than twenty-four hours. I mean to say; it is simply horrific! Although my mother always said these things happen in threes, so I've been very careful driving here. But, oh LaVonda, poor Royce!'

Sylvia always spoke quickly, and diverted on and off track, so LaVonda was used to her non-sequiturs, but this time she was sure she couldn't have heard right. Did Sylvia say poor Royce?

'Did you say poor Royce?'

'Oh, I knew it would be my duty to break the news to you, but I'm prepared for this. I had to tell Angela, and Helen, and Colin, because I heard the news first, being the only one in the office early this morning, and I did think young Angela was going collapse with shock, poor little thing; she is quite fragile-minded, isn't she? I mean, not in a bad way, but she's not very robust. You can tell just by looking at her.'

'Sylvia, what about Royce? What's wrong?'

'Sorry, I'm not going about this very well, am I? But it is just the shock. So completely unexpected. We're all terribly upset, and I've been crying all morning...'

LaVonda felt like screaming in frustration, but the thought of hurting her poor head stopped her.

'...and he was so young. Only forty-six. I'm mucking this one up, aren't I? LaVonda, I am so sorry to be the one to break the news, but someone has to... Royce passed away last night. HR came over this morning to let us know, and I was the only person in. I mean to say, I guess everyone else was a little worse for wear after last night, but I don't drink, and so I offered to break the terrible news to everyone when they finally arrived at work. Then when I heard about your accident, well I mean, that was just terrible too, so I wanted to come over straight away to check on you and tell you about Royce.'

The blood seemed to drain from LaVonda's brain, leaving her lightheaded. Royce dead? It wasn't possible. It *couldn't* be possible. Healthy, nasty men didn't just drop dead. Unless he had a brain aneurysm, or maybe a stroke, or some sort of accident. A terrible thought came into her mind.

'Syl, how... how... how did he die?'

'Excuse me. They're ready for you now.' Two orderlies had entered the room, and they moved to each end of the bed.

'Oh, well, I'll have to go then, I suppose. I was just telling LaVonda, one of our beloved colleagues passed over last night.' Sylvia moved her handbag to her other arm as she prepared to leave.

'That's too bad. I'm sorry for your loss, but we have to take her now. Excuse me.' One of the orderlies unlocked the brakes on the wheels of LaVonda's bed.

'Sylvia, how...'

Sylvia reached over and patted LaVonda's shoulder.

'I'll call tomorrow to check on you. Gosh, all this death and accidents business is very distressing. I might need to go and have a little rest myself.'

LaVonda's blood pressure had soared up to, and right through, the ceiling. She couldn't get a word in edgeways. If only Sylvia would shut up for one minute...

'Syl!' Her voice was a barely controlled shriek. 'What happened?'

'Sorry what? Now, I know you've had a bad experience yourself, LaVonda, so I'll forgive you raising your voice at me. It was a car accident like yours, well not exactly like yours. Dreadful business, though. Someone ran him over and then left the scene. A hit-and-run, they call it. Terrible. Just terrible.'

What on *earth* was she going to do? Well, confess, of course, but then she'd have to go to prison, and she wouldn't be around for the birth of her grandchild, and she'd definitely lose the house and... oh no, that wouldn't do at all. LaVonda couldn't be locked up in a tiny cell while Dave and Jemima moved into her home and played loving grandparents to her daughter's baby.

But she had to turn herself in, of course she did. There was no question. It was absolutely the right thing to do.

Her mind refused to remember what had actually happened. *Think, LaVonda, think!* She pleated the hospital sheets between her fingers. Her head throbbed incessantly, and her throat was dry and sticky.

*Come on. You were pulling out of the car park, and you saw Royce coming out of the restaurant, and then... what?* What had happened? Had she really put her foot down and driven straight at him? Had he bounced off her bonnet, over the roof of the car, and smacked down on the concrete? Had that happened?

It felt like it might have, but when she tried to fill in the details, her mind went blank. Maybe she was suffering temporary insanity? That was probably it. Ann might be able to get her off on a technicality, because she hadn't been herself when she drove over her newly appointed manager, and she'd obviously been traumatised from her own accident... well hang on... no, because that had happened afterwards.

LaVonda took a sip of water, then let her head drop back. She winced in pain. Oh god, she'd been drunk! She didn't remember anything because she'd been horribly, dreadfully drunk, and she'd driven a car. No wonder she'd run someone over. It was the most dangerous, stupid thing she'd ever done in her life. LaVonda lifted her chin bravely. She would take her punishment, and if that meant she missed out on seeing her grandchild being born and growing up, it was just too bad.

Maybe they would go easier on her if she confessed. Surely that would look better to the judge than saying nothing and simply waiting until the police caught up with her.

Although... would they catch her? Nothing connected her to the hit-and-run. As far as everyone else was concerned, she had gone home in a taxi. Of course, someone might have seen her car afterwards, but she owned a white Hyundai, one of several thousand on the road every day. And it was probably written off now anyway, after her own accident, so it wasn't like the police would be able to detect any Royce-sized bumps on the front of the car.

*Oh, don't be ridiculous. You can't possibly think you'll get away with this. You have to confess.*

Did she? It wasn't going to make any difference to Royce; he'd still be dead. Confessing wouldn't bring him back, would it? Well, no, it wouldn't, but she'd killed a man! And so many people knew how much she disliked him; someone was bound to think of her as a suspect.

Or maybe that wasn't the case. People disliked, even hated, each other all the time, but it didn't mean they went around killing them. Well, obviously some people did, but they were probably psychopaths, not friendly, polite, otherwise law-abiding women in their late forties.

She might actually be able to get away with it. But could she live with herself if she did? Knowing every day that she'd taken someone's life and never confessed. Never stepped up and taken her punishment.

God, her head was pounding so badly, and her thoughts were irrepressibly scattered. She needed strong painkillers, a decent sleep, and then this would all be straightforward in the morning. She didn't need to decide anything right now.

LaVonda closed her eyes. She could picture Royce standing in front of the restaurant and her little white car coming towards him. She watched in her mind as he looked up, just before she hit him. He barely had time to react; his face registered the beginning of surprise, then the car struck his side, throwing him into the air, the weight of his own body slamming him into the ground. Killing him.

She could visualise it all as an observer, but she couldn't *remember* any of it happening. She tried to place herself in the driver's seat and run through the scene again, but the images wouldn't come. She remembered *imagining* hitting him, but not actually doing it.

But of course, she had. She'd closed her eyes to stop from seeing the actual moment of impact, but there was no doubt she'd done it. She'd deliberately run into Royce. She was 100 percent guilty.

'LaVonda Robinette?'

LaVonda opened her eyes, and her gaze landed on a policewoman standing at the end of the bed. She nearly shrieked out aloud.

The policewoman looked down at the notepad she was holding.

'Are you LaVonda Robinette?'

LaVonda opened her mouth, but nothing came out, except a tiny squeak. She nodded. It was probably better if she didn't try to speak. She had the right to remain silent, after all.

'I'm Senior Constable Julie Day. I want to talk to you about your accident this morning. How are you feeling?'

How was she feeling? Apart from her heart still pounding hysterically against the wall of her chest, she felt momentarily relieved. This was about *her* accident, not Royce's. Concentrate, LaVonda! Stop thinking about Royce.

'What do you remember about the accident?'

'I... um... I was behind a truck. There was a car... driving too fast. I couldn't get out of the way... and then he hit me.' The self-pitying tone in her own voice both upset and disgusted her. She'd hit someone too, and he hadn't escaped so lightly.

'It was a *she*, actually. A P-plater. She escaped without injury, but she's taken full responsibility for causing the collision.'

As she should. Both the girl, and LaVonda, should take responsibility for their accidents. Oh, for heaven's sake. She needed to stop thinking about Royce!

'In the case of a major vehicle accident where there are injuries, it is customary to test both parties for alcohol and narcotics. The other driver had nothing in her system.'

The silly girl probably wasn't concentrating on driving. Undoubtedly, she'd been texting on her phone, or checking her social media. LaVonda had noticed a lot of young people playing with their phones while they were behind the wheel. It was obviously terribly dangerous; someone could be killed. She could have been killed.

'Your blood test results have come back, and it appears you had 0.034 alcohol units. That's under the legal limit but could have affected your ability to react defensively.'

*She'd still been drunk this morning.* LaVonda went cold with horror as all the blood in her body rushed to her face. She must have been completely paralytic last night to still have alcohol in her system more than ten hours later. No wonder she couldn't remember running into Royce. She'd been blackout drunk.

LaVonda didn't know what to say. Pain hammered at her head, and she reached up to touch the bump. The policewoman's expression softened.

'I know, you took quite a knock to the head. We'll need to get a statement from you, but that can wait until tomorrow. I understand you're being discharged in the morning?'

LaVonda nodded. Senior Constable Day placed her card on the bedside table.

'Just give me a call when you're ready, and I'll take your statement. I hope you feel better soon.'

LaVonda twisted the card between her fingers. It was looking quite dog-eared now. Senior Constable Julie Day. The number of the police station was written underneath, and LaVonda had almost memorised it. What would happen if she called and confessed? Would that nice Julie come straight back down and arrest her? Handcuff her to the bed, so she couldn't escape?

She looked up as Ann came into the room.

'Never a dull moment with you, is there? Maxie's on her way; she's been on night shift and just woke up. How are you feeling?'

*Horrible. Guilty. Embarrassed. Terrified.*

LaVonda heaved herself up in the bed and forced a smile. 'Better. I was hoping they might let me go this afternoon, but apparently not.'

Her headache had subsided in the past few hours and was now a dull, manageable ache. Her wrist was sore, but constant thoughts had distracted her from the worst of the pain. She looked down at the card in her hand again.

'I brought you a charger. Yes, I know you're going home in the morning, but in the meantime, if you need to make any calls...'

Why was Ann looking at her in a meaningful way? What did she know? Oh, heavens. Now she truly was becoming paranoid.

'...or check Facebook, or whatever. You must be so bored just lying around.'

'Thanks, Ann. That's... great.'

Should she tell her sister? She'd have to at some stage, and she definitely needed a good lawyer. Although... was Ann a good lawyer? Perhaps she was only mediocre. LaVonda had always assumed Ann was good, but she didn't actually know for a fact. Maybe for this situation she needed someone more ruthless, more cut-throat, than her older sister. Someone who could convince a jury that Royce was an evil monster who had almost *deserved* to be mown down in a restaurant car park.

'So what happened? Some arse rammed into you. Had he been drinking? I tell you, Von, there is a special place reserved in hell for people who drink and drive.'

Oh dear. Definitely a different lawyer.

'It was a young woman. She hadn't been drinking.'

'Texting? I'll bet she was texting. They all do it. The number of times I've seen young people fiddling around on their phones behind the wheel... it is a wonder more people aren't killed. Now, tell me, what happened last night?'

Last night? What did Ann know about last night?

'It was... fine. Nothing... happened.'

'Did you say anything to the man? When you rang me, you were all set to confront him about his behaviour.'

'I rang you?' She couldn't remember calling Ann. How drunk had she been?

Ann clicked her tongue impatiently. 'You called me from the restaurant about nine. You were there celebrating that man's promotion; Rhys, is it? You were going to confront him and his girlfriend about setting you up. I tried to talk you out of it, but you'd clearly had a few drinks, and you were pretty riled up. So, did you say anything?'

LaVonda stared blankly at her sister. She couldn't remember any of that. It did sound like something she would do though, and she *had* been imagining confronting Royce about his behaviour towards her.

'Royce. His name is Royce, and no, I didn't say anything. I must have changed my mind.'

'I'm glad to hear it. You sounded quite wound up, so thank goodness you came to your senses. This Royce character will eventually get what he deserves; you don't need to get yourself mixed up in anything awkward, or career-limiting.'

Well, it was far too late for that.

LaVonda looked up as Maxine came into the room and sat down on the end of the bed. Her eyes sparkled with mischief.

'First you pick a fight, then you go and try to get yourself killed, so I'd have to live with the guilt for the rest of my life. Nice work, Von.'

'Max, I'm sorry about what I said.'

Maxine waved her hand dismissively. 'Don't worry about it. I've already forgotten. A fading memory is just another of the joys of becoming old. How are you doing?'

'I'm alright, I just want to go home. Can you pull any strings?'

'No way. You have to stay until the staff are confident that you don't have a concussion. You'll just have to suck it up for one night.' She grinned at Ann, who nodded.

'She's right, Von, don't fight it. Just try and relax. Do you need anything?' She reached out and lifted the plastic jug on LaVonda's beside table, pouring water into a little paper cup. Her hand shook slightly with the weight of the jug, and water slopped out, knocking the cup over. Maxine frowned.

'Here, let me.'

'I can do it.' Ann picked up the paper cup and used her stump to support it while she tried again to fill the cup with water. Both Maxine and LaVonda watched her in mounting frustration. She looked so awkward and clumsy. Why couldn't she just accept help?

'There.' Ann handed the cup to LaVonda, who didn't want any water. She sipped it anyway.

Maxine spoke. 'Do you need a lift home tomorrow? Ines and I have a couples' counselling session in the morning, but I can check on you at lunchtime and see when you expect to get out of here. In the meantime, you should try and get some rest.'

LaVonda doubted she'd sleep, but she would take the advice to try and relax. After all, she couldn't do anything today. It was getting late, and she was tired, sore, confused, and emotional. She didn't have to try and deal with anything right now; she had plenty of time to work out what to do in the morning.

*To confess. There was plenty of time to confess in the morning.*

Oh, well, yes. That too. But the point was, she didn't need to worry about anything at this very moment. Tonight, she would rest, and then tomorrow... tomorrow, she would confess to Royce's murder.

# NINE

LaVonda glanced up at the clock on the office wall. It was mid-morning. Today. She would turn herself in today. Immediately after lunch. She just had to finish this urgent press release on fatbergs clogging up the national sewage systems, and then meet Ann for lunch and legal advice, then she would pick up the phone, call the policewoman who'd taken her accident statement, and confess.

It had been more than a week since the accidents, although she'd only just returned to work this morning, and there was such a backlog of emails and work, she couldn't possibly go to prison until it was all under control. Plus, she had Royce's workload to try and manage as well as her own.

She couldn't quite believe Royce was gone. His desk had been packed up, and no one, apart from Sylvia, spoke much about him. They were probably all still in shock. Angela hadn't returned to work; no doubt she was trying to come to terms with his death. LaVonda hadn't gone to the funeral, although everyone else in the office had. She couldn't bear to; after all, it seemed a bit hypocritical to join in the mourning for a man whom she'd deliberately murdered.

Had she really killed him? It seemed so... unlikely. So out of character for her. Yet she had, and clearly it wasn't *that* out of character. She'd let her own mother die just a few weeks earlier.

But, oh, the sheer relief of having both of them gone. No more anxiety on Saturday mornings; she could spend time pottering around in her garden instead of visiting Maude and listening to her abuse. And it was so pleasant to come into work this morning and not worry about what Royce might do next to embarrass or upset her.

*That was no excuse for murder though*, LaVonda told herself sternly. Royce might have been a horrible man, but she'd ruthlessly struck him down in the prime of his life. She had to pay the price for her actions, and she would. LaVonda was no coward, even if the thought of going to jail absolutely terrified her. She'd seen Orange Is the New Black. She knew what went on in a woman's prison.

There was just so much to do right now; it really wasn't a good time to be incarcerated. Deborah was leaving for Washington next Monday, so LaVonda had to help her get things organised, then on top of that she simply *had* to clear her enormous backlog of emails, and of course this fatberg report wasn't going to write itself.

Perhaps she should wait until the end of the week and confess then. Yes, Friday might be better, actually Sunday would be better still. Then she could empty out the freezer, pay the rates, and talk to Emmett, to help her daughter prepare for her new life as the child of a felon. She should probably warn Dave as well, in case reporters got wind of the story and started hounding him and Jemima. Although, really, that was the least of her problems right now. *So, scratch that. Dave, you're on your own.*

LaVonda glanced at the clock again. No, today was definitely out for a confession. There was too much to do. Plus, she had organised the Head Office site visit to the Murray Dam and water plant this afternoon; she couldn't pull out at the last minute just because she needed to have herself arrested. It would be completely *unprofessional* to leave the rest of the team in the lurch.

It wasn't that she was deliberately *avoiding* confessing. She had every intention of confessing. But she had a number of people depending on her, and how could she possibly resign herself into years and years of prison life when she had so much to organise? Sunday. Sunday would be the day. LaVonda opened her phone calendar and added a new reminder. *Sunday 9am. Call police and confess to murder.* There. Now it was official.

'Can I speak to you for a minute?'

Good grief! Deborah was standing next to her desk, looking down at her. LaVonda flushed and tried to cover her phone, but Deborah seemed too distracted to notice what she'd written. She stood with her arms crossed, drumming her fingertips against her biceps in a way that was quite disturbing.

'Of course. Here? Or...' LaVonda nodded towards Deborah's office.

Deborah didn't reply. She turned on her heel and headed back towards her office. Not out here then. LaVonda hurried after her.

Deborah waited until LaVonda had entered and then shut the door behind them. LaVonda could see Sylvia outside, leaning slightly towards the office. She would be desperate to know what was going on and was clearly trying to eavesdrop.

'Please, take a seat.'

LaVonda sat down and waited for Deborah to take her chair behind the desk, but Deborah remained standing. She looked unhappy and slightly flustered. LaVonda waited quietly. Eventually, Deborah spoke, her voice soft.

'Royce was killed by a hit-and-run driver.'

Oh god. What did Deborah know? Had she seen LaVonda drive into him? Was that what this was about? Deborah knew LaVonda was the murderer, and now she was about to announce she was going to turn her in to the authorities. Or perhaps she already had? Maybe the police were on their way, and she'd brought LaVonda in here to spare her the embarrassment of a public arrest.

LaVonda's breathing became shallow, and she shut her eyes. She refused to faint or have hysterics. Whatever else, she would remain dignified and upstanding.

'As you know, I had asked Royce to take over my role while I am in Washington.'

LaVonda nodded and opened her eyes. Deborah was taking the long way around, but okay. She could handle it.

'Obviously, with his untimely death, I'm in a bit of a bind.'

This wasn't panning out the way LaVonda expected. This sounded less like an imminent arrest, and more like an offer...

'I wonder if you might consider stepping into the role for a while. Just until we get everything sorted.'


LaVonda felt like singing, but of course that would be completely inappropriate under the circumstances. The hire bus rattled along towards the Murray Dam, while the twelve occupants played with their phones or simply stared blankly out of the window. LaVonda was much too excited to do either. Her heart soared like one of the magpies outside.

She was going to be Acting General Manager for the foreseeable future and, as Sylvia had pointed out, Deborah was unlikely to return and then she, LaVonda, might win the role permanently. It was almost too good to be true. Of course, there was the small matter of her imminent prison sentence, but LaVonda wasn't going to think about that right now. She was going to enjoy this moment, the promise of what could be. The thrill of finally being recognised and offered the managing role overcame LaVonda; all those years of hard work and dedication had finally paid off.

Deborah was going to make the announcement on Friday and had asked LaVonda to keep things quiet until then. Not an easy task. LaVonda felt like standing up and making an announcement right now, on the spot. After all, why wait?

Alright, she had promised Deborah she wouldn't say a word, but it was just so tempting. Imagine Colin's face when he found out she was going to be his manager. She could hardly wait.

The bus pulled up outside the Murray Dam water plant, and the employees filed off the bus. LaVonda did a quick head count. Perhaps they should pair up, do the buddy system so no one was left behind. Before she could suggest it, a young woman carrying a pink folder approached them.

'Hi, you're the Head Office crowd, right?'

'That's right.' LaVonda took charge. Well, she was the most senior person, and she was about to be the General Manager, even if no one knew yet. She reached out her hand for the young woman to shake.

'LaVonda Robinette. We spoke on the phone.'

'Ah yes, you're the one who organised this site visit?'

'I'm the one who always organises the site visits. You must be new?'

The young woman stiffened. 'No. I've been here ten months. Most of the staff at the plant have been here less time. I'm considered one of the old staff. I'm Amanda.'

LaVonda hadn't meant to offend the woman. She smiled broadly to paste over the tension.

'It is lovely to meet you, Amanda. I haven't been out for a while. How many staff do you have out here?' She knew exactly how many staff worked at the plant, she'd conducted the induction training for every one of them, plus she checked off their timesheets, but her tactic worked. Amanda visibly relaxed now she'd been given the chance to show off her knowledge of the operation.

'Fifteen of us in total, but we're not all full-time. Paul is the site manager, you probably know him, he's retiring next year, and Frank will likely take his place. Frank hasn't been here long, but he's the most qualified. Poor Frank. His partner died a few weeks ago, and we didn't expect him to come back to work straight away, but he's very dedicated. Then you have Michael, who looks after pipe maintenance; he's a terrific guy, but he has a glass eye, the left one, so when you meet him, try not to stare...'

LaVonda noticed the rest of the staff looking bored and fidgety while Amanda prattled on. She had to take charge again and cut off the gossiping.

'Perhaps we should make our way down to the plant room so the staff can get their hard hats?' Her gentle suggestion worked. Amanda stopped talking about the water plant staff and led the group across the car park towards the main building.

Paul was waiting for them and he greeted LaVonda warmly while the rest of the group were trying on their hard hats.

'Good to see you again, LaVonda. Thanks for organising to bring the staff down. Most of them look familiar, but there are a few new faces.'

'It is my pleasure, Paul. Head Office believes it is important our staff get to see some of the operations hands-on. It gives everyone an appreciation for the work the department does.'

Paul nodded. He was typically a man of few words. LaVonda glanced around the room, then lowered her voice.

'Paul, Amanda mentioned one of your staff recently lost his wife. We weren't notified in Head Office, although I assume HR was aware. How is he?'

Paul shook his head. 'Seems fine. I'd be in pieces, but some folks react differently. Probably keeping busy helps. You had your own tragedy out there, didn't you?'

'Uh, yes, yes, we did. Royce Butler. He died... he was killed, just last week.'

'I heard he'd only just started, but he was already making an impression?'

'Ah, yes, that's right. Quite an impression.' LaVonda wanted to get off the subject of Royce, so she clapped her hands like a schoolteacher. 'We'd better get moving. Is everyone ready?'

Judging from the sour expressions on several people's faces, her attempt at rallying the troops was not appreciated. Paul led them all back outside and then herded them, single file, up the walkway towards the dam. Already, the roar of water spilling through the pipes into the catchment was making hearing difficult.

Standing at the back of the group, LaVonda could hardly hear, let alone see Paul, as he stopped and greeted another man. He introduced the man to the group, but LaVonda had stopped paying attention. She wasn't particularly interested in the water plant. She did this tour every year, and she pretty much knew all there was to know about water. She preferred to use the time to think about her new promotion. Of course, she couldn't take it; she was confessing to murder on Sunday, but it was nice to daydream about the possibility for a while.

'Hey mate, don't know if you've met LaVonda Robinette from Head Office? She organises this tour for the Head Office folk each year. Be nice to her, mate, she's a good egg. LaVonda, this is Frank.'

LaVonda squinted up at the man standing in front of her. The sun was shining across his face, and at first, she couldn't make out his features. She shifted slightly to focus, as she held out her hand, and her broad smile instantly died. She had heard the expression 'blood ran cold', but she'd never before known how it felt. Her entire body was shocked stiff. Every hair stood on end, and her breath caught in her throat. It was him. The man from the bar.

He clearly didn't recognise her, but then again, why would he? He'd been drunk that night, angry, abusive, and the lighting in the restaurant was dim. He had no reason to associate the assertive woman who challenged him in the bar, with the middle-aged woman standing in front of him now, bundled in her fleecy jacket, pink beanie, and wearing her corporate security pass around her neck.

Blood roared in LaVonda's ears, and she thought she might faint. This was the monster who had threatened her, assaulted her, and then haunted her dreams for the past two weeks. Another spark of horror shot through her. Oh god, this was Frank. Frank with the dead wife. Had he killed her? Had he murdered the woman LaVonda had stood up for?

Frank took her hand in his heavy hot one and gave it a quick, hard pump. LaVonda was vaguely aware of the pain in her wrist, but the rest of her mind was in free-fall. As he turned back to the rest of the group, she started shaking violently and uncontrollably. She had to get away. Excusing herself quietly, she hurried back to the bus. She heard Paul call out after her, but she didn't stop until she was safely away from that terrible man.

'Peanut is doing well. How about you, Mum, how is everything with you? How is your wrist? How is your head? You don't know how worried I've been about you. Are you sure you don't need me to come there and look after you?'

Perched at her kitchen bench, and still bundled in her fleece, LaVonda put her daughter on speakerphone and poured herself another glass of brandy. So much for not drinking ever again. Although, this was an emergency, so obviously it didn't count.

'I'm... fine. No need to worry. Everything is absolutely fine. How are you? How's the baby?' She took a swig of brandy and braced herself as it stung the back of her throat. She still felt dizzy and anxious, and the brandy didn't seem to be helping the way it was supposed to help.

'You just asked me that, Mum, and you don't sound fine at all. You sound completely stressed.'

Well, yes, she was completely stressed. The dread of having to confess to Royce's murder (or was it manslaughter? What was the difference?), in two days' time had been supplanted by the trauma and distress of coming face to face with *him*.

Frank.

He had physically attacked her, and he had probably killed his wife, and LaVonda was the only person at work who knew the depths of his violence. Would he remember her? Would he come after her next? LaVonda shuddered and picked up her brandy again.

Emmett was still talking. 'You should consider letting Jaz take you through a STER session, Mum. It is designed specifically to relax your mind and clear your emotional baggage. You'll be amazed at how it will help you to become less stressed and more able to express your authentic self.'

If Jasper took her through his STER session, only one of them would come out the other end alive. Wisely, LaVonda chose not to share this thought with her daughter.

'Thank you for the offer, but I don't think so. Em, I need to talk to you about something serious.'

Even as the words left her mouth, LaVonda hesitated. Was this the right moment to tell her daughter she had killed someone, and she planned to confess this weekend, and she was probably going to jail?

No. Because she *wasn't* going to turn herself in on Sunday evening, was she? Not now.

There was something she had to do first.

'What is it, Mum? Do you need me to come home?' Emmett's voice held a tiny note of panic.

Oh, why had she blurted that out when she had no intention of confessing yet? Her thoughts were all over the place, and she needed time to think, to sort out what to do calmly and carefully before making any decisions, and certainly before telling Emmett what was going on. LaVonda cast about for something to say.

'Your dad wants to buy the house and move in here with Jemima.' The name sounded strange when she said it aloud. As though by saying her name, LaVonda was giving Jemima validation to be in their lives.

'Is that all? I think it's a great idea. You could buy something smaller, and cosier, and more suited to you.' Emmett's relief was clear, although her enthusiasm was entirely inappropriate.

'*This* house is suited to me. It is my home, and you grew up here. I love this house.'

'Do you, though? Do you? Mum, I've heard you complain about the house being too big for the two of you, and you couldn't wait to retire and downsize.'

'That's not true. I don't want to leave my home, especially not so your dad can move in and start a new family.' As soon as she said it, LaVonda wanted to bite the words back. She hadn't been planning to tell Emmett that particular piece of news.

'You don't want him back, anyway. It might seem strange now, but this is probably for the best. Let Dad get on with his life and you can get on with yours. I think you'll be much happier on your own, and maybe you'll even meet someone nice down the track.'

LaVonda shook her head.

'Em, you're not listening. Your dad is planning on having more children with her. Jemima.' It was no less strange the second time she said the woman's name. Jemima was real, though, wasn't she? She was an actual person in LaVonda's life.

'Good for him. It might be nice to have a little brother or sister. Although my own Peanut will be older than their aunt or uncle. That could be weird.' Emmett chuckled.

LaVonda wondered if she might be going mad. Didn't Emmett understand what this meant? She didn't want to be cruel to her own child, but Em hadn't thought this through. She spoke again, slowly. Clearly.

'Em, if he has another child, you probably won't see a cent of the Robinette inheritance. Your grandfather might cut you out of his will once he has a biological grandchild.'

'Oh, I don't care about that. Money isn't everything you know. Love and kindness are the foundations of life, and the rest is just noise and distraction. Besides, the STER program is about to take off in a big way, so we'll be fine. Mum, I have to go, but I'll call you next week, okay?'

She hung up, and LaVonda poured herself another brandy. It was all well and good for Emmett to say she didn't care about money, but she'd never had to do without it. LaVonda knew what it was like trying to raise a small child on a tiny income. It was irresponsible of her daughter not to consider these things.

A knock on the back door made her jump, and she nearly spilled her drink. Her heart thudded hard. Frank?

It was Doreen. Possibly the last person in the world she wanted to speak to right now. LaVonda held the door half-open, hoping Doreen would take the hint and leave.

'I saw your rental car arrive home a few minutes ago, and I thought to myself, I might just pop over and see how poor LaVonda's doing. It must be so hard on you, losing your mother, and your husband, and then your car, all at the same time. Were you forced to sell it? Lucy from number 9 had to sell all her assets when her husband left. He took all their money, too.' Her eyes gleamed, and she took a step forward, clearly angling for an invite inside. 'You must be in desperate need of some sympathetic company.'

It was obvious that Doreen had come over to sniff for gossip. LaVonda scowled and pulled the door towards her, blocking the entrance with her body.

'Thank you for your *sympathy*, Doreen, but I've never been better. Now, if you'll excuse me...'

'Oh, I'm so glad. Because I simply don't know how I'd *cope* in your situation. You're a better woman than I am, hahaha. Mind you, this is just the *storm* before the *calm*, as I like to say, hahaha. Once you get through all this trauma and pop out the other side, it will be clear sailing. Trust me.'

'Goodbye, Doreen.' She started to shut the door.

'Wait! I also wanted to see if you enjoyed my Tuna Mornay. I know I said not to worry about returning the dish, but it *was* one of my best ones... so perhaps I could just come in for a moment and grab it?'

'I threw it out.' LaVonda almost laughed aloud at the expression on the other woman's face.

'Well, goodness me! I don't know what to say.'

*That would be a first,* LaVonda thought meanly, and went to shut the door again. Doreen stuck out her hand to stop her.

'I mean, it *really* doesn't matter, but it does seem just a *little* rude, after I went to all that trouble for you. I won't say anything to the others, of course, because I don't want to make it awkward for you next time you come to book club. You will be coming back, won't you? Once all this drama of yours settles down?'

LaVonda opened the door wider and took a step towards Doreen, who quickly stepped back. She hadn't been to the book club since Dave had left. She was sick and tired of doing things because she felt she had to, rather than because she wanted to. And right now, she did not want to stand here talking to Doreen. She wanted to go back inside and have a good hard think about Frank.

'I've quit book club. So, if you ladies want to gossip about me, fine, go ahead. But please don't come around prying for information, Doreen, because next time, I won't answer you.'

She left her neighbour standing, mouth agape, on the other side of the firmly closed door.

Shrugging off her jacket, LaVonda picked up her brandy glass and walked into her living room. She put some classical music on her phone and synchronised it to Dave's expensive retro speakers, turning the volume down, just enough for background atmosphere. Then she snuggled into the sofa, pulled her new yellow throw over her knees, and opened her laptop. She took a deep breath, followed by a fortifying slug of brandy. She didn't want to do this next part, but she had to know.

It was all online, and LaVonda's horror mounted as she absorbed the facts. Frank's wife, Philippa, had fallen to her death from the couple's 10th floor balcony the same night LaVonda had publicly challenged him. It seemed he had made good on his threat to 'sort her out' when he got home. Frank had initially been questioned about the death by police, but then released without charge, thanks to a sudden alibi his cousin had provided.

LaVonda felt sick with guilt. There was no doubt in her mind that Frank had killed Philippa, and she, LaVonda, had infuriated him enough to commit that brutal act against his wife.

He had to be punished. She couldn't let him get away with murder. Closing the laptop, LaVonda shut her eyes and gave herself up to the thought she'd had in the back of her mind all afternoon. Her imagination took over; planning out the steps, working her way through the details.

She knew where he worked. She knew the hours he worked. She knew all she needed to know.

# TEN

The first two murders weren't deliberate. Not really. Neglecting to help until it was too late, well you couldn't call that murder, could you?

The second one, well yes, *technically* that was murder, but it was accidental... almost. She'd been a bit drunk and upset, and she hadn't realised what she was doing at the time. She was just fantasizing about killing him; she hadn't meant to *actually* kill him. It was just bad luck. Or good luck, depending on how you looked at it.

Not this time. There was nothing accidental about this time.

The musty stench of damp towels and sour milk made LaVonda wrinkle her nose in distaste. It was the first time she had been back in the house since Maude's funeral, and she felt apprehensive and uneasy. LaVonda knew she was being silly. Maude was well and truly gone; it wasn't as if she'd be waiting inside to hurl abuse and insults.

Still, LaVonda couldn't shake her apprehension as she walked briskly into the living room and opened the curtains to let in some light. It didn't help much. The room was still gloomy and depressing. A month of being locked up had made the house feel abandoned, and the sunlight, filtered by grimy windows, barely illuminated the furniture. Everything had been left exactly the way it had been on the day Maude died. Even the urine stain on the living room carpet lay untouched.

She should talk to her sisters about cleaning this place up, sorting things out, and putting the house on the market. That was the practical, responsible thing to do. But not now. Not today. Today she had a different reason for being in her mother's house.

A tiny rustling noise made LaVonda spin around in alarm. Nothing. No movement, no sound. She stood motionless, straining to hear. She'd definitely heard something, maybe a mouse? The house was deadly silent now, and she felt a chill of nervousness creep down her spine. She was starting to freak herself out. She should hurry up and get on with it.

Grimacing, she knelt down on the sticky carpet next to the old wooden cabinet that housed the television. The side drawers shrieked in protest as she pulled them open. LaVonda stifled a shriek of her own. The drawers yielded nothing more than old videos and a few power cords. She checked underneath the unit but found only dust and a few mouse droppings on the carpet.

She glanced around the rest of the room. There was nowhere else to hide them; they must be in the bedroom. As reluctant as she felt to go in there it *was* the most logical place to hide something illegal. Maude wouldn't have wanted to risk the nursing staff stumbling across her secret, so they were probably hidden at the top of the wardrobe or stashed under the bed. At least, LaVonda *hoped* they were in the bedroom. She didn't want to poke around in her mother's room, but the only other hiding place was out in the garden shed, and she couldn't bring herself to go into that spidery hellhole.

LaVonda paused in the doorway of Maude's bedroom. The bed was the same one her parents had slept in when she was young, but now the mattress looked saggy, and the room smelt of unwashed sheets and foot odour. LaVonda shivered and stepped inside. *Stop dawdling. Just get on and find them.*

One of the wardrobe doors was ajar. Tentatively, she pulled it open to reveal a row of faded dresses hanging like limp corpses. LaVonda shook her head. Why was her imagination so morbid? They were just musty old dresses, for heaven's sake.

She looked down at several pairs of shoes in varying stages of wear. She opened the other door and noticed a flat, metal tin tucked towards the back of the wardrobe. LaVonda knelt down and reached in, trying not to breathe in the stale stink of the shoes. She pulled the tin out, then hefted it onto the unmade bed, and wrenched open the tight fitted lid. Nestled inside, loosely wrapped in an old pillowcase, were several packets of cartridges and four guns.

LaVonda stared at them and a tiny thrill shot through her. These were evil-looking, dangerous weapons, all illegal and unlicenced, and it gave her a rare sense of power just to look at them. Guns meant control. When you held a gun, you could make people do anything you wanted them to do.

She'd known her mother had kept them, but she hadn't set eyes on them for years. She picked up the smallest one, an old-fashioned Derringer, and hefted it in her hand. This was the one she'd used all those years ago when her mother's father; their granddad, had taken her and Ann out one afternoon to shoot rabbits. He'd used a shotgun but given the girls his small, black handgun to practice their aim.

Ann had hated the whole experience and flatly refused to even touch the gun. But LaVonda had been fascinated as Granddad taught her how to cock the hammer and hold the piece steady, so when she pressed on the trigger, it didn't ricochet or rebound. Of course, she'd never actually managed to shoot a rabbit. Her aim was terrible and drew snorts of disgust from her grandfather. But she could still remember the sensation of discharging the weapon, the jerk to her arm, the smell of gunpowder, and the sudden bang that had shocked her every time.

She placed the gun carefully back into the tin and lifted up a much bigger, heavier, black pistol. She pointed it at the wardrobe door and tried to aim. Her arm shook, and she steadied her grip using her other hand. Her sprained wrist had healed, but it was still weak and a little sore. She'd never be able to hold this gun up long enough to aim and shoot Frank. The Derringer would have to do.

Carefully, LaVonda placed the small gun in her handbag. She bit her lip, then reached out and picked up the larger gun. It wouldn't hurt to be over prepared. Just in case.

LaVonda shifted the bulk of her handbag to her other arm, trying to make it look lighter than it was, as she joined the queue to pay at the petrol station. She should have left her bag in her rental car, but she didn't want to let it out of her sight, and now it seemed important to pretend to the world her plain, black bag held nothing more than a wallet, makeup, and a nice middle-aged lady's packet of tissues. Not that anyone else in the queue was paying her any attention whatsoever. She glanced up at the security camera mounted on the ceiling. This wasn't good. This seemed like the kind of rookie mistake that led to an arrest; running low on petrol and having to stop for fuel on your way to kill someone.

The cashier looked as bored as everyone standing in the queue. LaVonda, on the other hand, felt wide awake and alight with anticipation.

'Next.'

'Number 11, please.'

He barely glanced at her as he held out his hand to take her payment.

*You'd sit up a bit straighter if you knew what was in here*, she thought, reaching into her bag, past the guns, to retrieve her wallet. She could take this whole place hostage, Thelma-and-Louise style, if she wanted. Not that she would, but she could. *Then you'd pay a bit more attention to me.*

Despite her bravado, LaVonda's hands trembled slightly as she handed over cash, not her card, and she sent up another little thanks to the universe for the Valium she'd found in Maude's bathroom cabinet. One small tablet was the only thing preventing her from wailing aloud in horror at what she was about to do.

It was late on a Friday afternoon. LaVonda had spent several days planning, choosing and rejecting ideas until she arrived at the perfect solution. It was still terrifying, but it would work, providing she could keep her nerve. Today she should, by rights, either be rotting in a jail cell, or sitting in her new office having 'Important Meetings' with other department heads. Instead, she was carefully disguised in a headscarf and dark glasses, making her way back out to the water plant to carry out her plan.

LaVonda drove carefully through the entrance gates into the car park. It was empty apart from one car; just as she'd expected. The rest of the staff were at a team planning day she had organised for them at Head Office, but Frank had stayed behind to keep everything running at the plant. It was coming up to five o'clock. Knock-off time. *In more ways than one*, LaVonda thought grimly as she got out of the car, locking it carefully behind her.

She stood for a moment to gather her courage. Her legs shook, and she reached into her bag to touch the guns and reassure herself. From where she had parked, she could see the entrance to the main reception. The place was deserted and far enough away from town that no one would disturb them.

It wasn't too late to back out. She could turn around and leave right now, and no one would ever know she'd been here. But then Frank would go unpunished. LaVonda had read everything she could find on the death of his wife, and there was no doubt in her mind Frank had killed Philippa. The poor woman hadn't accidentally fallen from the 10th floor balcony; she'd been pushed.

LaVonda had looked into his furious eyes. She'd had his threats screamed into her ear, and she knew Frank was not only capable of murder, but that he had committed it, possibly because of the fury he'd felt at LaVonda's interference. She hadn't meant to, but she'd had a hand in Philippa's death, and now she was going to avenge her.

So, no. She wasn't going to leave. Frank wasn't going to get away with murder.

Filled with resolve, LaVonda marched up to the reception and pulled open the door. The room was empty. He could be anywhere. She eyed off the restrooms to the right of the reception desk. Did she have time for a quick loo break? It was nearly five; he would be coming through here any minute and if she missed him... She would just have to hang on.

She stood, waiting, her hand inside her handbag, resting on the bigger gun. The only sound now was the ticking clock above the front desk, and that was doing nothing to calm her nerves.

The internal door to the reception burst open, and Frank strode into the room, stopping in surprise at the sight of her. He was bigger than she remembered, more substantial, and despite the Valium, her heart pounded hard in fright.

'What do you want? We're about to close.'

LaVonda took a deep breath and removed her glasses. There was no immediate sign of recognition from the man in front of her.

'I know, but this won't take long.' Her voice shook slightly. She blinked. He took a step towards her, a frown on his face. It was time.

'Stop right there.' LaVonda drew out the larger of the guns and pointed it at him.

'What the fuck? What is this? Is this a joke?'

'No joke, Frank. Put your hands up.'

His hands remained at his side, curling into fists.

'Who are you? Hang on, you're the lady from Head Office who was out here a week ago. Is this part of the team planning? You kidnap me and the others rescue me? Sorry, lady. I finish at five and there is a cold beer at home with my name on it. I'm not playing your stupid game.'

'This isn't a game. Put your... damn hands up.' She motioned with the gun. God, it was heavy.

His eyes widened. Slowly, he lifted his hands above his head.

'Thank you. Now turn around.'

He let out a low growl but did as she asked. LaVonda lifted the smaller gun out of her handbag and carefully placed the other gun inside, sliding the safety back on. She set the bag down on the floor, well out of the way. Frank was made compliant by the bigger gun, but the Derringer would finish the job now.

'We're going to the dam. You go ahead. I'm right behind you. Don't try anything stupid.'

Frank opened the door and walked back through, lifting his hands high. LaVonda followed him. All her senses were on high alert. She felt sharper, brighter, and more dangerous holding the gun. Her eyesight seemed magnified. Even though he was several steps ahead of her, she could see every individual hair on the back of his thick neck. His shirt had come untucked, and one of the laces on his boots was flapping loose. LaVonda frowned. He obviously didn't care about his appearance, or perhaps he was slacking off at the end of a long week. Either way, he was quite unkempt. The smell of his pungent body odour sparked the memory of being pressed against him while he shook her until her teeth rattled.

Her resolve increased. He was a monster, and he deserved to die for what he'd done. She felt a sudden thud of sadness at what Philippa had gone through at the hands of this monster. *Concentrate,* she told herself sharply. *This is a dangerous situation, and you need to keep your wits about you.*

They walked silently towards the edge of the dam. Frank stopped at the wall. Far below, water poured thunderously from the catchment area into the dam.

'Who sent you? What the fuck do you want?'

'No one sent me, Frank. I know what you did to Philippa.' She raised her voice so he would hear her clearly. 'I know you killed her. So now you're going to die. Get up on the edge.'

'And then what? You plan on pushing me in?'

'No, you're going to jump. And if you don't jump, I'll shoot you. You might survive the fall. You won't survive my bullet.' She'd liked the line when she'd come up with it last night, and it sounded even tougher when shouted over the rush of the water. 'Your choice, Frank.'

He lowered his hands and slowly turned around. She kept the gun trained on him. He looked her straight in the eye and smiled slowly. Nastily.

LaVonda hadn't been expecting that. She didn't want him to turn around; she certainly didn't want to see his face. The gun trembled in her hand. His grin grew wider.

'Please don't kill me, lady. Pretty please? I promise to be a good boy from now on if you just let me go.' He was mocking her. How dare he? Her anger rose, making her voice loud and firm.

'Stop talking. Turn around and get up on the edge.'

'No. I won't turn around, and I'm not gonna throw myself in. You wanna shoot me, lady, you do it like this with me watching you. Go on. Shoot me right in my face. Is this how it's going to be?'

Nausea welled, and the gun shook again. LaVonda tightened her grip. This wasn't going the way she had planned. In her mind, it had been easy to bring this man out to the dam and force him to jump to his death. Or, failing that, shoot him in cold blood. It worked in the movies and on television, but this wasn't anything like she'd imagined; it was far more dangerous, and intense, and real. She took a step back.

'Can't do it, can you, bitch? Can't shoot me. Weak as piss, that's what you are. You're gonna pay for this. I'm not going to throw you off a balcony, no, I'm gonna kill you slowly.'

Now he was taunting her, trying to make her angry, which seemed like a stupid way to get out of the situation he was in. But then he knew she wouldn't do it, didn't he? He knew she didn't have the courage to simply shoot him.

*Oh, but I do*, thought LaVonda.

The shot was louder than she'd expected. It made her jump, and it made Frank jump too, even though the bullet flew safely past him. They both stared at the little gun in shock.

'What the fuck?' Frank recovered first and lurched towards her. There was no time to turn and run, and in her panic LaVonda did the only thing she could think of; she threw the gun right at his face. He flung his hands up to block it and stumbled backwards, stepping on his loose shoelace. As her own hands flew up in terror, he tripped and crashed to the ground, hitting his head hard on the edge of the concrete wall.

LaVonda's body had turned to ice. She was a statue, simply gawping at the man lying on his back in front of her. One minute he'd been flying towards her; now he lay still on the ground. Blood oozed from the side of his head.

Her gun lay off to one side. Not within his reach. But LaVonda had seen enough thriller movies in her time to know what happened next. He would regain consciousness, grab the gun, and come after her. On terrified jelly legs, she forced herself to step towards him, then bent and snatched up her gun. He didn't move.

She pointed the gun at his head. *Come on, just do it. Squeeze the trigger. This is what you're here for. This is what you wanted. One quick shot, then you can go home.*

She stared at him for several minutes. He wasn't moving at all. Perhaps he was already dead. She lowered the gun.

Frank let out a moan. LaVonda yelped in fright, turned, and ran back towards the office. She stopped just long enough to snatch up her handbag, then bolted from the plant.

From where she was huddled on her couch, LaVonda could see her front door. Her new yellow blanket was wrapped around her shoulders, and the big gun was heavy in her lap. LaVonda sat immobile, watching the door like a hawk, but her thoughts scurried around like frightened mice.

What had she done? Well, she'd wanted to get herself arrested, and that was almost certainly going to happen tonight. Unless Frank himself came looking for her. She wouldn't be hard to track down. They worked for the same company; he'd be able to find out where she lived.

She glanced down at the gun in her lap. She would shoot him. If he came to her home, she would shoot him, because she'd have no choice. It would be his life or hers. It seemed far more likely, though, that when he came around, he would immediately report her to the police. They'd be here soon, banging on the door and demanding she open up.

She should turn herself in. She had been planning to do that once she'd killed Frank. She was intending to go to the police and finally confess to Royce's murder, and possibly Frank's too, depending on whether she'd had to shoot him, or whether he'd cooperated and killed himself by jumping into the dam. But now, her body refused to move from the couch. Her legs were curled up underneath her, and she felt she couldn't move them, even if she tried. Any minute. The police would arrive any minute now.

She should call someone. Emmett, probably. Ann, definitely. She'd need legal help when the police arrived, and if it was Frank who arrived, and she shot him, she'd still need Ann's support. She should call her right now. Except she couldn't move. Once she moved, everything became real, and LaVonda did not want everything to become real. She wanted to stay in this temporary bubble, where nothing had happened yet, and maybe nothing would.

Was that a car pulling up outside? She strained to hear.

Thump, thump, thump.

LaVonda jumped. Even though she was half-expecting the knock on her door, she was still taken aback. This was it. They were here. Frank wouldn't bang on the door, he'd just fling it open, stride in, and attack her. It had to be the police arriving, without sirens or flashing lights. Nothing as dramatic as she'd been expecting. Just a couple of bored policemen working the Friday night shift, driving down to her quiet suburb to arrest her.

She stared in anguish at her side of the door. She didn't want to open it and see them on the other side. What would they do? Would they handcuff her? Would the neighbours, or heaven forbid, Doreen, notice the police car and come out to see what was going on? She didn't think she could bear to be marched down the driveway in handcuffs in front of Doreen. She should have gone in and turned herself in so she could retain a modicum of control over the situation. Why hadn't she done that?

Slowly, she unfolded her legs. She had to get up and answer the door before the police broke it down. The gun shifted in her lap. Oh god. She couldn't have a gun on her when she opened the door. They would see her armed and dangerous and probably shoot her on sight.

Thump, thump, thump.

Frantically, LaVonda stuffed the loaded gun down the side of the couch and stood up on shaking legs. It was only a few metres to the front door, but it seemed to take a lifetime to walk there.

'LaVonda? Are you in there?'

Maxine. LaVonda flung open the door, nearly bursting into tears at the sight of her sister. She managed to pull herself together as Maxine pushed past her and came into the house.

'God, it is freezing. What took you so long?'

'Sorry, I–'

'I broke up with Ines. You were right, she was too young. We were totally unsuited.'

'I never said–'

'I hope you have wine; I've had a shit of a day. Why is your phone switched off? I've been trying to call you since I finished my shift. I was starting to get a bit worried, and I don't do worried.'

Her phone. She'd switched it off before she'd gone out to the water plant, and she hadn't thought to turn it back on. The police might be trying to contact her.

Without waiting for a reply, Maxine unwrapped her scarf and dumped her bag next to the couch. LaVonda peered outside. There was no one else. She shut the door and followed her sister, who had gone into the kitchen.

Maxine already had her head in the fridge. She was wearing her uniform, so she'd obviously come straight from work. Her stockings had a ladder running up the back of her leg.

'No wine?'

'I have vodka in the freezer.' Dave's vodka.

'Tonic water? Orange juice? No, never mind. I'll have it on the rocks.'

'Max, I...'

'What is going on, Von? Why is your phone switched off?' Maxine dropped several ice cubes into a glass and poured herself a large slug of vodka.

'I... I turned it off for a meeting. I guess I forgot to switch it back on. Max, you can't stay. I'm expecting...'

Expecting to be arrested, or attacked, in the next hour. Either way, Maxine shouldn't be here.

'Gavin? Is Gavin coming over? I thought Ann said that hadn't worked out? I'll go before he arrives. I just need some sympathy... and alcohol.' She took a big gulp from her glass before heading back into the lounge room. LaVonda followed, trying not to flap her hands about in panic. How was she going to get rid of her sister before Frank or the police arrived?

Maxine flopped down on the couch, kicked off her shoes, and took another sip of her drink, smacking her lips together loudly.

'I was getting quite... well, not worried, but definitely concerned when I couldn't reach you. You never have your phone switched off.'

LaVonda grabbed for her bag, reached past the Derringer, and lifted out her mobile. She pressed the button to switch it on, her heart pounding as she did. What if the police were trying to reach her? Could this be construed as obstruction of justice?

The mobile screen lit up. Four missed calls and one message. One call was from Dave. The other three were from the same number. A number she didn't recognise. She didn't want to listen to the message, not while her sister was here, but she needed to know.

'I'll be back in a minute. I just need to make a quick call.'

LaVonda left the room and walked quickly back into the kitchen, the phone pressed to her ear.

'*You have one new message. Message received today, at 6.06pm.* 'Hello, LaVonda? This is Andrea from HR. There's been an accident, one of the water plant staff, and as the Acting General Manager, I thought you should know. Can you call me, please?' *End of message. To replay message, dial one. To delete...*'

LaVonda hung up, feeling shaky. Somehow, HR knew about Frank, and yet the police hadn't been in touch. Maybe everything was still being sorted. After all, it probably took a while to file a police report. She'd better find out what was happening.

Quickly, she dialled the number Andrea had called on. The HR woman answered straight away.

'Hi, Andrea, this is LaVonda Robinette. I've just received your message.'

'LaVonda, thank you for calling back. Look, sorry to bother you at home, but there was an incident out at the water plant this afternoon. One of the staff, Frank Crawford, was found unconscious and bleeding from his head. Paul went back late this afternoon to pick up his jacket, and he saw Frank's car, so he went looking for him and discovered him lying near the dam. Lucky he did go back, otherwise the poor guy might have been lying there until Monday.'

'Will he... will he be alright?'

'I hope so. The hospital wouldn't give me many details, but apparently, he arrived at the hospital unconscious, and he's in an induced coma due to swelling on the brain. Other than that, I don't know.'

'Right. Well. Thank you for letting me know, Andrea.'

She hung up, her mind whirling. Frank was still alive, but unconscious. He hadn't told anyone yet. So that meant...

It meant she still had time.

'Everything okay?' Maxine had followed her into the kitchen.

'What? Yes, just a guy at work. Had an accident and knocked himself out. HR was just letting me know.'

'With all due respect, Von, your department seems to be a particularly dangerous place to work. Your nemesis gets killed, you had an accident, and now some other poor bloke's sent himself to hospital. All in the same month. You sure no one's out there trying to bump you guys off?'

LaVonda's eyes widened, and heat soared into her cheeks. 'No, of course not!'

Maxine shrugged. 'It was a joke. Lighten up. So, are you still seeing this Gavin? What's he like? Oh, tonight's the night, isn't it? Now I know why you're so keen to get rid of me.'

LaVonda rolled her eyes. 'No! For your information, I'm not seeing Gavin or anyone else. I couldn't be less interested in men at the moment.'

Not live ones anyway.

'Okay, okay. Don't bite my head off. I'll be back in a moment. I need to use your loo.'

As Maxine left the room, LaVonda wandered back into the living room and slumped down on the couch. She gazed aimlessly around the room as she tried to concentrate on what to do next. The police weren't coming for her tonight. There was still a window of opportunity. But what could she do?

Her gaze landed on Maxine's open bag lying next to the couch and fixed on the hospital pass lying on top. LaVonda's thoughts started ticking. It was risky, but she was probably going to get caught anyway. Why not at least try to finish the job?

Maxine came back into the room, sniffing at the sleeve of her uniform.

'I smell like shit. Like actual shit. I was helping an old guy off the commode earlier, and his stinky hands clutched at me, and now I smell like faeces. Do I? Here, smell.' She thrust her arm towards LaVonda, who screwed up her nose.

'I'm not sniffing your top, you lunatic. Listen, why don't you go home and shower? This just isn't a good time; I really do need to do something.'

'Alright, calm your farm, I'm going. I thought I might get a little more sympathy, but clearly that isn't on the cards tonight.' She picked her glass up and drained it.

'I am sorry about Ines, and I love you, and you're always welcome. It's just... I've got some urgent stuff to do.' LaVonda picked up Maxine's bag and handed it to her.

'Are you going to tell me what is going on?'

'Not right now, but I'll call you tomorrow. Okay? Good night.'

LaVonda hustled her sister out of the house. She would have to think of some excuse for her strange behaviour and then call Maxine in the morning and explain. Unless, of course, she had been arrested by then, in which case her one permitted call would be to Ann.

LaVonda pushed open the hospital room door and glanced quickly at the face of the man lying on the bed with the curtain half pulled around him. It was Frank. Her breath caught in her throat.

Frank's head was bandaged, and a clear tube poked out of his nose. The other end connected to an oxygen pump. An IV bag hung above his head, dripping fluid into another tube. That tube snaked under the blankets, which were drawn up to his chin. A loop of clear plastic hung below the side bars of the bed.

From her own hospital stay, LaVonda knew someone would be in every fifteen minutes to check his temperature and blood pressure. She didn't have much time.

Hospital visiting hours were still underway when she arrived, and a quick call beforehand, pretending to be Frank's sister, had given her his room number. Dressed in her fleecy jacket, and with a slightly anxious look on her face, LaVonda blended in with all the other visitors to the ward. No one looking at her would suspect she carried a pair of scissors in her pocket.

Her anxiety had increased when she entered his room. What if he woke up and saw her? Well, there was no time to worry about what could go wrong. She had to move quickly. She had to cut his IV line so an air bubble would float through the tube, into his bloodstream, reach his heart, and kill him. Painlessly (probably) and quickly.

As LaVonda reached into her pocket, she realised to her dismay there was someone in the far bed. The curtain blocked the other bed, so she couldn't see him, but she could hear a man clearing his throat, and it reminded her instantly of Dave. She frowned in momentary irritation.

*Focus. Do what you need to do, then get out.*

She reached for the loop of tubing at the side of Frank's bed and took out her scissors. Quickly, she snipped the tube in half. Pale yellow liquid dribbled from the ends and the smell of urine filled her nostrils. She sucked in her breath. *Bugger.*

'Nurse? Could you pass me the bedpan please? I need to move my bowels.' A thin, reedy voice came from the other side of the curtain. *Bugger. Bugger.*

'Um. Just a minute,' she called back nervously, lifting up the side of Frank's blanket. Urine was pooling under the bed. She spread her feet apart so she wouldn't stand in it and pushed the blanket up further. The sheet was tucked in around him, so she pulled it free, finally exposing the cannula needle fixed in place on his arm.

She snipped the tube near the base of the needle, tucked the scissors back into her pocket, and stepped back, letting the blankets fall back into place. It was done. Air was now running through the tube and would reach his heart in a matter of minutes.

'Nurse?'

LaVonda glanced desperately at the curtain, where she could just make out the shadow of the patient pulling himself up in the bed. Her voice came out high and squeaky.

'Yes, um, hang on. I'll be back shortly.'

She hurried from the room, the plaintive voice of the unseen patient following her.

'Please? I need the bedpan right now.'

# ELEVEN

LaVonda leaned forward and gazed at her reflection in the bathroom mirror. Her eyes sparkled and her cheeks were rosy, but a glowing pink flush, rather than her usual hot, red stain. She felt alive, powerful, and fierce. That was the word; fierce. She was formidable, pulsing with female power and determination.

Frank was dead. She'd killed him. She'd struck a mighty blow for her gender. Cast retribution on behalf of the millions of women who had fallen victim to male violence. This was her role. This was her destiny.

She saw herself clad in fitted black latex, twisting and turning her body through security laser beams like Catherine Zeta-Jones, a stealthy assassin, her ruthlessness notorious throughout the country. A black business card embossed with silver calligraphy, flicked carelessly on the bodies of each of her victims: *Killed by LaVonda.*

Although... well yes, that would almost definitely give her away.

*Killed by the Black Widow.*

Hmmm.

*Killed by the Revenge Queen.*

Alright. She'd have to work on her moniker.

Meanwhile, she had never felt more vital, more in control. More powerful. She was driven by bloodlust, and LaVonda absolutely adored this version of herself.

What the hell had she done? LaVonda sat up in bed. On the far wall, her dresser mirror reflected the moonlight gleaming through the gap of her curtains. It looked like a huge, bright, accusing eye glaring straight at her.

She'd killed someone. Two *someone's*. Deliberately taken their lives as though they had no right to live, to exist. Who on earth was she to decide who lived or died?

This was terrible. She'd done a terrible thing. LaVonda felt slightly dizzy with regret. She swallowed, but the stubborn lump of shame in her throat wouldn't budge. For the rest of her life, she'd have to live with the knowledge that she'd deliberately taken someone else's life. Twice.

*They did deserve it though. Well, Frank at least.*

No, that was simply nonsense. The justice system existed for a reason. What sort of world would it be if people went around killing other people just because they felt like it?

*People like Frank do that.*

Yes, but did she want to be like Frank?

*Of course not.*

Well then, was she happy she'd killed Frank? Was she relieved that Royce was gone?

*Yes. Yes, I am.*


The resignation letter was neatly folded into an envelope and tucked inside LaVonda's handbag. She kept patting it nervously. Today was the day. It *should* have been her first official day in her new role, but only LaVonda knew it was the last time she would ever set foot in the building. She had a 9am meeting with the Managing Director, where he would formally welcome her to his executive team. Instead, LaVonda would hand him her formal resignation, and then she would go straight to the police station and turn herself in for both murders.

Technically, since she was about to be arrested, she didn't *need* to resign. Being sacked was probably on the cards anyway, but this course of action gave LaVonda a feeling of control. She appreciated the formality of it. Resigning, like confessing, was the *appropriate* thing to do.

She still hadn't told Emmett what was going on, but she'd sent Ann a text message telling her to meet her at the police station at 10am. Ann had immediately sent a message back asking why, but LaVonda didn't respond. Ann would find out soon enough. She would tell Emmett later today, once she had been released on bail and was back at home.

Surely, she would be released on bail. She wasn't a flight risk, and she wasn't a threat to society. Ann would make sure LaVonda didn't have to stay in jail until her trial. Then she'd hire the best criminal lawyer money could buy. That might be Ann, but it could possibly be someone else. Hopefully, Ann wouldn't be too offended.

LaVonda shivered in nervous anticipation as the lift stopped on the third floor and the doors opened. She stepped out and nearly collided with Sylvia. The other woman reached towards her, grabbing her arm, her long nails digging into LaVonda's skin.

'Oh, LaVonda. Guess what? They've caught him. They caught the guy who killed Royce.'

What? What was Sylvia talking about? What guy?

'I knew it had to be him; it was obvious. I was saying to my Ralph, just the other day, that I wouldn't be at all surprised if young Angela's ex was involved, and it turns out I was 100 percent right. I mean to say, I should be working on the police force because I have a real instinct for these things.'

Saliva filled LaVonda's mouth, and her heart thudded hard. She'd left it too late. The police had arrested the wrong person.

'How do you know, Syl? Who told you?'

'Angela herself. She rang this morning and said she wasn't coming in because her ex-husband had been arrested for Royce's murder, and she needed to stay at home. Her poor little boy isn't taking this at all well, and Angela is beside herself, as you can imagine.'

Oh hell. Angela's ex-husband? She had to clear this up. Right now. She reached into her bag and pulled out her phone. She tapped in the number for directory assistance and asked to be connected to the local police station.

Sylvia was looking at her, a confused expression on her face.

'I don't think they're going to tell you anything more than I've told you.'

LaVonda ignored her. 'Hello? Could I speak to the person in charge of the Royce Butler murder case, please?'

Sylvia harrumphed. 'I mean to say, if you want to try and get more information, that is up to you, of course, but you won't find out anything I don't already know. Angela gave me all the details, poor girl, she obviously needed to talk to a friend, and as I've often said; I'm always available if I'm needed.'

'Yes, I'll hold.' LaVonda gripped the phone and tried to control her breathing. In and out. If only Sylvia would shut up, so she could concentrate.

'Apparently, he, the ex-husband, I mean, was more upset about hurting the dog than anything. He'd tried to avoid it and just hit Royce, but the poodle got under the front wheel. I mean, the animal is fine, a broken leg I think, but according to Angela, her ex was quite distraught. I mean to say, don't get me wrong, I like animals as much as the next person, but you can't compare a dog's life to a human life.'

What was she talking about? What dog?

'This is Detective McInnis.'

'Sylvia, what dog?'

'Royce's dog. The poodle. He was walking it when Angela's mad ex-husband drove over him.'

'Hello? This is Detective McInnis. Can I help you?'

'Sorry. Wrong number.' LaVonda hung up and stared at Sylvia. 'Royce was walking his dog?'

'Yes, you know this, LaVonda, we all know the details. Oh... I suppose... actually, you were away then, weren't you? So you probably don't know. Royce was taking his dog out for a late-night walk, which he does every night, and Angela's ex was waiting for him in his car. He's supposed to have a terrible temper, but this is the first time he's ever killed someone. He broke down and confessed to her on Saturday night, because he was worried about the little dog, and she convinced him to turn himself in. I mean to say, fancy being worried about a dog?'

'Angela's ex killed Royce. You're sure.' She felt a stab of... disappointment? Surely not.

Sylvia looked taken aback. 'I'm absolutely sure. Are you alright? You look pale. Would you like me to get you a cup of tea?'

'No. I'm fine. Thank you.'

'Alright, well, you have your meeting with the Managing Director in a few minutes, so do you want me to put your handbag in your office? Then you can go straight up.'

The MD. Oh hell. She couldn't meet the MD right now; she needed time to think.

'Actually, Syl, I've just remembered something urgent I have to do. Could you cancel the meeting, please? Give the MD my sincere apologies, but I have to leave.'

'Of course. What is it? I mean to say, you don't have to tell me, but that's what I'm here for; to listen to everyone's problems. Just let me know how I can help.'

LaVonda sat in her rental car in the basement car park, thinking furiously. She hadn't killed Royce. She hadn't struck him at all. Angela's crazy ex was the culprit. That's why she had no memory of hitting him. Because she hadn't. She *wasn't* a murderer, after all.

*Oh. Right.*

Well, she might not have killed her colleague, and that was a very *good* thing, LaVonda reminded herself, but she had still ended the life of a terrible, awful man. She had some guilt, yes, of course she did, but that was well and truly overshadowed by the glow of satisfaction at having taken revenge on behalf of poor Philippa.

*And yourself*, a little voice inside reminded her. Well, yes, but she wouldn't have killed Frank simply for his actions in the bar. No. She had done what she'd done on behalf of an innocent victim, and LaVonda would *not* apologise. In fact, she wouldn't confess, wouldn't turn herself in, and she certainly wouldn't spend another moment regretting her actions. She *hadn't* killed Royce, thank goodness, but she *had* killed a man who deserved it, and that was that.

Her phone beeped as a new message came in, and she looked down at her lap. Dave. He was the last person she wanted to think about right now. She hadn't bothered to return his Friday call, because she had far too much on her plate right now to worry about *Dave*.

His message was short and to the point. *'The bank is sending a valuation agent to the house next Friday evening. 7pm. I'll see you then.'*

LaVonda read the message twice, her mouth dropping open in disbelief. How dare he? They were not going to get a valuation done, because she was not going to sell the house to him. Did he think he could just bully her into submission? Because if he did, Dave Robinette had one hell of a nerve.

Royce and Frank were forgotten, as she focussed on this new outrage. Fine, let him turn up on Friday. She'd get the locks changed. See how he liked that!

Better still, let him waste his time, go ahead and get the valuation, and then tell him to jam his offer up his bum. He couldn't *force* her to move out of the house. He would just have to find somewhere else to settle his new family.

She hated thinking of Dave having more children. LaVonda had desperately wanted another baby when Em was still little, and they'd tried, but after Mark's death, and her subsequent traumatic miscarriage, she'd been unable to carry another pregnancy.

Now Dave was going to get what he'd always wanted. He was casting his old wife aside to make room for a much younger, fertile woman who would provide him with the offspring LaVonda hadn't been able to give him. Granted, he'd been a good father to Emmett, but LaVonda knew he'd always longed for his own child. Maybe that was part of the reason for him finding such a young girlfriend. They'd probably have more than one child, too. Maybe several.

Brian would be pleased. Dave's father had wanted his only son to produce an heir, and now that looked likely to happen. The miserable old bastard would probably remove Emmett, who wasn't even a real Robinette, from his will, and insert his true-blooded successors.

Sodding Dave. This was all his fault. She could *kill* him.

Actually... she could kill him. She was still technically a murderer, even though she had one less death on her hands than this time yesterday. How would she do it? Something non-violent, but still painful. Maybe she could arrange for him to take an accidental overdose? Although Dave hesitated before taking an aspirin. She'd never be able to get him to swallow one sleeping tablet, let alone the twenty or thirty it probably took to kill someone.

Could she electrocute him? Drop a hairdryer into his bath? There was the added satisfactory bonus of watching him realise he was about to die at her hands, but her opportunity of being there when Dave took a bath had diminished significantly since he'd moved out of their house.

Her phone rang and startled her out of her pleasant daydreams. It was her sister.

'LaVonda, what on earth is going on? I'm at the police station. Where are you? What is this about?'

Oh heavens. LaVonda looked at the clock on her dashboard. She'd been sitting here for more than an hour.

'LaVonda? Are you still there? What are you *doing*?'

*I'm sitting in my rental car, fantasising about murdering my husband. Ex-husband.*

'Ann, I'm sorry. I don't, I mean I didn't... Look, I thought I needed to do something, but now I don't think I do. Sorry. I didn't mean to waste your time.'

'Seriously, Von, what is going on? You've been acting weird since your accident. Maxie told me you practically threw her out of your house on Friday night. We haven't heard from you all weekend. Then you send me on a wild goose chase down to the police station this morning, and you don't turn up. Is something wrong? Are you in trouble?'

'No, nothing like that. It's the change, I think. My... *(ugh)* menopause. It's making me a little crazy.' Did she sound convincing? She couldn't tell.

'You should see your doctor, get some hormone treatment. And maybe you should get another head scan. Check you don't actually have a concussion after all.'

'I'm fine, but I will go and see someone. I promise. Sorry, Ann.'

LaVonda sat in Deborah's old office, now her new office, with the door firmly shut. She stared at the scribbled figures on the notepad in front of her. Even with the pay rise from her new acting role, she wouldn't be able to afford a new mortgage on the house to pay Dave his half of the value. Her only option was to convince her sisters to try to fix up Maude's house and put it on the market. If they could sell it, then she could give Dave his fair share.

Of course, this all depended on Dave agreeing to sell her his half of the house. But as far as LaVonda could see, he didn't have much choice. She would *never* agree to move out and allow Dave and his girlfriend to move in. Never.

LaVonda looked through the internal office window to where her staff were busily working. Or at least pretending to work. LaVonda rubbed her hand across the back of her neck. Her team probably thought she was working hard on important General Manager tasks. The truth was, she'd been doing frantic, personal, financial calculations and fantasising about murdering Dave.

Could she hire a hitman? No. She didn't have the money, and she had no idea how to contact those kinds of people. Besides, if she was going to do it, she'd do it herself. A tiny thrill shivered through her as she remembered the high she'd felt after dispatching Frank. That powerful feeling of control, and pride in herself, was intoxicating. How ironic that she'd never felt more alive than when she had killed someone.

*Oh, stop it.* She wasn't actually going to murder Dave. It was just fun to think about it, that was all.

LaVonda sighed and reluctantly turned back to her figures. Maude's house was the only option.

She made an appointment to see Maude's attorney the following day. Her mother's little house probably wasn't worth much, as it was in a less-than-desirable suburb, and the property itself hadn't been maintained, but hopefully the land would be worth something. Maybe on Friday she could see if the valuation expert would come out and have a look.

Actually, why wait for him? What was stopping her putting it on the market right now? Ann and Maxine wouldn't care; they'd be happy to leave all the arrangements up to her, just as they had for Maude's funeral. They'd both agreed to turn up, but that was the extent of their involvement.

LaVonda brought up a search for local real estate agents and clicked through until she found one with excellent reviews. His profile showed a man in his early forties with blond, thinning hair and a thick, pale moustache. His name brought a smile to her lips. *Johnny Danger.*

She rang his office and made an appointment for 6pm. Even though she had no desire to set foot in the house again, she might as well get this over and done.

Johnny Danger looked exactly like his profile picture. Slightly heavyset, with a broad smiling face, he wore a powder-blue suit and a lurid, floral tie. He shook her hand vigorously. LaVonda felt her own smile drop. He was a bit much, wasn't he?

'So, this is the place?' He rubbed his hands together and beamed at the property.

*No, I thought we'd just hang outside this random house*, thought LaVonda sourly. She'd made a mistake. This man wasn't suitable at all.

'Lead on, MacDuff!' His tone was hearty and nerve-gratingly annoying. LaVonda hesitated. She could feel a headache coming on. Not only did she absolutely not want to go back into the house, but she did also not want to go in there followed by this fool.

'Actually... I've changed my mind.' To her horror, LaVonda realised she was suddenly close to tears. What was *wrong* with her?

Johnny looked at her for a few seconds, then walked over to his red Porsche. He opened his car door and removed a packet of tissues from the glovebox. Then he came over and handed them silently to LaVonda, who took them gratefully and blew her nose.

'I'm sorry. I don't know what came over me.'

Johnny's entire demeanour had changed, and when he spoke this time, his voice was soft.

'It's fine, normal even, to feel emotional about your home.'

'No, it's not that. It was my mother's house. She died recently.'

'I'm so sorry to hear that. I lost my mother a few years ago, so I know how utterly devastated you must be feeling.'

LaVonda looked up at him. He smiled. A gentle smile, not the beaming grin he'd worn a few minutes ago. Her heart fluttered. What kind eyes he had.

'I'm not devastated by her death. Not at all. She was an alcoholic, and she never made any attempt to get help or try and kick the habit. She was a nasty woman and I'm...'

Good grief. She'd been about to admit to this stranger that she was *glad* her own mother was dead. Clearly her personal filter was severely defective these days.

'...I'm just having a bad week. That's all,' she finished lamely. Johnny smiled and turned to look at the house.

'Well, listen, if you've changed your mind, it's not a problem. But since we're here, why don't I have a quick look around so I can give you an idea of what it might be worth? I can go in by myself if you prefer.'

LaVonda felt absurdly grateful for his sympathy. She nodded and handed him the keys. Then she leaned against her rental car, using his tissues to wipe her eyes. God, she must look a mess. She stooped down to look at her reflection in the side mirror. Mascara had collected under her eyes, and her nose was pink and shiny. Perhaps she had time to reapply some makeup before he came back out?

Oh, what nonsense. She didn't care what Johnny Danger thought of her. He was there to do a job for her, not pass judgement on her looks. All the same, LaVonda licked her finger and tried to wipe away the smudges so she looked a little less distressed.

She let her gaze roam up and down the street. Some tired old weatherboard houses remained, but there were a number of recent developments showing the neighbourhood held promise. LaVonda felt her spirits lift a little. Perhaps they would make a decent sale, and she'd have enough money to pay out Dave. She might even have some left over. Then, with the insurance money from her accident, she might be able to buy herself a fancier car. A Porsche, maybe, like Johnny's. Or a Mercedes. Doreen Worthington had a Mercedes.

Johnny Danger came out of the house, carefully locking the front door behind him. He walked over to LaVonda and held out her keys.

'It's a good-sized block, and the neighbourhood is up-and-coming.' His voice was normal, no sign of the earlier bluster, and LaVonda was grateful. 'The house itself needs a good clean out; I know a few companies that will do the job if you don't want to do it yourself. The fixtures are worn, and the kitchen and bathroom are dated. You can try and sort that out, but I'd recommend putting it on the market as a tear-down-and-rebuild. There are plenty of developers who'd love to get their hands on the block.'

Tear the house down? LaVonda blinked and prodded her feelings. Was it upsetting to imagine the house gone, a brand-new townhouse in its place? No. She didn't care at all. That part of her life was gone. Her father was long dead; he wouldn't be coming back to this place. Let them raze it to the ground.

'I think that sounds great. I'll need to check with my sisters, but I don't think they will care. Let's do it.' She held out her hand. Johnny shook it, this time far less vigorously. He smiled.

'I should reintroduce myself. John, John Dangerfield. The Johnny Danger flamboyancy works for a lot of people, but I think you need to meet the real man behind all this.' He gestured to his suit and tie. LaVonda laughed.

'It's nice to meet you, John. I look forward to working with you.' She did too.

John Dangerfield. It was a much nicer name than Johnny Danger. He seemed like a very nice man too. Nice eyes. LaVonda smiled as she drove home, clicking through the radio stations to find an upbeat song to match her mood. She wound down her window and let the breeze ruffle her hair, as she sang along loudly to the Spice Girls. She kept singing even as she stopped at red lights, feeling slightly embarrassed in front of the other drivers, but steadfastly ignoring them. LaVonda felt a rare sense of positivity, and she was going to enjoy it while it lasted.

Her good mood lasted another ten minutes. As she swung into her own driveway, her grin faded, and a horrible new thought occurred to her. What if her mother had written the three of them out of her will? She wouldn't put it past Maude to have left her estate to an animal refuge or a political party. Maude didn't like animals or politicians, but she would have enjoyed the idea of her daughters' disappointment. Still hurting them even after her death.

*You were expecting to get everything, and instead you get nothing!* She could almost hear Maude cackling.

LaVonda switched the engine off and pulled on the handbrake. In her rear vision mirror, she could see Doreen's house across the road and one of her blinds moving slightly. She got out of the car and hurried into the house before her neighbour could come out.

After dropping her handbag on the bench, LaVonda plonked herself down on a stool and looked around her kitchen. It was a little on the boring side; there was a distinct lack of colour, but it was functional, open, and airy. And spotlessly clean. Perfect.

LaVonda liked her kitchen; she liked her home, and she didn't want to move out. If Maude had cut them all out of her will, LaVonda would find another way to stay here. There had to be something else she could do. She would not let Dave force her out.

Well, there wasn't any point in worrying about it tonight. She'd wait until tomorrow, when she saw the solicitor, and found out one way or another, and then she'd work out what she needed to do.

'Yes, you and your sisters are definitely the beneficiaries.'

LaVonda released her breath in a rush. Thank god. She was going to be alright after all.

'But I'm afraid the probate and settlement of the estate will still take a while. You're probably looking at six months to a year.' The solicitor removed his glasses and began polishing them in a *lawyerish* way. He peered at her over his desk, a smirk wreathing his face.

LaVonda was surprised. 'But if we're the beneficiaries, then the house is ours, isn't it?'

She *knew* she should have asked Ann to come along. This man was definitely going to amuse himself by testing her lack of legal knowledge. Look at him sitting complacently behind his big desk like a fat, predatory toad, his manner close to contemptuous.

'It's likely, yes, but these things take time, and can be contested you know. You'd be surprised at the number of times we've had far-flung relatives crawl out of the woodwork, making claims against the estate.'

'There are no other relatives.' Maude had been an only child, and George's brother had died of a stroke ten years ago. There were no cousins, aunts, or secret siblings. LaVonda just wanted to wrap this whole thing up and get on with selling the house. 'No one will contest the will. How soon could we get the deed?'

The solicitor grimaced and replaced his glasses on his nose. LaVonda could see how this man would have appealed to her mother. He was a character straight out of a Dickens's novel; the dour, unfriendly lawyer who enjoyed making life difficult for his client's poor families. LaVonda would bet he was *hoping* to have someone come forward and contest Maude's will.

'As I said, six months to a year. Possibly longer.' Almost definitely longer, now she'd irritated him. 'You'll have to fill out these forms, and we can get the process underway.'

LaVonda pursed her lips and stood up to leave. She reached out her hand for the forms. How annoying. She wouldn't be able to sell her mother's house for another year, so she wouldn't have the funds to buy Dave out. Maybe she could persuade the bank to lend her the money based on her eventual inheritance?

In the meantime, she had to talk to Dave. He was not going to force her out of her own home. He needed to know that she wouldn't budge on this.

Once she was out of the building, she took out her phone and dialled his number. He answered straight away, as though he'd been waiting for her call. LaVonda was taken aback, but she recovered quickly and launched right in.

'Dave, I'm not selling you the house. You'll have to find somewhere else to raise your new family because I'm not leaving. Ever. Once we know the market value of the house, I'll give you your half, and you can be on your merry way.'

LaVonda was proud of her tone; slightly flippant but decisive. It left no room for argument.

Dave was silent. LaVonda frowned.

'Did you hear me? There is no need for you to come around on Friday. I'll pass on the valuer's report once I have it.'

'How are you going to afford to pay me out?' His voice was cool and restrained. Very un-Dave-like. LaVonda felt the tiniest prickle of fear.

'Not that it is any of your business, Dave, but I am expecting a sizeable inheritance from the sale of my mother's house, so the bank will happily lend me what I need.'

'LaVonda, half your inheritance is legally mine.'

What? What was the silly man talking about? Of course, it wasn't his.

'Don't be ridiculous. You're not a beneficiary. You weren't even mentioned in the will.'

'As your husband, I'm legally entitled to half your assets, including your share of the inheritance. I won't fight you for it, if you sell me our house.'

Did he say fight? LaVonda's mouth went dry. She swallowed hard before she replied.

'How could you possibly fight me for it? We're separated, Dave, and you left me before my mother died, so legally, you aren't entitled to anything I earn or inherit after we split.'

That was right, wasn't it? It sounded right. She'd have to ask Ann.

'Legally, we're still married, LaVonda. Trust me when I say that I can make things very difficult for you. I'm coming on Friday, and we can discuss it then. Goodbye.'

LaVonda's eyes widened. Good heavens. Dave sounded like a lunatic. Had he just *threatened* her? She stared down at the blank screen of her phone. He had. He'd threatened her and then hung up on her. How *dare* he?

He wouldn't dream of behaving like that if he knew what she'd done. Oh no. If he knew what she was capable of, he'd back right off. Her mind whirled as she considered, and then discarded, thoughts on how to deal with this new challenge. Suddenly, everything clicked into place.

*You want a fight, Dave? Okay, you've got a fight. But no one said anything about fighting fair.*

She'd have to be clever, though. Dave wasn't the sharpest knife in the block, but the man had lived with her for more than two decades. He'd never believe LaVonda had suddenly had a change of heart. No, she had to be far more subtle. She had to make him believe he'd won, then strike when he was least expecting it.

He'd given her no choice. She didn't want to do this, but she wasn't going to let him trample over her life. She would put a stop to *all* his plans; his plan to take her house and her inheritance, his plans to usurp her daughter from the family by starting another one, his plans for a long and happy life with his new partner.

Oh, she was going to stop him alright. Stop him dead.

# TWELVE

'Hello, LaVonda? This is John Dangerfield. I have the advertising contract ready for your signature. Would you like me to pop around this evening?'

Oh damn. She'd forgotten about the real estate agent. Between her preparations for tonight and the workload that was piling up on her desk, she hadn't thought to call him and cancel the deal.

'John, I'm so sorry, but it looks like we won't be selling after all.'

'That's okay. If you've decided to go with someone else...'

'No, it's not that. We don't actually own the house yet. I mean, I thought we did; we will eventually, but right now everything is tied up legally.'

John chuckled. He had a nice laugh.

'I understand. Well, I look forward to working with you when the house is yours to sell. Keep in touch, LaVonda, and I hope all goes well.'

'Could I... buy you a coffee sometime?' Why on earth had she said that? She didn't want to have coffee with him. It was true; she did feel a bit guilty about wasting his time, but she didn't need to make up for it by buying the man a coffee.

'Sure. I'm free now if you have time. I could meet you at Brew & Brew?'

'Alright. It will take me about ten minutes to get there.'

What was she doing? She didn't have time to go and have coffee. She had a pile of work to do and a murder to plan. Although, most of the planning was already done. She just had to rely on her powers of persuasion to carry it off. Was that why she'd invited John for coffee; to prove she had the ability to manipulate?

LaVonda grabbed her coat.

'I'll be back in half an hour,' she told Sylvia, who nodded and returned to her online shopping.

She had to do something about that woman. Between gossiping and browsing the internet, Sylvia did precious little work. LaVonda suspected the woman was taking full advantage of LaVonda's constant distraction. The rest of the staff were slacking off too. Colin had taken to calling in sick every Monday and often 'forgot' to submit a leave form. Helen was hardly ever at her desk, and LaVonda suspected she spent most of her time on the second floor where her boyfriend worked. Angela was taking extended leave, although LaVonda didn't blame her. She had to do something about the others though. Deborah had run a tight ship, and LaVonda didn't want anyone to think she wasn't up to the job.

John was waiting for her in the café, sitting at a small table facing the door. He wore a light tan suit this time, teamed with a brown shirt and an orange tie. He looked like an extra from an 80's episode of 'Miami Vice'. A beam of pleasure wreathed itself across his face as she approached.

'Hi, good to see you. What would you like to drink?'

'I'll get it.' She smiled at him.

'No, please. Let me. After all, you're the potential client.'

LaVonda's heart sank slightly. That's why he'd agreed to meet her.

'English Breakfast tea, please. Cold milk.'

'LaVonda, I'm joking. I know you're not a potential client. At least not yet. I'll be back.'

She watched him walk up to the counter to order. He gave his hips a little wiggle as though he knew she was looking at him. LaVonda grinned despite herself.

'So, is your week improving? You told me last week was rough, is this week any better?' John sat back down next to her.

It was far worse. Because tonight she had to kill her ex-husband, though that probably wasn't what John was expecting to hear.

'Hmmm.' She made a non-committal sound. John laughed.

'You don't have to talk about it. I'm happy to just sit and enjoy your company. Whereabouts do you work?'

This was more like it. Safe ground.

She told him all about her recent promotion and the work done by her division. She was probably boring the poor man, but he didn't seem to mind. He was genuinely interested in her, and it was a pleasant feeling to be able to talk about herself and have someone pay close attention. Dave had always tuned out whenever she started telling him about her work.

John was a much nicer man than Dave. Not bad looking either, apart from the floppy hair and his awful moustache, of course. The clothes didn't help either.

Their drinks arrived, and John grinned at the waitress.

'Why, thank you, Ma'am!' He tipped an imaginary hat. His fake American accent was atrocious. LaVonda cringed.

He waited until the waitress had left, then smiled at her across the table.

'I know what you're thinking. Why do I dress like this? And put on the mannerisms? And call myself this ridiculous name?'

'No, I wasn't...'

'Because in this industry, LaVonda, you've got to have a USP. A unique selling point. People hire Johnny Danger because he is a caricature of a bad salesman, and people find it hilarious. They like the absurdity of it all. They want to tell their friends they hired *Johnny Danger* to sell their house. It gets a laugh every time.'

Well, that did make sense. She'd laughed when she'd first seen his name too.

'When I do get the deed to my mother's house, I will hire you. I promise.'

He reached across and tapped her lightly on the back of the hand.

'LaVonda, I'm not here because I want to do business. I like you. I'm hoping you might want to have dinner with me tonight?'

LaVonda blushed. Good heavens. She was a mature woman, not a teenager. Why was she feeling all coy and silly?

She shook her head. 'I can't. Not tonight.'

He looked disappointed.

'But I'm free tomorrow.' Assuming she hadn't been arrested for Dave's murder.

She wouldn't be arrested. She wouldn't. No one would ever connect her to Dave's death. She knew the man; she knew his Friday morning routine. She had a foolproof plan. Everything was in place. She smiled across the table at John.

'I'd have loved to have dinner with you tonight, John, but I'm afraid I've already made other plans.'

'Would you kill me? If I'd done something to annoy you, seriously annoy you, would you have tried to kill me?'

Mark's voice was so clear in her mind, it was almost as though he were standing right there in her bedroom. She picked up the pale pink t-shirt lying on her bed.

'Of course not. I loved you, Mark.' Good grief. Had she just spoken out loud to her dead husband? She pushed her arms into the t-shirt and pulled it over her head.

'So, you don't love Dave? Never loved him?'

It was completely different. For a start, Mark would never have left her for another woman, and he certainly wouldn't have tried to boot her out of her own home, let alone threaten to take half her inheritance.

'This is wrong, babe, and you know it. This isn't you.'

LaVonda frowned. She did not need this prickling of conscience right now. She needed to remain focussed. Lethal. Right the wrongs again and come out on top. Ah, there it was. The surge of adrenaline she'd been waiting for.

*Mark, you don't understand. Now please go away and let me finish getting dressed.*

There was a knock on the door. Dave was early. Damn. She was hoping to have a glass of wine before he arrived to help steady her nerves. She picked up a bottle of perfume, gave herself a quick spritz, and then ran lightly down the hallway to open the door.

Her ex-husband stood outside, his arms folded across his chest, a scowl on his face. She was going to have her work cut out for her tonight.

'Hi, come on in. It's good to see you.'

Dave frowned and raised his eyebrows as he walked into the house.

*Careful, LaVonda, don't lay it on too thick.* She tried again.

'Well, it's not *great* to see you, and I wish we weren't doing this. But I've given it a lot of thought over the past few days, and I'm prepared to at least discuss some options.'

Dave's forehead cleared slightly.

LaVonda walked into the kitchen, calling back over her shoulder. 'Would you like a drink?'

'No, thanks.'

'Oh, come on. The bank guy isn't due for another ten minutes. We might as well relax while we wait.'

She poured him a glass of vodka, added two ice cubes and tonic water, then brought it back into the living room. She handed Dave his drink, and to her relief, he took a sip. He cleared his throat.

'LaVonda, I...'

'Let's not get into everything now. Let's wait until we have an idea of what the house is worth, then we can discuss what we're going to do.' She took a seat on the couch, angling her body towards his in a friendly manner. 'I spoke to Emmett yesterday. The pregnancy is going well. She is convinced she's having a boy, but I'm hoping for a little girl. What do you think?'

Dave's face relaxed a little, and he sat down on one of the armchairs. He took another sip. 'As long as it is healthy, I don't mind.'

LaVonda felt a stab of irritation. Well, *of course,* as long as it was healthy. That went without saying. God, the man was annoying.

'I wonder what they'll name the baby. Hopefully not anything too bizarre, although if Jasper has a say in it, who knows what kind of name our grandchild will get.' She felt a little pang at the word grandchild. They were going to be grandparents together. She shook her head. There was no room for sentimentality. She had to be ruthless.

Dave nodded and sipped his drink. He looked around the room, avoiding her eyes. Well, this was awkward. How had they stayed married for so long? They had absolutely nothing to talk to each other about. LaVonda thought about asking after Jemima, then changed her mind. She had no interest in discussing Dave's girlfriend. If only the bank man would hurry up and arrive so she could put her plan into motion.

'New cushions?'

'Yes. They brighten the place up, don't they? I love the colours.'

'Silence.

'How's work, Dave?'

'Fine. How is yours?'

'Good. I've had a promotion. I'm Acting General Manager while Deborah is away.'

'Congratulations.'

'Thank you.'

More silence. Dave took another sip of his drink. LaVonda glanced at her watch.

'New throw rug?'

'Yes.'

'Nice. Very... um, bright.'

Oh, this was excruciating. Where was the bank man? LaVonda exhaled in relief when a knock on the door signalled his arrival. He came in and introduced himself, and immediately went to work, measuring and making notes on his iPad.

Ten minutes later, he walked back into the living room. LaVonda and Dave had given up trying to make small talk, and they were sitting in silence.

'What's the verdict?' Dave asked.

'I'll write up my report in the next few days. You should have the final valuation report mid next week. Goodnight.'

'No, wait! Can't you just tell us now?' LaVonda glanced at Dave, who was sitting on the edge of his chair.

'Not with any degree of accuracy. I need to research the suburb, median house prices in the past year; a whole host of factors.'

'Can you give us a rough estimate? Please?' Dave sounded as desperate as LaVonda felt. They had to know now. This had to get this resolved tonight.

The valuation expert sighed. 'I can give you a rough estimate, but it is not much more than you'd get from a real estate agent. My final report will be much more accurate, and if you're thinking of refinancing, that is the figure the bank will take into consideration.'

'We understand. An estimate is fine.'

He sighed again and turned his iPad around to show them his calculations so far. LaVonda's gaze went straight to the number at the bottom of the screen. It was higher than she'd expected. Good. That would make it easier to pretend to negotiate.

Once the expert had left, LaVonda fetched the vodka and topped up Dave's glass. She poured herself a glass of red wine and took a mouthful to fortify herself. This was it. She had to give the performance of a lifetime. She was ready.

'It's worth more than I expected.'

Dave nodded. 'Yes. Quite a bit more.'

'I still want to stay here.'

'I know you do, LaVonda. But look, the house is too large for one person, and it makes no sense to have a big mortgage on your own.'

'I wouldn't be on my own if you hadn't left.' *Good, very good. Get a little guilt going.*

Dave looked down at his feet. 'I'm sorry I hurt you. I truly am sorry. But I'm doing this for both of us, in a way. We deserve the chance to be happy, don't we? And we haven't been happy for a long time.'

'Speak for yourself, Dave. I was fine. I was perfectly content in our marriage. Please don't pretend I ever factored into your decision. Because if I had, you wouldn't have dumped me on my birthday.'

Dave looked pained. 'That was a terrible thing to do, I know.'

'Yes, it was. I was devastated. I cried for a week.' *Way too much, LaVonda; pull back.* 'Well, I was very unhappy at any rate. The only thing I have left is our home. I live here, surrounded by old memories.'

Dave seized on that, just as she'd known he would. 'Wouldn't you rather live somewhere without the memories of us? Wouldn't it be better for you to make a fresh start somewhere else?'

He was so predictable. LaVonda sighed theatrically. 'I guess it would be nice to have my own place, to decorate the way I want.'

'And you could find something fresh and modern. If you stay here, the kitchen will need doing in a few more years, and probably the carpets replaced too. It's a lot of work for one person to tackle.'

'True. Oh, I don't know, Dave. I love this house, and I loved my old life. I don't want things to change and I don't want to move somewhere new.'

His voice was soft, cajoling. 'I understand, I honestly do. But imagine a fresh start. A lovely place of your own, a peaceful garden, a sanctuary of sorts. Somewhere Emmett and the baby could come and visit you.'

She pretended to mull it over. 'Maybe you're right. Maybe I should think about getting my own place. After all, if the house is worth that much, I could afford to get somewhere nice.'

'Yes, and look, I'd be happy to pay a bit more than half to help you out.' He was trying so hard not to look too eager; she almost felt sorry for him.

'How very nice of you, Dave, but I only want what's fair. I won't pay you more than half if I do decide to stay after all. I'm just not sure... I need a minute. This wine has gone straight to my head. I'm going to get something to eat. Would you like something?'

Dave shook his head. 'I'd better go. I told Jemima I'd be back by eight.'

'Okay. I thought you might want to stay for a bit longer and discuss this. I was starting to come around to the idea of maybe agreeing, but if you need to go, then go. I'll make my decision on my own.'

She could almost see the cogs ticking in his brain. He wanted to leave, but he also sensed she might be caving, and with a little extra pressure he might be able to persuade her... He cleared his throat.

'I can stay for a little while longer.'

'Okay. I'm just having soup for dinner, but you're welcome to join me.'

'No thanks.'

LaVonda left him in the living room while she went to heat up the soup she'd made yesterday. She stirred the big pot until it was hot, then dished herself out a small bowl. She put a thick slice of sourdough and butter on a tray alongside the bowl and carried it back out into the living room. Dave sniffed the air as she set the tray down on the coffee table.

'Is that your mushroom and chestnut soup?'

'Yes.' LaVonda knelt down by the table and busied herself, breaking off a piece of bread and buttering it. She took a bite and then dipped her spoon into the soup.

'Actually, I might have a bit, if you have some spare.'

LaVonda smiled and got up. It was his favourite, and she'd known he wouldn't be able to resist. In general, Dave thought soups weren't a proper meal, but this particular one was different. Hearty and creamy, it was a man's soup. Not one of those thin little consommés he used to tease her for liking.

If he'd been even the slightest bit switched on, he might have wondered why she was making his favourite soup for her own dinner. But then Dave didn't think, did he? He wouldn't suspect for one minute she had deliberately planned this, and that she had slipped a handful of death cap mushrooms into the dish.

She poured out a large bowl and put a couple of slices of bread on a plate for him. The poisonous mushrooms wouldn't show any symptoms immediately. They would start to take effect in the next few days, rendering Dave first unwell, then mortally ill, then dead.

Of course, the autopsy would show what killed him, but Dave was a creature of habit, and every Friday without fail, he treated himself to a full English breakfast at Café Bueno before work. Eggs, bacon, sausages, grilled tomatoes, and sautéed mushrooms sourced from the local markets. Unless he specifically mentioned eating LaVonda's mushroom soup to Jemima, it was unlikely that anyone would think to look further than his local café for the accidental poisoning of Dave Robinette.

LaVonda sat back down opposite her ex-husband and slowly buttered herself another piece of bread. Hopefully he wouldn't notice she hadn't touched her soup until he had finished his. She watched Dave pick up his spoon. Greedy anticipation lit up his broad face. He scooped out some of the creamy broth and brought it to his mouth, then blew gently on the steaming spoonful before opening his lips.

*Oh god, no.*

LaVonda flung herself across the table, smacking the spoon out of his hand and knocking the bowl of soup all over the coffee table. Dave stared in shock as the second meal she'd recently prepared for him went flying before he'd taken a bite. For a moment there was stunned silence. Then LaVonda spoke.

'I've changed my mind.'

It was true. She simply couldn't kill the man she'd been married to for twenty-five years. Emmett's dad. Yes, he was behaving like a complete tool, and yes, she absolutely hated his plans for the future, but she couldn't bring herself to end his life. They'd been married for decades, and despite herself, LaVonda still cared about him. If he died, Emmett would be inconsolable. LaVonda knew what it was like to lose a beloved parent. She couldn't do that to her daughter. She couldn't do this to Dave.

'I've changed my mind. You need to go now. I'm not selling you the house.'

Dave scrambled to his feet and eyed her warily. 'LaVonda, you need help. You've gone insane.' He picked up his keys and hurried out of the house.

LaVonda groaned. Had she ever actually intended to go through with murdering him? She loved the fantasy of killing Dave, but the raw reality was impossible. Imagine how distraught her daughter would have been, and if she had gone through with it, what then? Was she going to murder Jasper next, simply because she didn't like him? Would she put her daughter through the same suffering she'd endured simply because she, LaVonda, badly wanted those men out of her own life?

Thank god she'd come to her senses in time. It was a momentary spurt of insanity, irrational fury, and revenge, probably brought on by her impending menopause.

Oh, who was she kidding? It wasn't anything of the sort. LaVonda knew exactly why she was so angry lately, and it had nothing to do with her shaky hormones.

She was angry at a world she no longer understood. A world that seemed to have moved on without reserving a place for her. She wasn't young and attractive anymore, and she'd become invisible. Sidelined. Her opinions didn't count, her existence didn't matter. She was irrelevant in a society that only valued relevancy. It was a bitter concept to acknowledge, but it was true.

Why *didn't* she matter anymore? Just because she had a few more wrinkles and, okay yes, *chin hairs*, had she lost her worth as a human being?

LaVonda knew the unfortunate answer to that.

She also knew that her fantasies, where she threatened and even killed people, were about wanting to be powerful and wanting her voice to be heard. She raged against the unfairness of men becoming more powerful and more relevant as they aged, while women lost what little value they'd ever had.

LaVonda stood up and surveyed the grey soup spread across the coffee table, dripping onto the carpet. Another horrible greasy mess to clean up. She definitely needed to think through her decisions before putting them into action.

She took the broken bowl into the kitchen and tipped it into the bin. She looked at the leftover soup in her favourite saucepan. It seemed such a shame to waste it, because it had been a great idea. She just didn't have the fortitude to use it on Dave.

LaVonda shook her head. She was done. No more murdering people who annoyed her. If she was going to kill again, and she probably wasn't, but *if* she did, it would have to be someone who totally deserved it. Someone purely evil.

She poured the soup into a plastic container. She used a sharpie to write '*Scientific experiment—DO NOT EAT*' on the blue lid. She drew little skull and crossbones on for extra effect.

Now it wouldn't be accidentally eaten. If she did need to dispose of anyone else, and again, she probably wouldn't, but *if* she did, she had her method close at hand.

# THIRTEEN

The loud suits and lurid ties were gone, and in their place was a plain, grey polo shirt and dark pants. LaVonda couldn't get over the difference it made to the man sitting on the opposite side of the restaurant table, nor the effect on her own behaviour. When he was dressed as Johnny Danger, there was a power imbalance that worked in her favour; she was the more attractive one, while he was still a bit of a joke.

Perhaps it was partly the fancy restaurant, sparkling chandeliers, and romantic private booths, but tonight John looked handsome, even sexy. Of course, he still had the blond side swept hair (which was a little too Donald Trump for her liking), as well as his silly moustache, but despite that, LaVonda found herself acting a little tongue-tied, a little self-conscious. John Dangerfield was unexpectedly charming, and she was drawn to him.

'Are madam and sir ready to order?' She hadn't noticed the waiter arriving at their table. Across from her, John grinned up at him.

'Maybe a few more minutes?'

'Of course, sir.' With a flourish, the waiter departed, and John directed his smile back across to her.

'Sorry, what were you saying?'

She had no idea. The past few seconds were a blank because she'd just noticed a few dark blond hairs poking out of the neckline of his shirt, and they made her think about other dark blond hairs poking out of other clothing and, good grief, please don't let this be another hot flush.

'Sylvia,' she blurted out to cover her embarrassment, as though he could read her mind. 'I think I was telling you how I have to counsel one of my staff members, Sylvia.'

'Sylvia. Right. So how do you think it will go?'

Oh, why was she telling John about this stuff? It was so *boring*. Surely, he found it boring? He didn't seem to though; he seemed to be interested in everything she said. It was an unusual and heady feeling. LaVonda picked up her serviette and placed it in her lap.

'I don't know, probably not very well. I haven't had to deal with many staffing issues before. It's not my forte. The HR department have offered to assist, but this is something Deborah, my old boss, used to manage expertly. I just don't know if I'm up to the job.'

Where had that come from? She'd never thought that, let alone said it aloud. It was true though. She wasn't sure if she was up to the job. It wasn't just the preoccupation with the recent murders (attempted and otherwise) that had her doubting her abilities. The fact was, she liked her old job, and this one wasn't suiting her.

'I'm sure you are up to the job, but the question is, do you want to be?'

Of course, she did. Didn't she? The extra money was great and definitely needed right now, and she'd worked hard for the opportunity to manage the entire department. Anyway, this was hardly the time to stop and think about work. She was on a nice date, in the company of an attractive man, and she should be having a lovely time, not fretting about her career choices.

'How was your day?' It was an obvious attempt to change the subject and, to his credit, John smiled agreeably.

'Not too bad. I had six open homes, at least three of them will sell in the next few weeks, so it has been productive.'

It sounded exhausting. LaVonda was curious.

'Do you like your job?'

'I do. It isn't for everyone; the hours are long, and a lot of sellers and buyers have totally unrealistic expectations either of the value of their home, or the value of someone else's, but there is something about the thrill of the challenge. Bringing homes on, designing a marketing plan, negotiating back and forth, then finally closing the sale... it can be incredibly rewarding. Plus, the money is great.'

He was obviously good at his job. LaVonda wondered idly what else he was good at. Oh, for heaven's sake. Couldn't she keep her mind out of the gutter for even one minute?

She picked up her menu. The waiter would be back shortly; she *had* to concentrate. But she didn't feel the least bit hungry. She had an unsettling, fizzy sensation low in her stomach that felt vaguely familiar. She looked at John over the menu. He was looking back at her. The sensation intensified sharply.

Flustered by lust, LaVonda put down her menu and reached for her cocktail glass. Her fingers knocked clumsily against the stem, and bright blue liquid splashed onto the tablecloth. LaVonda looked at it in despair. Why had she ordered such a fluorescent drink? She'd wanted to seem sophisticated when John had asked what her favourite cocktail was, but her mind had gone blank, so she'd requested a Blue Lagoon. Blue Lagoons were her choice of cocktail when she and Ann visited Bali several years ago, (Ann loved Fluffy Ducks) and she'd remembered enjoying them back then. But now she wished she'd ordered a simple gin and tonic, or a martini... anything clear. LaVonda couldn't take her eyes off the blue mess seeping and spreading into the perfect white tablecloth.

'Don't worry about it.' John's voice was reassuring and held just a hint of amusement. He shifted in the booth, so he was closer to her. She looked up into his sparkling green eyes. Oh god, there was that lust again.

Would she sleep with him? LaVonda hadn't imagined she'd ever sleep with anyone other than Dave for the rest of her life. She stared down at the stain again.

Two waiters arrived at the table. One quickly picked up their drinks, cutlery, and side plates, while the other deftly whisked away the stained tablecloth and replaced it with a new one. The table was reset, and the whole thing was done so quickly and discreetly, LaVonda was slightly stunned. She needed these men around for those nights when she woke in a pool of sweat. They could whisk off the damp sheets and her nightie and replace them with fresh ones before she'd had time to come to full consciousness.

The thought of being stripped naked brought another flush to her cheeks and a pleasant tug low in her abdomen. John was close enough now for her to smell his aftershave. Fresh and clean; a hint of something masculine. Leather or wool, maybe? Dave always wore a citrus aftershave that reminded her slightly of rotting fruit.

Good grief, why was she thinking about her ex-husband? LaVonda refocussed her attention on her date. She made up her mind. She *would* sleep with John. Not tonight obviously, but once they'd had a few more dates, and if everything was going well... well, why not?

'May I take your order?'

John raised his eyebrows questioningly at LaVonda. She returned her attention to the menu.

'The salmon, please, and could I have a glass of wine too? A sauvignon blanc, please.' That seemed a safer choice than anything colourful.

John ordered the chicken risotto, and the waiter departed silently. John leaned back in the booth.

'Tell me about your family. You've got sisters, haven't you? I've got one older one, but we aren't particularly close. Do you all get on well?' His full lips under his bushy moustache stayed slightly parted after he finished speaking. There was definitely chemistry; invisible but real sparks whizzing between them. LaVonda drew in her breath sharply.

'Yes, we do. They're my best friends. They can be painful at times, of course, but I wouldn't swap them for the world. Ann, she's the older one, she's a lawyer and married with two boys. She's wonderful, and she has a wicked sense of humour. Maxine is my younger sister. She's a bit of a hard case, but she's great. They are both my best friends.'

This was better. Talking about her sisters was helping, and much to LaVonda's relief, the sexual tension between them started to dissipate. There was plenty of time for that later. Right now, they just needed to get to know each other a little better.

John grinned and leaned forward slightly. 'You're lucky to have them. I'd like to be closer to my sister, but we're too different. Every time we see each other it only takes a few minutes for us to start rubbing each other the wrong way. She hates my Johnny Danger persona; she thinks it is juvenile and stupid. But it works well for me. I've made nearly twice as many sales this year as my nearest competitor in our office and more than three times the average of everyone else.'

LaVonda felt her lips purse in slight distaste. He sounded a little boastful, didn't he? She took another sip of water to cover her discomfort.

'What about the rest of your family, John? You said you lost your mother?'

'Yes. My old man is still alive. He lives on a small property in the Blue Mountains with his second wife. He married her about ten seconds after Mum died.' His tone was bitter.

LaVonda understood. She knew what it was like to have a parent let you down. She felt very warm and understanding towards John. It would have been awful for him to feel like his mother had been replaced so quickly.

'That must have been hard on you.'

John shrugged. 'It's his life. I don't see him much anymore. Probably suits us both better that way. Family can be painful.'

'That's true. My father was a wonderful man, but my mother was neglectful and hurtful. She made life hell for me, and Ann, and Max. We're all better off now she's gone.'

'You lost your father too?'

'Yes. He died when I was in my early twenties.'

'That's rough.'

LaVonda nodded. 'It was worse than rough. A year after we lost Dad, my first husband, Mark, died in a car accident. Our daughter, Emmett, was a toddler. She hardly has any memory of him at all; as far as she is concerned, my husband, sorry ex-husband, Dave, is her dad. I wish she had more memories of Mark. He was a wonderful father to her.'

Over the years, LaVonda had learnt that when she was asked about Mark, it was best to quickly bring up his death and then keep talking for a few moments. It was a coping mechanism. By the time she finished speaking, most people had absorbed the news, arranged their features into politely sorrowful expressions, and then said how sorry they were.

John didn't say sorry. He simply reached out and took her hand in his warm one. 'It must have been a distressing time for you.'

LaVonda nodded. 'It was. Thank goodness for Ann and Max. They stepped in and mothered both of us until the grief fog lifted and I was able to start functioning again.' She didn't mention the baby she'd lost. That was her private pain.

'They sound wonderful; I hope to meet them one day. What was he like? Mark?'

LaVonda was slightly startled by the direct question. People generally didn't want to dwell on the subject of Mark, as though talking about him might upset her. Some people were nosy and asked for the details of how he died, but hardly anyone wanted to talk about what Mark was like when he was alive.

'He was... lovely,' she said slowly. 'He was kind-hearted, funny, and he never took himself or anyone else too seriously. He would sometimes do strange things like drag our mattress into the backyard so we could go to sleep under the stars. Or book us on a bus trip to some strange little country town because he'd heard the local shop made the best scones or something. I thought he was perfect. He didn't live long enough for me to get fed up with his quirks or tire of his jokes.'

'I didn't mean to upset you.' John looked concerned. Their waiter arrived, setting down their meals. LaVonda waited until he had left before she replied.

'You haven't upset me. I like talking about Mark, but I haven't spoken about him to anyone in a very long time. It's funny; I still miss him. All these years later, I still wish he'd walk through the door and come back to me.' She laughed. 'That sounds so stupid, doesn't it?'

John was still holding her hand. He gave a little squeeze, then pulled his hand gently away.

Of course, he had pulled away. What was she thinking, telling him all about Mark? That wasn't the sort of thing any potential new partner wanted to hear: *You're great, but you'll never be as wonderful as my dead husband.*

'No, it actually doesn't sound stupid. It sounds perfectly understandable. I've never suffered that kind of loss, but it makes sense that having someone ripped out of your life would cause a huge wound.'

John lifted up LaVonda's wine glass and handed it to her. Then he picked up his own, his green eyes looking deep into hers.

'To old loves and new beginnings.' He touched his glass softly to hers.

LaVonda smiled.

'Dad told me you're having a nervous breakdown.'

Oh, he did, did he? LaVonda pulled the phone from her ear and glanced at the time displayed on the screen. 7am. She sat up and yawned, propping her pillows behind her back. It had taken her a while to get to sleep last night, following her date. She had thought briefly about inviting John in but, thankfully, common sense and an abundance of leg hair (well, it was winter) had convinced her otherwise. She put the phone back to her ear.

'Em, I'm perfectly fine. It is *very kind* of your Dad, and you, to worry about me, but you can both stop. I've never been better.'

'Dad told me you invited him to the house, made him a meal, and then threw his dinner plate across the room. Twice.'

LaVonda's mouth twitched in a smile. Dave's face had been priceless both times. He had looked so ridiculously shocked. LaVonda quite liked having the power to shock. Actually, she was thoroughly enjoying this feeling of being unexpected and unpredictable. It made a pleasant change.

'This isn't like you, Mum.'

'Perhaps it is, Em. Perhaps I am a plate-hurling, tantrum-throwing shrew, and I've just managed to hide it extremely well for the past forty years. Perhaps you don't know me at all.'

Certainly no one knew what she was capable of doing.

'Mum!'

'I'm kidding, Em. I only threw the plates because your Dad is trying to kick me out of my home, and I don't think that's fair. Do you?'

'Maybe not fair, but why would you want to stay there, anyway? You've always talked about downsizing to a place on the coast. Why not do that now? You could get a lovely little two-bedroom place and decorate it exactly the way you want, using bright colours, instead of having everything in those boring neutrals that Dad likes.'

They were boring, weren't they? Perhaps Emmett was right. For the first time, LaVonda let herself think about moving out of her house. Maybe it could be part of her transformation into old age? After all, she was being forced to go through menopause and yes, she was losing her youth, her vitality, her *significance*, but perhaps she could come through this and find her own space in the world. Surround herself with colours, different experiences, and unexpectedly interesting people. Like John.

And maybe have the occasional fling with murder, just to keep up the adrenaline. But only for those people who deserved it, of course. Murderers, paedophiles, rapists; that sort of person. Monsters who didn't deserve to live anyway.

'Mum, are you still there?'

'Yes, sorry, I got distracted for a minute. Perhaps you're right. I'll give it some thought. Now, tell me, how are you and the baby doing?'

'We're good. Peanut is kicking all the time now. It's so cute and weird.'

LaVonda felt a pang. She could remember exactly what those tiny internal flutters felt like. If she put her hand on her belly, she could almost feel them, even though it had been thirty years ago.

'And Jasper?'

Emmett was quiet for a few seconds, and when she spoke, her voice had a slightly strained quality.

'Good, he's good.'

LaVonda's nostrils flared. 'What is it, Em? What's wrong?'

Emmett laughed, but to LaVonda's finely tuned senses it sounded forced.

'Nothing's wrong, Mum. Jaz is just spending a lot of time with this guy... Dane, who seems... nice, but he's a bit intense. He has a group of followers who are into some strange awakening stuff, and Jaz seems quite enamoured with the whole thing.'

A cult? Jasper was joining a cult?

'Look, it's not a cult or anything, Mum. It's just a group of people who have some obscure ideas... anyway, I'm sure it will be fine. Jaz will probably get bored of it soon. He doesn't have a long attention span.'

That was probably true, although the man had managed to keep his attention on her precious daughter for longer than LaVonda liked. And now he was joining a cult, and no doubt Em would get sucked into it as well. Couldn't anything around here stay normal for just five minutes?

'Why don't you come back home for a few weeks, Em? Jasper could spend time with his weird new friends, and I could look after you.'

'Now look who is worrying. Honestly, Mum, there is nothing to get in a flap about. I shouldn't have said anything. Now promise me you'll think about selling the house to Dad? It would be good for you to make a fresh start. And I promise I'll come down and visit you in your new home once Peanut is born.'

LaVonda agreed to think about it. She pursed her lips as she hung up. Emmett was referring to the baby as Peanut a bit too much for her liking. She'd thought it was the baby's pet name, but with Emmett and Jasper as parents, there was every possibility Peanut was her grandchild's *actual* name.

And it was all well and good to say don't worry, but *of course* she was worried. Even as she showered and dressed for Sunday morning shopping with Ann, LaVonda continued to fret about Jasper's new interest. Why couldn't he be an ordinary hippie (or what did they call them now? Hipster?) and get himself a normal hippie job making dandelion tea for tourists? Why did he have to invent his own enlightenment programs and hang around with other oddballs? And even more importantly, why was her clever, capable, otherwise intelligent daughter allowing herself to be so heavily influenced by him?

Jasper was going to be the father of her grandchild, and Emmett clearly loved him, so LaVonda should make an effort to try and understand him and his motivations. But he was just so *tiresome*. Wouldn't it be nice if he were to just disappear from all their lives?

LaVonda looked through the café window as she waited for Ann. She'd been lucky to snag the last free table, narrowly beating a young couple who were now standing near the counter, giving her the stink eye whenever she glanced in their direction. LaVonda happily ignored them. The only trouble was, she couldn't move from the table to order her tea, so she had to wait until her sister arrived.

She recognised Ann by her walk well before she could make out her features. A navy beanie atop russet curls bobbing quickly through the crowd. With her arms folded in front of her, her missing forearm wasn't at all noticeable. Ann was bundled against the elements, and as usual, she moved as though she were running late for an important meeting.

LaVonda felt a wave of affection at the sight of her sister. She might have a disability, but Ann was a little lioness, ferociously protective of her family. Good lawyer or not, Ann would defend her to the death. In that instant, LaVonda made up her mind; she would tell her about Royce, and maybe even Frank too. Ann was her big sister, her protector, the woman she was closest to in the world. Ann would stand by her. Theirs was an unbreakable bond, a bond between sisters. A love like no other.

'I hope you have a bloody good reason for standing me up outside the police station last Monday, you selfish bitch, because I'm about five seconds away from strangling you to death. Honestly, Von, what the hell has gotten into you lately?'

Ann unwrapped her scarf and glared at LaVonda, who shrank back in her seat.

'Ann, I...'

'Save it. Get me a latte, a big one. And a chocolate muffin. No, two. Then you can explain yourself.'

LaVonda closed her mouth and got up from the table. Ann clearly wasn't in the happiest of moods, so perhaps now wasn't a great time to confess her crimes. She hurried up to the counter.

'A large latte, a pot of tea, and two of those muffins please.' As she handed over her credit card, still deliberately ignoring the couple who'd missed out on the table, the female turned and stepped back into her.

'Oh, so sorry!' Sarcasm dripped from the girl's mouth. 'I didn't even see you there.'

Her male companion grinned, showing a missing tooth. LaVonda's eyes narrowed. She put her card back in her wallet, then swung her handbag forcefully onto her shoulder, deliberately hitting the girl's arm.

'Oh, goodness. I didn't see you either! How silly of me.'

The girl looked stunned. LaVonda smiled widely and quickly made her way back to her table. She sat down, feeling a little breathless.

'Did you just hit that kid?' Ann raised her eyebrows.

'No, of course not. I accidentally bumped into her. How are you doing? How is Sam? The boys?'

'They're all fine. Now, either you tell me what is going on, or *I'm* going to hit you with *my* handbag. Why did you make me go down to the police station on Monday? And why have you been avoiding my calls all week?'

Where to start? She wanted to be honest and upfront, but there was only so much she could tell Ann. Maybe a modified version of the truth?

'Okay, well, you know the guy at work who was harassing me?'

'Yes, Rhys someone?'

'Royce. Royce Butler. He died a few weeks ago. He was killed in a hit and run, Ann, and I thought I was the driver who hit him.' There. It was out now. No turning back.

'Why the hell would you think that?' Ann's eyes narrowed.

'Because...' *oh dear,* 'because I was drunk, and I was... driving, and I saw him standing outside the restaurant.'

'You drove into him?'

'No! I mean, I thought I had, but it turns out I didn't.'

'Seriously, Von? When I asked you to tell me what was going on...'

'I know, I know, it sounds bizarre, but I promise you it is the truth. I thought I'd killed him, and I was ready to confess, which is why I asked you to meet me. Because I needed your help. Then I found out someone else had killed him. I was in shock. I didn't even think to call you and cancel.'

Their drinks and Ann's muffins arrived. LaVonda was silent as the young waiter placed her cup and saucer, a pot of tea, and Ann's latte on the table. He then pushed the teapot over to one side so he could put the plate holding the muffins down, and some of the liquid slopped out of the spout. He looked flustered and grabbed the edge of his apron to wipe it up. Ann waved him away irritably.

'Just leave it, please.'

The waiter left and LaVonda picked up the teapot. She poured some of the tea into her cup, avoiding Ann's gaze.

'Bloody blue balls, Von, that's a hell of a story.'

'It's the truth.' Well, part of the truth.

Ann sighed loudly and picked up her mug. 'Okay, well, this does explain why you've been so weird lately. But why didn't you just tell us? Maxie has been on the phone to me every day, convinced your menopause is making you insane, and Em called me this morning to tell me that you've been throwing things at Dave's head, which incidentally is not a sign of insanity, but the point is, we've all been worried about you. If you'd just told us what was going on... but no. You have to keep it all to yourself and let the rest of us freak out in the wings. It's selfish and unfair, Von.'

LaVonda screwed up her nose. 'I was trying to *protect* you. It is my problem, after all.'

'We love you, you self-centred, irritating twit. Although god knows why. So, from now on can you *please* just tell us what is going on rather than hiding it all and dealing with it yourself? We're your family. What affects you, affects us. Okay?'

LaVonda nodded, even as she thought: *Oh, Ann, I can't possibly tell you everything.* But for now, they were good.

Ann broke off a piece of muffin as LaVonda added milk to her tea, so neither of them noticed the young couple at the counter coming over to them.

'Just watch yourself in future, you old bitch,' the girl spat at LaVonda. Her companion nodded in agreement. LaVonda jerked back in surprise at the unexpected attack.

Ann immediately stood up and shook her stump in the air. 'How dare you threaten me? I'm a disabled woman! Someone call the police!'

Silence fell in the café as everyone turned to look at Ann. She stood straight, her arm held high, her face furious. LaVonda's own face flamed red. She didn't know whether to be mortally embarrassed or proud. Her sister looked ridiculous, but also quite magnificent in her rage.

Okay, proud. Definitely proud.

The young couple scrambled over each other to get out of the café. One of the staff came over.

'Is everything okay?' He looked worried.

'Oh, yes. Those awful people were threatening me and my sister, but it looks like they've been scared off now.' Ann sat back down, demurely tucking her skirt underneath her.

'If you're sure?'

'Yes, all good, but if you felt like sending over a piece of that caramel slice, I wouldn't object. Now, Von, where were we?'

'You were telling me I have to be honest with you, and frankly, after that display of temper, I'm too terrified not to.'

Ann laughed. 'Effective, isn't it? People are so frightened of disabilities. Fuck it. Those two deserved a little public humiliation.'

'Ann! I've never heard you swear before, let alone twice in one morning.'

'Oh, I'm quite the potty-mouth when I want to be. I'm not going to sit by and watch anyone threaten you, or Maxie. You might not think you need your big sister's protection now that we're all old ladies, but you're wrong.'

LaVonda chuckled. 'I never realised I had a mob boss for a sister. You've probably scared those kids straight for life.'

'Hopefully you're right. I don't know, Von, I feel different these days. Less uptight, less concerned about what other people think. I'm turning into a grumpy old woman, and quite frankly, I'm embracing it.'

'Me too.' The sisters smiled at each other and LaVonda felt slighted elated. It was a relief to realise the changes they were experiencing weren't all for the worse. She felt very close to Ann right then.

'Does it ever... do you feel self-conscious, having people stare at your arm? Obviously not when you're waving it around like a maniac, but you know, just generally?'

Ann chewed thoughtfully on her muffin, then swallowed. 'Sometimes. It was better when I had the prosthetic, because people only noticed if they got close.' She picked up her latte and brought it to her lips. LaVonda took a sip of her own tea.

'Then why did you stop using it?'

'I've told you this a thousand times. It hurts to wear it, I don't like it, and if people can't accept my stump, that's their problem, not mine.'

LaVonda nodded, but privately she wondered. Ann was so much clumsier and less agile than when she wore her prosthetic arm. If it were LaVonda's disability, she'd *definitely* wear the arm, no matter how painful. But then what did she know? She'd never had to deal with the reality that Ann did. She cast about for a change in topic.

'Emmett and... er... another friend told me they think I should agree to sell Dave the house and move somewhere else. What do you think?'

'What do I think? I think I'm getting bored of hearing you carry on about it. Yes, you should move and the sooner the better. Let Dave stick with the past. You should be embracing your future. Speaking of which, I've had an idea, and it is a good one. I've found something for you, me, and Maxie to try tomorrow night, and I guarantee this will help us all unwind.'

LaVonda narrowed her eyes.

'Yoga? Ann, I've told you before I am not interested in doing that hippy-dippy stuff.'

Ann looked offended. 'Yoga is not hippy-dippy. You're being very narrow-minded. No, it isn't yoga; this is quite different, and I think you'll enjoy it.'

LaVonda let her breath out in a sigh. 'Okay, fine. I'm in. What are we doing?'

'You know what? I'm not telling you. Just meet me tomorrow at 6.30pm. I'll text you the address. Wear loose clothing and bring an open mind.'

'Does Max know about this plan of yours?'

'No, but I'll call her this afternoon. Have you spoken to her lately?'

LaVonda squirmed. She hadn't spoken to Maxine since the night she'd killed Frank, and she'd been so distracted by everything that had happened in the past few days, she hadn't even thought to check in and see how her little sister was feeling.


'Nice of you to call.' Maxine's tone was snarky.

LaVonda grimaced, set her mug down on the bedside table, and climbed back under the covers. This habit was a relatively new development. Usually when LaVonda got up, that was it; she'd immediately launch into getting ready for her day, but the last few mornings she'd made herself tea and gone back to bed for a few minutes. It was lovely and relaxing, propped up against her pillows, scrolling through her news feed, and giving herself a little gift of time each morning.

'Sorry, I've just had a lot on my mind lately. How are you feeling? Has Ines been in touch?'

'I'm pretty good. No, I haven't spoken to Ines, but we text and she's okay. So, tell me, are you coming to this mystery thing of Ann's tonight?'

'I'm not brave enough not to. Do you want to come back for dinner afterwards? I've thawed a chicken pie and there is too much for just one person.'

Maxine paused. 'Actually, I have a date.'

'Seriously? You just ended one relationship and now you're launching into another?'

'It is just one date, Von, I'm not marrying the woman. You'll be relieved to know this one is a fair bit older; she's my age.'

'I didn't care about Ines being younger than you. I just thought you two didn't seem happy together.'

'You're right. We weren't. Anyway, enough about my love life. How's yours? How is Gavin?'

LaVonda rolled her eyes. 'I have no idea. I'm not seeing Gavin. I had one disastrous date with the man, and I hope to never see him again.'

'What happened?'

LaVonda thought about telling Maxine the whole story, but something held her back. Embarrassment? Guilt? She wished she'd never tried to stand up for that poor woman. If she had simply minded her own business, both Philippa and Frank would be alive today.

'Nothing happened. He's just not my type. He's middle-aged, pleasant, and completely boring.'

Maxine laughed. 'Another Dull Dave?'

'Exactly.'

'See? This is why I date women. Chicks our age are still dynamic, sexy, fun. Boys are boring.'

'Max, are you trying to convert me?' She smiled at the thought.

'No, not at all. Frankly, I don't need the competition.'

LaVonda snorted. 'Nice of you to say, but I'm about as alluring as a bowl of cold porridge.' She couldn't help but feel pleased by Maxine's comment. It was quite flattering to be thought of as any kind of competition in the dating world. 'So, tell me more about this new woman.'

'Nah, it is too early. Let me go on one date, and if it goes well, I'll fill you in.'

LaVonda hung up the phone and smiled as she sipped her tea. She was pleased her sister sounded happy; she deserved to be happy. Hopefully, this new romance would work out for her.

LaVonda stretched her legs and her smile grew wider. She had always privately thought she'd make an excellent lesbian. She related better to women than men, and she preferred female company in general. The only thing stopping her was the whole having-sex-with-a-woman thing. Which was probably a bit of a deal-breaker.

Obviously, that wasn't an issue Maxine had. LaVonda drank the last of her tea and frowned. She didn't want to think about Max's sex life, any more than she wanted to think about Ann's or anyone else's, but she couldn't quite imagine what it must be like to have sex with another woman. It seemed a little... clammy?

LaVonda shook her head to clear her thoughts. As long as Maxine was happy, that was the main thing. She'd had such a bad run in the romance department. The longest she'd ever dated anyone was Ines, and that was less than a year. LaVonda would love to see Maxine settle down. Although she couldn't quite imagine her sister in a loving, cheerful and relaxed relationship. Max seemed to thrive on drama and passion; she was far happier at the very beginning, or very end of her relationships, when there was excitement and conflict, than during the partnership itself.

She'd been like that as a child too; forceful and intense, refusing to show any weakness. LaVonda remembered her chasing an older boy across the school oval because he'd dared to bully one of her classmates. God knows what she would have done if she'd actually caught him. Still, no one would describe any of the sisters as laid-back and easy-going. Even Ann, the most relaxed of the three of them, didn't exactly suffer fools gladly. Yet she had married the lovely, high-voiced Sam, and they'd been happily married for years. And LaVonda herself had had two successful long-term relationships, one ending in death, the other because of a stupid middle-aged crisis. So, there was no reason why Maxine couldn't settle down with a nice partner just because she was a little... forceful.

Unless... unless the rape had affected her more deeply than they realised. What would it have been like to have something so momentous, so utterly devastating, happen to you at such a young age? How could anyone, even someone as strong-minded as Maxine, not be traumatised and subsequently negatively affected by that? Poor Max. LaVonda wished with all her heart she could go back and stop what had happened that night. Or at the very least taken steps to help her sister afterwards. They'd ignored it; pretended it had never happened. How completely irresponsible and stupid of them all.

She and Ann were practically adults at the time. Why did they think they were so powerless? They should have marched straight down to their mother's room and demanded she throw Walter out of the house. They should have called the police, taken Max to hospital, hired a hitman. They should have made that man's life the living hell he'd made Maxine's. Yet they'd done nothing. Merely comforted their younger sister and then tried to put it behind them.

LaVonda pursed her lips. If there was anyone who deserved to die, it was the monster who had hurt her younger sister. If she could punish anyone else in the world, it wouldn't be Dave, or Jasper, or even the awful young couple at the coffee shop. It would be Walter Durbin.

# FOURTEEN

$W$alter Durbin.

LaVonda typed his name into her Google search, selected Images, and leaned forward to peer at her screen. Everyone else in the office had left for the night, and she was on her own for the first time all day. This morning had been spent in tedious back-to-back meetings. Then she'd had a counselling session with Sylvia over her work performance, which had *not* gone well. Meanwhile, dozens of emails were flooding her inbox and she didn't want to deal with any of them right now. LaVonda scrolled down the list of pictures, her heart beating fast because, although she wanted to find him, she didn't want to see his face.

He wasn't there. That wasn't at all surprising, because he would be an old man by now, and old men didn't tend to have a high social media presence. But there had to be some way to find him. She could always hire a detective. No, it probably wasn't a good idea to connect herself to a man she planned to murder. LaVonda would have to do the legwork herself.

She picked up her phone and dialled Emmett for the third time that day. There was still no answer, and LaVonda felt the faint stirring of anxiety in the pit of her stomach. Emmett was far too easily influenced by Jasper, and if he were into a bizarre new cult, it was only a matter of time before her daughter was sucked in too. LaVonda would probably have to stage an intervention, although she had no idea how to organise one. Maxine would probably know. She'd ask her tonight.

LaVonda glanced at the time on the bottom of her screen. She was due at this secret stress-relieving thing of Ann's in half an hour. What were the chances Ann had booked them in for spa treatments tonight? LaVonda closed her eyes briefly. Perhaps she had a lovely luxury evening of pampering to look forward to, with a glass of champagne sipped in a hot tub before being treated to a soothing massage.

Her eyes popped open. It was a pleasant thought, but LaVonda suspected Ann had something far less restful in mind. As long as it wasn't some type of yoga. She'd tried a yoga class once, a few years ago, and that was quite enough thank you very much. She had no desire to pose like a tree or salute the moon or whatever else she was supposed to do. She hadn't found the class relaxing at all. The teacher had reminded her of Jasper, and there was nothing at all comforting about that.

The address Ann had given her was a small community hall behind a supermarket, and LaVonda frowned as she pulled into the car park. She was starting to feel uneasy. She parked her car near several others and took a deep breath before she marched up to the dimly lit entrance. This didn't look promising.

Inside the small foyer, Ann and Maxine were waiting for her. They were both dressed in loose clothing, although Ann's t-shirt hung almost to her knees, covering her rounded torso, while Maxine's was short enough to be a crop top. Maxine was bouncing on the balls of her feet in an agitated manner.

LaVonda looked over at the woman seated next to the hallway entrance collecting money from people passing through into the dark hall. A slightly crooked sign above her head read 'No Limits No Lights'. What on earth was going on here?

She walked up to her sisters, a frown on her face. Maxine reached out and grabbed her by the shoulders.

'Run! Save yourself. It's too late for me, but you can still make it.'

Ann punched Maxine's arm.

'Very funny. You both promised to keep an open mind, and it is only an hour out of your lives. Maxie, please stop fidgeting, you can have a cigarette afterwards. This will be good for all of us, you in particular, Von. You look completely stressed out.'

'I *am* stressed out. Jasper has joined a religious cult, and he's trying to brainwash Emmett. She's not answering her phone, so it is probably already too late to save her.'

Maxine chuckled. 'I spoke to her last night, and it isn't a cult. Although they do practice lingam awakening.'

'What on earth is that? And why did you call Emmett?' LaVonda felt unreasonably annoyed at this revelation.

'I didn't. She called me. We do speak regularly, you know, especially when you go flying off the handle.'

LaVonda snorted. She didn't fly off the handle. And why was her daughter confiding in her aunts and ignoring her own mother's calls? Before she had time to give voice to these thoughts, the woman at the entrance stood up.

'Everyone in now, please. We're about to start.'

Ann stepped forward. 'Come on, I've already paid for us. Let's go.'

'Ann, what is this? What are we doing?' With growing trepidation, LaVonda followed her sister into the dark hall, Maxine prodding her from behind. 'Will you stop poking me? What is this?'

The only light came from the foyer, and as they entered the room, LaVonda could just make out a number of people standing against the walls. Some appeared to be stretching or warming up, rolling their necks and shoulders. As Ann walked further into the room, she seemed to be swallowed up in the darkness. LaVonda stumbled slightly and looked back at the doorway in irritation. Why hadn't they turned on the hall lights?

Ann stopped near the far wall and turned to face LaVonda. LaVonda could hardly see her features, but she could hear a note of apprehension in her sister's voice.

'Now, you promised to keep an open mind. We're here to dance. In the dark.'

What kind of madness was this? Dancing in the dark? In a hall with complete strangers? Oh, no. She did not want to do this.

'Come on, let's just go with it.' Maxine grinned. LaVonda could see her teeth gleaming. She glanced around the darkened room. What was Ann *thinking*? This wasn't relaxing at all. In fact, she could almost *feel* her blood pressure rising.

LaVonda shook her head in the dark, then turned and strode back across the room towards the foyer. She was halfway there when a heart-thumping beat started, and suddenly LaVonda found herself surrounded by people twisting their bodies and waving their arms. She froze, but no one crashed into her. They were dancing wildly and enthusiastically around her.

LaVonda's eyes had adjusted to the dark, but she couldn't see her sisters anywhere. They were lost in a sea of writhing dancers. The beat opened up into a Beyoncé song, one of her favourites, and despite her self-consciousness, LaVonda felt herself moving slightly in time to the music. Well, she was here now, and she couldn't escape, so she might as well go along with it, although she was still going to kill Ann when this was all over.

As a rule, LaVonda enjoyed dancing. But in private, at home on her own, with no one else around. Not in public, where people could stare at her. Although... no one was looking at her in here, and she couldn't really see what anyone else was doing. She shuffled from side to side, then as the song hit the chorus, LaVonda did a little experimental spin; a move she enjoyed at home but had never done in front of anyone else. It felt good, so she did it again. She tried a couple of prancing steps, then bounced on the spot and pumped her fists above her head. Good grief. This was actually fun!

The song ended as another one started. LaVonda gave up and let herself go. No one paid her any attention as she bobbed and swayed and even kicked one leg up. She could hardly see anyone else, but the energy coming from the other people in the room was pouring into her. She felt energetic and alive. She didn't need to stop and rest; she could keep dancing all night.

An hour later, the music slowed, and the foyer lights were turned up, casting a dim light into the dark hall. LaVonda filed out with the rest of the crowd, happy and sweaty, exhausted, but exhilarated.

Maxine was already outside, her own face shiny, and she was still panting slightly as she drew in on her cigarette. The tip glowed red in the gathering darkness of the evening.

'That was surprisingly... fun,' LaVonda conceded, as Ann came up and joined them. Ann's t-shirt was soaked, and she shivered as she pulled on her puffer jacket.

'I knew you'd both enjoy it once you loosened up. You're both way too uptight, and god knows we all need a bit more movement in our lives. Maxie, how can you smoke after all that exercise?'

'Sheer dedication,' Maxine answered, dropping the cigarette and grinding it underfoot. 'Von's right. That actually wasn't too bad. You can sign me up for another one. Anyway, I'm off now. I'm meeting Tracy for dinner, so I'll see you both later.' She strode off towards her car, her long legs covering the distance in no time.

'Who is Tracy?' Ann asked, as LaVonda reached into her bag to check her phone. She hoped Emmett might have called and inadvertently smiled when she saw one new message. John. She sent back a reply, confirming yes, she would love to meet him for lunch tomorrow, and then she sent another quick text to her daughter: 'Call *me, please.'* If Emmett had called Maxine last night, that probably meant she hadn't been completely brainwashed yet.

'Who is Tracy?' Ann repeated. LaVonda looked up.

'Her new girlfriend, I think. She mentioned last night she'd started seeing someone. I hope this one works out.'

'She doesn't waste any time, does she?'

'That's what I said. I don't think she was particularly happy with Ines though; they never seemed well suited.' LaVonda was cooling down now, so she pulled on her own jacket. They both walked towards the car park.

'A bit like you and Dave then?'

'Ann! Oh, alright, yes. Like me and Dave. Did I tell you I've decided to sell the house to him?'

Ann smiled. 'I'm glad to hear it. Where are you parked?' It was getting dark, and the temperature had plummeted.

'Over near that van.' She paused. 'Ann. Has Maxine ever spoken to you about... Walter Durbin?'

Ann's eyes narrowed. 'No. She doesn't talk about any of that, ever. Why do you ask?'

'I've been thinking about the impact it must have had on her. I guess I just feel guilty we didn't do more to help her.'

'We didn't do anything to help her,' Ann snapped. LaVonda looked at her in surprise.

'It's true, Von. We didn't do a bloody thing, except help that monster get away with it. For years I've hated myself for not speaking up. Yes, I know, Dad had just been diagnosed, and we were scared that you and Maxie would be put in foster homes, and I didn't think I could support the three of us. But I should have tried. I didn't even bloody try.'

LaVonda was shocked. She'd always felt slightly guilty about not reporting Maxine's rape to anyone, but she hadn't realised the depths of Ann's remorse.

'But Ann, you were only nineteen. Even if you could have supported me and Max, child support services wouldn't have agreed to it. And we didn't know how long Dad had left... it wasn't your fault.'

'I know it wasn't my fault. I feel terrible for not doing anything afterwards, but I'm not blaming myself for her being in that situation. That was all on Mum. She brought him into our lives, and I'll never forgive her.'

She had, hadn't she? LaVonda remembered her mother bringing home her new friend, Walter. Their father had been in hospital, and Maude had broken a tooth tripping over drunk one morning. She'd gone to the dentist, been gone all day, and when she finally returned, she brought the dentist home. Walter Durbin.

'I'm sorry, Ann. I didn't realise you felt so badly.'

Ann waved her hand dismissively. 'Look, it's in the past and there is no point in dwelling on it. We can't change things now.'

*Oh, but I can*, thought LaVonda.

Walter Durbin was a dentist.

LaVonda carefully shut her office door and settled herself at her desk. She'd been expecting to be as stiff as a board this morning, but instead she was pleasantly sore and mildly euphoric. Whether that was from last night's exercise or her discovery, she wasn't sure.

After leaving Ann, she'd gone straight home and tried again to track down Walter, adding '+ dentist' to her search. This time his face showed up straight away. He'd looked older, his curly black hair sparse and grey in the photo, but it was definitely him. LaVonda shuddered. It looked like he was still practising dentistry, although he lived in another state. The man must be at least seventy by now.

She picked up her phone and dialled, then promptly hung up as Sylvia knocked on the door.

'Come in.'

'Sorry to interrupt, but the recruitment approvals urgently need your signature, and tomorrow's board presentation has been moved to this afternoon. I told the secretary I'd send your slides through this morning. I hope that's okay? I mean, I assume you've finished them?'

LaVonda was pretty sure Sylvia knew that she hadn't even started the presentation slides. Sylvia was still upset after their discussion yesterday when

LaVonda had politely asked her to lift her game. The conversation hadn't gone down too well.

'Yes, of course. I'll have them to you in the next hour. I just want to check some data first.'

Sylvia smirked and left, closing the door behind her. Great. Now she had to produce something quickly or risk losing face. Why hadn't she at least given herself until midday?

Sighing, LaVonda switched on her computer and began working. Outside, the wind picked up, spitting rain against the windows.

Several hours later, the light morning showers had given way to a storm, and LaVonda absolutely did not want to go out to meet John for their lunch date. She shivered even though it was toasty warm and bright inside. Perhaps she could cancel? After all, she still had two meetings this afternoon to prepare for, plus a string of emails to read, and now the board presentation to deliver. She didn't have time to go out for lunch.

She tried calling Emmett again. The phone went straight to message bank. LaVonda's anxiety increased. It wasn't like her daughter to ignore her calls, and they hadn't spoken since their phone call on Sunday. Should she drive up to see if she was okay? It was a five-hour drive, so it seemed overly dramatic to get in the car and rush to her daughter's side. But if she didn't and Emmett needed her...

LaVonda would never forgive herself, *never*, if she stood by waiting again, while one of her loved ones was in trouble.

Her phone pinged as a new message came in. '*Hi, I'm fine, just busy. Will call tonight.*'

That was a relief, although it didn't set her mind totally at ease. LaVonda glanced at her watch. The presentation slides had been delivered, the recruitment approvals signed, and her speaking notes prepared. She might as well give herself a short break.

The wind had turned spiteful, thwarting every attempt LaVonda made to close her umbrella. She wrestled frantically, trying to get the damn thing to close so she could open the café door and get inside, out of the rain. The umbrella refused to budge. Come on!

'Allow me.' John appeared at her side, dressed in a pale green suit and a nubby yellow tie. A tiny flicker of annoyance flared, and LaVonda quickly squelched it. He was working today, so of course he would be dressed like this. Why had she expected otherwise?

John took the umbrella and managed to close it. He pushed the door open and LaVonda walked into the café. It was warm and cosy inside and smelled like cinnamon. Usually this would have soothed LaVonda, but a large drop of water had fallen from the café awning as she stepped under it. So now she had a big wet spot on her hair and any minute it would start to frizz.

'What would you like? I'll get it.' John grinned down at her. He wasn't putting on his overbearing twang, but for some reason the sight of him made her feel irritated and slightly embarrassed.

'No, I'll get it. You paid for dinner the other night.'

As she waited at the counter, LaVonda tried to reason with herself. John was still the same nice man, even if he was dressed as Johnny Danger. She knew it was part of his work image, and there was no reason at all to feel annoyed. She ran her hand over her hair. Definitely frizzing.

'Two roast beef rolls and a flat white to takeaway, please.' The man behind her placed his order. LaVonda frowned.

'Excuse me, I think I was next.'

The man smiled and shrugged. 'Didn't see you there.'

How could he not see her? She was standing right in front of him. LaVonda's blood pressure rose. Let it go, it doesn't matter, she told herself. She drummed her fingers against her thigh, while the woman at the counter prepared his order.

'Who was next?'

LaVonda raised her hand, but the woman had already turned to another customer. Oh, for heaven's sake! LaVonda stomped back over to the table where John was sitting.

'Perhaps you'd better order for us, because I'm being completely ignored as usual. Here's my credit card.'

John looked up in surprise.

'I'm not taking your card. Are you alright?'

'Yes, just tired of being overlooked, which is not a problem you seem to have. Can you order for us or not?' LaVonda knew she sounded rude and petulant, but she didn't care. She was so *sick* of being treated as though she didn't exist.

John gave her a concerned look but didn't argue. He got up and walked over to the counter. There was no bum wiggle this time.

LaVonda took out her phone and sent Emmett a message. *'Do you want me to come up?'*

As she pressed send, she felt her face start to burn. *Oh no, please not now.* She held her breath and gripped the edge of the table, as though this could possibly hold back the flush. The heat came on relentlessly. LaVonda yanked her arms out of her jacket and used the café menu to fan herself. Oh god. This was a bad one. Maybe she should head back out into the wind and rain where it was cooler? John returned to the table as she was undoing the top two buttons on her blouse.

He smiled as he sat down. LaVonda scowled. If he made one stupid joke about her stripping for his benefit, she was getting up and walking right out.

He didn't. He poured her a glass of water and handed it over. LaVonda gulped it gratefully. Now if he would just pretend this hadn't happened...

'Are you alright now?' The concerned tone in his voice irritated her.

'I'm fine,' LaVonda snapped. 'It is a hot flush, that's all.'

'I know what it is, my older sister is going through the change at the moment too.'

Great. So now he was reminding her that she was older than him. LaVonda glanced at the door. Perhaps she could fake a headache and leave? This date was turning into a disaster.

'I was asking if you're alright because you seem a little tense.'

LaVonda gritted her teeth. 'I am not tense.'

John nodded and poured her some more water. Wisely, he kept quiet.

Their food arrived just as LaVonda's flush subsided. She looked down at the salad roll. She had no appetite. She felt foolish and irritated, and tension had made her jaw ache. She wanted nothing more than to go straight home and sink into a bubble bath, followed by bed.

'Thank you for lunch, but I'm not up to this now. I have to get back to work. I'll call you later.'

Back in her office, LaVonda still felt irritated, but now also guilty for rushing off. John hadn't done anything wrong, poor man, and he didn't deserve to be treated like that. She would call him later and apologise, but for now she *had* to get her emotions under check and make her way through the pile of work on her desk. This job was more complicated than she had realised, and every day it felt like she was falling further behind. There was no time for hormonal mood swings and personal dramas, even though those were taking up most of LaVonda's time and energy these days.

She opened one of her emails and clicked on the attachment. A proposal for her review and comment. She sighed. Writing proposals had been quite enjoyable; reviewing other people's proposals was mind-numbingly boring. She took a deep breath and tried to focus on the words.

A message appeared on her phone. Emmett. *'No need to come up. All is well. Talk soon.'*

What did that mean? All is well? As far as LaVonda was concerned, all was far from well. Maxine and Emmett might not think Jasper's new cult was anything to worry about, but something felt off. It was her mother's intuition alerting her to possible danger.

*Concentrate! You'll talk to her tonight. For now, you have to concentrate on this proposal.*

LaVonda read the first paragraph. Then she read it again. The words made no sense. She tried a third time. It was no use. She simply couldn't concentrate. Her mind whirled. Emmett. Jasper's cult. Frank's murder. Royce and Maude's deaths. The attempt on Dave. Not that those were *all* her fault, and of course, she *hadn't* actually gone through with dispatching her ex-husband.

No, but she had killed a man. Frank was dead because of LaVonda. She was a murderer. A cold-blooded killer without regret or remorse.

Inappropriate pride flared. LaVonda wanted that feeling again. She *craved* the sense of power and justice she'd experienced when she killed a monster, when she took justice on behalf of those who couldn't.

She dialled quickly, before she changed her mind.

The phone rang several times. LaVonda took a deep breath to calm her pounding heart. She wasn't committing to anything yet, she was just making some enquiries. Once she had tracked him down, then she could decide what needed to be done.

'Welcome to Open Smiles. You're speaking with Lindsay. How may I help you?'

'Hello. I was hoping to make an appointment to see one of your dentists please. I'm a new patient.'

'Certainly. I can fit you in with Tamir next Wednesday or Bruce on Friday morning.'

'I was given a recommendation... I was hoping to see Walter Durbin.' His name was like wet ashes in her mouth. She swallowed hard.

'I'm afraid Walter doesn't work here anymore. But all our other dentists are excellent.'

'I'm sure they are. I just wanted to take the recommendation my friend gave me... are you able to tell me where Walter is working now?'

LaVonda heard a sharp intake of breath down the other end of the phone.

'I'm so sorry to have to tell you this, but unfortunately Walter passed away more than a decade ago. I don't know when your friend last saw him, but he hadn't worked at this clinic for almost a year before he passed.'

'He's dead?'

'I'm afraid so. He had a stroke, I believe. Now, I can make you an appointment with any one of our dentists. We have a number of spots available...'

LaVonda hung up the phone. Walter Durbin was dead. A stroke. It seemed like too easy a death for such a monstrous man. She wondered how Maxine would feel when she heard the news. Relieved?

She explored her own feelings. It wasn't relief she felt. No, her feelings hung a little lower. It would have been satisfying, and poetic somehow, to have evened the score and avenged her little sister. To have taken the life of another terrible, dreadful man. What LaVonda was feeling, if she were *perfectly* honest, was savage disappointment.

# FIFTEEN

'I'm sorry about walking out on our lunch date the other day, John. I was in a bad mood, but I didn't mean to take it out on you.'

Most of her phone conversations these days seemed to start off with an apology of some kind. It was getting tedious. LaVonda glanced out of her office window. Monday's rain had given way to a sunny, pleasant week. Not that LaVonda had spent any time over the past few days enjoying the weather.

'That's okay, we all have off-days. Are you good now?'

'Yes, well mostly. I've decided to resign from the General Manager role. I'm just not suited to it.'

It was true, she wasn't enjoying the new responsibilities, and frankly, she was making a pig's ear of things. Her presentation on Tuesday had been a disaster from start to finish. She'd forgotten her notes and tried to improvise, but two slides in she realised she was completely lost. She'd fumbled, blushed, read a few lines off the screen, and finally given up and clicked through the rest of the slides in silence. Sylvia had been at the Board presentation to take the minutes, and LaVonda couldn't bear to look at her. Afterwards, she'd simply packed up, collected her things from her office, and driven herself home.

Wednesday and Thursday had passed in a state of mild panic at her ever-increasing workload, before LaVonda finally made the decision to resign. She wanted her old job back; the job where she knew what she was doing, where she was competent and reliable instead of floundering. She planned to tell the Managing Director today, after lunch.

'If you're unhappy in the role, then you've probably made the right decision. Is there anything I can do to help?'

If LaVonda was perfectly honest, it wasn't just the job making her feel anxious. Emmett was almost certainly being brainwashed by Jasper and his band of merry cultists. She denied it, but LaVonda wasn't easily fooled.

Then there was the whole business of finding somewhere to live now that she'd decided to sell to Dave, and on top of that, she still had the occasional nightmare about Frank. Add her hot flushes to the mix and it was little wonder she had started grinding her teeth in her sleep.

'Actually, there is something you can do. Can you find me somewhere to live? I've decided to sell my half of the house to Dave, so I need a new home. I'd like to stay in this general area, and I need two, or maybe three, bedrooms, two bathrooms, and it must have a small garden, and preferably a modern kitchen.'

John laughed down the phone. 'You're not going to believe this, but your timing is impeccable. I think you may be in luck.'

Well, that would be a first.

'Do you have something like that?'

'I do. A nice modern duplex two suburbs from your place. It just came on the market, and I haven't shown it to anyone yet. Are you free now? It's empty and I have the keys, so we could go and take a look.'

LaVonda looked at her email inbox. 312 unread emails. 313. 314. Most of them were marked *Urgent* or *For Immediate Attention*. LaVonda puffed up her cheeks and exhaled. She should at least try to make a dent in the pile, but wasn't it more important to organise a roof over her head?

Oh, who was she kidding? She wanted to see John, she wanted to see the house, and she definitely didn't want to sit here and tackle this mountain of work. She'd stay back tonight and get some of it knocked off then.

John gave her the address and hung up. LaVonda snatched up her bag and coat and walked out of her office.

'Are you going out again?' Was there a slightly accusatory tone in Sylvia's voice?

'Yes, I am.' *Not that it is any of your business, Sylvia.* 'I'll be back in an hour.'

As she drove out to the house, LaVonda wondered what her staff's reaction would be when she returned to her old role. Everyone had seemed supportive when she started as Acting General Manager, but as time had gone on, it was clear she didn't actually have the respect of the rest of her colleagues. It would be a relief to go back to her old job, where she was confident in her skills and ability. The MD would understand. At least, she hoped he would.

John was waiting for her outside the house. This time, his loud, flamboyant suit didn't bother her in the slightest. It seemed almost appropriate. He greeted her warmly, leaning in for a quick kiss on her cheek, his moustache scratchy, the scent of his aftershave triggering a small stroke of inappropriate desire. LaVonda turned away quickly so he wouldn't see her blush. She focussed her attention on the house.

Set well back on the flat block, it looked fresh, modern, and clean. A white pebbled path set with large pavers wound through the neatly mown lawn to the front entrance, where two potted topiaries flanked the front door. The impression was tranquil and inviting, and LaVonda felt a rush of excitement. She followed John through the doorway into the foyer, where a modern light fitting hung from the ceiling.

Together they walked into the large open-plan kitchen and tiled living area. Both bedrooms were freshly carpeted, with mirrored wardrobes and attached bathrooms. John explained that the owners had bought the duplex as an investment, but their marriage had recently broken down, so they were selling their assets and splitting the profits.

LaVonda could picture herself in this lovely little home. The garden was small, but well maintained. A cherry tree and two lemon trees stood proud in the back yard, and a passionfruit vine, heavy with fruit, ran along the back fence. It was private and perfect.

'I'll take it.'

John raised his eyebrows and grinned at her.

'Would you like to put in an offer?'

'No, I want to buy it. I'm happy to pay full price, but I want to move in by the end of the month. Can you make that happen?'

'I don't think a short settlement will be a problem, but you can probably get it for several thousand less than the asking price. I shouldn't tell you this, given I am working for the owners, but they're very motivated to sell.'

'I'm happy to pay full price.' LaVonda repeated. With the money she'd get from selling her half of the house to Dave, she could afford to pay for this house and still have enough for new furniture and furnishings.

'Well, if you're sure, I'll give them a call now. Excuse me.' John took out his phone and dialled as he walked back into the kitchen. Left alone, LaVonda opened the folding glass doors and stepped onto the back deck. She would buy a garden swing chair; it would be lovely to sit out here reading a book and sipping a glass of chilled wine on warm summer evenings.

She wandered down to the end of the garden and picked a passionfruit off the vine, lifting it to her nose to inhale the fragrance.

'Congratulations! You're the proud owner of this lovely home, and the vendors are happy to settle in the next four weeks.'

Just like that. She had taken another step out of her old life and into the new one. The impulsiveness of her decision made her feel a little breathless.

'Are you free tomorrow night?' John was asking. 'Because I think we should go out and celebrate.'

LaVonda grinned back at him. 'Sounds great.' She could feel a bubble of excitement inflating her chest. A brand-new home and a date with John. Just three months ago, this would have been inconceivable, and the thought of it would have completely rattled her. But now? Now it did sound great.

'I'll get the paperwork started as soon as I'm back in the office. Shall we say 6pm tomorrow for dinner? I'll make a reservation somewhere special, and I'll pick you up.'

He moved towards her, took her hands in his, and then leaned forward. She looked into his eyes, nodded, and lifted her face as he kissed her. A quick, light kiss that was over within seconds. His moustache brushed her upper lip in a strange, but not unpleasant way.

LaVonda was still smiling as she got back into her rental car, waving as John drove away in his Porsche. She touched her mouth and shivered. There was definitely chemistry between them.

She looked back at the house, then picked up her phone and dialled Dave's number. His hello was tentative, cautious, and her smile fell. Why was he behaving so nervously towards her? What on earth did he think she was going to do to him over the phone?

'You can have the house.' No preamble, just straight to the point. 'I want half the current value, and I want everything settled and in my account in the next four weeks.'

Dave was silent for a moment. LaVonda's heart gave an extra-hard thud in her chest. What if he'd changed his mind? No, surely not. Dave cleared his throat and then spoke.

'Um, terrific, are you sure though? You're not going to change your mind?' The unspoken word 'again' hung between them. Well, she couldn't fault him for being sceptical; she'd been a little inconsistent lately.

'Yes, I'm sure. I've found another property I want to buy. So, you and Jemima can move in at the end of next month if you can get everything squared away by then.'

'That won't be a problem. I'll speak to the bank tomorrow. Thank you. This is very gracious of you, LaVonda.'

It *was* gracious of her, although she had to admit it was quite gracious of *him* not to give her a hard time. She had been acting somewhat erratically in the past few weeks, and admittedly, Dave had borne quite a lot of the brunt of her behaviour.

Well, as he should. Let's not forget who caused all this upheaval in the first place. If he hadn't left her, hooked up with a younger woman, decided to create a new family, and tried to kick her out of her own home, she wouldn't have gotten so stroppy, and she wouldn't even have *considered* murdering him.

She was glad she hadn't gone through with her plan though. Dave was an idiot, but he wasn't a vicious man, and he didn't deserve a horrible death just because he was making some stupid, and okay yes, rather upsetting decisions.

Men like Durbin, Frank; those men *deserved* to die. They had deliberately and viciously harmed other people. So LaVonda had no qualms... well, very few qualms about killing them. If only Walter Durbin hadn't had a stroke, because LaVonda would have just loved to take his life.

Sylvia stood up as LaVonda came back into the office, and she hurried over to meet her. 'Oh, LaVonda. The MD came down to speak to you, and I had to tell him you were out of the office. Again. He wants to see you immediately.'

It took all of LaVonda's acting skills not to react. She smiled at Sylvia.

'Thank you for letting me know. I'll go up in a minute.'

'Well, I mean, he did say straight away...'

LaVonda steeled her voice. 'I'll go up shortly, Syl. I need to do something first.' She actually needed a minute to get her nerves under control, but that was none of Sylvia's business.

Perhaps she had left it too late. Being summoned to the MD's office wasn't a good sign. LaVonda's legs trembled slightly as she took the lift to the top floor and walked towards the double doors of the MD's office. She knocked and waited politely. The doors swung open.

'Come in, LaVonda.' The MD spoke quietly, sounding far more menacing than if he'd bellowed for her to get inside.

LaVonda swallowed and stepped into his enormous office.

'Have a seat.'

She sat, smoothing her skirt down with damp hands. Her cheeks felt hot. She watched as he took a seat at the conference table opposite her. He regarded her for a few minutes in silence. She'd seen him do this before; when he wanted to intimidate someone, he stayed quiet until the other person was practically squirming. Well, LaVonda wasn't daunted, and she wasn't going to break down and start talking, even though it was an effort not to babble out an apology.

Finally, he broke the silence, and LaVonda's small, initial flutter of triumph promptly shrivelled and died as his words filled the space between them.

'LaVonda, I'm afraid your performance in Deborah's role has been well under par, well under.'

LaVonda tried to smile genially, but her face felt frozen. She should have come to him earlier. Now he was going to suggest she step down and someone else take her place, and she would lose the opportunity to control the situation.

'I realise I haven't been managing things quite as well as I could have—'

'A number of your staff have made complaints about your lack of leadership and support. According to them, you are unfocussed and easily distracted, and you've spent more time out of the office than in it.'

Hang on, that was a bit rough. She hadn't done a great job, and she had let the work get on top of her, good heavens, she was the first to admit it, but she hadn't been that bad, surely. Was this some petty payback from Sylvia and Colin because she'd recently spoken to them about their own lack of engagement? She swallowed and opened her mouth to defend herself, but the MD wasn't finished.

'I spoke to the Director of Security this morning, and he advised me that, in the past, he has found you difficult to deal with and incompetent.'

*Oh, how dare he?* LaVonda went into a slow burn. She fixed her gaze on the MD in his expensive suit, strands of oily hair brushed over the top of his pate. Who did he think he was? She'd killed a man, for heaven's sake. She could just as easily kill another. If only he knew the danger he was facing across his desk, he wouldn't be sitting there frowning at her so arrogantly. The only thing standing between him and certain death was LaVonda's decision *not* to murder him.

'What have you got to say for yourself, LaVonda?'

She knew she hadn't done well in the role; she had been distracted and overwhelmed at times, and she could have tried harder. Perhaps she could have handled the staff situation better as well by being more open and listening to concerns, instead of shutting the office door and pretending they didn't exist. She had made a lot of mistakes in the past few months, and she was sorry she hadn't put more effort into the job. She'd been so excited when she'd been asked to step in, and instead, she had let Deborah and the rest of the team down. She wanted to return to her old role, where she was confident and competent, and where she added value to the organisation.

LaVonda opened her mouth to tell him all of this, but only two words came out, surprising both the MD and herself.

'I quit.'

LaVonda kicked off her shoes and dropped her shopping bags on the kitchen bench. There was only one thing on her mind.

Wine.

Yes, it was all very well to moderate one's drinking to avoid the slippery slope of alcoholism, but there were occasions when a cold glass of white wine was called for, and today was definitely another one of those days.

Once she'd poured a glass, she rummaged around in her shopping bags and pulled out a small wheel of brie and expensive, but delicious, rosemary and parmesan crackers. It seemed entirely appropriate to hold herself a small party to celebrate finding her new home and leaving her old job.

Of course, she would need to find another job, but that was a problem for the future. Tonight, she would relax and simply celebrate. She felt empowered and delighted as she hugged her arms around her own waist. A huge smile wreathed her face. She felt ridiculously pleased with herself. Who would have thought quitting her job would feel so gratifying? The look on the MD's face! As if he couldn't believe his ears. It had been one of the most satisfying moments of LaVonda's life. She only wished the rest of the staff could have seen her.

LaVonda took her plate and wine into the living room and curled up on the couch. She flicked on the television, but the noise was so jarring she quickly switched it off, opting for her 80s playlist instead. LaVonda sipped her wine, then closed her eyes as music filled the room, allowing herself to be taken back to the early days of her first marriage. LaVonda and Mark had both loved Dire Straits and would often spend Saturday nights in their tiny flat, drinking cold beers and singing at the top of their lungs until the neighbours hammered on the walls.

Would Mark have been proud of her today? Probably. He used to think everything she did was wonderful, and he'd supported every decision she'd ever made. He'd been so excited by her second pregnancy. Although he adored Emmett, LaVonda knew he was secretly hoping their second child would be a boy. He'd kept talking about possible names for boys until LaVonda pointed out their daughter had a 'boy's' name, and if they had a son, it was only fair to call him something feminine. Mark had growled in mock anger, then launched himself at her as she lay stretched out on the couch. He pretended to wrestle her, but instead covered her face with kisses and nuzzled into her neck.

'Get off me, you big bear!'

'I can't. You're irresistible.'

Dave had never called her irresistible. Their relationship had been largely devoid of the passion and laughter and fun she'd shared with Mark. They'd had a good relationship, and they'd still had fun times, of course they had, but after Mark died, something in LaVonda died with him. Colours faded, sounds became muffled, and

LaVonda moved through the next stage of her life feeling slightly detached. If she didn't care too deeply, she couldn't be hurt so completely. She'd loved Dave, but it had been a grateful, friendly, companionate love. He'd provided security and stability, he'd been (up until recently) a loyal husband, and he adored Emmett as if she were his own child.

But he wasn't Mark, and she couldn't love him as though he was. Theirs was a once in a lifetime love, and LaVonda was glad she'd had the chance to experience it, even for just a few years. Staying up late to talk, waking up early to make love, calling each other throughout the day because they could hardly bear to be apart. Even when Emmett was born, and it seemed like they were tired all the time, and they'd had no money; even then they'd had fun, teasing each other and laughing and rolling around like puppies.

'We're not calling him Josie.'

'Why not? You got your choice with Emmett. I also quite like Matilda for a little boy...'

'Or we could call him Emmeline, and then we could have Em and Ems. Your favourite chocolate!'

LaVonda smiled at the memory, and then her face fell. The baby had been a boy, but Mark had never known.

How different her life would have been if Mark hadn't died. Or maybe it wouldn't be so different. Perhaps she and Mark would have drifted apart, locked into a marriage like the one she and Dave had found themselves in. LaVonda would never know how things might have turned out if Mark and her son had lived.

A knock on the front door startled her. It was almost 7pm, and she wasn't expecting anyone. It must be Maxine; no one else she knew would just turn up on Friday evening without calling first.

She walked over to the door and paused. What if it wasn't Maxine? LaVonda felt vulnerable and a little frightened. She forced some confidence into her voice.

'Who is it?'

'Mum! Open the door, it's me.'

At the sound of her daughter's voice, LaVonda yanked the door open. Emmett was standing on the doorstep, looking forlorn. Good grief, what had happened?

'Jaz is losing the plot, Mum. I'm not dealing well with all the new stuff he is getting into. I want to be supportive, but it's all getting a bit too weird. I need a break.' Emmett flung her rucksack on the floor and plonked herself down on the couch.

A thrill surged through LaVonda, curving the edges of her mouth into a broad smile, which she immediately tried to suppress. This must be why she had been compelled to resign today; some inner intuitive part of her must have known her daughter was in trouble and needed her. LaVonda didn't generally think of herself as particularly intuitive, but clearly, she was.

Emmett could move straight back into her old room, and then, in a few weeks' time, they could both move into the duplex. Once the baby was born, Emmett could find a job teaching, and LaVonda would stay at home and look after her grandchild. For the first year or two, at least. It was perfect. She inadvertently beamed at her daughter.

Emmett pouted. 'Mum? Are you even listening to me?'

'Yes, of course.' Drat, she couldn't keep from grinning. She turned away and tried to compose herself, before turning back. 'Do you want something to eat?'

Emmett shook her head. She looked upset, and LaVonda immediately sobered up. Her daughter was distressed, and she had to provide her with comfort and support. And try very hard not to give in to the overwhelming temptation to disparage Jasper.

'Tell me what happened.' She sat down next to Emmett, reaching forward for the box of tissues on the coffee table. Emmett took several and dabbed at her eyes.

'He's okay. He's still a totally amazing human being; it is just that he has become so obsessed with this new lifestyle, and I feel like Peanut and I don't matter as much anymore.'

Lavonda patted her daughter's green muslin-covered knee. As usual, Emmett was dressed in droopy, unflattering layers of material. This skirt had sequins and rice-looking beads scattered over it. Hopefully she would return to her former tasteful style once she'd settled back in at home.

'Em, I'm sure that's not true.' Oh, why on earth was she defending *Jasper*? 'Well, maybe–'

'Mum, he spends all his time with Dane and the group, and they're into some bizarre stuff. The other day I came home to find Jasper and Dane, and a few of their followers meditating in the sunroom–'

'Well, that doesn't–'

'Naked.'

*Good grief.* LaVonda tried not to react, but a tiny shudder ran through her.

Emmett sighed. 'Look I can deal with that; yes, it is a bit weird, but it's not the weirdest thing he is into at the moment.'

*It isn't?*

'But the point is, even after they were done, Jaz ignored me. He invited everyone to dinner; he'd made a huge pot of lentils, and he knows I hate lentils, and then he spent the whole evening making plans to combine the STER program with Dane's '4 Rs' program...'

'For *arse* program?' LaVonda goggled.

'Four R's, Mum. Relax, Release, Resolve, Revive. It is very popular; Dane has a blog and a weekly podcast. Anyway, I understand this is a huge opportunity for Jaz, but I'm tired, sore, huge, fed up, and I need support right now, but he doesn't seem at all interested.'

'I'm here for you, darling.'

'I know, Mum. Thank you. I'm so tired, I just want to sleep for days.'

LaVonda could relate to that.

'You're welcome to stay as long as you want. Perhaps after a week or two, when things calm down, we can talk about your future?'

'I'm just here for a few days, Mum. For a little break. I'm not home for good.'

'Well, you don't need to make any decisions now. How about I make you a cup of tea while you put your feet up and relax?'

'Thanks.' Emmett swung her feet up onto the couch and leaned her head back, closing her eyes. LaVonda blanched at the sight of her daughter's grubby black boots resting against the cream material.

'Could you just...' She broke off and bit her tongue. Em had enough on her plate without LaVonda's nagging. 'Never mind.'

She left her daughter lying on her couch while she went to make tea. Her heart felt light and happy. Emmett was back home, where she belonged. And if LaVonda had her way, they would never have to set eyes on Jasper again.

# SIXTEEN

She should have known it was too good to last.

It was only 7am on Saturday morning but already Jasper had been here an hour, closeted with Emmett in her bedroom while LaVonda sat up in bed, sipping her tea, and straining to hear the sound of the front door opening, and Jasper leaving.

It didn't seem that was likely to happen though. Emmett had been very quick to welcome Jasper in when he'd arrived earlier that morning. LaVonda, who'd still been asleep, had woken, frowned, groaned, and then gone back to sleep. When she awoke again, she'd gone into the kitchen to make tea and peeked outside. Sure enough, Jasper's van was leaking oil all over the driveway. Well, that would soon be Dave and Jemima's problem, not hers.

LaVonda took her tea back to bed and tried not to listen to the faint sounds of talking coming from down the hallway in Emmett's room. What were they doing in there? How long did it take to say, 'no I'm not coming back, and you won't change my mind'?

Surely, they wouldn't reconcile? LaVonda badly wanted her daughter to be happy, really, it was all she wanted, but she would be so much happier married to a smart, hard-working lawyer or doctor, or even a bus driver. As long as he had a steady job and could support his family, LaVonda wouldn't care. But Jasper, with his ridiculous lifestyle and his propensity for alternate realities, simply wasn't the right partner for Emmett.

A door opened and closed, and someone padded down the hallway to the bathroom. LaVonda heard the toilet flush and then the shower running. It didn't seem at all like Jasper had left or was leaving anytime soon.

LaVonda let out her breath in a huff. If Emmett did take him back, then she was consigning herself and her child to a life of uncertainty, of potential poverty. If Em went back to work, she could make a reasonable living as a primary school teacher, but it wouldn't be enough to single-handedly support herself, her child, and a man who refused to settle into a proper job.

If only Dave wasn't planning to have more children, Emmett would almost certainly inherit his father's estate. Brian had cut Dave off years ago when he refused to go into the family business, and he had written him out of the will. All his money would skip down to the next generation, in this case, Dave's stepdaughter, Emmett. Until he had biological children with Jemima, of course. There was a chance Brian would still keep Emmett in his will, but who knew? If she were to inherit the Robinette money, Emmett would never have to worry about money again, and LaVonda wouldn't have to worry about Emmett.

What if Brian were to die before Dave and Jemima had children? Surely then Emmett would still be in the will. A tiny flame of excitement flashed in her chest. LaVonda placed her mug down carefully on the glass coaster next to her bed, then slid further down under the covers. The heating hadn't kicked in yet and the house was still cold. She wriggled her toes and bit her lip.

She could do it. She'd actually have no qualms about it. She'd do it to protect Emmett's future and the future of her unborn grandchild. Brian wasn't an evil man like Frank had been, but he was nasty, unpredictable, and selfish. LaVonda wouldn't take any *joy* in killing him, but she would be happy with the results of his death.

Actually, she might take a little bit of joy.

How to do it, though? She hadn't seen the man in years, and he probably wouldn't even recognise her, so there was no point in going to his house. He'd never let her in. She didn't know much about him, other than he played golf twice a week and had a dating profile on one of those apps Maxine was always banging on about.

Finder? No, Tinder! That was it. What if LaVonda were to match up with Brian on Tinder? She could set up a date, disguise herself, meet him for a drink, and then suggest going back to his place for a nightcap. She could easily slip something into his drink and no one would ever know who she was.

On impulse, LaVonda installed the Tinder app and looked at the instructions. It seemed easy enough. She needed to make a profile (she could use her middle name), upload a picture, then she was set. She could find Brian, swipe on his profile, and hope he swiped on hers. Perfectly easy.

There was a knock on her bedroom door, then it opened, and Emmett poked her head around.

LaVonda sat up, locked her phone, and picked up her tea, beckoning her daughter to come in.

Emmett smiled, a slightly shamefaced smile, as she came in and sat down on the edge of the bed. LaVonda tried to rearrange her features into an understanding expression, but she could feel frown lines on her forehead giving her away.

'Is this really what you want?'

'Yes, Mum. He's my soulmate. He came for me straight away, so I must matter. He may not be able to articulate his feelings, but it is obvious by his actions that his devotion is real.'

LaVonda resisted the urge to snort. 'You're thirty, not thirteen, Em, and you're behaving like a love-stuck teenager. You have your baby to consider now.'

'Our baby. The baby is half Jaz's.'

LaVonda waved her hand dismissively, as though she could flap away Jasper's right to parentage.

'Babies take commitment and effort. You can't just ignore their needs because you've got a new interest. He turned away from you, Em, when you needed him. What if that happens again? What if this new arse thing takes off and he decides he is more into that than you and the baby? What then?'

Emmett pulled a face and reached up to push a strand of hair off her face.

'Stop trying to be funny, Mum. It's R's, not arse.'

'Alright, I'm sorry, but my point is that babies need stability, both financial and emotional, and it doesn't look like Jasper will be able to provide either of those things.'

'We have each other. We have love. That is enough.'

This time LaVonda did snort. 'Love doesn't buy nappies, Em, and it doesn't buy groceries. You were such a good teacher, and you seemed to love it. Why not go back to that?'

'There aren't any teaching jobs where we live, and anyway, I want to be at home with the baby and supporting Jaz. We're fine, Mum. We're mostly self-sufficient, and Jaz makes some money from STER. There is more than one way to live, you know. You like a conservative life, whereas we're happier living an alternative lifestyle, and there is nothing wrong with either choice.'

LaVonda thought there was quite a lot wrong with her daughter's lifestyle, but she didn't want to waste her morning arguing about it. She threw back the covers and swung her legs out of bed.

'It is your choice, Em. I just want you to be happy and safe and secure. Is Jasper out of the shower? Because I've got quite a lot to do today.'

'I'll go and hurry him along. Is it okay if we stay for a couple of nights? He's tired from the drive, and I'd like to see Dad while we're here.' Emmett paused in the doorway.

'That's fine. You'll have to fend for yourselves tonight, though. I have plans.' LaVonda walked towards her en-suite bathroom.

Emmett's eyes lit up. 'A date?'

'No, not a date. Just dinner with a friend.'

'A male friend? Will you be bringing him home afterwards? Did you hear that, Peanut? Grandma has a boyfriend.'

'Em!'

'Alright, calm down, I'm going.'


'Any special plans for tonight?' The beautician spread wax along the inside of LaVonda's right thigh and pressed a strip of cotton on top.

'Um, no, not really.' How was she supposed to answer that? And wasn't it a little inappropriate for someone who was waxing off her pubic hair to enquire as to her evening plans? LaVonda wanted to close her eyes and pretend this wasn't happening. The pain, and the lying down half-naked, were bad enough. She didn't want to make idle chit-chat as though the two of them had run into each other at some boring function.

'Would you like me to do underneath?'

What was that supposed to mean? LaVonda thought they'd already done underneath. Wasn't that the awful part from ten minutes ago when she'd almost shrieked out loud and called a halt to the whole proceedings?

'Some ladies like their bottoms hair-free.'

Only some? Who on earth *wanted* a hairy bum? LaVonda didn't think hers was particularly furry, but what if it was? What if John accidentally came in contact with a tuft of fluff and was turned off?

'Yes, you'd better do it all.'

LaVonda held her leg up in the air and tried to think of something pleasant, anything really, as the beautician went to work. Gosh, she was being very thorough, wasn't she? Even finishing off by using her tweezers on a few strays, which seemed unnecessarily fussy. After all, no one was taking a torch down there to inspect her handiwork.

The rest of the waxing hadn't been too bad. She usually had her legs done every couple of months anyway. But as far as everything between was concerned, she'd always settled on the occasional trim before wearing her swimsuit in summer, and that was about it. Now she'd upped the ante and was the owner of a small, neat, dark triangle framed by pink, plucked chicken skin. Possibly the least sexy look in the world. Hopefully the redness would subside before tonight.

LaVonda thanked the beautician, paid, and walked out of the salon, trying to move normally instead of bow-legged. Next stop was the lingerie shop across the road. She wasn't planning on seducing John in a marabou-trimmed camisole and suspenders, but she wanted something a bit more glamourous than her usual control-top pants and underwire bras.

Good heavens. She felt ridiculously excited and nervous. Should she get condoms, or would he have that covered? Best to assume he would; she didn't want to look like she'd planned every detail of this. As if the freshly waxed bikini line and new underwear wasn't already giving the game away.

Would they go back to his place? They couldn't come back to hers, not now that Emmett and Jasper were there. She wasn't ready to share the news about John with anyone yet, and particularly not her daughter and son-in-law.

'Can I help you?' A middle-aged saleswoman was smiling at her. LaVonda smiled back.

'I'm fine, thank you.' She looked at the rows of bras hanging on the wall. There was a dazzling array of colours and sizes. LaVonda reached out and picked up a hot pink bra in her size. Could she get away with wearing something like that? All her bras were white, black, or beige, and her underpants were plain cotton briefs. She hadn't worn underwear like this since she was a teenager.

She replaced the hot pink bra and lifted out a pale green one. This was more like it. No need to go overboard. Small changes. The saleswoman was hovering next to her. She nodded at the bra LaVonda was holding. 'There are matching panties for those. Would you like to try the bra on for size?'

'No, I'll take it, and the pants.'

'You're sure you won't try it on first? No refunds or exchanges for incorrect sizes, I'm afraid.'

'I'm sure.'

Was she sure about sleeping with John tonight? LaVonda felt a flutter of excitement, or was it nerves? She didn't have to do it; she could always change her mind, even at the last minute. Of course, that meant her waxing and the new underwear would go to waste. She watched the woman ring up her purchases and handed over her credit card, trying not to wince at the price.

'Your husband will love these.' The saleswoman beamed as she handed over the bag containing LaVonda's new, expensive underwear.

Good grief. What an inappropriate thing to say. LaVonda wasn't buying underwear because of a *man*. Well, she was, but she could just as easily be buying them for herself. It was annoyingly presumptuous of the woman to assume she was buying them with someone else's reaction in mind.

She opened her mouth to tell the woman off, then closed it again. What good would it do? The woman was trying to be friendly. She didn't need LaVonda ruining her day by pointing out what a silly remark she'd made. Still, LaVonda didn't like the idea that people were looking at her decisions and judging her intentions. It was extremely unsexy to have everyone assume you were going to have sex tonight.

Was she going to have sex tonight? Look, she'd play it by ear. If the mood felt right and she wanted to, then at least she'd be prepared. And if not, there was always next time, assuming John was agreeable. LaVonda bit her tongue and smiled as she took the bag. Tonight, she would simply relax and enjoy herself, whatever happened.

An unpleasant surprise was waiting for her when she arrived home. LaVonda was greeted by the unwelcome sight of Jasper walking nude down the hall into her kitchen. She stopped short, suppressed a scream, and immediately went looking for her daughter. Emmett was curled up in the living room watching something on television. Had Jasper been watching it with her? Had his bare bum sat against LaVonda's lovely new cushions? She'd have to burn the couch.

'Jasper is wandering around the place completely starkers!'

'He's a naturalist now, Mum.'

'Not in my house, he's not. Either he puts on pants or he leaves. Immediately.'

Emmett laughed, (laughed!) and headed towards the kitchen. LaVonda went into her bedroom, shut the door, and sank down on her bed. Honestly, the entire world seemed to be conspiring against her plan to feel sexy and seductive tonight for her date with John. Now she'd have to concentrate extremely hard to get the image of a naked Jasper out of her head. Fully clothed, he did nothing for her libido. Naked, he just about destroyed it.

She shook her head. Regardless, she was looking forward to seeing John. But first things first. She had something more pressing to take care of, and then she could focus on her date. LaVonda went into her en-suite and shut the door. Normally she didn't wear much makeup. A little foundation, a few brushes of mascara, and a touch of pale lipstick. But not for this. No, for her Tinder profile, she needed to go all out.

LaVonda swept thick foundation all over her face, blending it in. Using an old brown makeup pencil, she drew thick brows onto her own neat ones and used the same pencil to line her eyes, adding a dramatic flick at the outer corners. It was all coming back to her; the way she'd made up her face in her early teens, when subtlety wasn't at all valued. She sucked in her cheeks and drew her reddest lipstick across her cheekbones in two vivid slashes. She rubbed the lipstick in, then applied a thick coating to her lips. Several sweeps of mascara finished the job.

LaVonda looked at herself in the vanity mirror. She looked tarty and slightly ridiculous. Mostly tarty. Perfect.

Back in her bedroom, she opened her wardrobe and fumbled about on the top shelf until she came across a large floppy sunhat, bought years ago and never worn. She fitted it on her head, tucking her hair back. Then she held her phone up, sucked in her cheeks and took her first ever selfie.

Several pictures later, LaVonda was satisfied. She looked unrecognisable; garish but alluring enough to appeal to an elderly man. She opened the Tinder app, uploaded the best photo, and adjusted her profile preferences to 'men over seventy'.

She flicked through possible matches and nearly skipped straight past Brian. She paused, staring at his ugly, but slightly familiar, face. It was him. He looked older than she remembered, but he still wore an expression of arrogance, his eyebrows knitted together, his top lip curled into a slight sneer. Ugh. How did the man ever get any dates? She swiped right on his profile. There. That should do it.

LaVonda ran a bath, scrubbed her face clean, then spent the rest of the afternoon in her room trying to relax and prepare for her date. The chicken pimples had subsided, much to her relief, and as she washed her hair, shaved her armpits, and plucked a few stray hairs from her chin, she couldn't help but feel her excitement build. Just before 5pm, she pulled on her towelling bathrobe and wandered out to pour a glass of wine to sip on while she finished getting ready.

Emmett and Jasper were lounging in her living room. Emmett was curled up and playing on her phone. At the other end of the couch, Jasper appeared to be doing some kind of meditation, sitting cross-legged, his eyes shut. Thankfully, he was fully clothed now, although, like Emmett, dressed in ill-fitting layers of fabric. There did seem to be a few layers between him and the couch, so perhaps she wouldn't need to burn it after all.

Although maybe she should let Dave have the couch. In fact, he could have all the furniture. LaVonda wasn't particularly attached to anything in the house, apart from her new soft furnishings. Dave could have the house and everything in it. She'd only take her own personal things. Make a fresh start. The thought made her smile, and Emmett looked up, saw her, stretched, and yawned.

'What time are you heading out, Mum?'

'In a little while. Will you be alright for dinner? There isn't much in the fridge, but I do have plenty of eggs, and I bought asparagus and zucchini today. And cheese.'

'Stop fussing, Mum. We'll be fine.'

She hadn't been *fussing*, she'd been exhibiting *concern*. LaVonda turned and stomped into the kitchen. *How sharper than a serpent's tooth it is to have a thankless child.* And the thankless child's moronic partner. She had just twisted the top of a bottle of merlot when she heard someone knock on the front door.

LaVonda looked up at the kitchen clock in dismay. John was more than an hour early; she hadn't even put on her new underwear yet. She certainly didn't want him to see her in a bathrobe, but she couldn't have Emmett answering the door. Her daughter would have all kinds of questions that LaVonda wasn't ready to answer.

She hurried towards the front door. Could she ask him to go and wait in the car? She didn't want to leave him in the living room with these two while she got ready. She glanced from Emmett to Jasper and back again. They looked like a couple of bohemian bookends. As though she'd called a casting agency and requested two authentic 1960s hippies, complete with unkempt hair and patchouli oil aroma.

No, she wasn't ready to introduce John to them, or vice versa. He would have to go on ahead to the restaurant, and she would meet him there. As she reached the door, another knock came.

Why was he so impatient? And for that matter, why was he so early? Her breath caught in her throat. Perhaps something had happened, although she couldn't imagine what. Frowning, LaVonda pulled open the front door and gasped aloud in surprise.

# SEVENTEEN

By 10am on Sunday morning, LaVonda felt she couldn't wait another minute for her sisters to arrive. If she'd been a nail-biter, her fingernails would have been bitten down to the quick; if she'd been a smoker like Maxine, she'd have chain-smoked her way through the past sixteen hours.

But being neither of those things, LaVonda had merely scrubbed the bathroom, vacuumed all the carpets, and repeatedly set and reset the outdoor table for brunch. Ann had agreed to forgo their Sunday shopping, and Maxine wasn't working, so she was able to join them. LaVonda had been far too rattled to cook; instead, she'd gone to the markets earlier and bought a salmon quiche and fresh croissants. That, and two bottles of Prosecco, would have to do.

Emmett and Jasper had gone to visit friends, so she'd had plenty of time to clean the house and get ready before Ann and Maxine arrived. LaVonda had set up everything on the back patio even though the morning was still cool, because at least this way, Maxine could smoke to her heart's content, and they wouldn't be interrupted by her rushing off every ten minutes to feed her addiction. The awning was retracted, and LaVonda's outdoor setting was in the sun, so it should be warm enough, but she'd draped a couple of brightly coloured blankets across the back of the chairs, just in case.

She opened the front door and peered out, scanning down the road for any sign of their cars. Her next-door neighbour was outside his house, watering his garden even though the forecast had predicted hot weather for this afternoon. He should be watering his garden in the evening, not the morning, when the water would evaporate too easily. Ordinarily, LaVonda might have gone over and said something, but today she was far too distracted. She merely smiled and waved, then went back inside.

The quiche was bubbling away in the oven. It smelt incredible, but LaVonda had quite lost her appetite after the events of last night. She slipped on an oven mitt and removed the quiche, setting it on the bench to cool. Then she opened one of the bottles of Prosecco, before placing it back in the fridge. It was probably a bit early to start drinking on her own.

A sharp knock signalled that at least one of her sisters had arrived. When she opened the door, both Ann and Maxine stood on the doorstep. Ann clutched a bottle of champagne that she held aloft. LaVonda's face broke into relief at the sight of her sisters. She pitched her voice dramatically low.

'Thank god you're here. You will not *believe* what has happened.'

Ann raised her eyebrow quizzically at LaVonda, who shook her head.

'Come in first. I've got brunch all ready. We're eating outside so Max can smoke.'

'I've quit.'

'What?' Both LaVonda and Ann swivelled towards Maxine, who shrugged.

'I'm trying, anyway. Tracy doesn't smoke, and she hates it, so I'm cutting down.'

'Is it serious? You and Tracy?' Ann dropped her bag on an armchair before continuing out to the back patio.

LaVonda left them chatting as they headed outside, while she went back into the kitchen to put the quiche on plates. By the time she joined her sisters, juggling the plates and a big bowl of fresh salad, Maxine was already fidgeting and tearing her serviette into tiny pieces.

'Oh, just have one,' Ann said impatiently. She tucked the champagne bottle under her arm and used her hand to try to twist the cork out.

Maxine reached over and snatched the bottle out of her hand. 'For fuck's sake, Annie. Let me do it. If you're not prepared to wear your helper arm, you can damn well accept a bit of assistance once in a while.' She popped the cork expertly and filled their glasses.

Ann accepted hers without comment. She took a sip, then leaned over the table to take her plate.

'The quiche smells amazing. Is it your salmon and dill one?'

'No, I bought it at the markets. I'm too wound up right now to bake.' LaVonda slumped back in her seat.

'Why? What's happened now? Honestly, Maxie, either have a cigarette or eat some of this. Either way, stop fidgeting. Bloody balls, between the two of you it's like hanging out with a couple of moody teenagers.'

Maxine reached into her bag and pulled out a packet of cigarettes. 'This is my first one for the day. I've definitely cut down a lot.'

Ann picked up her fork and stabbed at her quiche. 'Good for you. And good for Tracy for convincing you to try to quit. She sounds like a keeper, and I'm looking forward to meeting her. Now, Von. What is going on?'

LaVonda quickly filled them in on the events of the past few days. She explained that she'd quit her job and told her sisters about Emmett turning up out of the blue, followed by Jasper.

'You've quit your job? What are you going to do?' Ann put down her fork. She looked worried. LaVonda waved her hand dismissively. She didn't want to talk about her job, or the fact that she was about to become unemployed. That was a problem for her future self; her current self-had quite enough to deal with right now.

'Are Em and Jasper still here?' Maxine looked around the garden, as though she was expecting her niece to pop out of the hydrangea bush.

'No, they're out visiting friends. But something else happened last night.'

Ann picked up her fork again.

'Are you going to tell us or just make us guess?'

'You'd never guess in a million years.' LaVonda paused for dramatic effect. 'Last night, Dave and Jemima came over.'

'You're kidding?' Ann's fork clattered against her plate as Maxine turned in surprise and coughed a face full of smoke at LaVonda.

'I'm not. Emmett invited them because Jemima wanted to take a look around her new home, and they thought I'd be out for the evening.' LaVonda waved her hands about to disperse the smoke.

'Why would you be out?' Ann frowned.

'Because I... it doesn't matter.' She didn't want to derail the conversation by bringing up John because then that was all her sisters would want to hear about, and she needed to get this latest outrage off her chest first. 'Anyway, the point is, they were coming over to deliberately skulk around my house while I was away.'

'It will be their house in a few weeks,' Ann pointed out. 'Although I agree it is bad form to come over when they thought you'd be away. Why not just call you and arrange a time?'

'Exactly my point. I wouldn't mind if Dave wanted to show his girlfriend around the place, but he could have done me the courtesy of calling and arranging a mutually convenient time. But no, they just showed up out of the blue. I was still in my bathrobe.'

The sight of the two of them on her doorstep had been a shock, and Jemima herself had been quite unexpected. She was a young Asian woman, short and slim, with shiny dark hair and a big smile. She'd been friendly too, reaching out to grab and shake LaVonda's hand before LaVonda could react and pull away. She smelled like warm vanilla, and her eyes sparkled, and LaVonda, who had for some reason pictured Jemima as a thin, washed-out blonde, was taken aback. She couldn't reconcile her imagined Jemima with the real one standing in front of her. Emmett had jumped up from the couch, hurried over, and reached out her hands.

'Dad, Jem, come in.'

No, hang on, don't come in. This was still LaVonda's house after all, and *she* got to decide who entered her home.

But before she could object, Jemima walked straight in, following Emmett into the living room. Dave had hung back, looking sheepishly at LaVonda. She'd glared back at him.

'Em said you'd be out tonight. She invited us so Jemima could have a quick look around the house.'

LaVonda had looked over to where Jemima was hugging Jasper. There was simply no way she was going to leave them all alone together in her home. No way in the world.

'So, what did you do?' Ann pushed her plate away and leaned over to refill her glass. She passed the bottle to LaVonda.

'I cancelled my plans and made everyone coffee.'

LaVonda had dashed into her bedroom and quickly dressed. Then she'd rung John and cancelled their date, telling him she had a family emergency. Well, it *was* an emergency in a way. She had no intention of leaving her house and allowing Jemima and Dave to prance around as if they already owned the place.

By the time she came back into the living room, everyone was seated. LaVonda had beckoned to Emmett. They'd left the other three in the living room and gone into the kitchen together, where LaVonda quietly shut the door, then turned on her daughter.

'What were you thinking? Inviting them over when you knew I'd be out?'

'I thought it would be better than inviting them while you were here. You don't have to cancel your plans, Mum. They won't stay long.' Emmett might have sounded relaxed, but she had the good grace to look slightly abashed.

'I'm not going anywhere now.' LaVonda had felt outraged. She wasn't overreacting, was she? No, not at all. It was absurdly rude of Emmett to invite her father and his girlfriend to poke around her house at a time when she knew LaVonda wouldn't be home.

Still, now that they were here, she would behave in a way that was both dignified and gracious. She would make them coffee and then offer to show Jemima around herself. Just to be clear, she had no intention of befriending the woman, but undoubtedly, Dave had already painted LaVonda as his crazy ex-wife, and she was *not* letting that label stick.

After the coffee was made, she'd sent Emmett back into the living room with the mugs, while she tipped a packet of biscuits onto a plate. This was a ridiculous situation, but she would rise to the occasion, demonstrating how mature and calm she could be, even though she was still seething inside.

'Biscuit, Dave?' She'd thrust the plate at him as he shrank back.

'I'm not going to throw it at you,' LaVonda had huffed, although at that moment, nothing would have given her more pleasure.

'So, what is she like? This Jemima?' Maxine's eyes flashed with interest. She stubbed out her cigarette on the grass and immediately lit another one.

'Alarmingly pleasant. Surprisingly attractive, and she seems to be completely devoted to Dave. She plonked herself down, started chattering away, making herself at home as though she had every right to be there. It was completely unnerving.'

'I'll bet. What did you talk about?'

Apart from Jemima and Jasper, who didn't seem to have a perceptive bone in his body, they'd all been a little tense and awkward. The conversation had centred mostly on Emmett's pregnancy and speculation about the gender of the baby. It wasn't until Jasper decided to fill them in on his latest interest that the evening took a sharp turn for the worse.

Ann made a face and put her glass down. 'What the bloody hell is vortex healing?'

LaVonda reached over, picked up her own glass, and drained it. 'Some sort of ceremonial life-affirming rubbish; part of the new cult thingy he is into. But that wasn't the worst part.'

She reached out for the bottle. There wasn't enough bubbly wine in the world to help her come to terms with what had happened next.

Jasper had been more animated than she'd ever seen him as he explained how vortex healing worked. He described in detail the spiritual riches he'd gained from his new program. To her endless credit, LaVonda hadn't rolled her eyes even once, although her jaw ached for an hour afterwards.

'These shamanic practices are thousands of years old.' Jasper had thrown his arms up energetically. 'They heal, and empower, and liberate your life forces.'

He was like a different man; talkative, lively, and enthusiastic. It was very disconcerting. LaVonda had glanced at Dave, who was perched awkwardly on the edge of his seat, a death grip on his coffee mug. She knew that look; he was itching to leave, but naturally he wouldn't say anything. Meanwhile, Emmett was smiling, but it was definitely forced. Only Jemima appeared riveted, and when Jasper finally paused for breath, she'd practically applauded him.

LaVonda had sat rigidly, her legs freshly waxed, thinking about the night she *should* have been having with John and contrasting it with the night she *was* having with her daughter and these three idiots.

Jemima's eyes shone as she encouraged Jasper. Clearly bolstered by her interest, Jasper went into even more detail about his newfound interests.

'It got worse than that?' Maxine laughed and drew deeply on her cigarette.

'Much worse.'

Jasper had looked directly at Dave. 'Man, Dane and me, we're holding a lingam awakening workshop next Saturday. You should come up and join us. It's a full day of lingam activation and awareness; pretty ground-breaking stuff. Opening our manpower.'

'Oh, I don't think Dad would–' Emmett started.

'Davie! What a lovely idea. We should drive up early in the morning, and I can spend the day with Emmie while you go to the workshop. That sounds perfect.'

LaVonda had looked from Jemima to her ex-husband to Emmett. What on earth were they talking about? Lingam awakening?

Emmett had sighed and leaned forward...

*Oh, good grief.*

Ann's eyebrows raised as she lifted her glass and brought it to her lips. 'What the bloody hell are lingams? And why do they need to be activated? Is that like activated almonds?'

LaVonda sighed and leaned forward...

'Penises?' Ann spluttered into her wine. Maxine burst out laughing.

'You knew about this, didn't you? Why didn't you say something?' LaVonda glared at her younger sister.

'I was going to, but I thought you might react badly, and I didn't want you flying off the handle again.'

'Would you stop using that expression? I don't fly off the handle!'

'You don't seem to have a strong grip on it right now.'

Maxine was enjoying this far too much for LaVonda's liking.

'I'm upset! My grandchild's father is some kind of penis pervert, and no one else seems at all bothered. Dave was actually considering going up there for it.'

'Dull Dave? At a lingam awakening? Oh, I'd pay to see that.' Maxine started giggling.

'I'll get you tickets,' LaVonda said sourly. 'I'm sure they have a spectator section.'

'How do you even know what a lingam is?' Ann was frowning at her youngest sister.

'I used to date a doula.' She looked at their confused faces. 'A doula is someone who supports women giving birth. Anyway, she was heavily into all that stuff. Tantric sex, divine energy, yoni massage. A yoni is–'

'Never mind, I don't want to know,' LaVonda interrupted, as she poured the remainder of the champagne into her glass.

Ann looked perplexed. 'But why do grown men need workshops to become aware of their penises? The twins were only about three months old when they started lunging for their own joysticks.'

It was a good point. LaVonda had only ever slept with two men, but even in her limited sample size, she was pretty sure that male penis ignorance wasn't a thing.

'Do you want me to explain it?' Maxine asked.

'No.' LaVonda shook her head as Ann nodded hers enthusiastically. LaVonda held up her hand.

'Seriously, Max. No. I got an overview last night, and that was quite enough. I don't need the details. Ann, you can look it up online if you're that interested. I need your advice. What am I going to do about this?'

'There isn't anything you can do, Von. Em isn't in any danger or trouble. You'll just have to let it go.'

That didn't sound at all satisfactory. She couldn't just 'let it go'. Surely there was something she could do, some way to get this back under control.

Could she kill Jasper? As soon as the thought popped into her mind, LaVonda dismissed it. She couldn't possibly cause her daughter that much distress. She frowned. Why did she keep leaping to murder as the first option for dealing with things? It was as though she'd opened a door following Frank's death, a door she kept returning to again and again. Bloodlust. She'd activated her own bloodlust.

It had been an incredible feeling though; killing Frank. She couldn't deny it to herself. Strangely enough, she'd had that same sensation once before in her life. It had been when she had given birth to Emmett. After hours of labouring, an anxious Mark by her side, she'd emerged. Exhausted, sweaty, and emotional, LaVonda had looked down at the red, squalling baby on her breast and felt a rush of something incredibly powerful and wonderful. It was an overwhelming feeling, delivering a brand-new life into the world. And it seemed taking a life could deliver the same exquisite adrenaline rush.

Ann was looking at her askance. Maxine wandered down to the end of the garden, a cigarette in one hand, her phone in the other, and she was tapping out a message. Probably texting her new girlfriend.

LaVonda shrugged. 'You're right. There isn't anything I can do. Dammit, Ann, why are children so annoying?'

Ann laughed. 'I've got all of that to look forward to. Unsuitable girlfriends, I mean. At the moment, my home dramas consist of remembering whose school project is due on what day and making sure everyone has clean undies. I'm quite looking forward to being the annoying, demanding mother-in-law. I feel like I was born to play that role.'

'Trust me, it is no fun. Do you think Max is texting her new girlfriend? She seems pretty keen on this one.'

Ann looked over at Maxine, who was now talking on the phone. 'She seems keen on all of them. But good on her. I'm looking forward to meeting Tracy. If I have to wait years before the twins start dating, I might as well hone my judgemental skills on Maxie's partners.' She lifted the bottle, and it slipped in her hand. She reached out and caught it with the nub of her other arm, wincing as she did. LaVonda resisted the urge to reach out and help her. She knew from experience that wouldn't go down well.

'What about me and Dave? You were pretty judgy there. Did you ever approve of him?' LaVonda frowned at her sister. Ann looked up.

'Look, he has been a good father to Emmett. I'll give him that. But as far as the two of you are concerned, well, no. Dave is so... careful, and he seemed to stifle, rather than enhance, your joie de vivre. You lost your lust for life, Von, but I think you're starting to get it back.'

Of course, she'd lost her joy. Within twelve months she'd lost her father, then Mark, then her baby. Dave wasn't the cause of her pain, and it seemed a bit unfair to blame him for the fog she'd been living in.

But Ann was right about one thing. LaVonda was starting to get her mojo back. Maybe it was the murder, maybe it was Dave leaving, or maybe it was her decision to move to a new house. Perhaps it was John. Whatever the reason, she was feeling more alive and more vital. The veil had lifted, and the world jolted into life, becoming sharper and brighter. Despite the frustration of her daughter and Jasper, the concern over her future, and the ever-growing list of things she had to sort out, LaVonda had a low-level excitement coursing through her. Something was about to happen. She didn't know what it was, but she knew without a shadow of doubt, it was coming.

# EIGHTEEN

'We're so sorry to hear you are leaving, LaVonda. This place won't be the same without you.'

Sylvia looked genuinely contrite, and LaVonda was moved. She could let bygones be bygones.

'Thank you, Sylvia. I'll miss you too.'

'But I mean to say, what will you do? Surely you are too young to retire?'

Yes, she was too young to retire! She wasn't even fifty yet, for heaven's sake. Her smile tightened.

'I'm not sure, Syl, but I know I need a change. Maybe I'll try my hand at something completely different.'

Sylvia looked doubtful. 'It will be very difficult to start a new career at your age. Oh, I mean, not that you're old or anything...'

'I'm sure I'll be fine.'

She would be fine. Not only had she saved up several weeks of leave, but she also had three months of long service leave, so there was no real hurry to find another job. She would take a little time to herself to set up her new home, then start looking for something after that.

Truthfully though, she was only interested in pursuing one particular career path, and it wasn't something she could admit to Sylvia. Although it *would* be fun to see the look on the other woman's face if she admitted that she'd like to become a professional hitwoman.

Well, why not? She had successfully committed her first kill, and goodness knows she already had the perfect assassin camouflage. After all, who would suspect a plain, middle-aged, conservative woman? There had to be *some* advantage to becoming invisible.

But how on earth did one get into it? Would she have to get entangled in the murky and frightening criminal underworld in order to practise her craft? LaVonda shuddered. She had no idea how any of that worked, and she didn't relish the idea of following her dream by associating with actual criminals. They probably didn't have a mentoring program, anyway.

Sylvia left, and LaVonda indulged in a little daydream. She could picture a small hole-in-the-wall reception staffed by a young woman. Em, perhaps? No, better to keep her family out of it. An anonymous young woman then. A line of bedraggled women and children stretched from the front desk along the street (for some reason they were all dressed like paupers from 18th century London). As each person approached the desk, the receptionist would busily take down their details, whispering reassurances that brought hopeful, nervous smiles to their coal-streaked faces.

Behind the reception, tucked away in her inner office, LaVonda sat at a large, polished oak desk, a huge picture window at her back. As the information rolled in, LaVonda studied the details on her laptop, peering through her glasses, making notes, and jotting down plans. Her methods would include poison, gassing people in cars, and cutting brakes. Nothing too messy or unsavoury, and certainly nothing where she herself would be put in danger again.

It was a delightful fantasy. Terrible people, the scourge of society, receiving their comeuppance at her skilful and deadly hands. LaVonda smiled wryly. *If only.*

Outside, Sylvia was bustling about, collecting her things before she went home. LaVonda glanced at the time on her computer screen. It was almost time to leave for No Limits, No Lights. She was looking forward to it. Perhaps she could persuade her sisters to join her for a drink afterwards? LaVonda was in no hurry to return to her home, where Emmett and Jasper would be lounging around. She grimaced as she pictured Jasper pressing his naked bottom into her couch.

No, not her couch; Dave's couch. LaVonda was going to decorate her new home in exciting, vivid, flame colours, orange, red, yellow. Maybe some cool blues and pinks in the bathrooms. She wanted different textures; fluffy, knobbly, plush, and silky smooth. Paired with delightful scents of jasmine, vanilla, and orange blossom. Perfect. LaVonda hugged herself delightedly. It was time for a change.

Once again, both Ann and Maxine had arrived first and were waiting for her just inside the hall foyer. LaVonda weaved through the queue to reach her sisters. Ann turned to greet her.

'We were beginning to wonder if you were coming.'

'I got held up at work. I'm trying to get everything in order for the person who will replace me.'

'I don't know why you bother.' Maxine's tone was contemptuous. 'You've given that place everything for the last twenty years. Why not take some time off?'

'I'm leaving in a couple of weeks, and I want to leave on good terms.' She dropped her shoulder bag on the floor next to her feet.

Maxine shrugged. 'Whatever.'

Ann reached out and cuffed Maxine lightly on her head.

'Stop being a brat. She's right to try and leave on a high note. Von, Maxie was just telling me about Tracy. Apparently, she's a detective.'

'Police officer,' Maxine corrected. She looked more content than usual; she wasn't fidgeting or twitching or looking like she wanted to bolt.

'Where did you meet a police officer?' LaVonda made a big deal of shrugging off her coat to cover the fact that this information had her rattled. It seemed a bit too close to home in light of what she'd done, and the new career she was (idly) contemplating, to have an officer of the law dating a member of her family.

'At work, of all places. She was one of the officers rostered on to guard a patient, and we got talking. She's great. Newly out, married for ten years before that, and has two kids. It's early days, but this one might be a keeper.'

'That's great news.' Ann smiled, but LaVonda thought she looked a little uneasy, and probably with good reason given how often their sister fell in and out of love. Hopefully, Tracy was a good match, and this relationship would work out.

LaVonda picked up her bag, and the three women joined the crowd, making their way into the dark hall. Maxine stood back to let a woman pass in front of her as Ann asked, 'So, why was she guarding someone? Did you have a dangerous criminal admitted?'

'It's a funny story actually,' Maxine said, striding confidently into the hall. 'We had a guy brought in, unconscious, and the first night he was there, someone tried to kill him.'

'Really? Bloody balls, Maxie! That doesn't sound funny, it sounds dangerous.' The sisters reached the far wall and set down their bags. LaVonda straightened up as Maxine laughed.

'No, not at all. The would-be-assassin cut his IV line, which kills people in movies, but doesn't work in real life. The idiot also cut his catheter line too, so obviously they didn't have a clue what they were doing. Anyway, the guy was under police guard until this morning, when he was finally released from hospital, so it was lucky I made my move on Tracy when I did, otherwise I might not have seen her again.'

'That *was* lucky.'

Ann and Maxine's voices faded away into the dark, as freezing cold water dripped down LaVonda's back. Her veins turned to ice. Frank wasn't dead. *He wasn't dead.*

The heavy beat started thudding through the room, and as people began to move around her, LaVonda stood stock still. She hadn't killed Frank after all, and now he'd been released from hospital, and he'd know. He'd know full well who had tried to murder him, twice, and failed.

The pounding beat turned menacing. The dancers became sinister slow-moving zombies, lurching towards her. Her throat closed up. Frank was in here somewhere in this black room with her. She couldn't see him, but he had followed her inside. He was one of the shadowy people moving around her, and any minute he would reach out and seize her. LaVonda's heart threatened to pound its way out of her chest. Her breath was coming in short, panicky gasps. Oh god. She had to get out of here. He was going to *kill* her.

Blindly, she stumbled towards the exit, pushing her way through the dancers, expecting to feel his hands on her any second, his hot breath on her face. Someone moved in front of her, waving their arms, engaging her. She ducked and twisted to her left. Another person materialised, turning towards her. LaVonda gasped as the person twisted and spun away. She was nearly at the exit; just a few more steps...

Once outside, she ran to her car, glancing back in terror as she wrenched open the door. He wasn't behind her, and she felt momentary relief that he wasn't hunched inside her car, waiting for her. But he was out there somewhere.

*He's not dead. He's not dead.* The refrain beat like a drum in her head the whole way home. She felt foggy and unfocussed; her mind unbalanced by the shocking news. Just one thing stood out clearly. This was a life-or-death situation, and one of them was going to die. Frank. Or LaVonda. She had to make sure it wasn't her.

Oh god. Emmett. Em was at home with Jasper, who would be worse than useless in a dangerous situation. What if Frank was at her house right now? LaVonda pressed her foot down harder on the accelerator. She had to get there before he did. She had to protect her daughter.

The house was empty, and the gun was gone.

LaVonda flung open her pantry doors, scanning the shelves frantically. What had she done with it? She still had the little Derringer, now tucked inside the pocket of her jacket, but the big black gun had disappeared.

Had she left it at the water plant? No, she distinctly remembered placing it back in her handbag, so she must have brought it home. But where on earth had she put it?

LaVonda yanked open her kitchen drawers, although why she thought she would have placed a loaded gun inside her cutlery drawer was a complete mystery. It wasn't under the sink, or in any of the cupboards. She hadn't stored it in the laundry or behind the vacuum cleaner. The gun was nowhere to be found.

Her breathing was ragged, and her mind whirled. She'd already checked her bedroom drawers and her wardrobe, twice, and she couldn't think where else it might be. She forced herself to stop and think. She'd been holding the gun the night she'd tried to kill Frank...

The couch! LaVonda charged back into the living room and dug her hand deep into the side. Her fingers touched cold metal, and she drew out the gun just as someone knocked on her back door. She yelped in fright. Holding the gun, she stumbled back into the kitchen. Through the glass on the door, she could see a shadowy figure. It must be him. LaVonda felt faint, but she managed to pull herself together. Gun in hand, she approached the door.

'Who is it?'

'LaVonda? It is me, Doreen.'

Oh, good grief. LaVonda pulled the door open, tucking the gun behind her at the same time.

'What is it?' She didn't have time for Doreen's nonsense. Not when her *life* was at stake.

Doreen looked slightly fretful, but this was her default look, wasn't it? Enquiringly concerned. An ill-concealed cover for sheer nosiness.

'I thought you should know, LaVonda, I saw a strange man here earlier today. He was wandering around in your front garden. Now, normally, I wouldn't have even noticed, but I just *happened* to be looking out of my window, and I thought to myself, *Good heavens, that doesn't look like Dave Robinette.* So, naturally, I thought I should let you know. Just in case. Because you can't be too careful now, LaVonda; you being a single woman without male protection.'

LaVonda drew in her breath sharply. A strange man. Oh lord. She steeled herself, the comforting weight of the gun heavy in her hand. She managed a reassuring smile at her neighbour.

'Thank you for letting me know, Doreen. There's the phone; I must go.'

She shut the door and hurried back into the living room, snatching her phone out of her handbag. She didn't recognise the number. Maybe it was Frank, trying to track her down. She took a deep breath, which did absolutely nothing to calm her, and held the phone cautiously up to her ear.

'Hello?'

'Hey, it's me.'

Me? Who on earth was *me*? It wasn't Frank, but she didn't recognise the male voice.

'Who is this?' She didn't have time for this nonsense. She looked at the gun in her hand. Black, heavy, and dangerous, it was the only thing standing between her and certain death.

'Me. Jasper. I'm at the hospital with Em.'

Emmett was at the hospital? Oh no. She was too late. Blood roared in LaVonda's ears as she sank to her knees on the carpet, squeezing her eyes shut. She couldn't bear it if anything had happened to Emmett. She simply wouldn't be able to go on.

'Tell me. No, don't tell me. Oh god, I can't bear it. Is she alright? Jasper?' Her voice dropped to a whisper.

'So, she went into early labour. Like, the baby was coming, but now it's okay. But, you know, it might be soon.'

'I'm on my way.' LaVonda dropped the big gun onto the couch, stood up, and flung her phone into her handbag. The smaller gun in her pocket clunked painfully against her hip as she raced towards the door. She pulled it open, revealing Ann and Maxine on the doorstep, matching frowns on their faces. Ann's hand was raised to knock.

'Emmett's gone into labour.' She didn't have time to stop and explain. She had to get to her daughter.

'I'm coming with you.' Ann spoke immediately.

'I'll come too.' Maxine's voice was decisive, but Ann reached out and put her hand on her sister's arm.

'No, you stay here and find Emmett's birthing kit. If she's in labour, she'll want her things. As soon as we get to the hospital, I'll let you know what is happening.'

Part of LaVonda's brain registered gratitude that Ann was taking charge, but her main focus was her daughter. How would she cope if anything happened to Emmett? She just couldn't.

'Come on.' Ann yanked her towards her own car.

The sisters barely spoke the whole way to the hospital. LaVonda concentrated every fibre of her being on her daughter. It was like Dad's death all over again, and LaVonda had to focus furiously on keeping death at bay. Back then, it hadn't worked. Now, it simply *had* to.

The hospital loomed, brightly lit and busy, in front of them. Ann dropped LaVonda off at the entrance and went to park the car. LaVonda's legs were shaky as she made her way to the front reception. The woman behind the counter was pleasant but distracted. She checked her computer, then directed LaVonda to the sixth floor where another receptionist pointed her to Emmett's room. She stumbled through the door, her heart in her throat.

'Mum! You didn't need to come. I'm fine.' Emmett didn't look fine at all. She looked tired, and her skin was grey against the white of her hospital gown. Her hair tumbled over her shoulders, and her eyes were red rimmed from crying. Jasper was slumped in a chair next to her. LaVonda ignored him and sat down on the bed, reaching for her daughter's hand.

'What happened?'

'I started getting pains on and off all afternoon, and by dinnertime, they were getting worse. Jasper brought me in, and they told me I was in early labour. Mum, Peanut is only seven months along.' She looked fearful, tears welling in her eyes. LaVonda summoned all her strength and smiled reassuringly at her daughter.

'You'll be fine, darling. Peanut will be fine too. You're in the best place, and you don't need to worry. If you do go into labour, the baby has an excellent chance at survival.' She didn't know this for a fact, but surely it was true.

Emmett smiled weakly. 'That is what the doctor said. Oh, Mum, I can't bear it if anything happens to the baby. I'll just die.'

*No, you won't*, thought LaVonda. *You'll want to; you'll feel like you will, but you won't die. You'll keep going, just like I did.* She didn't say any of this to her daughter. Emmett swivelled her head towards the door.

'Ann, what are you doing here?'

LaVonda turned to see her sister bustling into the room.

'Saving you from your mother. How are you feeling, sweetheart?'

'Better. They're looking after me well. Peanut is being monitored and they've got me on drugs to suppress the labour. It will still happen soon, but we're going to try and keep our little one inside for as long as we can.' She stroked her belly. 'Aren't we, Peanut?'

'Do you need anything?' LaVonda felt a sudden urge to tuck her lovely, dishevelled Emmett into her pocket and take her home. She wanted more than anything in the world to keep her daughter safe and protect her from all the pain and anguish she was facing. But she couldn't do that, any more than she could stop her living the life she wanted. Emmett was a grown woman, and although LaVonda would always be there for her, she had to let her daughter live her own life and experience her own joy and her own pain. She had to accept that she simply couldn't control this.

'I just need some rest. Jaz will call if anything happens. Don't worry, Mum. Okay?'

'I won't.' But, of course, she would.

'Come on, Von.' Ann leaned past LaVonda and kissed her niece's forehead. 'Let's let this mum-to-be get some rest.'

LaVonda allowed Ann to lead her back to the car. She climbed into the passenger seat, leaned back against the headrest, and closed her eyes. She didn't want to leave, but Ann was right. Emmett needed her rest, especially if she was going to go into labour in the next few days.

Her eyes popped open. *Max.* They'd left Maxine alone at the house, and Frank was out there somewhere, on the loose, and coming for her. He could be at her house right now!

Fumbling with her phone, LaVonda called her sister. There was no answer. Fear drenched her body, and she started to shake. She pressed down on the call button again. The phone rang and rang. Then, just as she was about to hang up and call the police, Maxine answered. Her voice was flat.

'Von. You'd better get back here. Right now.' Max hung up.

LaVonda stared at her phone in horror. A moan escaped her throat.

'What is it?' Ann kept her eyes on the road, but her voice trembled. 'What? Von?'

'Max. She's... in danger.'

'What?'

'Just drive, *please*. We need to get back.'

Ann sped up.

'What sort of danger? Von, what is going on?'

LaVonda shook her head. She couldn't speak. Fear and tension wove knots into her neck and shoulders. Her head pounded and her jaw ached with stress. What was happening back at the house? Was Frank there? Was he holding Maxine hostage? She reached into her pocket, her fingers touching the Derringer, but it failed to bring her any comfort. What good would that stupid little gun be in this situation? She'd need to get far too close to Frank to shoot him. Perhaps she could throw herself at him and tackle him to the floor?

When they pulled into the driveway, LaVonda was out of the car before her sister could bring it to a complete stop. She raced towards the front door, Ann hurrying behind her. LaVonda wrenched open the door, then stopped short.

'What are you doing?' Ann stepped around her and then saw what had made LaVonda stop. Maxine was holding a gun and pointing it straight at them.

'Max.' LaVonda wanted to scream, rush over, and snatch the gun out of Maxine's hand, but she forced herself to keep still. If her sister was startled, she might accidentally squeeze on the trigger.

Maxine was staring down at the gun, a look of anguish on her face, as if she couldn't quite believe what she was holding. Ann looked warily from the gun to LaVonda and slowly stretched out her hand. She spoke softly but firmly.

'Put the gun down, Maxie.'

To LaVonda's enormous relief, Maxine obeyed, setting the gun gingerly down on the couch. All three of them stared at it as though they were in a trance. Maxine recovered first.

'LaVonda. Crystalline. Robinette. Why the *fuck* do you have a gun on your couch? What the hell is going on?'

LaVonda looked from her youngest sister to her oldest sister and back again. She couldn't possibly tell them. She had to get them out of the house. Quickly. Before Frank arrived. He could be here any minute.

'You have to leave. Now. I can't tell you why; you just have to trust me.'

Ann snorted. 'We're not going anywhere until you tell us what is going on. I mean it, Von. Whatever it is, we have a right to know.'

Maxine narrowed her eyes at LaVonda and nodded. 'Stop fucking around, Von, and tell us what the hell is going on with you.'

Again, LaVonda looked from one sister to the other. Both chins jutted out, both foreheads held matching scowls.

Fine. They were all in danger here anyway. She might as well give them the full story, then perhaps they could help her when Frank arrived.

'Alright. I'll tell you everything. You'd better sit down though.'

Ann took a seat on the end of the couch, well away from the gun. LaVonda sank into a chair. Maxine stayed standing.

'Max. Please sit down.'

'Not until you tell us what the hell is going on. Why do you have that thing?' She folded her arms across her chest and fixed LaVonda with a furious stare. Oh dear. This was not going to be easy. LaVonda reached into her pocket and pulled out the Derringer, setting it on the coffee table. Maxine took a step back and threw her arms in the air.

'Are you kidding me? Do you have a whole arsenal of weapons in here? A machine-gun behind the couch? A machete in the chimney? This is unbelievable!'

'Maxie.' Ann's voice was soft. 'Let her explain.'

'Okay, sure, because I'm dying to hear this. Why, Von? Why are you stockpiling weapons in your living room? Are you planning to kill someone?'

'I *have* killed someone. At least I tried to kill him. The man in the hospital you were telling us about earlier. I... I cut his IV line, after I shot him... because he murdered his wife.'

Both Ann's and Max's mouths had dropped open. They looked almost comical in their shock, and LaVonda wanted to laugh aloud. She could feel hysteria bubbling up. Hysteria that was threatening tears, giggles, and an overwhelming desire to scream.

Her sisters remained frozen for an endless minute. Ann recovered herself first.

'How do you know that? How do you even know him?'

LaVonda explained about the altercation in the bar and meeting Frank afterwards. She described her plan, getting the guns from their mother's house, and driving out to the dam. She told them how she had failed to kill Frank and then gone to the hospital to finish the job.

'I can't believe this. Is that why you were trying to get rid of me the other night? So, you could go and kill someone? Fuck. I need a drink.' Maxine strode out of the room, returning a minute later brandishing a champagne bottle and three glasses. Ann raised her eyebrows.

'It was all I could find. Keep going, Von. I believe we were up to the part where you tried to kill this guy again?'

LaVonda nodded and swallowed. 'Yes, I thought cutting his IV line would do the job. It works... in the movies.'

'Ha!' Maxine snorted as she popped the champagne cork. Ann held her hand up. 'Just let her finish.'

'Well, that is pretty much it. As far as I was aware, he was dead, so I left him there and came home.' LaVonda looked at her sisters, who stared back at her. Maxine had finally taken a seat and was chugging her champagne as though it were water.

'Why do you still have the guns?' Ann asked finally. Her voice was measured and calm.

Maxine spun to look at her. 'That's your question? Not *'What the hell were you thinking, Von?'* or *'What made you think you could kill someone?'* or *'What gives you the right to decide that someone deserves to die?'* She looked absolutely furious. 'Just, *'Why do you still have the guns?'* But yes, okay, why do you have them, Von? What are you planning to do?'

LaVonda lowered her voice as though Frank might be outside, listening in. 'He's going to come after me. Now that he's been released from hospital, it is only a matter of time before he tracks me down and comes to exact his revenge. You shouldn't be here. You're in danger while you're with me.'

Maxine shook her head. 'He's not coming after you, you stupid woman. He's in jail.'

'You said he'd been released!'

'Released from hospital into police custody. He was arrested while he was still in hospital for murdering his wife; there was an eyewitness. As soon as we released him, he was taken away in a paddy van. He's not going to come after you, Von; he suffered a severe concussion and has significant memory loss that he will probably never fully recover from. But even if he does remember what happened, he's going to be locked away for a very long time.'

LaVonda stared at her sister in disbelief. Frank had memory loss. He wasn't coming for her. Ann reached out and topped off their glasses.

'Right. Well, a toast would probably be out of the question in the interests of good taste, but I think we can safely put that one behind us. Von, do you want to tell her the rest?'

LaVonda did not want to tell either of them anything else, but her relief was almost palpable, and she did owe them the truth. Reluctant at first, she filled Maxine in about Royce's accident, and then told both Ann and Maxine about Maude and her attempt on Dave's life. It felt almost liberating to talk about it, and although she wasn't exactly *glad* she'd shared all of her terrible secrets, it was a relief to get them off her chest.

'You tried to kill Dave?' Maxine spluttered. It was probably the first time in twenty years that she hadn't referred to him as Dull Dave. That, in itself, was quite disconcerting.

'I didn't though. He's still very much alive. And at that point, I decided that I would only kill people who weren't directly related to us.'

'What a fucking relief.' Maxine's voice dripped with sarcasm. Clearly, she wasn't taking this very well. Ann, on the other hand, was being disturbingly calm considering a lot of this was news to her too. She was quietly sipping her drink and staring at the gun next to her on the couch. LaVonda glanced at her quizzically, then turned back to Maxine.

'No, I mean, I know Dave doesn't deserve to die. I thought if I was going to kill anyone in the future, it would only be terrible people. People like Walter Durbin.' She said it deliberately, hoping her sister might understand. Because surely if anyone would want that man dead, it was Maxine.

Maxine scowled. 'You planned to kill Durbin? For me?'

'Well, yes, but I was too late. He's already dead. He had a stroke a few years ago.'

'No, he didn't.'

LaVonda and Maxine spun around to look at Ann, who was sitting motionless, not taking her gaze off the gun. Her cheeks were flushed, and she had the strangest expression on her face. Sort of an anguished fury. She clearly wasn't coping well with LaVonda's revelation either. LaVonda reached forward and placed her hand on Ann's knee, in what she hoped was a comforting way. Poor Ann. She was obviously in denial. She spoke quietly, but firmly, to her sister.

'He did, Ann. He's dead. I spoke to the dental practice he used to work at.'

Ann shook her head.

'Oh, he's dead alright, but he didn't have a stroke. He died of a drug overdose. I know, because I was there. I killed the bastard.'

# NINETEEN

LaVonda was stunned. This wasn't possible. Ann? She stared open-mouthed at her sister. Ann refused to look at either of them. She kept her gaze firmly fixed on the gun.

'Obviously, I wasn't ever going to tell you, but now, well what the hell? Since we're doing true confessions, you might as well know the truth about me.'

LaVonda shook her head. Her mind felt fuzzy and slow. Ann was confessing to murder. But why would she tell them she'd killed Walter Durbin, when she couldn't possibly have done that?

'Ann, what are you talking about? Are you making a joke?'

'No. It's not a joke. About ten years ago, one of my colleagues was the prosecutor in a rape case that involved that... that man. Durbin was accused of raping a sixteen-year-old. Anyway, the defence argued that the victim had been drunk and therefore confused, and Durbin was acquitted. My colleague told me that there had been several other accusations of rape against him, but none of those women would come forward. After the trial, the victim tried to kill herself.'

'Jesus.'

'I know. I kept thinking of you, Maxie, and what you'd gone through, and how badly we handled it back then.'

Maxine looked ill. LaVonda was in turmoil; her mind was spinning. She reached out to her older sister.

'Ann, we were all young, and we didn't know any better. It didn't occur to any of us that he could hurt someone else.'

'Well, it occurred to me then. The bastard had gotten away with it, and god knows how many times. I decided to put a stop to it.'

Maxine got to her feet and ran her hands through her hair. 'I cannot believe this. Both my older sisters are murderers?'

'Well, technically I'm not–'

'You!' Maxine spun around and stabbed her finger towards LaVonda. 'You have spent the past few months running around trying your level best to kill any number of people. And you!' The finger stabbed towards Ann. 'You actually went out and murdered someone. And never said a word.'

All three women fell silent and stared at each other in turn. Moments passed. The tension rose.

'I'm dating a cop,' Maxine said softly. 'How am I supposed to introduce her to my family now? You think your family is fucked up, Tracy? Try being related to a couple of middle-aged wannabe assassins.'

Ann's face broke into a grin at the same time LaVonda let out a snort. Maxine put her hands on her hips as the other two started laughing uncontrollably.

'It's not funny!'

'I know, I know!' LaVonda tried to say between gasps. Ann doubled over. 'Oooh, stop, I'm going to wet my pants!'

'Stop laughing. Both of you. I mean it. Oh, for Christ's sake!'

LaVonda and Ann clutched at one another, tears of mirth streaming down their cheeks. The harder LaVonda tried to stop, the funnier the situation seemed. She couldn't stop.

'Bloody balls.' Ann straightened and grabbed her crotch. 'I've wet myself.'

'Oh, Ann, you haven't.' LaVonda let out another snort.

'I bloody have.'

'Never mind, it's Dave's lounge now. Feel free to pee on it all you like.'

'Shut up!' Maxine's voice rose to a yell. She looked utterly furious, and her expression was enough to make both LaVonda and Ann instantly sober.

'I don't know why you're both finding this so amusing. You do realise that not only have you committed the worst possible crime, but you've made me an accessory to murder? So perhaps you could stop treating this like a giant fucking joke.'

She snatched up her bag and stormed out of the house, slamming the door behind her.

LaVonda and Ann looked guiltily at each other.

'She's right, you know, Von. I've made you both accessories to murder.'

'Yes, but in light of my recent activities, that seems pretty minor.' LaVonda drank the last of her champagne. It tasted sour.

'Trust me, it's not minor; it is actually very serious. Do you think we should go after her?'

'No, leave her to cool off.'

Ann looked worried. 'What if she goes to the police?'

'Ann, she won't. Not without talking to us first. Did you really kill Durbin?'

'Yes, I did. I'm not particularly proud of doing it but, Von, I'm not sorry either. Sometimes the legal system simply doesn't deliver justice. So, I did.'

'Believe it or not, I understand. Tell me, what happened?'

Ann reached forward and picked up her glass. She brought it to her lips, draining the contents, then looked directly at LaVonda.

'Are you sure you want to hear this?'

'Yes.'

'Okay. It was about a year after the boys were born, shortly after I'd gone back to work. My bloody emotions were all over the place, and when I found out that young Henry Whiu had tried to prosecute Durbin on a rape case, and he'd been acquitted... Von, I flew into an absolute rage.'

LaVonda leaned forward and looked directly into her sister's eyes. 'I know. I know that feeling.'

Ann nodded. 'And I thought about Maxie; how she was so young when that happened, and how maybe if we'd said something then, Durbin might have been punished. But we kept quiet, and god knows how many other people, children, he'd gone on to rape and then... then I reached a new level of rage.' She paused. 'It's weird but being that utterly furious actually calmed me and helped focus my brain. I knew what I wanted to do, and once my mind was made up, I was absolutely determined.'

LaVonda understood. It was the same feeling she'd had when she'd found out what Frank had done. A feeling that, no matter what, this was something she needed to do. She nodded encouragingly.

Ann took a deep breath. 'Okay, well, I did some investigating and found out where he was and that he'd been fired from his job for drinking. I tracked down his address, told Sam I had a work conference, and drove interstate to his house.'

'And you gave him an overdose? Ann, how? Where did you get the drugs from?'

'That was actually the easy part. Between my job as a public prosecutor and Sam's job as a crisis counsellor, we probably know every single heroin dealer in town.'

'Does Sam know about this?'

'No, of course not. Bloody balls, Von. I'm worried about Maxie. Should we just try to contact her? What if she tells Sam?'

'She won't do that. We'll call her in a minute. Just tell me how you managed to do it.' LaVonda was intrigued, fascinated, appalled, and slightly in awe of her sister's confession. It was so unexpected.

Ann exhaled. 'I got to his place about four in the afternoon. The curtains were all closed, and the place looked deserted. I tell you, Von, I was so scared, I was about to throw up. I very nearly left. But I thought of Max, and how I'd already let her down once, and so I knocked on the door.'

LaVonda shook her head. 'Good grief, Ann. That was so dangerous.'

'Oh, really? More dangerous than taking a homicidal maniac out to the dam and trying to get him to kill himself? Because, frankly, that is the stupidest murder plan I've ever heard of. What did you think would happen?'

'I don't know, I guess... look, it works in the movies.'

Ann rolled her eyes. 'Maxie is right; for a smart woman, you can be incredibly stupid sometimes. Those things are scripted, you know? Real life doesn't work like it does in the movies.'

LaVonda smiled despite herself. 'I know that, I do know that, and you're right. It was a ridiculous plan, but at the time, it seemed quite clever and fail proof. I didn't think... anyway, we're talking about your murder, not mine. What happened then?'

'I knocked, and after a few minutes, the door opened, and he was standing in the doorway.'

LaVonda held her breath, picturing the moment. Ann, coming face to face with Walter Durbin. She must have been terrified. If only she'd told LaVonda what she was doing. She'd have gone with her; helped her commit the crime.

Would she, though? Ten years ago, LaVonda wouldn't have *contemplated* the idea of killing someone, would she? Not back then. Now, though...

Ann was still speaking.

'He looked older, smaller, and less monstrous. But it was him. He leered at me. I told him I was the daughter of an old friend and was passing by, so I thought I would look him up. Then I held up the bottle of whiskey I'd brought, and his eyes lit up. That was my ticket in the door.'

Ann paused and picked up the bottle. She shook it, realised it was empty, and put it back down again. LaVonda shook her head.

'Sorry. There is still some vodka in the freezer.'

'No, never mind. Anyway, I went inside and waited while he drank the whiskey. He kept making suggestive remarks, but it was easy to ignore them because he was drunk and slow. Then it was just a matter of waiting until he was so drunk that he wouldn't resist. I had a syringe, I found a vein, I laid him out on the couch, and I left.'

'He died.'

'Yes, he did. His funeral notice was in the paper the following week. I'd do it again, even though I have to live with the guilt of taking a man's life.' She paused. 'Von, I don't regret killing him. I don't.'

LaVonda nodded. Ann took a deep breath and looked down at her feet.

'I couldn't turn myself in, because the twins and Sam needed me. You understand, don't you? I couldn't confess. But I needed to be punished for murdering a human being. Von, I found a way.' Her voice dropped almost to a whisper. 'I found another way to punish myself.'

She lifted her amputated arm slightly.

It took LaVonda a moment to realise what she meant. When she did, she was horrified.

'Ann! You stopped using your prosthetic arm... because of Durbin?'

Ann nodded. 'I loved that thing. It helped me live normally. But afterwards, after I'd killed him, I felt like I needed to suffer myself. This is my penance; living without my super-arm, but at least I didn't have to go to jail. Although now...' She looked towards the front door where Maxine had exited a few minutes before.

'She won't tell anyone.' LaVonda tried to inject a note of optimism into her reassurance to her sister.

'You don't know that.'

It was true. LaVonda didn't know what Maxine would do. She knew she would protect Ann's secret, and she understood why Ann had done what she'd done. But Maxine obviously felt differently.

'She's not answering.' Ann put down her phone and turned her face to LaVonda.

'Try not to get upset. We'll get hold of her, and I promise you I will convince her not to say anything.'

After Ann had left, LaVonda continued to try to reach Maxine, who steadfastly ignored the calls and messages. It wasn't until after LaVonda had fallen into an uneasy sleep that her phone beeped a message. She snatched it up, blinking as she tried to focus. The message was brief. *Meet me at Hogan's pub at midday on Saturday.*

LaVonda immediately sent a reply. *'Are you okay? Can you please call me? We're worried about you.'* She waited ten minutes. No reply.

So that was that. LaVonda and Ann would have to wait four more days to find out what was going on and whether or not Maxine was going to turn them in.

Somehow, LaVonda managed to get through the next few days. Focussing on winding everything up at work helped, and when she wasn't at work, she was at the hospital visiting Emmett and reassuring her. Every day the baby stayed in utero increased its chances of survival, and every day, Emmett seemed a little brighter and more positive.

'At this rate, I might go full-term,' She chirped as LaVonda unpacked fresh fruit and juices from the bag she'd brought. LaVonda thought it was unlikely that the pregnancy would continue for much longer, but she nodded reassuringly at her daughter, who was shifting around on her bed, trying to get comfortable. LaVonda picked up a pillow and helped place it behind Emmett's back.

'Thanks. This bed is so uncomfortable. I can't wait until I can go home and sleep on my own mattress.' She rubbed her bump thoughtfully. 'Actually, I can. I'll put up with all of this to keep Peanut in me a bit longer.'

LaVonda smiled and pulled a chair up to the side of the bed. There was a clump of matted hair just under Emmett's ponytail, and LaVonda longed to attack it with a comb. She could almost feel the knot untangling under her fingers. Reluctantly, she looked away.

'How is Jasper going?' She was surprised to find she actually did care how he was. It must be hard on him too, worrying about his partner and child.

'He's fine. When he knew you were coming, he decided to go and have a smoke and give us some time together. Mum, I know you don't like him, but he is a wonderful, loving man. He does get these obsessive ideas sometimes, but he's a good person and I love him. Did you know he's spent every night sleeping on the floor in here, so I don't have to be alone? The nurses told him to go and get some rest, but he refuses to leave me. One nurse took pity on him and gave him some blankets to lie on. So you see, he does love me, and I love him. He reminds me of Daddy Mark.'

Mark? How could Emmett remember Mark? She was so young when he died.

'I don't remember him, exactly.' Em answered LaVonda's unspoken question. 'More the way he made me feel. He was a big, warm, comforting feeling, that went away one day. I didn't think I'd get that again, but Jaz gives me that same warm feeling. The sensation of being loved, and adored, and taken care of. And he'll give our baby the same feeling.'

LaVonda felt tears prick at her eyes. She knew exactly what Emmett meant. Mark had wrapped them both up in his love and made everything feel safe and secure. Until he left.

She could feel her face getting hot and tight; too hot; too tight. Damn the timing of these things.

'Mum, are you alright?'

'Yes, fine. It's just a hot flush.' She hurried into Emmett's small bathroom to splash cold water onto her face. She'd recently started carrying a makeup bag so she could patch herself up after these incidents.

Emmett sat up higher in her bed and called out. 'Are you sure you're alright, Mum? You look like you're boiling.'

She was. It was one of the rare, but terrible flushes, just like her first one, the kind she still got from time to time. LaVonda pulled off her shirt and bra and used Emmett's facecloth to slop water onto her chest and the back of her neck. Slowly, she started to cool down.

She gazed at her reflection in the small mirror above the sink. If Jasper loved Em in the same way that Mark had loved her, then perhaps he wasn't that bad. Oh, not that he was in Mark's league, not at all. But perhaps it wasn't a complete mystery as to why her daughter loved him.

She heard a knock on Emmett's door, then someone talking, so she quickly pushed the bathroom door shut. She wiped her torso down with one of the towels, but her face still burned. She ran more cold water on Emmett's washcloth and used it to wipe her face and the back of her neck again. The heat was slowly subsiding. Quickly, she opened her makeup bag and took out her small comb, fixing her hair first. Then she dressed, before turning her attention to her face. She smoothed foundation over her skin, blending it in with her fingertips. A spiky hair poked out of her chin. Oh, the indignities of old age. As fast as she dispensed with one issue, another one cropped up. LaVonda took out her tweezers and dealt swiftly with the errant hair.

By the time she walked back into Emmett's room, her daughter was alone again, sitting up in bed, a look of concern on her face.

'You just missed Max. She came by to check on me, and I told her you were in the bathroom, but she got all awkward and said she had to leave. Mum, what's going on? Why are you and Max acting so weird?'

LaVonda smiled weakly. She couldn't possibly tell her daughter anything right now. Perhaps later, once the baby was born...

'Nothing. Well, nothing important. We... we had a little argument about...' About what, LaVonda? She cast around in desperation. '...about onions.'

Emmett laughed. 'Onions? Seriously? Oh Mum, who argues about onions?'

'It doesn't matter, it was just a silly argument that got blown out of proportion. You know what Max is like.'

'I know what you are both like. You're the two most stubborn, controlling people on the planet. You'd both benefit more than you could imagine from doing something like STER.'

'I'm not doing STER, not now, not ever. And for your information, Emmett Louise Robinette, I am *not* stubborn and controlling. I'm your mother, and I care a lot, that's all.'

'You care about onions.' Emmett's face broke into a grin, and LaVonda rolled her eyes. 'Look, Mum, just make up with Maxine, please. You're about to be a grandmother, and she's about to become a great-aunt, and I'd like to bring this baby into a family where people aren't fighting each other over onions. Is that too much to ask?'

'Actually, I'm having lunch with her and Ann tomorrow, so we'll sort everything out then. Don't worry. Just concentrate on keeping Peanut safe, and I'll visit you in the afternoon.'

LaVonda was the first to arrive at the pub when it opened, so she was able to grab the rare coveted seating right in front of the open fire. She dumped her bag on one chair and her jacket on another, and took the third for herself, pulling it closer to the warmth of the flames.

The heat soaked into her skin, warming her down to her bones. How lovely it would be to curl up here with a good book and maybe even doze off. But there was no time for daydreaming. It was critical that she and Ann convince Maxine to keep their secrets.

Her phone beeped. LaVonda glanced down at it. A Tinder notification. Glancing around quickly, she opened the application. Dave's father had swiped right on her profile; they were a match. He'd sent her a message, but she didn't have time to look at it right now. Brian would have to wait.

Ann arrived a few minutes later, her face breaking into a weak smile at the sight of the fire. She shivered as she removed her coat, placing it carefully on the back of her chair, then leaned forward towards the flames.

'Isn't this gorgeous? I wish I could enjoy it, but I'm so nervous. Do you think Maxie will agree to forgive us?'

LaVonda nodded decisively, even though she was far from confident. 'Yes, don't worry. You've said yourself; she burns fast and furious. She'll have calmed down by now and, look, she loves us as much as we love her; she's not going to turn us in.'

Ann still looked worried. 'I hope you're right. Anyway, we can only try. Do you want a drink?'

'I'll get it, you stay here and thaw out. What would you like?' LaVonda rummaged around in her bag for her wallet.

'Just a Coke or something; I want to keep my head clear for this.'

As she stood up, LaVonda saw Maxine's white-blonde head coming through the pub entrance. She looked tall and imposing in her long black coat and high boots; her mouth outlined in bold red lipstick. She looked armed for battle. The second thing LaVonda noticed was that she was holding hands with a slightly shorter woman who was similarly clad in black. Before LaVonda could warn Ann, Maxine spotted her and headed towards them, tugging the woman behind her.

'Ann, Von, this is Tracy. I asked her to join us for lunch.'

LaVonda felt her chest constrict. What was Maxine playing at? Had she brought her policewoman girlfriend to arrest them? Were they supposed to confess? She glanced at Ann, who looked ill but had gotten to her feet to greet Tracy.

'It's nice to meet you.'

Tracy looked mildly disconcerted and awkward, as everyone did when they first shook hands with Ann, who was holding out her left hand. Maxine should have warned her, but clearly Ann's disability wasn't foremost in her sister's mind.

'Nice to meet you too. And Von, is it?'

'LaVonda.' She might be arrested by this woman before the end of lunch, but only her sisters were allowed to call her Von. Nobody else.

'Take a seat, Trace.' Maxine motioned to the free chair as LaVonda hurried to remove her coat from it. 'I'll get us drinks. Wine for everyone?'

Ann nodded as Tracy sat down in the chair and beamed at them. LaVonda hadn't been planning to drink either, but now she couldn't wait for the soothing effects of a large glass of wine. She tried to catch Ann's eye to smile reassuringly, but Ann was staring into the fire, seemingly mesmerised by the flames.

Tracy didn't seem to notice their discomfort. She grinned widely and leaned back in her chair.

'What a great place. Maxine told me this pub had a fireplace; good on you for grabbing the best seats in the house. Is there another chair we can steal?' She looked around, then got up and went over to a man sitting nearby who was resting his briefcase on the chair next to him. Tracy picked it up and placed it on the ground. 'Are you using this? No? Excellent, thanks.'

She seemed particularly self-assured, but then again, why wouldn't she be? She was a police officer, used to dealing with the very worst of humanity, so of course she wouldn't balk at being assertive. If LaVonda had gone over and asked for a chair, the man would have probably ignored her.

Tracy plonked herself back down, rubbing her hands towards the fire.

'Maxine tells me you're a lawyer, Ann, and Von, sorry LaVonda, you work for the government?'

'I did, I mean, I recently resigned though, so I'm not sure what I'll do next.' It probably depended, in no small part, on the outcome of this afternoon. If Maxine was planning to tell Tracy what her sisters had done, then LaVonda's next few years were definitely spoken for.

'You could think about joining the police force! I've only been in for a few years, but I absolutely love it. Sure, the paperwork and some of the beat work can get a bit boring, but you can't underestimate the satisfaction that comes from seeing justice served.'

Ann snapped out of her trance. 'Is that why you're here?' Her face had turned from pale to blotchy red, and her breathing was rapid.

Tracy reeled back. 'I don't know what you mean. Maxine invited me to lunch to meet you both. She talks about you all the time, and she told me she thought it might be a good time for us to get together.'

'I bet she did,' Ann muttered and went back to staring at the fire. LaVonda looked over at the bar. What on earth was taking Maxine so long?

Tracy had obviously written Ann off, because she turned her chair slightly away and towards LaVonda. She smiled in a hopeful way.

'I understand you have a grandchild on the way. You don't look old enough! You must be so excited.'

'I am.' *And I'd like to be around to see her grow up.* She forced a strained smile at Tracy. She might as well be nice to the woman who held her future in her hands.

Maxine arrived back at their little group, carrying an ice bucket holding a bottle of wine and four glasses. 'I've ordered wedges, chicken skewers, and pork buns. That should keep us going for a while.' She placed the glasses down on the table and started filling them. Tracy shook her head.

'Not for me thanks; I'm on duty in a couple of hours. I was just telling LaVonda that she should consider a career in policing.'

Maxine smirked. 'I don't think that would suit you at all, would it, Von? Being a police officer? I find it fascinating though. Babe, tell them about that couple you arrested for embezzlement.'

Tracy laughed. 'Oh yes, that was so funny. This dear little old couple in their eighties. Honestly, to look at them you'd think they'd never even had so much as a parking ticket, and yet there they were, embezzling thousands from the charity where they were both volunteers. I tell you; it was one of the best moments of my career when I got to put them away.'

LaVonda caught Ann's eye; she looked as aghast as LaVonda felt. A couple in their eighties going to prison, and Tracy took pleasure in that?

Tracy must have noticed their exchange, because she immediately became defensive. 'Look, I'm not saying it's ideal to lock up octogenarians, but this couple had been deceiving the charity for years. I don't care how sweet and lovely you are or what your motivation is; 'do the crime, pay the time' is my motto.'

LaVonda's stomach churned.

A waiter brought their food over and placed it on the small table. The smell of the satay chicken would have normally had LaVonda practically drooling, but right now, she thought she might choke if she tried to eat. She took a plate and loaded one skewer and four wedges on to it. Perhaps Maxine and Tracy wouldn't notice if she just pushed the food around on her plate. Across from her, Ann steadfastly ignored the food and picked up her wine. Her hand trembled as she brought the glass to her lips.

Suddenly, LaVonda felt angry. What was Maxine playing at? She put down her plate and glared at her younger sister.

'Max, can I see you for a moment?' Without waiting for a reply, she stalked off towards the toilets. To her great relief, when she turned to check, Maxine had followed her.

LaVonda glanced around the toilets; all the stalls were empty. She turned faced Maxine.

'Just what are you doing? Are you trying to torture Ann and me? Because this isn't funny, Max. Ann is literally shaking out there, and I'm on the verge of throwing up. Turn us in to your girlfriend if that is your plan, but don't play with us like a cat toying with mice.'

Maxine turned and looked at herself in the mirror. She ran her fingers through her hair, then dropped her hands to the sink.

'I'm not going to turn you in. I just wanted you to see what you've done. Awkward, isn't it? I'm an accessory to murder now, thanks to you two, and every time Tracy and I are together, all I can think is that if she knew, she'd arrest me. If I don't say anything, then my choices are to be in a relationship where one of us is keeping a huge secret from the other or to break up with her. It isn't fair that you two put me in this situation, and I thought you should realise the impact it has had on me. If I keep Ann's secret, and yours, then I have to end this thing with Tracy, and I really like her.'

'I'm sorry, but Ann did what she did for you.'

'Who the hell asked her to? I certainly didn't want her to kill him. I didn't ask you to let our mother die either. She and Durbin were horrible, destructive people, but what the hell gives you or Ann the right to mete out justice?'

The toilet door banged open, and a woman came in, pausing when she saw the two of them.

She smiled hesitantly, then hurried into one of the cubicles, while LaVonda and Maxine stared at each other in silence. They heard a rustle of clothing, a snapping of elastic, and then a noisy stream into the bowl.

'Let's finish this conversation later.' Maxine turned to leave. LaVonda reached out and grabbed her arm.

'No. You need to reassure Ann that you're not going to say anything. She's in pieces.'

Maxine exhaled. 'Fine. Send her in. I'll tell her.'

LaVonda hurried out. Ann and Tracy were sitting by the fire in silence. Tracy was nibbling at a chicken skewer, while Ann stared into the flames.

'Ann, Maxine needs a quick word. How is the chicken, Tracy?'

Tracy smiled at her as Ann got up and headed towards the ladies.

'Terrific. Here, have one.' She picked up the plate and held it out. LaVonda picked up a stick and bit into the end.

'Mmmm. Lovely.' She couldn't taste a thing. Surely, Tracy must be able to read the guilt on her and Ann's faces. Despite Maxine's reassurance, LaVonda still half-expected Tracy to reach behind her, pull out a pair of handcuffs, and snap them onto

LaVonda's wrists. Would she try to handcuff Ann? LaVonda pictured Tracy putting one handcuff on her sister's left wrist and then stopping awkwardly as Ann held out her other arm.

LaVonda gave a short, involuntary snort. Tracy looked at her in surprise.

'Sorry, nothing. Have some more wedges.' LaVonda could feel hysteria building underneath, and she smothered another grin. She was going to burst out laughing, she just knew it. 'Will you, sorry... could you excuse me for a moment?'

She hurried back to the toilets.

Her mirth died immediately. Ann and Maxine were facing each other at the end of the room. The peeing woman had left, and the toilets were empty. Ann looked tiny and vulnerable as she stood opposite her much taller youngest sister, who was hissing at her.

'And just who made you God? What gives you the right to dole out justice? Who the hell are you to decide that Durbin had to die and then carry out the sentence all by yourself? And you!' She caught sight of LaVonda in the mirror and wheeled around. 'Sheer goddamn incompetence is the only reason you can't call yourself a murderer.'

'I'm sorry. I feel horribly guilty,' Ann pleaded. 'It is, without a doubt, the worst thing I've ever done in my life. But I couldn't turn myself in, Maxie. I had two babies at home, a husband just starting a new job, people depending on me. They still depend on me, and if you send me to jail, you'll destroy my family.'

'I'm not going to tell anyone. You have my word. But if either of you ever try anything like this again... are you listening to me, Von? If you ever do anything like this again, I will go straight to the police.'

'What about Tracy?' Ann's voice was quiet. Maxine turned back towards her.

'I'll give it a few weeks so she doesn't suspect this lunch had anything to do with it, then I will break things off.'

'Surely you don't have to–'

'I will break up with her.' Maxine's tone brooked no argument. 'I can't risk her finding out what you two have done.'

'What have they done?'

LaVonda spun around. Tracy was standing just inside the door, her arms folded across her chest, a scowl on her face. LaVonda's heart dropped like a stone. It was all over.

# TWENTY

'**A**re you going to answer me? What have they done to make you want to break up with me?'

LaVonda looked back at her sisters, who were wearing matching expressions of dismay. Maxine took a step forward. 'Babe–'

'Don't 'babe' me. Just tell me what is going on?' Tracy's voice was curt.

Maxine bit her lip and looked at LaVonda. Her eyes seemed to be pleading for help. LaVonda looked back in despair. What could they possibly say without Tracy arresting them all on the spot?

Tracy unfolded her arms and placed them squarely on her hips. LaVonda felt faint. Tracy looked furious.

'Ann's a kleptomaniac.' The words burst out of LaVonda's mouth, surprising her. Where on earth had that come from?

'What?' Tracy glared at LaVonda, who shrank back. Her voice trembled as she repeated herself.

'She's a kleptomaniac. She steals things.'

'Yes, I know what a kleptomaniac is.'

'She's getting help though. She sees a counsellor twice a week, and she's almost completely cured.' LaVonda was frantically building on her story. Out of the corner of her eye, she could see Ann slumped against the sink. *Don't give up*, she thought desperately. *Please don't give up.*

Tracy looked past LaVonda towards Maxine, who looked like she was about to crumble too. 'So, your sister is a klepto... sorry, *recovering* kleptomaniac, and that's why you want to break up?' Tracy almost spat the words out. 'What a load of crap. Tell me the truth, Maxine.'

Ann looked up; her face resigned. 'Tell her, Maxie. Just tell her the truth.'

No! LaVonda wanted to leap in front of her sisters and protect them. *Don't say anything, Max. Please.*

Maxine was pale, but she stood straight, her mouth set in a tight line. She shook her head slightly. Ann sighed and pushed herself up from the bench.

'I'm a murderer, Tracy.'

'So am I.' LaVonda jumped in before Ann could say anything else. 'We like to kill people for fun, and Maxine is worried that we might kill you, or that you might arrest us for murder. That's why she wants to break things off.'

Tracy's upper lip curled in a sneer. She jammed her hands into her pockets.

'Well, that's original. I haven't been back in the dating scene long, but a simple, 'I'm not that into you' would have sufficed, Maxine. You didn't need to stage an elaborate scene in a pub toilet using your sisters as props to get rid of me.'

'Trace–'

'No, forget it. I don't know what stupid game you're all playing at, pretending to be kleptomaniacs and murderers, but clearly you think my job is a joke. That I'm a joke. Well, you know what? I'm not interested in your opinions of me. I don't need this grief. You can all go to hell.'

Tracy banged the door of the toilets behind her. The three sisters stared pale-faced at each other.

'Ann, why?' LaVonda whispered. Tears formed in her eyes. 'Why did you say that?'

'I don't know. I'm just tired of lying and keeping secrets, I guess. Perhaps it would be better if I did confess.'

Maxine's hand thumped down on the sink top, making both Ann and LaVonda jump.

'No. There will be no more random confessions. What is done, is done. Durbin and Mum are dead, may they rest in torment, and there is nothing to be gained from turning yourselves in. You'll just have to learn to live with the guilt.'

LaVonda didn't feel guilty. She knew Ann felt guilty, but given the chance, LaVonda would have done the same thing to Walter Durbin. She'd wanted to kill him. She still did, and she couldn't understand why the thought had never crossed Maxine's mind. After all, she was the one who had suffered at Walter's hands.

'Max, aren't you glad he's dead? After what he did to you?'

Maxine turned her head and looked steadily at LaVonda.

'What do you think he did to me?'

Had she gone mad? They all knew what Walter Durbin had done. Thirteen-year-old Maxine had sobbed in their arms all night afterwards, although she'd refused to give them any details aside from telling them that she was no longer a virgin.

'Technically, he didn't rape me.' Maxine spoke so quietly they had to strain to hear her. LaVonda reeled back in surprise.

'Of course, he did. You were only a kid. You may not have fought him off or screamed for help, but that doesn't mean you consented.'

'I could have cried for help. I didn't want to.'

'But you couldn't have. He might have hurt you.' LaVonda blinked at Maxine.

'You don't get it, do you? I seduced *him*. I deliberately put on a little satin camisole and shorts. I was flirting because I wanted him to look at me, look at my legs and my new breasts and admire me. When he'd touched me? I liked it. I could have fought him off or cried for help if I'd wanted to. But I liked it. Okay? At the time, the things he did to me felt good. Afterwards, I felt ashamed and upset and creeped out, but at the time, I didn't try to stop him.'

LaVonda and Ann were stunned silent for a few seconds, then both burst out in protest.

'You were a kid!'

'You were thirteen. Who cares if you flirted with him or not?'

'He was the adult; he should have stopped it. It's not your fault!'

'It's not your fault!'

Maxine nodded and lit up a cigarette. Neither of her sisters tried to stop her. She inhaled deeply, then blew out the smoke in a long stream.

'I know that now. I didn't know that then. My point is, he didn't technically rape me. He didn't deserve to die.'

LaVonda shook her head. 'He did rape you, and as far as I'm concerned, he got exactly what was coming to him. You weren't the only one, and maybe if we'd spoken out back then, we might have saved other girls...'

This time, Ann shook her head. 'I doubt it. Mum wouldn't have believed us, and Dad would have told us to simply try and forget about it.'

Maxine nodded and took another drag on her cigarette as LaVonda cried out.

'No!'

Ann fixed her with a look. 'Von, Dad was a lovely man, but he was weak. He never stood up to Mum, and he wouldn't have supported us doing anything about Maxine's rape. You know that.'

She didn't know that at all. Dad had been a wonderful man, honourable and loving. He would have done anything for them. Anything... except leave their mother. LaVonda looked at her sisters in sudden anguish. He *had* been weak, hadn't he? Loving but weak. How had her sisters seen that side of him, when she hadn't? Why had she been so blind to her father's faults? She'd loved him so much; she still did, but Ann and Max were right. By refusing to leave Maude; by failing to protect his daughters, George had let them all down.

The toilet door opened, and two girls came in, stopping short when they saw the three women. One of them frowned.

'Oh, I don't think you're allowed to smoke in here.'

Maxine glared at her and inhaled deeply on her cigarette, blowing out the smoke defiantly. The girl who had spoken up looked at her sceptically.

'You'll set off the—'

She didn't get a chance to finish her sentence before the overhead sprinklers burst into life, soaking all of five of them.


Brian wasn't going to die. At least, not at LaVonda's hand. She sighed as she picked up a pair of tiny, pink cotton socks and added them to her shopping basket. She would have loved to do it, not only for the sake of Emmett's inheritance, but also because Brian was a horrible person, and it would have been most satisfying to send him to his eternal rest. But she'd promised Maxine. No more murders or, more accurately, attempted murders, so that was her chosen future down the drain. Reluctantly, she'd deleted her Tinder account so she wouldn't be tempted to follow through with her plan.

LaVonda picked up a six-packet of bibs and then replaced it on the pile. Peanut wouldn't be eating solids for months, in fact knowing Emmett, she'd probably breastfeed until the child was eight, so it was pointless buying bibs yet. She could get that little sheet set though. It would look adorable in the crib she'd ordered to be delivered this week. She didn't know whether or not Jasper's uncle Kelvin had finished the monstrosity he was making, but at least LaVonda's grandchild would have somewhere to sleep when it came home. Emmett and Jasper were planning to stay with her after the baby was born, until the little one was strong enough to leave hospital and travel home.

LaVonda looked longingly at the little baby dresses hanging on the rack in front of her. She would love to buy some of those, but she'd probably be wasting her money. Instead, she put more muslin wraps and cloth nappies into her basket before taking it up to the counter.

Shopping was a lot more fun than working, LaVonda decided, as she popped open the boot of her new car to add her purchases to the growing pile of things already bought. The insurance money from her car crash had finally come through, and LaVonda had treated herself to a bright red Renault. It was time to redefine herself in middle age, and the car was just the start. Besides, it was somewhat poetic for this time of her life given her regular hot red flushes.

She wasn't going to hide anymore. LaVonda Robinette had come out of her shell.

She had spent her last week at work cleaning out her emails and typing up notes for her replacement, who was starting at the end of the month. She'd felt no regrets about leaving; it was quite satisfying to close the door on this chapter of her life, and although she had no idea what the future might bring, she felt relaxed and positive for a change. Perhaps she was finally learning to 'go with the flow' as Emmett would say.

Still, it would be strange to wake up on Monday morning and not have to get ready for work. No more driving alongside idiots in the morning traffic, no more tedious strategy meetings or PowerPoint presentations. No more pretending to laugh at Colin's lame jokes or listening to Sylvia's endless chatter.

She would probably miss her colleagues a little bit. They weren't all that bad, and look, they'd put on a lovely farewell for her yesterday afternoon, complete with balloons, tinsel glitter, and a giant cake. Farewells were big at the Department of Environmental Services: Land, Waste, and Clean-up Division.

LaVonda drove out to her new townhouse and pulled into the driveway. A few more weeks, and she would own this place. Dave had deposited the house funds into her account on Friday, and next week, John would organise the payment to the vendors, and then that would be it. She would be the new owner. The deal had taken longer than she'd expected; there was a lot of paperwork, but Dave had been extremely accommodating about the probability of LaVonda needing a few more weeks.

'Take as long as you need,' he'd declared magnanimously. He'd come over early last week, on his own thankfully, to talk through the details of the purchase. LaVonda had grinned a wicked grin.

'Oh, well, in that case, perhaps I should wait to move out until after Christmas? Have one final Christmas dinner in my marital home? I mean, as long as you don't mind?'

Dave's face had fallen, and he'd cleared his throat nervously.

'Dave. I'm teasing you.'

Honestly. Why had she ever married him? The man had absolutely no sense of humour.

'You're sure you don't want to take any of the furniture? Not even the couch?'

Especially not the couch.

'I'm sure. You can have it all.'

She was looking forward to buying things for her new home. Filling it up using colours and textures, soft, oversized couches, and chunky wooden tables. LaVonda got out of the car and walked up to the front door. It was locked, but she cupped her hands against the glass, trying to see in. The place looked bare and drab. But once she'd moved in, it would come to life. She could hardly wait.

She walked around the side of the property, opening the gate and letting herself into the garden. It was so peaceful and private. The back deck had dappled shade on one end from the overhanging trees, and the sunny end would be perfect for her pots of herbs and geraniums. Maybe she could set up a little swing set on the grass for the baby when Emmett came to visit. She'd hang wind chimes near the side fence where the breeze could catch them. Dave didn't like wind chimes, but it no longer mattered what Dave liked. Perhaps she could even install one of those little bubbling water features like Ann had at her place. LaVonda bit her lip. Actually, scrap that. Ann's fountain always made her feel like she had to pee quite urgently.

LaVonda's phone beeped with an incoming message. She snatched it up, anxious as always, these days that it might be Emmett going into labour. She had made it to thirty-two weeks, so the baby had a good chance of survival now. Still, the longer Emmett could keep the pregnancy going, the better the odds for her child.

It wasn't Emmett, it was John, confirming their date for tonight. LaVonda smiled. After cancelling their last date, the night that Dave and Jemima showed up, she hadn't spoken to John for several days. He'd sent a couple of messages that she hadn't replied to because, of course, there had been all that business with Ann and Maxine and finding out Frank was still alive, and she'd been far too preoccupied to think about John.

But in the days that followed Saturday's pub lunch with her sisters and poor Tracy, LaVonda had thought about contacting John again. At first, she was hesitant. After all, her life was quite complicated right now, but then again, how many nice, attractive men who were also interested in her was she likely to meet? John might be her new soulmate, and was she ready to throw that away simply because she was embroiled in murders and attempted murders, and about to become a grandmother, and also unemployed, and buying a new house? LaVonda didn't think so.

Earlier this week, she'd finally called him, and John had sounded happy to hear from her. After talking for a few minutes about her new house, she'd casually invited him over for a drink and pizza tonight. He seemed keen; a little too keen if she were perfectly honest, but it was nice that he was still showing interest in her considering that she'd cancelled their date at the last minute. LaVonda wasn't sure if she would be quite so accommodating if the tables were turned. Yes, it was flattering that he was still interested, and if things went well tonight, who knows?

She tapped out a quick message to John, then dialled Emmett's number.

'How are you feeling?'

'Not too bad, although I've had a few cramps this afternoon. Peanut is fine though, heartbeat strong as a baby ox and no signs of distress. Are you coming in later?'

'I want to clean the house this afternoon, and I have plans for this evening, so I thought I'd come in the morning. Unless you need something?'

'We're fine, we don't need anything. What are you up to tonight? Are you seeing that guy again?'

'No, nothing like that.' The lie slipped too easily off LaVonda's tongue. She should just tell Emmett, for goodness' sake. *Yes, I've met a nice man, and he is coming over tonight*. Easy. And yet, something held her back. Was it because she'd only been single for a few months, and it was a little unseemly to have started dating so soon? No; Dave had left *her*, no one would blame her for trying to move on with her life. Although women did tend to get judged harder in situations like this than men did, didn't they? A man could move on straight away, and everyone would be sympathetic and supportive, whereas women were seen as a bit too loose if they launched from one relationship to another.

But Emmett wasn't judgemental, and even though Ann and Maxine definitely were, LaVonda knew they'd all be delighted that she had met someone.

But that was the problem, wasn't it? They'd be so happy. Well, perhaps not Maxine, who was still stinging from the whole Tracy event, but Emmett and Ann would immediately get overly invested in her relationship, and LaVonda wasn't entirely sure how she felt about John. Not yet anyway. Yes, he was pleasant and attractive and thoughtful, and they had chemistry, but was she moving too fast? After all, she didn't know the man. He might have all kinds of strange or unsettling skeletons in his closet, and god knows she had more than a few of her own rattling around.

'I bought Peanut a few more things this morning, some more muslin wraps, singlets, and nappies.'

'Thanks, Mum, but we definitely won't need nappies. You see, we plan to use the Elimination Communication method. It's where you look for cues that the baby needs to wee or poo, and then simply hold them over the toilet or a bucket. It's a better method, more sanitary and holistic than using nappies.'

LaVonda was aghast. 'Emmett, I–'

'Gotcha! I'm teasing you, Mum. I know you think we are weirdo hippies, but we're not quite as alternative as you think. I have to go now; the specialist has arrived, but I'll see you tomorrow. Enjoy your date and don't forget the condoms!'

Cheeky sod. LaVonda felt her cheeks heat up as she dialled Ann's number.

'My daughter is a rat.'

'All children are rats. The best way to get your own back is to embarrass the hell out of them whenever you get the chance. I'll give you a demonstration tomorrow while we're shopping, if you like?'

'I'll look forward to it. As long as it doesn't involve your stump. How are you doing?'

Ann was quiet so long that LaVonda thought the call had dropped out.

'Ann?'

'I'm still here. I'm... fine. Surprisingly fine. I can't quite believe what a relief it is to have gotten that off my chest after all these years. Even if it did almost cost me my relationship with you two.'

'It would take more than one little murder to get rid of me.' LaVonda laughed. 'Okay, that came out wrong. What I meant was, I completely understand why you did what you did, and I know Max is a bit upset now, but she loves you Ann. We're family. We've always looked out for each other, and that won't change, no matter what. Have you spoken to her lately?'

'Yes, she called me this morning. I think she is okay. She seemed pretty calm, at any rate. As calm as Maxie gets.'

'There you go. Now. One other thing.'

'Make it quick, Von. I have a client meeting in a few minutes. We don't all have the luxury of endless time.'

'I'm unemployed, Ann, not retired, and I'm going to look for another job. Soon.'

LaVonda had actually thought she might wait a while, at least until after the baby was born and she'd moved into this lovely place. She didn't want to tell Ann that though. She could do without the lecture.

'Was that what you wanted to tell me?'

'No,' LaVonda spoke quickly, before her sister could interrupt with objections. 'Ann, I've been doing some research, and there are some amazing myoelectric prosthetic arms available now. Even if you didn't want to wear one all the time, it might be useful occasionally. Anyway, before you say no, I just wanted you to think about it.'

'I already have. I'm seeing my GP tomorrow to discuss some options.'

'Really?' LaVonda was surprised and delighted.

'Yes, really. Perhaps I've punished myself long enough. I'm going to consider it anyway.'

'What does Sam think?'

'Well, he doesn't know the reason behind my decision, but as usual the man is completely supportive. I'm pretty lucky.'

'You're very lucky.' Sam was a wonderful husband to Ann. Would LaVonda ever have that again? A supportive, loving partner?

John's face popped into her mind. Oh, it was a bit too soon to be casting him in that role, surely. But maybe one day...? She inhaled deeply.

'Ann, there is something else. I've met...'

'Sorry, Von. I really have to go. I'll see you tomorrow for Sunday shopping?' She hung up.

LaVonda frowned at the phone in her hand, before dropping it back in her handbag. She'd been about to tell Ann about meeting John, but look, perhaps it was better that she hadn't said anything. Not until after tonight, anyway. If their date went well, then she would tell her sisters, and Emmett, all about John. After all, she couldn't keep him a secret forever. Sooner or later, they'd have to know she'd met someone nice.

Reluctantly, LaVonda took one last look around the garden before walking back to her car. In just a few more days this place would be hers, and her new life would begin.

It was a shame she couldn't have an exciting new career to go with her new life, because, quite frankly, any job other than professional assassin, now seemed quite dull. But that couldn't be helped. She'd promised Maxine she wouldn't try to murder anyone again. And look, as much as she'd enjoyed believing she'd killed Frank, it had been a terrible shock to find out she'd failed. Perhaps she wasn't cut out for that career after all?

But it would have been *so* satisfying to do away with Brian Robinette. Horrible man, with his grabby hands and his awful fishy breath. LaVonda thought back to her wedding day. Brian had been a nightmare. He'd leered at her constantly, making suggestive remarks, and he kept pulling her in for a hug. Finally, she'd twisted away and stomped on his foot, and he'd stormed out in a fury. From that moment on, he'd despised her almost as much as his own son. They probably shouldn't have let Emmett anywhere near the old man, but Dave had been hopeful his adorable little step-daughter might help heal the family tensions. And it had worked, to an extent.

Emmett was the only person in the family Brian still spoke to, and she was currently the only beneficiary of the old man's extensive fortune.

What a shame LaVonda wasn't allowed to kill him.

# TWENTY-ONE

LaVonda's hands trembled slightly as she finished drying herself and hung her towel back on the bathroom rail. Nerves? Excitement? If she was honest, it was probably a bit of both. She'd only ever slept with Dave, and Mark before him, and it was strange and slightly unsettling to imagine being naked in front of another man.

She looked at herself in the mirror. Would he be turned off by her body? She was still fairly slim, but her waist had thickened over the past few years, and everything had become a little softer and even droopy in places. LaVonda hoisted her boobs up to where they used to sit, then let them drop back into place. Hmmm. She held one arm up and gave it a shake. Definitely jiggly. What did Maxine call them? Tuck-shop-lady arms. Yes, that was it. Well, she couldn't do much about that right now, except refrain from waving her arms about tonight.

She'd leave the lights off. Although, then it might be too dark, and she'd quite like to see his body. LaVonda felt a little kick of excitement that she hadn't experienced in years. Not since the early days of dating Mark. She could clearly remember that shivery thrill of anticipation before each date, followed by the happy delight of seeing his face. His eyes had always lit up at the sight of her too, and the world seemed to fall away whenever they were together.

LaVonda shook her head. Why was she thinking about Mark? She was bringing another man into the home she'd shared with Dave for decades; if she was going to reflect on anyone else right now, it should be *Dave*. Not her dead first husband.

LaVonda rolled on deodorant (two applications, just in case), sprayed perfume, and then put on her new underwear. The lace under the bra cups was a little scratchy, but she probably wouldn't be wearing it for too long anyway.

Heels or flats? High heels worked better with the floaty black dress she was wearing, but that seemed oddly formal for entertaining at home. Normally, she kicked off her shoes as soon as she came through the front door, and she never wore anything but slippers, or occasionally socks, in the house. Oh, why was she dithering? Just put the heels on. Now, dangly earrings or diamond studs? Long earrings might get in the way if he tried to kiss her neck, but they had the advantage of making her neck look longer and more kissable.

LaVonda frowned at her reflection. Was she being ridiculous? Undoubtedly.

At least the living room looked cosy and inviting. She'd turned on both lamps, so the room was lit with a welcoming glow, and music played softly in the background. Even though it wouldn't be her couch for much longer, LaVonda was pleased with the effect of her new cushions and throws. The room no longer looked like a bland, beige catalogue picture. The deep reds and bright oranges she'd chosen gave the room warmth and charm and worked much better against the polished golden wood of the coffee and side tables.

She had set out a dish of nuts and a small plate of cheese and crackers, plus a bottle of expensive cabernet sauvignon. She glanced at her phone. He would be arriving any minute. Jittery excitement fluttered again; perhaps she still had time for a quick nervous wee?

Too late. Even though she was expecting it, the knock still startled her. He was here. She paused for a moment, took a deep breath, and pulled opened the door.

John was standing on the doorstep, holding a bottle of wine, and dressed casually in faded black jeans, a grey polo shirt, and sneakers. LaVonda immediately felt overdressed, middle-aged, and fussy. She should have worn jeans herself, or at least a top and skirt. She smiled widely to cover her discomfort.

'Come on in.'

'Thanks. You look great.'

He walked in and leaned forward to kiss her cheek. His moustache scratched against her skin. He was wearing a new cologne tonight; it smelled woody, masculine, and expensive. LaVonda's stomach gave a little squirm of anticipation.

She led him into the living room. 'Make yourself comfortable and help yourself to wine. I won't be a moment.'

Back in her bedroom, LaVonda unclipped her dangly earrings and dropped them back in her jewellery box. She yanked the dress back over her head, kicking it swiftly under the bed in a way that was very un-LaVonda-like. She pulled on a soft cotton skirt and a gauzy red top. That was better. Not too dressy, but not completely casual either. She stepped out of her heels and into ballet flats, then hurried back into the living room.

John was standing near the French doors, holding a full glass of wine, and looking at the black-and-white scenic photos hanging on the far wall. He turned and grinned when she came back into the room.

'Did you take these? They're very good.'

'No, my daughter, Emmett, is an amateur photographer. She's a primary school art teacher, but photography is her passion.' Was it still her passion? LaVonda had no idea.

'They look great. I especially like this one.' He reached out and touched the picture of a dandelion, close up, its spores starting to float away as though someone had just blown gently on it. LaVonda had always thought that one was a little clichéd; too obviously staged, but she didn't voice that opinion. Instead, she moved closer to look at the picture and again was treated to a whiff of his cologne. She felt a sudden urge to throw her arms around him and sniff deeply. Good grief.

'How is your daughter? She's due to have her baby soon, isn't she?'

'Yes.' LaVonda moved away quickly and went over to the couch. 'She's in hospital, hoping to keep the baby in until closer to her due date.'

'That must be stressful.' He walked over and sat down on the other end of the couch. Not too close, but she could have reached out and touched him if she wanted to. She thought she probably did want to, but nervous, excited butterflies were making her feel slightly sick. She watched him set his glass down on the coffee table.

LaVonda leaned over and picked up her glass, taking a sip that almost turned into a slurp. She hadn't meant to swallow quite so much. Flustered, she took another sip. The air felt charged somehow; their conversation happening on one level while sexual tension pulled at them both from underneath. LaVonda cleared her throat.

'It is a bit concerning, but she is being well looked after. I visit her every day, and she is in good spirits, all things considered. My sister is a nurse at that hospital, and she checks on her frequently too.'

John nodded and reached for his wine. LaVonda's eyes were immediately drawn to his crotch. She caught herself and quickly looked back up. His green eyes were shining, and a slight smile played on his lips. LaVonda's own lips parted.

'Would you like some more?' Her voice came out a lot higher and squeakier than normal. Good grief, LaVonda. Get a grip.

'I'd better not, in case I need to drive us to dinner. Are you hungry?'

'No. Not particularly. But we could order pizza?'

His eyes lit up.

'Pizza sounds great. I don't let myself have it too often because of the effect on my waistline.' He patted his stomach, then held out his glass. 'I will have another one, thanks.'

She picked up the wine bottle, leaning towards him to pour. Her hand was steady as she topped up his glass, but then she glanced up at him, and her hand wobbled. John smiled, lifted the bottle out of her hand, and set it down on the table. He reached out and gently took hold of her chin, turning her towards him. Oh god. It was happening. He leaned in even closer, his breath warm and spicy on her face, his moustache and full bottom lip coming closer. LaVonda closed her eyes... just as the music stopped, and the harsh ringtone of her phone cut in through the Bluetooth speakers. They both drew back sharply.

'Sorry, sorry. I'll just get rid of this.' She picked up her phone. Maxine. Why was Maxine calling her? Was it about Emmett?

'Max?' The sound of the fear in her own voice scared her even more as she hurried into the kitchen.

'Relax. She's fine, although she's had a bumpy evening. But congratulations, Grandma; you have a little grandson.'

A grandson! LaVonda was a grandmother. She tasted the word as it came into her mind. It wasn't old and fusty, as she'd feared. It was elegant. Almost regal. She was a grandmother, and she had a grandson. Mark had a grandson.

'How is Emmett? The baby? Is he okay? I'm on my way.'

Maxine laughed. 'Slow down, granny. Em is fine. She gave birth earlier this evening, and she's resting comfortably. The baby is doing well. I've seen him, and he's a little on the small side, but otherwise perfect. He's in NICU right now because he is still a premmie. But he is healthy. There's no point in you coming in now. Emmett needs her rest, Von, and you won't be able to see the baby until tomorrow.'

'Can I talk to her?'

'Sure. Hang on.' She heard a rustle on the other end of the phone, then Emmett's voice, weak but happy.

'Mum? He's here, Mum. Our little Peanut. He's so beautiful, I can't believe how beautiful he is. We're utterly smitten.'

LaVonda's face broke into a smile.

'That's wonderful news, darling. I am so proud of you. I cannot wait to meet him. Do you have any pictures?'

Emmett laughed. 'Quite a few, actually. Great-auntie Max took some, so I'll get her to send them to you.'

'And you? Are you feeling okay?'

'A little sore. They've given me painkillers, but I'd rather just use some homeopathic remedies and see how I go.'

Oh, Emmett. Take the damn pills. LaVonda rolled her eyes.

'Does the baby have a name?' She held her breath.

'Declan.'

Declan. Well, that wasn't too bad. Quite a normal name, really.

'Declan Serenity Wisdom Brown.'

Of course.

'Mum, I know you were hoping for a girl...'

'Nonsense, darling, I couldn't be more thrilled. I'll let you get some rest, but I'll be in first thing in the morning to see you and meet Declan. I'm so excited.'

'Thanks, Mum. See you in the morning. I'll hand you back to great-auntie Max.'

Maxine's voice growled in her ear. 'I'll send you some photos on one condition. Never, ever, call me great-auntie Max. Okay?'

LaVonda laughed. 'Okay. Tell me, how are you doing?' They hadn't spoken for a few days, and she hoped her sister wasn't still upset about losing Tracy. Maxine was resilient, but she'd taken quite a blow.

'Me? I'm fine.' Maxine lowered her voice. 'Emmett's doula is rather gorgeous. Single too. I'm thinking of asking her out.'

LaVonda grinned. Maxine was incorrigible. She hung up, and within a few seconds, the photos started popping into her phone. She opened the first one up.

A tiny, red-faced baby screwed up his nose at the camera. His eyes were closed and spaced wide apart, and above them, his sparse eyebrows were scrunched together. The baby's tiny lips were pursed in annoyance at being born. He looked like a small, furious alien, and LaVonda fell instantly, unexpectedly, and whole-heartedly in love. Her grandson. Her boy.

Declan looked a little like Mark in the next photo. His face was calmer in this one, although his eyes were still tightly shut. He had Mark and Emmett's slightly flared nostrils and Mark's high cheekbones. Tears pricked at LaVonda's eyelids, and she sniffed them back with a smile. Mark would never meet this little boy, but his grandson carried his genes on in another generation.

The third photo was of Emmett lying in bed, staring in wonder at the baby in her arms. Jasper lay next to her, one arm around her shoulders, the other circling his tiny son. LaVonda beamed. She might not *completely* approve of Jasper and his strange, unorthodox lifestyle, but the picture of this new little family was delightful. Love shone from Emmett and Jasper as they looked at their baby.

LaVonda stood in the kitchen staring longingly at the photos until she realised, she'd left John alone in the living room for far too long. She took one last look at little Declan, then hurried back into the living room.

'Good news?' John was eating peanuts and leaning back against her cushions. His feet rested on her coffee table, which was surprising and a little irritating. He sat up straight as she came into the room.

'Wonderful news. Emmett has had a baby boy. Declan. They're both doing well.'

'Congratulations! Do you want to go and see them? I'm probably still alright to drive you.'

LaVonda shook her head. 'No, they're all resting quietly tonight, so I'll go and see them tomorrow.' She beamed at him as she sank back down on the couch and lifted her glass towards him.

John reached over and clinked his against hers. 'To Declan!'

'To Declan.'

The undercurrent of sexual tension had drained away, and LaVonda knew it wouldn't return. Not tonight. Her mind was occupied with thoughts of Emmett and Mark and the bittersweet joy of Declan's birth. How wonderful that he was here safely, yet how sad that he'd never know his grandfather. She shook her head. Now was not the time to get all maudlin. Tonight, she just wanted to relax, eat pizza, and enjoy John's company.

John seemed to have picked up on the change in mood. He leaned back and grinned, somewhat ruefully, she thought, but he looked content and comfortable. And really, so what if he'd put his feet on her coffee table? If he did it again, she would politely ask him not to. It was no big deal.

'Tell me more about yourself. Where did you grow up?' She reached over and cut herself a wedge of cheese, then curled up on the end of the couch, her legs tucked under her. She felt warm and happy. She had a new grandson to meet tomorrow, and right now she had some nice wine and an attractive man sitting next to her. Everything was lovely, apart from her slightly scratchy bra, but she could cope with that minor annoyance. At the other end of the couch, John smiled and reached out to help himself to more nuts.

'Here, actually. I've lived here all my life, apart from some brief trips overseas when I was younger. I was born in the local hospital, went to Sunnybank Primary and Southern Heights High School.'

LaVonda had gone to the same schools, but she decided not to mention that. She didn't remember him, and he would have been a few years behind her. No need to make a point of the difference in their ages.

'My folks lived here pretty much their entire lives too. I think that's what makes me such a good real estate agent. I know this place like the back of my hand. I don't think I'd ever want to live anywhere else. Except maybe Bowral. I wouldn't mind retiring in Bowral. Have you been there? It's a great little place. I sometimes go there to escape from the rat race. Hey, we should take a trip next weekend after I finish work. We could stay Saturday night and come back on Sunday.'

A tiny alarm bell went off in LaVonda's head. Surely it was a bit soon for the two of them to go away for a weekend together. Their relationship was brand new, and they hadn't even had sex yet. She hadn't told anyone that she was seeing someone, and yes, she was attracted to him, but she hardly knew the man. It was way too early to be planning trips away together.

Although, things did seem to happen a bit more quickly these days. After all, look at Dave. A few months with Jemima and he was already talking marriage and babies.

'I'm not sure, John. We don't know each other very well yet.'

'No, you're right. Sorry. I didn't mean to make you feel rushed.'

LaVonda relaxed. Clearly, he liked her, and that was why he was being a little overly keen. She smiled widely.

'I do want to get to know you better, and for you to know me.'

Although how much did she *really* want him to know about her? Probably not much about her recent activities anyway.

But maybe Maxine was right. A relationship based on deception would never work. LaVonda had a feeling that this night might be the start of something special, but if she told him some of the things she'd done, he might be scared off for good.

Although, wasn't it better to have that happen now, and not down the track after they had slept together, and she was way more invested?

*Don't overthink it*, LaVonda told herself. *Just do it, otherwise you will start fretting and worrying, and putting it off, and making it into a much bigger deal than it is.*

'John, I need to tell you something. I've done... well, some things I'm not proud of...' She paused.

His chuckle was deep and throaty and reassuring as he reached over and took her hand. His skin felt warm and firm against hers.

'Haven't we all? I don't think anyone can get to our age without a few skeletons in the closet, but unless you're going to admit to being a serial killer, I think we can probably get passed it.'

Hmmm.

'Not a serial killer... as such.' Good grief, was she actually going to do this? Yes. He needed to know the truth. Some of the truth, at any rate. 'But I have done some... unpleasant things, and I'm not sure that you're going to like hearing this.'

He squeezed her hand in a way that was probably meant to be reassuring, but she noticed a tiny frown appear on his forehead. Look, if he was scared off, then so be it. They had to be honest and open with each other from the beginning. Although... maybe she shouldn't be too honest and open all at once. Perhaps she could start off small and work her way up to the Frank murder attempt.

'I let my mother die.'

Way to go, LaVonda. Just blurt it out. No filter, no subtlety, just a bald statement of the facts. Nice work.

John recoiled, but just a little. Then he smiled gently.

'Right, well that's... do you want to talk about it?'

She did. She told him about Maude's alcoholism and her abusiveness. How her sisters had firmly rejected their mother, while she'd kept visiting her for years. She told John about her fantasies of her mother dying and how, when Maude actually was dying, she'd left her lying on the floor instead of immediately calling for help. When she finished talking, she searched his expression for a reaction. He was silent, but he seemed calm. So that was positive. Finally, he spoke.

'Look, it probably wasn't your finest hour, Von, but I do understand.'

She wished he wouldn't call her Von, although now didn't seem to be the right time to bring that up.

'Really? You don't think that is unforgivable?' She was a little surprised at how accepting he was. After all, she'd dropped a bit of a bombshell, yet there he was, still chewing on nuts, and sipping his wine as if she'd just revealed she used to be a Girl Guide, or something equally as innocuous.

'No, I don't. Besides, even if you had called for help straight away, chances are it wouldn't have made any difference. At least, that's what I tell myself.'

'What do you mean?'

John's gaze dropped to his lap. He let go of her hand and picked up the cheese knife. He carefully cut a piece and put it on a cracker, then bit into it. He chewed and swallowed, his movements slow and precise.

'Von, I've done something similar. Years ago, when I was very young.'

Well, this was a revelation. LaVonda felt quite shocked, but mentally shook her head. He'd listened without judgement to her story, so she would do him the same courtesy. She moved slightly closer towards him in a gesture of support.

'I was just a kid, well almost; I was seventeen, and I was dating a girl named Susan.'

Such a drab name, Susan. Susie, now that was cute, in a little girl way. Suzanne was sophisticated and glamorous. But Susan? Oh, for heaven's sake, LaVonda. The man is pouring out his secrets to you. Try to stay focussed.

'She was my first girlfriend, and we were madly in love; at least I was. She led me on, I can see that now, but at the time, I thought we were both crazy about each other. Turns out, I was the one who was crazy.'

LaVonda was aware of her heart rate picking up in slight excitement and dread. Good grief, what had he done? Had Susan died? Had he killed Susan? Surely not.

He was still holding the cheese knife, and she deliberately flicked her glance away from it. For heaven's sake, either cut a piece of cheese or put the knife down. LaVonda picked up her wine and took a quick swallow. To her great relief, John leaned over and replaced the knife on the board.

'We dated for almost a year. She was gorgeous, long dark hair, bright blue eyes, the best smile. She used to laugh all the time. She thought I was the funniest guy in the world.' His eyes went dreamy as he reflected. LaVonda felt her patience slip, along with one of her scratchy bra straps. Discreetly, she hauled it back into place. John hadn't noticed. His eyes had taken on a faraway, unfocussed look as he talked about his past.

'One night, we went out to see a movie; I can't remember which one now. It might have been Rambo. No, Susan hated violent movies, so it must have been a romantic one, or a comedy? God, my brain. Why can't I remember? Oh, it doesn't matter anyway.'

No, it doesn't. LaVonda's glass was empty, and she wanted to get another bottle from the kitchen, but the poor man was telling his story, and it seemed a bit insensitive to get up in the middle of it. She rearranged her face into an expression of interest, indicating *Please, do go on. Please.*

'I thought she'd been a bit quiet, because usually she loved comedies. Yes! It was a comedy; I do remember that much. Anyway, afterwards she wanted to go somewhere quiet, so I drove us out to Pine Forest because that was our special private place. I thought she was in the mood for some loving. Turns out it was quite the opposite. She wanted to break up.'

LaVonda shuddered involuntarily at the image. A beautiful young woman alone in a dark forest with a man she was dumping. Good grief, Susan. Perhaps you should have watched a few violent movies. Then you'd know you never put yourself in a situation like that. But surely John hadn't...

'I didn't react well. Remember, I was just a kid. I cried, I begged her to reconsider, I got angry with her. I... I...'

*What? John, what did you do?* LaVonda's chest started to hurt, and she realised she'd been holding her breath. She let it out slowly and carefully.

'I... tore off the watch she'd given me for my birthday and hurled it into the trees.' He rolled his eyes. 'Dramatic, right? Then I told her to get out of the car.'

Oh, John, you didn't. LaVonda's mind had leapt ahead in the story, and she was already watching Susan being raped and killed by some crazed murderer because John had abandoned her all alone in the forest. Her hand flew to her throat. She didn't know if she wanted to hear what happened next.

'She refused to leave the car. So, I drove her home.'

Wait, what?

'You drove her home?'

John grimaced.

'Yes, I took her home, and we didn't speak to each other until we got back to her place. I was hoping she might reconsider. But when we arrived, I turned off the ignition and looked at her. She looked sad and guilty, but also as though she couldn't wait to get away from me. She said, 'Bye Johnny,' then she got out of the car and went inside.'

LaVonda was bewildered. This story was not going as she'd expected, although of course, she was quite relieved to hear John hadn't been responsible, directly or indirectly, for an ex-girlfriend's horrible murder.

'So, then what happened?'

'I didn't want to go home, so I drove around for a while, miserable and upset. I kept trying to convince myself I could win Susan back. Finally, I went back to Pine Forest to try and find my watch. *Clueless!* That was it. To this day, I can't stand that movie.'

LaVonda needed to pee, and her bra was becoming unbearably scratchy. He wasn't particularly concise at telling stories, was he? That wasn't a reason to write someone off, but you'd have to admit, it was an annoying habit. And how could you not love *Clueless?* The film was brilliant. She and Mark had seen it together at the movies, and they'd both loved it.

John shook his head. 'I never did find the watch, and I never got back together with Susan. This is embarrassing to admit, but I stalked her for a while. Hung around her house, called her, that sort of thing. Then she hooked up with another guy, who threatened to punch my lights out if I came near her again. I was pretty distraught at the time. Anyway, I decided that the only way to get her attention was to kill myself. I imagined her coming to my funeral and being full of regret and wishing she'd stayed to save my life. Like I said, I was distraught.'

The urge to pee had passed as the story got interesting again.

'What did you do?'

'One evening, I took a rope out to Pine Forest, to our place. The plan was to hang myself from a tree. I managed to throw the rope over a branch, but when I put my weight on the noose to test the strength, it snapped. I was such a loser I couldn't even kill myself successfully. Then I heard a car coming, and I had another idea.'

He lowered his voice, and LaVonda had to lean forward to hear him.

'I went back up near the road and watched as the car approached, and I decided to throw myself in front of it. I think I knew, even then, that I didn't seriously want to die; I just wanted Susan's attention. If I was injured and taken to hospital, that would probably achieve the same result. I waited until the car was close, then I shut my eyes and ran straight out in front of it.'

LaVonda was breathless.

'What happened? Did it hit you?'

'No, the driver must have spotted me just as I dashed out, and he swerved. I heard the tyres squeal, then an almighty bang, and when I opened my eyes, I saw the station wagon crumpled around this huge tree. Smoke pouring from the engine; the whole front was smashed in. I just froze in shock. I could see a baby seat and one of those baby capsule things in the back, and I was terrified, but when I approached the car, thankfully, they were both empty. There was just a little pink stuffed animal on the back seat. The driver was crushed up against the steering wheel. He had blood on his face, and at first, I thought he was dead, but then he began moaning. I panicked and took off.'

'You left him?' LaVonda's voice was barely a whisper.

John nodded his head ruefully.

'I know. Pathetic, wasn't it? But I was partly in shock, and I was also worried about getting in trouble. Imagine what Susan would think if she found out I'd tried to kill myself and ended up causing an accident. I still feel guilty though. That guy might have died, and that would have been my fault. He was probably okay...' he shrugged, 'but who knows?'

Adrenaline, pure and cold as ice, shot through LaVonda, alighting all her senses. The room was suddenly brighter, the music amplified, the smell of John's warm skin and fresh aftershave intensified. She looked steadily at him.

'You didn't try to help the driver? You left him all alone to die?'

John dropped his gaze and picked up his glass.

'Yeah. I was going to call for help as soon as I got home, but the telephone was in the hallway, right next to the kitchen. I was afraid my mother would hear me if I called the police. So I figured someone would find him sooner or later and get help, and then I just tried not to think about him anymore. I do feel bad though.'

*Do you, John? Do you feel as bad as I have for the past twenty-seven years?*

LaVonda searched his face. He smiled at her, a tremulous, but hopeful look, his green eyes clear and wide and innocent. It wasn't possible... except that it was.

It hadn't been a kangaroo. It was never a kangaroo.

LaVonda stood up. John seemed smaller and less tangible somehow. As if he were already a ghost perched on her couch. Even his voice seemed... insubstantial.

'Are you okay? I know this is a lot to take in.'

'I'm fine, John. More wine?' Her voice was calm, measured.

He grinned, a look of relief spreading across his face.

'Sure, thanks. So, what were the other things?'

'What do you mean?'

'You said you'd done 'some things.' What were the other things?'

LaVonda smiled. 'It doesn't matter.'

*Not anymore.*

He looked slightly uncomfortable as he looked up at her. 'Are you hungry? Should we order a pizza now?'

She looked down at him, in her living room, sitting on the couch, her cushions behind his back. She'd invited him into her home and into her life. John Dangerfield. Johnny Danger. He had no idea. Her voice was smooth and light as she spoke.

'I don't feel like pizza anymore. How about I make us a cheese toasted sandwich and heat up some soup? I hope you like mushroom and chestnut?'

He looked momentarily disappointed, but quickly rallied, giving her a big reassuring smile. 'Sounds delicious. Can I give you a hand?'

'No. Relax. I'll be right back.'

It is funny the way things happen; the choices we make in life.

LaVonda watched John scrape his spoon around the bottom of the bowl and then wipe it clean using the crust from his sandwich.

A tricycle turned into the wrong driveway. A late-night request for chocolate. Dating a co-worker with a possessive and violent ex-husband.

Making the choice to turn and run away.

So many little decisions. With such astonishing consequences.

'That was amazing.' John pushed his empty plate away and leaned back, lifting one ankle onto his knee and linking his hands behind his head. 'My mother used to make mushroom soup, but yours is better.'

LaVonda held her smile fast.

'I'm glad you liked it. It is getting pretty late, though, so perhaps you should go.'

Disappointment clouded John's face. How could she have ever thought him handsome? He looked like a sulky child. A spoilt, selfish brat who never once thought about the terrible consequences of his actions. Perhaps tomorrow, when he was writhing on the floor in agony, cramps tearing at his dying body, his breath coming in short, pointless gasps, perhaps then he might have some regrets?

She allowed him to kiss her cheek as he left. She waited until she heard his car leaving, then carried his empty dish and plate out to the kitchen. She pulled on rubber gloves, filled the sink with boiling soapy water, and then carefully washed the bowl, his spoon, the empty container, and the soup pot. She placed everything in a plastic bag, tied the handles, and took it outside. Tomorrow was rubbish collection. So that was handy.

LaVonda opened her mouth and yawned. The adrenaline was subsiding now, leaving her empty and worn out. She'd done it. Funnily, she felt no sense of triumph in the moment, just mild satisfaction, as though she'd done something minor, but important. Like pulling out a stubborn, nasty weed.

It was very quiet in the living room. Peaceful. LaVonda glanced around at the home she was about to leave behind for good. She plumped up the cushions, picked up a piece of red fluff from the carpet, and readjusted the pile of home-decorating books on the coffee table. Everything was neat and tidy, just as it should be. As her gaze roamed around the room, she noticed something else ever so slightly out of order. LaVonda frowned, then walked over, reached out, and straightened Emmett's dandelion photo.

There. *Now* it was perfect.

Thank you, lovely reader, for reading and finishing this book. Please take the time to leave me a rating or a review on Amazon or Goodreads or connect with me on Facebook: *Kirsten Maron author.*

I'd really love to know what you think of LaVonda Robinette.

Thank you to the talented Shawline Publishing team for designing the book cover concept, and to the amazing Steffi Dryden for editing the story. Thank you to the wonderful Rachel Steele for providing the initial critique.

Thank you also to my brilliant beta readers, Laura, Cate, Servane, and Sarah, for your thoughtful feedback and suggestions.

Thank you to all my girls, young and old. You all inspire me every day.

Finally, a big thank you to the real Lavonda Robinette, and Ann Avenell, for lending their fantastic names to these fictional characters.

I am so grateful to have such an amazing group of women in my life.

**WHAT WOULD LAVONDA ROBINETTE DO?**

Copyright © 2021 by Kirsten Maron.

All Rights Reserved.

Shawline Publishing Group Pty Ltd

www.shawlinepublishing.com.au

SHAWLINE
PUBLISHING
GROUP

CPSIA information can be obtained
at www.ICGtesting.com
Printed in the USA
LVHW041626010221
678031LV00018B/3268

9 781922 444424